The King's Sword

First paperback edition August 2021

Book design by Kate Absher Myers
Edelweiss design by Jazlyn Myers
Illustrations by Rebekah Simmers
Illustrations' copyright © 2021 by Rebekah Simmers

ISBN 978-1-7372620-0-8 (paperback)
ASIN B094V49ZYW9 (eBook)

The King's Sword

the first novel of the

Metzlingen Saga

Rebekah Simmers

DEDICATION

For my children,
my everything,
& my husband,
my always.

Love you.

PART ONE
LEUCERIA

AUGUST 7, 1479
WANING HARVEST MOON

CHAPTER 1

THE PATH TO FREEDOM

Matthias - Battle of Guinegate - August 7, 1479

MATTHIAS GINGERLY STEPPED AROUND THE grotesquely tangled limbs of men, his face long and sour, as he guided his prince's destrier to do the same. Hooves splattering the reddened mud, the great horse snorted and tossed his head but acquiesced when a hard tug of his reins brought them at last to uncluttered ground. His muscles twitching, Matthias squeezed his fist tighter around his pike, eager for his arm to cease trembling at his side. Heart ramming against his breastplate, he gritted his teeth and ascended the last leg of the hill with his precious cargo.

It was time.

Every day he'd struggled. Every battle he'd fought. Every vow he'd made. Every step he'd taken had led to this moment. One final mission and he was to be free. *Free.* Yet now his dreams hung about his neck, no more than a weighted noose, mocking him, waiting for his legs to be kicked out beneath him.

Numb, Matthias arrived at the king's tent, where the flag atop thrashed angrily in the wicked wind. The summer air had grown muggy, carrying with it the stench of the spilled bowels and the last cries of men, dead or dying in the thousands behind him. The battle had raged for six hours; the search for wounded, looting, and burials would last long after.

Halted by the guards, Matthias side-eyed the limp body carried on the back of the horse beside him. He reached and adjusted the cloak to better cover the prince's ashen face.

"The king's nephew, Prince Siegfried," Matthias said.

The long poles of the guards' halberds remained crossed. Clean and crisp in their unblemished royal colors, the guards didn't move, not even an eye, for their prince. Matthias shook his head, irritated at the slight shown the dead.

Bastards.

"I'll wait." Beyond exhaustion, Matthias snorted and spat the line of bile burning the back of his throat. It always lay there after a fight when his body and mind became his own again. He slammed the butt end of his pike into the ground and wiped his forearm across his chin.

Matthias removed his iron helmet and tucked it into the crook of his arm. He removed his bloodied gloves. *Ach.* Though he liked the fit of these, he would need a new pair. Worn thin and frayed at the fingers, they were beyond another patching, but *still.* He stashed them inside his helmet.

Matthias wiped aside the hair matted to his forehead and then squeezed the back of his neck, exhaling. He was bruised. His body was battered. But he was *alive.* The prince, whose green banner soared beneath the king's and whose body he'd brought from the field, was not. Whether or not the king already knew—and how he would respond—was something else altogether.

Between Siegfried's personal guards and Matthias's men, they'd managed to keep the prince surrounded and had seen him safely through battle, though several had died to do so. The battle won; Matthias had turned to the prince. Cheering uproariously within a group of nobles some ten paces away, Prince Siegfried had met Matthias's eye and raised his helmet aloft. Thrilled for what had passed and, Matthias guessed, the promise of what was to come.

As was Matthias.

Until, with a single step, Prince Siegfried had suddenly slipped from sight.

Yells of shock had escaped the crowd and the nobles tumbled back, retreating. Matthias had broken into a run, racing toward his prince. His boots sloshing, each step had slid or sunk into the slick, muddied ground, frustrating his effort. Diving around a guardsman at last, Matthias's heart had frozen in his chest, horrified.

His prince had lain at his feet, twisted and still, in his armor.

Matthias had crouched beside him, stricken. All of that fighting and the man had somehow managed to lose his footing, fall upon the rocks, and split his skull.

"*Scheiße,*" Matthias had cursed.

His prince was dead. The promise he had made to grant their freedom surely with him.

Matthias waited, until commotion at the tent's entrance caught his attention and pulled him from his reverie. Several of the king's advisors exited. Relief washed over him when Matthias saw his own brother, Reymund, safe among them. Clutching his carved cross to his chest in one hand and his walking cane in the other, Reymund gave him a crooked smile and continued with the others. They'd meet later. First, this.

Matthias exhaled the tightness sitting in his chest and looked skyward. The sky was open here. Calm. Clear of banners and arrows in flight. A raven flew alone above him. Wings feverishly flapping, it cawed, flitting about until it found and joined its mate.

"*Quatsch,*" Matthias muttered as his vision blurred. Matthias blinked furiously, eager for his eyes to adjust to the evening light. They'd long given him trouble, growing red and irritated in the late days of summer. Today was no exception. Bathed in sweat, his eyes were tired and pained and in need of rest. Frustrated, spinning on his heel, he rubbed the back of his hand across his eyelids rigorously, hoping to drag the veil-like cloud from his eyes, and opened them wide.

Finally. His eyes acceded, no longer fighting him.

The last of the fog cleared, and Matthias could clearly see the grounds before him.

The lowing sun, burning the horizon, cast an orange glow over the sea of carnage. The valley below and the opposing hills, once swarming with soldiers, were now trampled and almost still. He shuddered, remembering the steel stream of horses and men erupting and tumbling toward him. Men and swords funneled together by terrain. Barreling toward him in a fury where he had stood. On foot. Pike in hand. Ready. The memory, as real as the horror only hours, moments before, reignited him. His blood pumped harder. His thighs flexed, his legs anchoring him, answering the charge that no longer came. He clamped his eyes, harder now, and their battle cries raised, echoing around him.

"Matthias," Crown Prince Zane called from behind him, drawing him back.

The king's son and heir, standing at the tent's entrance, filled the frame with both body and presence. His face severe, Prince Zane wore his richly detailed armor, muddied and bloodied from battle. A few years older and classes above Matthias, the prince was grounded in the way few men of importance were. In comparison with his father, the prince was approachable. A mentor of sorts. Friendly to the common man. Well-liked and respected. Any agenda, if it existed, was well hidden.

Prince Zane strode toward him, and the halberds parted at his approach. He met Matthias and clasped his forearm in greeting. "Well met, my friend. Hell of a fight." Shoulders slumping, Prince Zane laid a hand on the horse's neck. "My cousin?"

Matthias frowned and nodded.

"Christ. This is . . . This grieves me much," Prince Zane said. He moved his hand, gently placing it on his cousin's back, and then drew the blanket covering him into a tight fist. He cleared his throat, blinking back tears, and then sharply exhaled. "God rest him." He crossed himself and shook his head. "Thank you for bringing him back to us. Come. Come inside. There will be a time for lamentations, but today, there is much to do. Siegfried may be dead, but the King may still have need of you."

Leaving the horse with the guards, Matthias followed Prince Zane into the tent. The king's tent held a miniature court, spirited north and rebuilt here on the soft grass of the Burgundian Netherlands. The curved walls were hung with red banners. The room stuffed with carved oak furniture laid upon woven rugs. A poster bed to the side offered respite and sport, should he choose.

King Girault stood hulking behind a table clustered with scrolls and platters of food. Having retired with some speed from the field at victory, he no longer wore his armor, looking refreshed and triumphant. His attention remained on the map his palms were spread across.

Crossing his arms at his chest, Prince Zane planted himself at the table's end. Matthias stopped, centered directly before his king. Dropping his chin, he swallowed, trying to assuage the gnawing dread of who would pay for the prince's death.

King Girault snorted and plucked a chalice from the table. "This is how you dare greet your king? Bringing the broken body of a better man?"

Matthias mustered his words. "You have my greatest sympathy for the loss of your kin, sire. Prince Siegfried fought valiantly, as always, alongside your men. In the end, it was an unfortunate accident . . ."

The king's jaw tightened, and he raised a palm to Matthias, silencing him.

"I know of Siegfried," the king said. Taking a long drink, his eyes hardened over the brim. "How is it a baseborn foot soldier returns my kin to me? Siegfried's guard should've carried that burden."

Matthias shifted his stance, working to stretch his right leg. Fire blasted through his hip, seizing from the fresh pain creeping along his nerves. "The prince's guard was gone."

"So they were. A few torn apart on the ground while the rest fled the field. Gutless, either way," the king said. "Now those cowards find themselves stripped and chained and awaiting my judgment."

Prince Zane rubbed a hand across his chin. "You come alone? Where are your men?"

"Caring for our dead," Matthias said.

"Hmpf." The king grunted and settled into his high-backed chair.

"You commanded me to report after battle, sire," Matthias said. "I knew not to hesitate."

"I did, didn't I? *With* the prince. One way or another, you came." The king drummed his fingers on the chair arm, then he gestured at the open bench across from him. "Better to come before the winds change. Have a seat, son. Let us toast the memory of my nephew."

Son.

Matthias was no son to the king, and neither was the king father to him. Nor was Matthias blood brother to Prince Zane or Prince Siegfried, though they'd become battle brothers, drinking companions, friendly, through years of endless campaign. Matthias was no one—a single mud-spattered face amongst thousands—yet the king treated him with familiarity, a hint of respect, a greater curiosity, and always a slur of mockery and condescension.

Leery, but grateful for rest, Matthias sat as instructed. The prince followed suit, straddling the opposite end of Matthias's bench, and picked up a chalice. The king reached forward and pushed another toward Matthias.

"To Siegfried," Prince Zane said.

Matthias took it and held it aloft. "To the prince."

"To victory," King Girault answered with a tilted brow.

Matthias drank, thankful for the rich wine coating his parched throat. He exhaled, surveying the table. The map was of the continent, with their kingdom, Ewigsburg, drawn at its center. Abundant wine and platters of food were within reach, but nothing freshly baked or stewed that tempted or cramped his soured stomach.

All he smelled was trampled ground and iron and death.

The king curved his back into his seat and balanced his chalice on his stomach. "Siegfried was my nephew, so I grieve him for my sister's sake, but I did not care for him."

"Father," the prince growled. "My cousin is not yet cold."

"No, I will tell you both." The king pointed his finger at them. "Your cousin was loyal, but he was a fool. His mind was as loose as the rocks he broke upon."

Matthias stiffened, as the layer of sweat on his limbs chilled. There was already a slur to the king's speech, and therefore his appetite for all manner of things would be increased. King Girault took another long sip and wiped his knuckle across his lips.

"Now. We came here to Guinegate to support the archduke's claim. We've done so. The inheritance Maximilian earned through his marriage to Mary of Burgundy is secure, should he not let down the line from here. That man . . . dismounting his horse to stand the square with the soldiers. What a show of bravado that was," he said, raising an eyebrow. "After our artillery was captured and the Burgundian knights were routed, I feared us doomed." He shook his head and made a fist. "But when the French cavalry gave chase, and their archers proved disastrous, France lost the day to our infantry. You—*both of you*—held firm in the square to victory."

Prince Zane lifted his chin. "We did what needed to be done,

Father."

"You did. And not for the first time." He leaned toward the prince. "You are a warrior to your bones, Zane. A leader. A true prince. Someday all I have earned will be yours, and your rule will be one of just strength."

"Thank you, Father," Prince Zane said.

The king rolled the base of his chalice to-and-fro on the carved arm of his chair. "You, Matthias, are an enigma. You puzzle and interest me. I know not what to do with you."

"I serve you at your will, sire," Matthias said. "I do not seek accolade."

The king's nose wrinkled. "Yet here you sit. A small man among giants."

"At your summons, sire," Matthias said.

"Ha!" The king grinned. He bent forward and shifted a platter. A pile of deep purple blackberries shook loose, and he snatched a few, popping them into his mouth. He swallowed and wiped their juice from his stained lips. "You're no one of consequence, yet you bewitch and inspire other men. They look to you. Follow and respect you. You've proven yourself, again helping to carry our allies to victory. A natural fighter—as skilled as those trained from birth in the great houses—and you lead, anchoring yourself as a shield between death and lesser men."

Matthias shifted on his seat, and the king's chin lifted.

"Speak true, Matthias," King Girault said, his voice low. "I would hear what you have to say."

"They are good men, sire. All, from prince to pauper. They are yours, are they not?"

"Hmpf," the king said with a half-smile. "They are indeed. Regardless of rank or whose retinue they ride in, it is *my* army. They are *all* my men."

Matthias tilted his chalice to the king. He took a last drink and set it aside. This was not a conversation for a thickened head.

"The battle was well fought, but war is changing," King Girault said. "The world with it. The swords of our chivalrous past are now met with ceaseless innovation. I must straddle them both and always look ahead, for my sake and my son's." He shifted forward on his seat, laying his hand over his vividly sketched kingdom.

His fingers dug into the border lines, claiming it as a cat would mark a bush. "Now. We've aided the archduke. The Hapsburgs are endlessly ambitious, and with the Holy Roman Emperor's back along our borders, it's an alliance we mean to maintain. But that doesn't mean we bow to them, like the princes scattered along the Rhine. *I am a king*; Ewigsburg bows to no man but me. To keep it so, I must always be faster, smarter, stronger than the glory hounds who spar with one another for scraps around me. While Maximilian must turn and press his advantage against France, my own eyes turn south, toward an old alliance. Forgotten, or abandoned, by most. The Kingdom of Leuceria."

Point made, the king narrowed his eyes at Matthias, waiting.

"Prince Siegfried mentioned a mission there." Matthias flashed his eyes to Prince Zane, who sat silently, solid, an oak trunked in the tense air.

"There is. A delicate one of some personal importance. With Siegfried's death, I find the circle of those I trust to see my will done smaller," the king said, reaching for more berries. "How long have you been in my service, Matthias?"

Matthias cleared his throat, not wishing to remember the day he'd been sold into the king's army or the farmer who'd done so. "Almost nine years, sire."

"That long now?" The king cocked his head. "You've come far and could go farther still. What is it you seek? Armor? Horse? Go on. I want to know what *drives* the foot soldier."

The king meant to toy with him. Matthias dug his heels into the rug, grounding himself.

"I bought my horse. A good horse, from the stud farm in Swabia. I've earned my armor. My sword," Matthias said.

"Do you desire a home? Perhaps a wife?" the king said, his lip curling.

"I have no want for a wife," Matthias said.

"Ha! Yes, few men genuinely want them, but many men, especially kings, find they *need* them. More coin, then? You spend meagerly. Live modestly. Every month you have your wages sent to the *kloster* at Maulbronn. Tell me why."

"For the kindness they showed my brother, Reymund."

And others like him.

"Ah yes, young master Reymund," the king said, tapping his fingers. "You are most loyal to him. I wonder, are you as loyal to me? And your men?"

"I fight and serve at your word, sire," Matthias said. "As do the men. They are my brothers, through battle and blood, but they are loyal to their king."

"*Hmpf.* Are caged dogs ever truly loyal, or do they only appear so? Walking the periphery of their cage as they wait for the sound of the latch?" The king snarled at him. "Tell me, Matthias, if I open the door, will you hunt for me, or will you run?"

Matthias straightened in his seat, answering the challenge. "I gave you my oath, sire. My word is all—*everything*—I have."

The king smirked. Exchanging nods with his son, he splayed his palm upon his map. "My nephew's death doesn't pain me as much as it inconveniences me. You know of Leuceria?"

"I do, sire," Matthias said.

"Then you know it's falling apart from within. The once great kingdom is only a shadow of what it used to be, with its borders crumbled to only surround the city itself. Though I could fit its riches inside my pocket, the land still holds opportunity." The king picked up a parchment bearing an unfamiliar broken seal. "Prince Zane must remain here, but he's recommended you, Matthias, to speak for Ewigsburg."

Me? Matthias turned to the prince and locked eyes with him.

The king rolled the parchment and slapped it against his palm. "The bastardized princess is to be bartered. You will bring her to me," he said. "Had she a throne to claim, half of Christendom would be there, as they fought for the inheritance of Mary of Burgundy. This princess is disinherited and sows discord, giving reason for the regent to be rid of her to take the crown." He took a drink from his chalice and wiped his hand across his bottom lip. "I seek to resurrect an old alliance with the General."

"The General?" Matthias's blood pumped harder, thudding in his neck and into his ears like drums. Known across borders and generations simply as "the General," still legendary on the whispers of soldiers, he was known by all yet spoken of by few. The only thing greater than his glory had been his sudden and renowned downfall, when he plummeted from grace and earned the hatred of kings.

"*Genau.* The very same. He is regent and will be king," King Girault said. "I want the mountains between us conquered. I want the trade routes reopened. I want access to the Leucerian coast. Besides, the princess may be disinherited, but she offers a womb to fill, and I need more sons. A full cradle is as much a show of strength as any."

Prince Zane glanced at his father. "What of your mistress, Lilith? And her fruited belly?"

"*Hmpf,*" the king said, his face falling. "For all her efforts, the lady bears me nothing but daughters. Dead ones." He paused, grinding his teeth, and landed a dark eye on his son. "A man needs sons to secure his house, and a prince needs brothers to support him. The loss of your cousin is a great one. I will do what I must for my kingdom and for you. Now that Siegfried can no longer marry her, I will."

Matthias was dumbfounded. It was one thing to accompany his prince as guard, another to represent his sovereign. "And for this task, you wish to send me?"

"Your master is dead. You will wear your sword in my name and stand in my stead." The king laid the parchment before Matthias. "This letter guarantees your safe passage. Take Reymund to stand as advisor. He can speak intelligently enough, and I require a report back with his . . . level of detail. Take men you trust and make haste. The barter is soon to begin, and I anticipate Rome has already sent delegates."

"Rome?" Matthias baulked.

"They'll feign to appear in her interest only to marry her to a puppet of their own," Prince Zane said. "Illegitimate, the throne transfers to the General; legitimate, to whomever the Princess is married. It may be all well and based on the law, but the Pope is seizing this long-awaited opportunity to acquire the kingdom for themselves. Leuceria in their hands is the bridge connecting France to the peninsula, giving them the coastline."

The king drank. "Siegfried was strong, but his mind was weak. His heart was loyal, but his tongue was loose. The fool would've risked offense, incurring the wrath of the church, and mucking our chances to claim this bride."

A barter. With the General. Against the church. The pope. *With Reymund.*

Matthias stood, stepped around the table, and took a knee before his king. "Send me, sire. I will not fail you. I only ask you send me alone and leave my brother here."

"Ha! You do not know the law, nor could you speak their language. Reymund must go." The king's face hardened. "You cannot fail me, Matthias. You must bring her back."

"Reward, Father, should he succeed the task you set for him?" Prince Zane said. "You were prepared to offer our cousin an ample reward."

"I was." The king scooted to the edge of his seat. He leaned his elbows on his knees and folded his hands before him so that they rested before Matthias's bowed head. "Every man wants something, Matthias. Now you, you're not every man, though you wear that mask well." His boot pushed forward, his body arching closer still, and he hissed into Matthias's ear. "Tell me. Tell me what it is you desire, and I'll see it's yours—should you not fail me in this."

Matthias's chest tightened. This mission seemed insurmountable.

But what if he did succeed?

What if this princess, whoever she was, was his hope? *Their hope.* To live and die as free men. The chance he'd been chasing for years and had never been so close to attaining. However impossible this mission truly was, he would not stop. He would see it through, for *them*, even if it killed him.

And then he would disappear.

Get far enough away. Lay down his sword and find silence. Replace the half-timbered roofs with the limbs of an ancient tree, still alive and climbing toward an open sky. Where the sun bathed the fields, thick with crisp gold grain, bending and weaving in the breath of angels. A sleep restful enough that the ground around him would grow around his own limbs, and he'd feel rooted. Centered. Until the day his body rotted into the earth, his name was forgotten, and he would know peace.

But first, this.

Matthias glanced at the prince from the corner of his eye. Prince Zane was watching Matthias, chin raised, his head ever so slightly nodding with encouragement.

Matthias summoned the words. "My oath."

The king snickered. There it was, that hint of mockery.

Matthias balled his fist, his knuckles straining still from the grip of the pike. "Prince Siegfried promised to grant our freedom. That my oath, those of my brothers and my men, be fulfilled."

King Girault looked to his son, who nodded, affirming the promised claim. Snarling, the king slammed his hand on his knee and swiftly stood. He strutted back around the table and ran his fingers along the bottom edge of the long map of the continent. Over Spain. Over France. Stopping at the coast of Leuceria, where the mountains fell into the sea.

"The set of stones you have on you, boy," he muttered. He tapped his fingers. "Very well. I'll honor my nephew's word and hold your oath fulfilled. But *only* if you succeed." The king's voice grew harsh and heavy. "Bring her to me. You, your men, will be free."

CHAPTER 2

LAST OF HER LINE

Avelina - Kingdom of Leuceria - One Week Later

IT SHOULD HAVE BEEN A day of anticipation. Full of excited whispers and flirtatious suitors with grandiose offers and promises as they bartered for the chance to wed their princess. It should have been a day of joy. One much reveled, with shared secrets between giggling ladies under the watch of the kind, radiant eyes of her mother. It should have been a day of awe. The day the people of Leuceria crowded the halls to behold the sole heir in a dynasty of thirteen great and powerful kings open the door to the rest of her life.

It wasn't.

Instead, Princess Avelina, in calm yet screaming silence, steeled herself for General Niro's order. The irony was not lost on her that the man sworn to protect her could be the very one to send her to her death. Born simply at the wrong time, and of the wrong sex, her fate hung on the whim of the man who treated her as both treasure and troll.

"Crown Jewel" or "the Bastard."

The general's hand had been forced, and the decision would finally be made. Her day of judgment, masquerading as the traditional bridal barter. Avelina expected once this charade of a barter was over, she would conveniently *disappear*, just as her parents had, and the crown would then freely—finally—be his.

For Niro to wear the crown and rule with absolute power, her dynasty had to be obliterated. Completely. She knew this.

Unless she could escape.

Crouched on the chapel floor, Avelina struggled to fasten the ornery hook that kept popping open. Successful at last, the old riding boot tightened around her calf. Stolen from the stables, the pair of boots fit well enough. She could wiggle her toes, and with the extra pair of hose, they didn't slide on her feet.

"Perfect."

Avelina faintly smiled in satisfaction and exhaustion. She spread her luxurious skirts back around her, and the boots disappeared. Another secret hidden beneath her silks. Lacing her fingers together, she leaned onto her knees for prayer. Lost in swirling, dusty, solitude, Avelina found her sanctuary.

The chapel door creaked open, and a warm wisp of salted wind swept past her. Avelina had expected him, but the sound of his voice still broke her peace.

"I see you've gone with the lavender?" General Niro's political advisor, Dolion, said, approaching her from behind. His steps were light, softly shuffling against the stones, but she heard each one as his cloak swished around him. Tall and dapper, with a head of distinct golden mahogany curls against his copper skin, he would be handsome except for the malicious snarl always coiling his lip and the hands oddly too big for his frame.

Breathe, Avelina. Just breathe.

The ribs within her breast constricted, but Avelina managed an even voice. "It seemed a fitting choice."

Yes, Dolion. Today, the lavender.

Whose rich skirts wouldn't betray her secrets. Especially the boots.

Her hands folded, Avelina pressed her elbow against the pocket she'd sewn into her underskirt. Needle and thread, patiently gathered from her embroidery basket and hidden away for weeks, had been used to sew what small treasures she had into her seams. There, secure at her hip, lay the most precious item, her mother's book of hours. Ornamented in gems held by tiny prongs, it was an intricate and brilliant design of pearls and semiprecious stones.

It was beautiful. Delicate. And her lone connection to her mother.

Avelina's eyes closed. She tried to lift the weight her parents' deaths had cemented into her chest and imagine them, but she'd only been four years old, and the details that remained were few. Their faces, scarcely remembered, and their voices, lost to time.

"Of course. Yesterday you were nothing but a disinherited disgrace. Today you're to be a bride. Though it does seem a waste of such fine silk," Dolion said, snickering. He slowly ran his fingers along the back of her neckline, a lone fingertip brushing against her bare skin. "The nobles' offers will be of no consequence, no matter how grand they may be. General Niro will never allow you to marry."

Avelina straightened her back, repulsed.

"Well then. Let us go quickly. The negotiations will soon begin," Dolion said. He clapped his hands and gestured toward the door. "I do look forward to the great houses turning on one another. I hate to miss a bit of blood sport."

Avelina didn't move. "Surely, this day does not have to end in blood."

He looked down his nose at her with a mischievous grin. "For someone, yes."

"Then I would once more say my prayers," Avelina said. "For all of us. One never knows upon whom the General's temper will fall."

Dolion's cheek spasmed. General Niro's temper was vicious and unpredictable. His son Marcus's was much worse.

"A moment," Dolion said, leering at her. "I will allow you *one* moment." His breath crawled across her open shoulder and along the slant of her neck until it curled behind her ear. "But, child, do not confuse me for an ally."

Determined, she steadied herself, fighting every urge to retreat. "Never."

For the thirteen years since her parents' murder, Avelina had stood opposite him, a prisoner held tightly at Niro's left side. With words slippery and sweet on his serpent tongue, Dolion had slithered into position, posturing as Niro's advisor in a court disrupted by tragedy. Dolion was witness, if not party, to all those struck down in Niro's name.

This man was no ally to her. To anyone. Like the tiny lizards running through their gardens, Dolion changed color to suit whatever thorny flower he stood beside. But as slick as he was, he valued the placement of his head and didn't trust Niro either. A fear she could use to steal this precious, last liberty.

"A single moment," Dolion said, backing away.

"Is all I need."

In this cold room, the watch of the dead afforded her privacy from the living. Once elaborately decorated and host to a congregation, the chapel now stood abandoned. Unused and ignored but for her. Large men stood at the threshold when she came for her prayers, worried their sins followed and would curse them to hell. Raiders had upturned the tombs, cracking effigies and scattering bones, leaving their spoils spread for the taking. Priceless holy relics pirated away. The high altar stripped from the apse, its centuries old carvings axed and burned.

"Such a shame," Dolion said, strolling nearby with exaggerated leisure. Only he ever followed her, probably convinced his wit would serve him well in either heaven or hell. "When your father died, they ruined this place."

Inching closer on her knees toward the tomb before her, Avelina shuddered at the mention of her father. Leuceria had erupted upon his death, blackening the sun with a midnight fog thick with loss and, for those who dared to seize it, rich opportunity. Houses had battled. Houses had fallen. Few families lay intact, and their victors had stood atop their towers watching, waiting, as a vast array of heirs and usurpers rose from the ashes to claim the empty titles left around them. The ground had eventually settled within the city, but the aftershock still rippled through her daily life.

Even in this period of political turmoil and perpetual darkness, where men erased history as it suited them, one monument lay undisturbed. Here, centered in the nave of the chapel where the old kings held court, lay the Father of Leuceria.

The tomb of their first king, Maximus the Bear.

"Great king," Avelina whispered, lifting her folded hands to her mouth.

The stately gate that had once surrounded the tomb had been pulled down. The flowering golden vines that had adorned the iron grille were now only a part of her memory. The destruction had ceased at the tomb itself. Tall and wide as his warhorse, sealed in painstakingly carved marble, the sarcophagus told the stories of his life that had become legend. The aged history of their kingdom. The men who built it. Fought and died for it . . . loved it. The stories of the old men.

"Forefathers. Father. God in heaven," Avelina said. "I beg of you. Give me strength."

Eleven generations followed the Bear. Ten kings had been memorialized. Five on opposing sides of the tomb in a circle never to be complete. Cast in Corinthiacum and twice her height, their black eyes fixed, eternally holding court for the first of their line. Empty pedestals marked where the majority had once stood, their likenesses smelt for the valued metal.

"It must vex you that your father's likeness was never here," Dolion called from where he sauntered amongst the bones. "The only Leucerian king never immortalized."

Her poor father. Uncast, unmentioned, unwritten. His body buried in shame in an unmarked grave. All trace of him, save her, vanquished.

Only a pair of her ancestors remained, standing testament to their history. Dressed for battle, fearless warriors in meticulous detail, head to foot in blackened bronze, their presence humbled her. Each king's crested shield sat at his feet and his sword against his hip. Mail snugly guarded and traced the limbs of their tall bodies, and intricately detailed plate armor covered their broad chests. Each man was proudly adorned with unique jewels; they both wore the crown that had been passed from one king to the next. Their faces hung in perpetual grief for their lost ancestors, and the last of their long line, the young princess, knelt before them.

"Such a rich dynasty," Dolion said. His head listing to the side, he stood before the platform where her grandfather's effigy had once been. Dolion hopped upon the empty stone and postured, pleased with himself. "Such history. Reduced to almost nothing."

Avelina ignored him. Her gaze fixated on the rounded ends of her knees and the glistening tiles beneath them. The last sparkling rays of sunset filtered through her chapel windows and dusted them in gray-rose. At first dainty strands of silk, the beams thickened, darkening, and coagulating into a red pool.

Avelina blinked furiously, trying to stop the hallucination, but to no avail. Blood seeped from beneath her knees and slowly spread across the floor. Her cheekbones burned as her cheeks iced below them, and the stench of iron flooded her nose. Avelina gagged, its taste tickling her tongue until it poured into her lungs. She bit her lip, grasping at a sense of reality, and she closed her eyes against the illusion.

No. Please. Not today.

Avelina couldn't help when the visions would come. Long barred from her mind and buried in her bones, the memories surrounding her parents' murder used to only haunt her at night. Lost in a dream when her heart betrayed her. With the commotion of the circling court and the general's increasingly intense moods, details from that night had begun breaking through and seizing her with crippling anxiety.

The flurry of motion as men raced her father's halls. Blurry and muted voices, as if muddled through water. The coldness of the tiles against her tiny seated bottom through her nightshirt. The stickiness when she drew her hands from the floor and wiggled her stained fingers. Being carried away in Niro's bloody arms. The last glimpse over his shoulder of her mother's body, sprawled naked, twisted, and brutalized.

"Breathe, Avelina," she whispered.

She had to maintain control. Quell her feelings and play their game, by their rules.

Be the stone-cold, stoic crown jewel. Again, as always, to protect herself, but she would not kneel and lay her neck across the block. This would be her one chance to escape, and she would take it. One deep last breath and she stood, locking her wobbly knees straight. She adjusted her gown around her waist and smoothed the fabric against her stomach.

It was time.

Avelina walked past Dolion through the door toward the Great Hall. Mindful to keep her boots hidden, she clasped her hands in front of her instead of lifting her skirt, as she so often did out of habit.

Dolion was quickly beside her. Leaning in, he prodded her. "Do they speak to you?"

"Who?" Avelina said curtly. Even on this summer eve, an icy

avalanche rode her skin, prickling her hair, curving along her back and running along her legs. Her calves seized; the muscles shocked against the leather of her boots.

"Your kings," he said.

"My Lord in heaven? Or my ancestors whose bones lay scattered?" Dolion snorted.

Avelina kept her chin parallel to the floor. Throngs of onlookers lined the loggia. Servants. Guards. Families too poor, or without the right name, to gain entrance to the barter. All gathered along the open-air corridor, eager for a glance. Not one amongst them had ever offered her help. Spoken for her. These long years. Yet today they arrived en masse for this farce. Their collective silence was deafening, beating against her eardrums.

"Any. All," Dolion said, his breath so close it lay on her lips like red paint. "I'd love to know what they say. Or will they not speak to the Bastard?"

"That I am a pawn in the political games of men."

"Ha! Aren't you a clever girl? Then they're honest with you."

"Always," Avelina said, quickening her step.

Dolion frowned. Eyebrows furrowed, he crept closer. His chest bumped her shoulder. "Don't play with me, child. I want their secrets. Tell me what wisdom the old ones share with you."

Scrutiny from all sides landed heavier on her with each step. No deference to her rank, their boldness smacked across her face. Their slippery stares traced down her until their weight pooled around her ankles. She pushed forward harder.

"Grace, only grace," she said. "In all things."

"Then they are silent. Such men would not waste their time on you," he seethed. "You're as wicked as your harlot of a mother. Weak as the king you claim as your father. You feign innocence while you would suckle the veins of your country dry beneath your veil. We will be rid of you soon enough, one way or another."

Avelina choked, fear lodged as a misguided bite.

Show them nothing, Avelina. Scream inside but show them nothing. Nothing. Swallowing the bile burning her throat, she dammed the tears threatening her eyes.

This bridal barter. For how many daughters before her had this been their *kairos*? Their opportunity to find a future. Family.

Perhaps even love. But that was not the case for her. These people came to witness her, the thirteenth of her line, climb as many wooden steps to the hangman's gallows.

"This is where I leave you," Dolion said as they reached the outer doors. "Until I see you at Niro's side."

Avelina refused to look at him. Taking a slow breath, she trapped the wail of the broken child within her. She squeezed her hands together, trying to ebb the shaking, and pressed her fists against her stomach when it wasn't enough.

The guards slammed their heavy poleaxes against the floor, and the doors opened. Avelina stepped across the threshold, leaving Dolion and her past behind her.

An ocean of boisterous voices and movement broke apart and fell silent. All attention culminated on her. Battering into her, it knocked the air from her lungs.

But Avelina stood anchored, a rock against the crashing wave.

Her chin began to quiver, but she kept it raised.

She was terrified yet resilient. Ready to stand witness at the negotiations and earnestly hopeful that somewhere within this room was her chance—to escape her lonely childhood, to escape into the unknown, and to escape with her life.

With practiced perfection, Avelina swept one foot behind her and dropped into a controlled, elegant curtsy. But this time, she would not lower her eyes. Instead, with shaking breath, she boldly stared into the room head-on.

Grace. And to remember who she was.

That's what they said.

Their voiceless words rattled her bones and rode her quickened pulse, pushing purpose and hope through her veins.

In a world racing to define who she was, or who she wasn't, she was to never, ever forget. She was Princess Avelina Elisabeth. Heir to the throne. Last of her line.

And beyond that, stripped of silks and naked of titles, she was her father's daughter.

She had been loved.

She, alone, was enough.

And it was she who would determine her own destiny.

CHAPTER 3

SINS WE COMMIT FOR
THE SAKE OF OUR SONS

Matthias

BACK PLANTED AGAINST THE WALL, Matthias squeezed the bridge of his nose between his fingertips and exhaled, hoping to expel the crushing weight his success or failure carried. His muscles were strained and fatigued, and a dull aching bound his bones. "What the hell are we doing here?"

"We're here to kiss an old man's arse," Jorn said, pacing. His cape, worn and dirty from traveling, whipped behind him like an angry beast's tail. "If they allow us in front of him, that is."

Matthias smirked and rolled his neck, welcoming the crisp cracks of his bones' release.

It was true. He knew exactly why they were here.

They were here at the will of his king, yet they'd come to Leuceria willingly. Hell, he'd have come by himself to see this through if he had had to, but his brothers would not have it. And Reymund, never one to be swayed by a challenge, would've gone alone.

Their trip had been a long one.

Matthias and his men had left Guinegate immediately. Determined to avoid any lingering components of the French armies, they'd sailed down the Rhine and taken what tributaries they could through the Alps. When they could sail no more, they'd ridden. They'd taken lesser trails and paid a heavy toll to protect the purse they secretly carried in their king's name. Through mountain valleys. Along crumbling Roman roads. Beyond the

Duchies of Milan and Genoa until they reached the border of Leuceria.

While their treasures, their king's seal, and the curiosity surrounding them leveraged safe passage and entry to Leuceria on behalf of their king, there was still no guaranteed invitation to barter. They were a motley crew, torn and tattered from travel. Without occasion to change, they stood in marked juxtaposition to the nobles filling the palatial hallway from one end to the other.

As varied as the colors, cuts, and crests on their patterned robes, the nobles were united in their flamboyant finery. Their garments trimmed in fur and their jewels heavy around their necks, they stood in clusters, talking amongst themselves. Their languages clattered like coins. Still, it was easy to pick out the suitor within each as their entourage circled and groomed them, waiting for the guarded doors of the palace's Great Hall to open.

Matthias met their stares openly. He kept his face courteous without deference.

These were grand men. From grand families. And grand kingdoms.

But so was the king for whom he stood.

As were his brothers—great men, *good* men, if not grand.

Matthias's solid frame doubled in size as he stepped forward, straightened his back, and rolled his shoulders wide. Catching Jorn's attention, he said, "Be still, brother."

"I sat long enough on my horse." Jorn's nose twitched above his red mustache. As if to emphasize, he stretched each leg beneath him.

Dressed up for the occasion, Jorn had tied his hair back off his face, though random auburn curls, whose shades seemed to ebb and flow with his mood, plotted their escape. Akin to Matthias in size and stature, Jorn was always a step behind him. An insatiable hunter. Quick. Skilled. Lethal. Loyal. And truly a pain in his arse.

"I'll wager your arse is as bruised as mine, but you're restless as a hare caught in a net," Matthias said, half-smiling. He tilted his head to the empty space beside him. "Too many eyes are upon us here."

Jorn snorted and steadied himself.

A quick count placed the number of men waiting for admittance at twenty and two hundred. Their weapons having been stored in the armory upon arrival, Matthias was uneasy around so many. He dropped his chin, twisting the new ring on his right hand. The large garnet, held by an etched sword that wrapped around his finger, felt odd to him, a man who made heavy use of his hands. The weight of what the ring represented—showing he stood as the "King's Sword," a makeshift title thrust upon him as quickly, and nonchalantly, as the mission itself—sat wearily on his mind.

"The king should've sent one of his nobles," Matthias said. "In place of Prince Siegfried."

"King Girault sent the men he trusts," Reymund said, laying a hand on Matthias's shoulder. "Any of our nobles may have used this to challenge him or press their advantage. Perhaps taken this bride for themselves."

Matthias smirked and adjusted Reymund's disheveled burgundy cape where the medallion of the king's crest glinted against his shoulder. Reymund smiled in thanks, realigning the wooden cross necklace back to the center of his chest. The king's trusted advisor, whose crooked body housed an unrivaled learning capacity, Reymund never forgot a thing, his mind absorbing what his muscles could not. That and his pure heart were his power.

"Are you ready, Matthias?" Alif said. The youngest amongst them, his straw-colored hair was plaited behind his lean but strong shoulders, leaving the thin mustache he was trying to grow to match Jorn's his most prominent feature. A full head shorter and thirteen summers young, Alif was the runt of their mismatched litter. "Did the king give you specific instruction?"

"Bring her back," Matthias said, raising a brow. "Emphasized rather ardently."

"I have a hard time believing they need the money here," Jorn said, gesturing at a statue. "If they have so much, they can drape gold on a man's limp—"

"Brother." Reymund interrupted him, at which Jorn gave a sheepish smile.

Carved from white stone, smooth with bits of glittering gray, the figure was nude except for the lavish leaves that gave it its lone bit of privacy. Several littered the corridor, towering in various poses and stages of dress. One with stag and sword, another twirled in a lovers' embrace. The abundance of gold they wore uniting them all in a curious, gross display of wealth.

"Or that they'll part with her so easily," Matthias said. "Especially to ruffians like us among these civilized men."

"Don't confuse dress for civility," Reymund said.

"*Genau*. Not all wolves bare their fangs," Jorn said. "These men are hawks. Circling in plain sight."

Matthias spread his shoulders. "Still, I don't like this. Bartering like she's an animal at market."

"'Tis the way of the rich," Reymund said. "Marriage done so. Love's a poor man's luxury."

"If anyone's," Alif said.

"Or curse." Jorn shrugged. "And you think the king offers her more?"

"It's not for us to say, Jorn," Matthias said, looking at him. "We're here to secure her in marriage. The king's business is his own."

"*Genau*. Never question your king," Jorn jeered. *"Duty before self. Honor above all."* He grinned and smacked Matthias's arm.

"These men pitted against one another works in our favor," Reymund said, shuffling between them. "Having you two bickering like housemaids does not. Especially here." Matthias moved to support him, but Reymund waved him off, steadying himself.

The doors to the Great Hall opened.

An opulent room of ornate walls and windows was a blinding change to the exposed stone masonry of the castles they knew. Woven tapestries and iron candelabras were replaced here with dripping chandeliers, mirrors wrapped in still more gold, and richly painted ceilings. A raised throne at the head of the room was set with a banquet table before it with jugs of ales and wines and glasses the same colors as the fruits overflowing on platters. Sets of similarly staged tables mirrored one another, covering the floor's length to accommodate the gathered crowd.

While most men flowed toward seating at the center of the hall, Matthias led his men to a front corner table. Close enough to observe negotiations. Backs protected against the wall. Covered. Where he could see everything.

"As I stand, that's got to be the General," Jorn said, nodding toward the towering man who entered through a door behind the throne.

The myth became man. Each confident step the General took thundered his presence. Face like a badger, his beady, black eyes peered from beneath tightly pulled eyebrows. His head was covered in thick ebony hair, slicked back and streaked with silver. A dark scar ran the length of his face, from his left eye, disappearing into his pointed beard. He spoke to no one, yet all turned in his path and bowed in submission.

Matthias dropped his chin, though he did not bow as he would have to his own king.

"And the dance of powerful men begins," Matthias muttered.

Had they been in a tavern, they might've measured their cocks. Here the men strutted like roosters in the yard, posturing, feathers ruffled and wings thrown wide to increase the ground they occupied. The air was heavy with both muffled and exaggerated conversation and laughter. Pride and insults were hurled between tables wrapped with kin, standing on their names, their money and the swords it bought them. Young suitors peacocked in their best robes—shoulders pinned back, spines pulled from their hips, and chins jutted—while their elders stroked their round bellies. Dinner and more drink arrived, fueling their sport, carried by servants wrapped in loosely draped linens, hair piled high and the plates piled higher.

Matthias grimaced. "General Niro's chokehold on the kingdom is weak. That he even agreed to the barter shows how slippery it's become. The nobles have called his bluff."

"The church as well," Reymund said, gesturing to those seated at a table of honor before the nobles. "Pope Sixtus IV's legate. The Holy Father may be at war with Florence, but he means to intercede. His attendance here speaks to the issue of her legitimacy."

"Or her inheritance," Matthias said.

"Exactly that," Reymund said. "He who has the girl, has Leuceria. Either by marrying her, to put themselves on the throne—"

"Or maintaining control by putting her in the ground," Jorn spat.

A sharp pain crossed Matthias's forehead, and he pinched the bridge of his nose, willing it to disappear. He needed a drink. A few drinks. Rest. *Someday*. He took a large swallow from his cup and coughed. "*Gah*, this ale is strong."

"It's better than the wine," Jorn said, sniffing a glass. Eyebrow raised, he handed it to Reymund, who paired it with a cheese tartlet.

Matthias smiled and watched the room while his men refueled. The hall grew increasingly tense, thick with braggadocio and thin on air. If he meant to take the princess home to his king, he needed to win this room. He needed to find the room's vulnerability and strangle it in his fist.

His eyes returned to the General. Matthias knew a losing fight when he saw one, and this was one the General was set to lose. Renowned on the battlefield, General Niro held no command authority here. He was lost and drowning in this sea of names and wealth and politics. Any love, respect, or fear of him seemed replaced with emboldened wagers and emerging defiance. Once his insurance to hold the regency, the princess had become Niro's greatest threat. Because here, the blood in her veins and any child she bore could raise an army with a claim for the throne.

There was a heavy clang, and the far doors opened. A shockwave rippled past them. Men stilled. Conversation ceased. All attention fixed on the small figure centered in the threshold.

Bring her to me. You, your men, will be free.

There she stood.

His hopes wrapped in silk.

"It's her," Reymund whispered behind him. "The Crown Jewel emerges."

"The princess?" Jorn said, setting down his ale.

"There." Alif pointed. "That has to be her."

Matthias's fingers traced the line of his beard and his knuckles settled against his mouth, watching her. Compared to the nobles garishly bedecked head to toe in their wealth, she was dressed simply. Wrapped in a dress too big for her frame, her only adornment a thin circlet of colored stones upon her dark hair. She lowered into a flawless curtsy, bravely, boldly staring at them all.

The room became hers, frozen in her wake.

"She's exquisite," Reymund said.

"She's only a babe," Matthias said.

"She's of age," Reymund said. "Recently seventeen."

"She was only a babe when her parents were slaughtered," Jorn said, ripping apart a seeded roll. "And you know that loathsome man had a hand in it."

The princess walked to General Niro, curtsied, and sat beside him. Forearm laid vulgarly across the table, his palm opened, and she placed her fingers within it.

Matthias watched as one by one each group was led to General Niro's table, beginning with the legate from Rome. The subdued conversation followed a general pattern. They presented their suitor. The nobles spoke directly to the curly-haired man who stood at Niro's side and appeared to handle negotiations. General Niro merely listened. None acknowledged the princess.

"Who do you think he is? By the general. He's a pretty one," Jorn said, rolling his eyes.

"Advisor," Matthias said. "His reputation as a general is legendary, but his political one is a disaster."

"Which is to our advantage," Reymund said. "His claims of her illegitimacy are trivial. Even a defamed princess holds prestige, and marriage raises one family above all others."

"None are here for the lady herself?" Alif asked.

"She's no more to them than a means to an end," Jorn said.

"Poor lamb," Alif said.

Matthias's jaw smarted. Alif was right. She didn't appear as a royal, knowing luxury and privilege, standing in the glory afforded her by birthright. She was the lamb, alone, terror-stricken, knowing itself to be soon gutted and sacrificed upon the altar.

She sat still. Silent. Her striking eyes the only feature betraying her. Glittering amber jewels. Darting. Flitting about. They met his, and for a time they were locked on one another. Staring at him, helpless, almost pleading, shocking in their raw honesty. The amber stones pierced his chest, seizing the chambers of his heart like talons.

This lamb was no prize. She brought no lands. No rank. No inheritance. Merely a vessel, her only offering her unseeded womb. Her esteem lay in her lineage, legitimate depending upon loyalty, and in what sons she could bear. If she lived long enough.

Matthias leaned toward Jorn's ear and muttered, "There's too much at stake. The time's come to be rid of her, but how? I fear there's no peaceful solution to be had here."

"Do you not remember Blutburg, brother?" Jorn said, looking down.

Blutburg.

"Of course I do." Matthias's nose wrinkled. The mere mention of the name flashed the memory of that horrid scent past his nose. He'd only been a boy then, but those memories were bone-deep and haunted him still. His mercenary father, enraged by the lack of promised payment for a siege under his command, had taken out his wrath on the city. Butchering and burning every soul, but those few who escaped, including Matthias himself, and the red-headed child he'd saved who now stood a man before him. East along the Danube river, it was where the fields had become a marsh of ash and blood, the first dynasty of many had ended and their brotherhood had begun.

"Then you know you finish it. Then. And there," Jorn said. "If he's kept her alive. Protected. All this time. Something else drives him."

"*Hmpf,*" Matthias said. "And therein lies the riddle."

The men exchanged glances and ate in silence, watching the rounds of suitors. When beckoned for their turn to barter, the men stood.

"You know what to do," Matthias whispered to Alif, who nodded and left the hall.

Matthias, Reymund, and Jorn advanced. The General stared at them and grunted.

With a hand on his chest, Reymund began speaking in Latin.

Raising his hand, the General interrupted him. "Enough. You may speak in your own tongue."

"May I approach, General? The journey has been long, and these legs withered beneath me do me no favors," Reymund said, slipping back into German.

The General nodded and, with a wave of his hand, a chair was brought for Reymund. Matthias offered his arm for support, led Reymund to it, and remained at his side.

"My thanks, General," Reymund said. "We come from Ewigsburg to negotiate on behalf of our king."

General Niro covered his mouth with his knuckles. Having openly measured each of them, he spoke. "Soldiers, aren't you? Girault's men?"

Matthias gave a deep nod of acknowledgment and motioned to Jorn. "*Ja*. My brother Jorn and I."

"You come from the field, then? Against the French?" General Niro asked.

"Directly," Matthias said.

"Is it true what they say? The young archduke charged the field amongst the foot soldiers?" Niro tilted his head.

"It is. Only a halberd's length between himself and my men, General," Matthias answered.

"Gallant indeed," Niro said.

There it is.

Barters were part negotiation, part heckling, but *that* was how to reach him. As a man on the field. Conceding the stakes, speaking plainly, pointedly, and with respect, from one soldier to another.

Crossing his arms at his chest, the curly-haired man shuffled his foot forward and looked down his nose at them. "I am Dolion. Political advisor to General Niro." He raised an eyebrow at Reymund. "Who is the monk? We've already spoken with the church."

"He's no monk," Jorn said. "Though he holds esteem with his God, for sure."

"General, we come at King Girault's behest. Our eldest brother, Reymund, is a valued advisor to our king," Matthias said. He laid a hand on Reymund's shoulder, drawing General Niro's eye to the crest pinned there. "And I am Matthias, the King's Sword."

"But there are three of you?" Dolion said. "King Girault sends a crippled monk, his sword, and what are you?" He turned his attention to Jorn. "The ass he rode here?" He laughed and stroked his chin. "The monk, his sword, and his ass. I like it."

Matthias drew a slow breath. He didn't care for this advisor. Slim and well-groomed, he looked like a fancy dog. Too lazy for the hunt, yet another man who supped on the labor of others and tucked his tail if threatened.

General Niro side-eyed the blond, who smirked and pulled himself straighter.

"I know Girault." General Niro shifted, leaning his shoulder toward the princess, who sat rigid on the edge of her seat. "His army was allied with mine. Long ago. A soldier like me, sitting as king. Tell me, how does he like it?"

"He thrives, General," Reymund said.

"Good on him, then." Niro's lip twitched. He rubbed his forefinger across his chin, then wiped his hand over his beard. "Where is the nephew? Prince Siegfried? I find it troubling others have been sent to barter on his behalf."

Matthias exhaled, considering his words. "Fallen. At Guinegate."

Niro's face fell. The news was a surprise, and from General Niro's reaction, an unwelcome one. He leaned forward, propping his elbow upon the table's edge, and ran his thumb across his bottom lip. He exhaled slowly.

Matthias maintained eye contact. Waiting. Watching. Witnessing the General's initial shock swing into decided reaction. Calculating, reassessing, strategizing, as his king had done only days before. *But to what end?*

Weighing him, Matthias found General Niro's struggles evident. It was obvious he lived well and indulged in too much drink, but not so much in pleasures. Worry lines trenched deeply around his sagging mouth showed how often a scowl sat there. Another trio of lines dug between his eyes. He sat hunched, protecting his belly, in the way men did when they had much to lose. He solidly gripped the hand of the princess at his side, lest she run, though she looked as if she wouldn't dare breathe without his permission.

How long had the General lived like this?

Wanting the crown, but not wearing it. Playing at regent, but being called usurper. Surrounded by beauty, but plagued by uncertainty. King Girault sat tall on his throne, looming over his court, ready for any challenge. This man of former greatness sat crumpled in his.

Waiting. But for what?

General Niro pulled the fist that avariciously gripped hers closer to him as his other hand fumbled a two-handled embellished cup. Steadied, he drank, a line of wine escaping the corner of his mouth and slithering into his beard. The General wouldn't let go of her even to properly take a drink.

"I'm sorry to hear that. That changes things immensely." General Niro's tongue ran over his teeth. "Then why are you here, Sword? Speak plainly, soldier. I will have your confidence."

"King Girault offers his own hand in marriage," Matthias said.

"Ha!" General Niro laughed and then just as quickly scowled. "He offers to make her his breeding mare. Why would I let her wither beneath some pretender older than myself?"

"After the man's sarded every other maiden at his own court? Even if your king prefers his bed full, there are plenty here as well who find theirs cold," Dolion said, cocking his head of curls.

General Niro coughed and tilted his cup toward Reymund. "He already has his heir, does he not?"

"He has a son, yes," Reymund said. "The Crown Prince Zane."

Matthias signaled Jorn, who placed their treasure on the table in front of Niro and opened the chest.

"We bring you this gift from King Girault," Matthias said, stealing a glance at the princess. Like a fawn, she stared blankly forward, focused and frozen in her seat amongst her prey, while her ears were perked, listening to every spoken word. His biceps tightened, and a tremor ran down the length of his body, his own muscles clenching in response to the fear he read emanating from hers.

"You bring only this chest of jewels in exchange for mine?" General Niro said. He ran his hand through the coins and let some drip between his fingers, clanking down upon one another. "Others bring me treaties and agreements of trade. Promise me land and great riches. What do you offer me, monk?"

"Our king makes an offer worthy of the princess and her most impressive lineage," Reymund said. "She will be queen of Ewigsburg."

"It doesn't seem right to raise her so," Dolion said. "Here she is ineligible to inherit any title. She's nothing but a girl."

After standing mute beside him, Jorn grunted. "Truly? Only a girl?"

Dolion glared at the princess. "She's no one. Nothing but a nuisance who should've been dealt with long ago."

Matthias's teeth vised. Dangerous influence rode the buttery tone of that pretty devil.

"Then why didn't you?" Jorn's expression did little to hide the disdain he held for the advisor. "Why take her in, General?"

"Because the king was my friend," Niro said sharply, wine-streaked spittle hitting his beard. "You know nothing of the man. We were raised together. He to wear the crown and I to be the soldier. As our fathers before us."

Niro frowned and wiped his hand across his mouth.

Dolion took a step forward, leaning over the General's shoulder.

"But it was *you*, General, who brought glory to Leuceria." Dolion turned a slanted eye to Matthias and raised an open palm. "The king was a simpleton. He married a harlot and was foolish enough to claim the babe she bore was his."

"Was the queen not also a noble by birth?" Reymund said. His right arm twitched in marked agitation. Matthias stepped forward, again placing a hand on Reymund's right shoulder, and pressed down firmly to help ground him. "From a respectable lineage here?"

"The queen was no great lady. She was treacherous and loose, and her depravity cost them their lives," Dolion said. He crossed his arms, his mouth twisting into a grin. "Every day the girl's grown, she becomes more a reflection of her mother. Reminding us daily of *who she truly is*."

"Mighty generous of you, General," Matthias said in a calm tone. "To raise her. *Protect* her."

Niro's cheek twitched.

"As you assumed the regency," Jorn said.

Matthias rounded an eye at him, and Jorn's lip tugged to the side against his beard. He rose on the balls of his feet and then back onto his heels, straightened himself, and exhaled.

"What was General Niro to do but assume the throne for the sake of our kingdom?" Dolion said. "It was a time of great chaos, as you can imagine." Darkness gathered around his eyes. "It is no matter. The time has come. The girl is of age. We will tolerate the Bastard no longer."

There was a marked shift in the volume of the nobles behind him, and Matthias looked over his shoulder. A younger man strode through with a group close at his heels.

This must be the son, Marcus.

Same dark features as Niro, he strutted with the ignorant confidence of a man who'd never been tested. Nose raised high, he plowed through the crowd, hand playfully rested atop the hilt of the sword that swayed as he walked. An adornment. This was a man who wore his father's achievement as his own. The invincibility of one great only by birth but coddled since. Hadn't learned to protect his backside. Or heed his words.

"Hai iniziato? Senza di me?" Marcus said, approaching the table.

"Yes, Marcus, the barter's begun," General Niro said, resting his back against the throne.

"Your bride price?" Following his father's lead, he traded his Italian for German. He leaned toward the chest and scoffed. "You come into my father's house and insult him?"

"There is no insult here, only opportunity," Matthias said. He leaned forward and closed the chest, edging it toward General Niro.

"Why are you even entertaining this?" Marcus said. "You've gone mad, Father."

"Show some respect for your elders, boy," Jorn said, stepping toward him. "Your father was cutting down armies at the knees when you were cutting teeth on your maid's tit."

Marcus turned to Jorn, looked him up and down, and dismissed him. Marcus's mouth opened, but Niro interrupted with a raised palm and gestured toward Matthias.

"Son, these are King Girault's men. From Ewigsburg. This is Reymund, the monk. Matthias, the King's Sword, and their friend . . . John," General Niro said.

"It's Jorn," Jorn said, arms crossing at his chest.

"Yern," General Niro said.

"No. *Jorn,*" Jorn said.

General Niro waved his hand dismissively and turned back to his son.

"And he's no monk," Jorn said, pointing to Reymund.

"I don't care who they are," Marcus hissed.

"They're soldiers, Marcus," General Niro said. "Warriors. Like me."

"Like us, you mean," Marcus said.

"Boy, wearing a dagger doesn't make you a soldier," Jorn said, rubbing his chin.

Marcus seethed. "If they are soldiers, make use of them. Pay them to stand with us."

"No thanks," Jorn said, taking a sidestep.

"Our king has made an offer," Reymund said. "A legitimate one."

"Only somewhat legitimate," Dolion said.

"Father, this pretense has gone on long enough. How many generations of our family have to stand in the shadow of their dead kings?" Marcus said. "Take the crown. It's our turn to rule. *My turn*. Or it was all for nothing." He smiled widely as he leaned toward the girl. "I should slit her throat myself. She is a complication left alive too long, and every breath she takes vexes me."

"You're of a vile humor, boy," Jorn said.

"There's no need for cruelty," Reymund said, shaking and pushing against the arms of his chairs. "Especially in front of the lady."

Matthias's lips pulled tight, and he shifted his weight from one foot to another. The situation was deteriorating rapidly. The boy could be brought down easily enough. The arse's mouth seemed his most dangerous weapon. Matthias stepped directly in front of General Niro and placed both palms down on the table. This barter needed to be between them. One soldier to another. He needed to take command, as General Niro had clearly lost his.

On Matthias's own terms, or he would lose the princess.

And he would not leave without her.

"You must have a strategy here, or she will become your undoing," Matthias said.

"Don't test me, Sword," General Niro said, lashing out like a trapped dog.

Matthias's heart thumped in his chest. The man floundered as he toyed with her fate. Dangerous in his uncertainty and lack of a clear plan. General Niro's grip on her hand was as desperate as it was furious. Matthias could see his fingers alternating, the tightness of his grip, squeezing and grinding her bones together, though not once did she wince.

She sat still.

Poised. Perfect. Painfully so.

Smile expertly crafted. Chin up. Emotions guarded but for her bottom lip, which trembled under her shortened breaths. Her shoulders tense. The pulse at her rigid neck flicking quickly against her olive skin. Like the rabbit held, pinned down against the ground, she was anchored under the full weight of the sentence, between the piercing sickle-shaped claws of the hawk. Waiting to be stabbed and ripped apart. Waiting to be thrown from her cage to the nest full of vultures. In sheer terror. Utter exhaustion. The impending surrender.

But there, almost unrecognizable, around her eyes lay a flicker of hope. Waiting, praying, under the full weight of defeat, for the slimmest chance of escape.

It lit a fire that roared through his veins.

"I can offer you more than my king," Matthias said, taking a step forward.

"Then tell me, soldier," General Niro said. "And tell me now."

CHAPTER 4

UNTIL DAWN

———— ∾∾ ————

Avelina

BREATHE. *BREATHE.*

Slowly, consciously, deliberately, Avelina drew each breath across her drying lips. Her eyes darted from one man to the other while the rest of her sat still, silent, chiseled in fear. She was determined to keep up with the chaotic argument around her. So many years, days, and hours of her life had gone by almost painstakingly slow, yet today, she knew it would be a matter of mere, manic moments that would have the most consequence.

"Hear me, General," the seated man, Reymund, said. "There is another way."

"You've done nothing but insult this house with your nonsense, monk," Dolion said. "A weak offer from a cripple."

"From a *king*," Reymund said. "Any advisor knows to listen to every offer. You cannot weigh information you have refused. That is, if your intention is truly to *advise*."

Though seated, the man's body moved in the chair from head to foot in some kind of fit. His chin jerked under a painful frown as he leaned forward in his seat. Forearm pressed against the chair arm, his hands still moved beneath him, as if the beating of his heart depended on it. Avelina felt a pull deep in her chest toward him she could not explain. A familiarity she couldn't place. As if they were kindred spirits, both trapped in their own way.

The flame-haired man, Jorn, stepped behind him and firmly gripped Reymund's shoulders. It didn't stop his fit, but the pressured weight of his hands seemed to comfort him, as Reymund reached and squeezed Jorn's hand.

Matthias stood firmly planted in front of Niro. "General, if you've no strategy, they've beaten you already."

Niro was cornered, and he knew it.

The closer Matthias leaned toward Niro, the tighter Niro's grip became on her hand, squeezing her bones together. Avelina shuddered, waiting warily for the sound of a snap. Her statuesque strength faded against the intensity of her pain. Screaming through her wrist. Climbing her arm. Tears pooled at the corner of her eyes. She wanted to rip apart from Niro and cradle her bruised hand against her.

"Tell me, Sword. My patience grows weary."

"Keep our king's chest. Offer every man here the chance to barter their highest price," Matthias said. "When you've chosen your winner from amongst them, I will challenge them to single combat."

"A duel?" Niro said.

"Nonsense, brother," Jorn said. "The ale's taken hold of your tongue."

Niro held his hand aloft to silence him and nodded at Matthias to continue. Niro may have the throne, but the soldier had laid claim as the head of this group of men. Across from her, Dolion leaned toward Niro, both intrigued and agitated by the group standing before them.

"You will come out ahead of every man here and be paid thrice over," Matthias said. He retreated slowly from the table, pulling all attention on him. He broadened his step and rested his hands on his hips. "First, by the chest from our king. Second, by taking the chest of your wealthiest adversary here. Thrice over when I defeat his house. And you'll be rid of the girl."

"Why not take the nobleman's head?" Marcus quipped.

"Now *that* would be a daring plan," Dolion said.

"His sword is enough," Matthias said gruffly.

Avelina's empty stomach tightened as she stared at the soldier. This Matthias was intent on Niro and Niro alone. She'd never seen someone speak to Niro in this way. Eye to eye. Building a dialogue instead of cowering to him or working to influence him. Dolion was always perched near his shoulder, aiming to feed Niro as if he were a babe. A small bite. A taste. A tease. And then another. Until Dolion was shoveling his words so rapidly their poison slipped by unnoticed.

Not this Matthias. His words, and the man himself, seemed different.

A moment of silence fell between them.

Niro rubbed a hand across his mouth and sighed loudly. His grip had begun to loosen on her hand, and the pain within it slowly ebbed. Niro was listening. *Listening.*

Avelina's pulse fluttered, her nervous heart hopping within her.

Good heavens, could this be it? This man before her. Her chance to escape.

If he could at least take her beyond the walls of Leuceria. Safely. At least that far. And then once beyond the walls . . .

"Look about you, General. Your tables are full of crows," Matthias said. "The rebellion's begun."

"Perhaps your largest reward, General, is not losing face with a court who questions your right to the throne," Reymund said. Calmer, his back crooked but tall against his chair, Reymund gestured toward the legate, watching with much interest from their table nearby. "You must remember, General. Those who call her legitimate have the support of Rome. They come here bearing his seal. By stating the princess is to be recognized as such, the pope declares Salic law is applicable. The king declared her his heir, leaving Leuceria as her inheritance."

"The pope's desire is only to see her married to one under Rome's control. To see Leuceria's throne absorbed into the empire. They wish control of our port. The coast from Italy to Spain. And to connect the Mediterranean to our mountains," Dolion said. "They make their threats plain, but the line they wish to command *is dead.*"

"Should I refuse, Leuceria's people will be excommunicated. Cut off in this life and the afterlife. We would be considered doomed and find no salvation outside the church." Niro's eyes narrowed. "But I do not fear Rome. I've been alive long enough to see her as both friend and foe. They say they speak for God. Or act on His behalf. Yet with this pope's connivance they dare to slaughter one another at Mass as they did in Florence."

"Medici," Reymund whispered, crossing himself.

Avelina shivered, remembering the cathedral attack in Florence the year before, and crossed herself as well with her unrestricted hand. The news of the murder at God's altar had left her shaken and had seeded a growing distrust of Rome in Niro.

"Pazzi or pope. I am finished with men. Their deeds and words too often betray one another," Niro growled. "I make my peace with God alone."

"Then it should reason for the General to be rid of them all," Dolion said, looking out across the crowded hall, then to Avelina. "And take a position that eliminates *every* threat."

"You can't, General, and you know it," Matthias said. He looked at Avelina and then quickly away. "Even if her blood is muddied, enough royal blood has been spilled. In death, you'd make her a martyr and unite them against you."

"And against your boy," Jorn said.

"You're a wise man, General," Reymund said, squeezing the arms of his chair. "Don't let yourself be so blinded by your riches upon this throne that you lose the wits that bore them for you. Once she crosses the border and marries our king, she loses her citizenship and any rights within Leuceria are rescinded."

"Satisfy your nobles with a negotiation and outcome that is legitimate." Matthias spread his arms wide with his palms open. "And let me remind them that *you* hold the power here, General."

Niro's eyelids darkened, turning a circle around his black eyes. Niro glared at them and wrinkled his nose. The vein sticking out on his temple thundered. Looking down on Reymund in his chair, he nodded and said, "Your mind is as crooked as your body, but it serves your king well. Your argument has merit."

"She cannot live, Father. I will kill her myself," Marcus said. "Why won't you do what must be done? Or did her harlot mother take your manhood from you too? Is that it?"

He started toward her, but Jorn's forearm thudded squarely in the center of Marcus's chest, stopping him. Jorn hissed at him and Marcus scowled, stepping away.

"You walk a narrow bridge, son," Niro said, voice low and cold as ice. "Your insolence threatens our reign. You will remember who you are and remember to whom you speak."

"*The General.* The General who belonged to his king. No better than a pageboy. And then betrayed him." Marcus's face was full of spite and his stance light, shuffling between feet in his anger. His gaze kept finding her, as if anticipating his strike. "It is you who threatens everything. Every breath she takes threatens my crown."

"That's enough," Niro said.

"They followed your orders, but they *loved* their king," Marcus said. "But their weakling king is long dead, and the only reason they haven't unseated you sits at your side." Again, Marcus stepped toward Avelina, but Niro stood and stopped him in his tracks.

"I'm not dead yet, son," Niro said. "You'd do well to remember that."

"You'll be dead soon enough, old man, and I will not make your mistakes," Marcus spat. "No. The nobles will know I alone am their king, that I mean to rule, and they will fear me."

"My mistakes? You're the fool," Niro shouted. "You will need their money, their men, and their allegiance, if you ever, ever want to wear the crown."

Marcus stepped back and looked at the floor, chewing on his reply.

"Time and again, you've chosen her over me. The time of her kings is over, as is yours," Marcus said. "You were great—*once, Father*—but now you do nothing but warm my seat."

"Ha!" Niro laughed. Glancing at Avelina, he let go of her hand, and she quickly pulled it into her lap.

Avelina's legs betrayed her urge to run, Marcus's words having struck them lame. *You have chosen her over me* resounded with each step Niro took around the table.

Matthias laid a hand on Jorn's chest, and they both took a step back as father moved eye to eye with his son. Barely any room between them, Niro leaned in toward Marcus's ear.

"I ensure you have a throne to sit on," Niro seethed, his nostrils flaring. "While I pray you have enough sense not to lose it for your own sons."

Niro walked to Matthias and held out his hand.

"I accept your terms," he said. "The duel must be to first blood and before any ceremony. You must earn the right to marry her by proxy for your king."

"As you wish," Matthias said.

Avelina's stomach dropped in disbelief.

Matthias met Niro's hand with his own, shaking it firmly.

"No, Father! This is a mistake," Marcus said, hand quick on the hilt of his sword. "I challenge the Sword. I will fight him for her, and then I will cut her heart from her breast."

"Halt your tongue, boy." Jorn's arms went wide as he stepped in front of Marcus, between him and Avelina. Like a stag with antlers down, he was ready and anxious for a fight.

Avelina slammed back into her chair, fear overriding her composure.

"Do you want to die, boy? This man will cut you down in one blow. Challenge me again and I will let him," Niro spat.

Marcus fell silent, and his head hung low as he looked at the floor. Taking a few steps back, he straightened his clothes, pulling his cuffs at his wrists. Lips pursed, Marcus pointed to Avelina. "Take heed, men, and hear my words. No matter what happens on the morrow, she dies." He stepped to Matthias, where he barely came to his shoulder, and added, "And I will bathe in your blood, soldier." He spun on his heel and left through the stricken crowd.

Ashen, Avelina corrected herself in her seat. The blood long drained from her cheeks, she knew she was as pale as the white marble statues lining the hallways. Determined, she mustered her strength.

"You will retire now," Niro said to the group of men. "Your King's Sword will face the chosen suitor here at dawn. He'll need to rest if he means to hand me the victory he has promised."

"I trust she will be here?" Matthias said.

Niro nodded. "They all will."

Matthias boldly stepped before her. His eyes flicked to her lap, where her trembling fingers tried to cover the bruises darkening from Niro's grip. The soldier drew himself tall, then presented a leg and bowed to her, his chest low and chin tucked with great respect. It was a grand move, made grander by the fact that no one had ever so dared. When he corrected, his brown eyes fixed on hers. The corner of his mouth tugged into a small smile.

"Until dawn, Princess."

CHAPTER 5

A MAN'S WORD

Matthias

"BETROTHAL BY PROXY. ONCE THINGS are finished, as the king's representative I will wed her in his name," Matthias said. His stomach wrenching, he nodded at the guard as they strode by, hoping no one would question them. He and Jorn supporting Reymund on either side, the trio reached the palace courtyard. Spying a stone bench, they set Reymund upon it to rest.

Alif should have been here. A handful of men dotted the area before them, but Matthias saw no sign of the young one.

"You're putting too much trust into this entire process." Jorn raised an eyebrow at this and shook his head. "They will never let her leave this place."

"Niro will honor his word," Reymund said.

"Niro is compromised," Jorn said. "Marcus is the problem, as is any man here who cows to that arse. Marcus lives in fear and anger, and he will lash out like a cornered dog. Drawing first blood won't serve their purpose, and he has too easy a taste for it."

"I will not leave her here," Matthias said.

He pictured her, readjusting herself to the edge of her seat. Patching together any crack that dared appear during the barter, the princess had expertly recovered her presentation. But he had seen it. The fear. The screams beneath. He had wanted to reach for her, gather her in his arms, and carry her from the room. As he had done for others, helping them escape an immediate threat—fire, war, attack. But this time, something, everything, was different.

This "Crown Jewel."

What terrors had this young thing seen that, under such pressure, she did not break?

"I gave my word to King Girault I would bring her back," Matthias said, pacing, searching the courtyard for any sign of Alif.

"This is dangerous. Too much so," Jorn said.

"I'm ready to do what is right, brother," Matthias said.

"What is right and what is possible aren't always the same thing." Taking a seat beside Reymund, Jorn stretched his long legs out in front of him. "We aren't meant to succeed. Mark my words, your king doesn't expect us to return."

"He gave his word," Matthias growled. "I'll take those odds on our behalf, and your stubborn arse can thank me later."

"Hmpf," Jorn scoffed. "You and your king. The man throws a ring on you and you're as wide-eyed as the first time a maid let your hand up her skirt." Jorn scowled and crossed his arms. "If something happens . . . I'll try to get her out of here, but I won't promise you I can. *Gah*, if only you weren't as stubborn as a two-headed mule. You rotting, *rotting* bastard."

Matthias lifted his head. A small carriage rolled toward them, its wheels crunching across the loose stones. As it approached, Matthias spotted his man Harock beside the coachman, and pumped his fist in relief. The carriage door opened and young Alif hopped out. Lars's long body unfolded itself, lumbering out behind him. A man of few spoken words, his unnatural size screamed loud enough as he hit the ground.

"Well done, Alif," Matthias said, squeezing him on the shoulder. "Lars, Harock, well done indeed."

Lars tilted his thick neck toward the carriage. "We've found passage with some merchants."

"Good. Reymund carries the king's letter of safe passage, but I'll feel better knowing he travels with you two devils at his side," Matthias said.

"Ach. He'll be fine, though he may not like the company." Frame stretched tall to survey the courtyard, Harock snorted and hopped down to the ground, dagger locked in his hand as always. There was a reason the man had lived as long as he had. Always ready,

never settled, the old man had the zeal of ten youths. "Won't you come with us, Matthias?"

"Just get my brother out of here." Matthias's stomach dropped as he guided Reymund to the carriage. At the door, Matthias wrapped Reymund in a hug and lightly kissed the crown of his head before letting go. "I'll see you soon."

Reymund smiled and laid a palm on Matthias's cheek. "Soon."

Not wanting to watch him leave, Matthias turned abruptly, determined to outpace the doubts and horses behind him. Back within the palace, Matthias found refuge behind a column and slid to the floor.

Jorn settled beside him, and Alif stretched on the floor before them both. Alif was soon asleep, and Matthias smiled, happy that Alif could sleep so easily anywhere. Jorn's arse, though, remained afire. He kept his thoughts to himself, but his leg bounced endlessly. His brother's nerves were unsettled, as usual before a fight, even when it wasn't his own. Especially when it wasn't his own.

Matthias set his head back and stretched his legs. He retrieved a *gulden* from his pocket that Reymund had given him years ago. *For luck*, he'd said. *Keep it near your heart and know I pray for you.* He ran his finger across the hammered image of the Madonna and Child and then the other side, of the imperial orb of the Holy Roman Empire.

Hmpf. He closed his eyes and resumed flipping the coin, hoping to find solace in the mindless repetition.

CHAPTER 6

TO BLOOD

Avelina

IT HAD COME DOWN TO this.

A duel. And this soldier, Matthias.

Avelina's breasts heaved against the front of her dress. The pain in her hand was excruciating. She bit the inside of her cheek, trying to deflect it, as Niro again ground her bones together. His knee bounced next to hers, knocking into it.

"This day will be remembered," Niro said, leaning his head toward her.

They sat next to one another at the head of the courtyard, a makeshift throne and stool set in the center of the green. The flat earth in front of them was surrounded by courtiers whose figures she could barely see through the morning mist. Breaths of dawn crept toward them, setting the dewy air aglow. In a moment, the sun would rise and roll its light across the gardens.

Her body ached from the chilled air and the stress of having sat rigidly awake, ready, all night to the dawning hour. Her stomach rolled within her, hunger pangs calling out, sorting themselves with raging nerves. Niro squeezed her hand one last time, let go, and stood.

Avelina pulled her wounded hand into her lap, covering it protectively with the other. She strained to swallow, her throat dry from thirst and vexed by the thick stench born from the hours of debauchery.

"Make the square," Niro called out.

Soldiers marched along the periphery, meeting across from her, creating an open square. The soldiers sectioned themselves off, keeping the masses of nobles clear. They turned their poleaxes parallel to the ground and held them aloft, daring someone to challenge them.

Hours of drink and argument had culminated in the announcement of the duel. First, breathless they stood. Once heavy with showmanship, an air of finality permeated the crowd. Igniting murmurs of desperation. Impatience. Foreboding. Then, with the sun at the horizon, a resounding roar rose through the crowd. They barked like a pack of dogs against the plan they called "folly."

"Insulting."

"Outrageous."

"Sinful."

Their voices raised together in protest; their curiosity had them tripping over themselves to reach the boundary. No longer separated into houses, they merged into one crowd, pushing against each other for the best view and to align themselves next to the elder of the House of Connaire. All attention fixated on the soldier who had commanded the attention of the General.

"The challenge has been set," Niro called out. "This man, Matthias, who stands on behalf of his King, Girault of Ewigsburg, has challenged the House of Connaire to single combat."

Avelina turned toward the man, standing alone in the square.

Matthias paced back and forth, turning his sword in his grip, swinging it occasionally from side to side. Surely intimidating in battle, his broad stance and hulking chest created a powerful display of self-assurance. Hair black as a raven, with beard wrapping around his rock-hard jaw, his face was guarded and intense.

When his step took him in her direction, he looked openly upon her. His large brown eyes locked on hers, as they had hours ago across the hall, and she could not look away.

It wasn't warmth. Or friendliness.

No hint of seduction or impropriety drawing her in.

There was a nakedness to him. An honesty. Nothing like the men she had known prior. The cryptic coldness they wore as masks, shrouding their ulterior motives and leaving her dangling, retreating, and alone in the dark.

For once, she felt no threat. No reason to flee.

Having lost regard for modesty, Avelina's gaze openly followed the soldier. She did not know him, but she depended on him, as he had become her means of escape. For the moment at least; the rest she could figure out later.

"They will choose their weapons," Niro continued. "There will be no armor."

Avidius, the elder of the House of Connaire, stepped to the poleaxes. He was a man of distinction here at court. Almost as old as Niro and with rivaling bright silver hair and beard against his umber skin, he only came to Niro's shoulder in height. They knew one another well. Avidius had fought under Niro's command, and at one point there had been a friendship, though the details of it and its demise, she wasn't privy to. Since the wars, the House of Connaire had quietly retired, making few enemies and acquiring much wealth by producing abundant wine on their lands, which included the ancient vineyards that had once belonged to her mother's family.

"There is no honor here," the elder of the House of Connaire said.

Niro raised his hand, and the poleaxes before Avidius were parted. Stepping into the square, his irritation was palpable, but his demeanor remained dignified. He turned on his heel, ensuring he had gathered attention, turning last to Avelina. Without moving his chin, he lowered his eyes, paying her respect, before turning to Niro.

"There is no honor here," Avidius said. "This is not the way of civilized men."

"No, old friend," Niro said. "But this is my court, and we will settle this as soldiers. They will fight until blood is spilled. The girl's fate will be decided."

Avidius folded his hands in front of him and tilted his head back, staring Niro in the eye. "And the throne of Leuceria?"

"The throne of Leuceria is mine," Niro said. "Let there be no doubt."

Marcus entered the square with one of his soldiers, Barreth, at his heel and paced back and forth. Rubbing his bald chin, Marcus landed loathing looks on her and the Sword. His lips were pulled tight, exposing his teeth; Marcus's distaste for the Sword was obvious to all.

"My father lacks the stones for what must be done," Marcus said. "But I don't."

Let him try.

Good heavens, let Marcus be fool enough and be cut down in front of me.

Avelina stifled the thought, lest they see it on her face. He'd killed many a man before, without arms to defend themselves, limbs pulled hard at their sides to offer a larger target. He had an endless taste for blood, but not the courage to fight for it.

"I present the challenger," Marcus said, gesturing to his soldier beside him. "Barreth will stand for the House of Connaire."

"What do you play at son?" Niro asked.

"This soldier belongs to the House of Connaire now," Marcus said, lifting his palms and shrugging.

"You speak to *me* of honor, Avidius?" Niro said, turning to the elder. "Where is your son?"

"I remain within the law." Avidius stepped forward. "According to custom, the challenged House can choose which man will fight for it. He may not be my blood, but he will fight in my stead."

"Barreth was sold for a fair price, Father," Marcus said, sneering.

Niro put his hands on his hips, and his jaw hardened.

Matthias pumped his arms, shoulders large and turned side to side, gaining their attention. "It is no matter. Let us fight and finish this."

Niro nodded and said, "According to custom, the challenged House also has the right to choose the weapon for both fighters."

Barreth snickered and swung a spear forward. As tall as himself, the spear was long with a leaf-shaped sharp metal edge. He slammed it's end on the ground, and a cheer roared through the crowd.

"Let's see how the King's Sword does without his little dagger," Barreth said.

Matthias lifted his sword, turned it over in his grip, inspecting the flat of the blade. Flipping the sword over, he presented the hilt to Niro. Niro took it and presented Matthias with a spear.

Avelina's stomach flipped as she slid forward to the edge of her seat. Avidius left the square, and Niro and Marcus took spots opposite one another at the square's edge, leaving the two soldiers to fight. Marcus openly cheering for his man, while Niro stood silent, arms crossed.

Looking about, she couldn't find either of the soldier's companions, and it surprised her. The redheaded man and the monk? Where were they? Matthias was as alone as she was.

The men walked around each other, sidestepping in a circle. Barreth spread his hands on his spear and lunged toward Matthias. Stabbing toward him, the sharp metal cut through the air. Matthias answered quickly, blocking the blow and knocking it away, but did not answer with his own thrust.

Barreth again lunged, fiercely thrusting his spear directly at Matthias's torso, and Avelina's heart jumped into her throat. Matthias blocked it, pushing the spear away. Barreth continued to move about, pumping his arms and letting out loud guttural grunts. Matthias took much smaller steps, watching silently.

Matthias was defending himself, but not answering.

Studying how Barreth moved, he turned his spear in his hand, as if testing its weight.

Each step he took looked preplanned. Calculated and brilliant.

Like every muscle in his body reflexively knew how to react.

Like he could fight without thought or emotion.

Like he had been born to this.

Barreth charged him, yawping, swinging his spear, and did not stop.

Every strike he took, every aim made at Matthias's head, his arms, his thigh, was answered again and again. Matthias's spear would break the thrust, denying impact. Then, in a flash, Matthias deflected and thrust his spear forward, slashing Barreth's leg. The man screamed, cowering back as blood spilled down his leg.

Blood had been drawn. The crowd shrieked, a few hands raised at the triumph, while most shook with rage, cheering on their champion.

Matthias took a step back and looked to Niro. Niro said nothing. Matthias's grip loosened, and the spear turned in his hand as his attention turned back to Barreth.

With a roar, Barreth again charged Matthias.

Taking several quick steps around Barreth, Matthias moved skillfully to defend himself, knocking the man backward.

It was a dance. Each step as important as where their hands were.

Each move quicker than the next.

Their spears wrestled with one another. Crossing. Thrusting. Retracting and realigning to begin again.

In swift succession, Matthias's spear at once deflected a strike, knocking Barreth's point toward the ground, and Matthias charged, slicing across Barreth's chest. The man's body shook as blood spattered from the wound. Matthias drove forward, knocking the spear from Barreth's hand.

Barreth fell to his knees.

Matthias dropped his spear to the ground and turned toward Niro.

She was breathless, watching.

A pair of men worked to tend Barreth's wounds. He was neither dead nor dying. Nor victorious.

Matthias had won. She had been won. And now, she would be wed.

Matthias turned to Niro. "Your greatest enemy is vanquished, General. Your place is secure now, and I will take my prize for my king."

Niro handed him his sword, and Matthias strode before her.

The mob rumbled behind him, lifting their voices and fists in protest. While the soldiers at the periphery held firm, a handful of Niro's personal guard closed in behind Matthias, forming a tight arch at his back.

Matthias was covered with blood and sweat, straining, his breaths haggard, yet she caught a hint of a smile. His brown eyes traced over her face and form. Not hungrily or rudely; just so. He threw his shoulders back and took a knee before her. His eyes sharpened, then his chin tucked down against his chest.

"My lady," Matthias said.

Avelina blinked and stood. Though her legs wobbled, she perfected her stance. Raising her chin defiantly, she looked about the square, the entirety of which stared at them in shock. She saw Marcus, making note of where he was. Red-faced at the edge opposite her.

Avelina stepped down to the soldier. So close to him now, she saw how truly massive he was. An energy pulsed around him. To her surprise, she was not afraid.

Matthias offered her his hand, and she slipped her fingers into the palm of his bear-like paw. The friction of his warm skin, his fingers against hers, the power in his large hand, all shocked her. She gasped when his thumb lightly traced the curve of her knuckles. Sore and bruised from Niro's grip, his gentle touch consumed her. The intense kindness soared through her into the pit of her soul.

"Princess Avelina, I, Matthias, as King's Sword, present an offer of marriage on behalf of my king, Girault of Ewigsburg," he said. "On my honor, I pledge you my service and my oath of protection. My sword is yours. I will remain faithful to you and to my pledged word."

The sincerity, the conviction, with which he spoke was enthralling. His deep voice rolled across her skin. From her ears, along her neck and below, she was bathed in a calmness that had escaped her for years.

In that moment, his steadiness calmed her. Her panic abated, and she finally breathed.

In that moment, hope, renewed, barely recognizable, grounded her.

But only for that moment; for in the next, a pair of Niro's guards ripped her from where she stood and carried her back toward the palace. In her last glimpse of her beloved gardens, while the court mob pushed past the soldiers and charged after them, Niro and his guards closed in around Matthias and seized him.

CHAPTER 7

HOLD ON

———— ∾ ————

Avelina

SPIRITED AWAY FROM THE DUEL, Avelina was hurriedly dragged through the palace and into the ancient tunnels beneath it. Hidden, dark, and secret, they were a natural maze only known by a few. She wrestled within the soldiers' arms to no avail until they emerged from the passageway at the coastline beyond the seaport.

Thinking herself to be thrown into the sea, she was astonished when Niro's guards instead shuffled her along the rugged rocks at the water's edge until they reached the beach. There, waiting expectantly, was the wild redhead, and without word or incident, she was thrust towards him. Jorn's hand clamped on her upper arm, pulling her along as she sank into the beach's white sand. They advanced the rocky cliff and met a young man waiting for them at the edge of the hunter's path that led toward the mountains.

"The horse, my lady," the young man said, holding his hand out to her and gesturing to the horse beside him.

Avelina hesitated, fearful of them.

"There's no time for this," Jorn said. With a sour look of determination, he placed his large hand roughly between her shoulder blades and pushed her forward. "Give me your hand."

"But the other man, Reymund," Avelina said. "You cannot leave him here."

"He's gone," Jorn said, pushing her again. The horses stepped about, front legs pawing at the ground.

"Matthias?" Avelina said.

Where was he? He'd been behind her in the tunnels until they'd seen Niro.

"The arse is behind you," Jorn said. "Alif, hold her still." Jorn swiftly climbed onto a horse. He reached his hand to her, palm open and voice authoritative. "Your hand. Now. We must ride."

She placed her hand in Jorn's, and his fingers tightened around it, pulling her forward. Alif was beneath her, heaving her astride the animal. The horse snorted, and she grabbed Jorn's shoulders tightly, afraid to lose her center. Turning toward the sea, she saw Matthias, barreling up the cliff toward them and her heart tripped, surprising her with her guttural response to him.

Face severe, Matthias's arm thrashed over his head, pointing down the road. "Go! *Go!*"

"Hold here. Tightly, my lady," Jorn said, guiding her hands down to the center of his chest.

Jorn nudged his horse and it quickly left the others behind. The thundering of the hooves rattled through her bottom and thighs, as she slammed onto the beast. All propriety gone and terrified of falling and being trampled, she thrust her hips forward, molding her chest against the back of the strange man. Her cheek smarted against the thick braided leather of his vest as she buried it between his shoulder blades.

Avelina's chest constricted, and tears stung her eyes. Keeping them tightly shut, she lost herself to the sole, desperate purpose of holding Jorn. Counting sets of four. Hooves beating. Rhythmically repeating as they rode.

The distance passed beneath them at a steady pace. The muscles in her arms screamed from the effort. Her palms were sweating, making it increasingly difficult to hold on. She grabbed frantically, pawing at the man's chest until she regained a firm grip. Finally, she felt the horse jerk, slowing down to a trot, and she opened her eyes.

At first, a blurred mix of colors, then she began to focus, picking up details. The towering cypress trees that had lined the coastal path were gone. They had entered the northern forests, where fir trees grew taller, closer together. Slithers of static yellow-gray evening light streamed down between them upon the path, less structured but still rolling beneath them. Eventually, they turned from it, cutting through the woodland until they reached a thick crop of rocks. They stopped beneath an overhang that jutted fiercely into the night sky and disappeared within its shadow.

"We rest here," Jorn said.

Dazed, she felt Jorn pull at her hands, loosening them from his chest. He turned and slid down from the horse.

Avelina plied her eyes open farther, the crust of dried tears splitting at the corners. She leaned forward onto her belly, legs braced, wrapping her arms on each side of the horse, and clung to him, exhausted. Even though it was summer and the animal's heat radiated against her, she felt frozen, unused to the harsh realities of the world outside the palace.

She'd been awake for two full days.

Sitting rigid by Niro, starved sick by stress, unable to eat. Taunted, threatened, and teased. Tossed from her home into the arms of strangers. Bounced for hours on the horse. Her hands were cramped and stiff, but she had held on, and she was alive.

Pulling her leg over the horse, her foot caught in her skirts and she slid sideways.

"Whoa, my lady, there are better ways to kill yourself," Jorn said, catching her midfall. Alif was quickly there helping her to the ground. Her legs shook. Her muscles twitched, strained and burning. Her tailbone was sore, but the intense pain she felt along her inner thighs astounded her. She squeezed her legs together, and it only worsened.

"You've done well, Princess," Alif said, patting her arm. "Don't weep."

She took a step back, stumbling, and Jorn reached for her, steadying her.

"She needs rest," Alif said. "I'll set a place."

"Only briefly. We cannot linger." Standing with his back to her, Matthias was unbolting something at the base of the saddle.

"*Genau.*" Stepping back, Jorn rubbed his beard, watching her. "The General spoke true enough where to find the pair of you, but we daren't stay long near the path the man himself put us upon."

Avelina shivered, surrounded by so much unknown. Strange smells and sounds battled one another, flooding her senses.

"I don't know what you have planned, my lady, but don't be a fool," Jorn said.

She startled, turning toward him.

"The boots." Jorn took a drink from a waterskin at his hip. "Be wary of running off."

Alif looked at her boots sticking out beneath her skirts. A wide smile spread across his face, and he chuckled. "Well done, Princess. They're sure to make the trip easier."

Jorn, however, was not chuckling. He stared at her, his harsh eyes thin and catlike in the dark. Clearing the distance between them, each of his determined strides cornered the breath within her lungs. She gasped, but her throat squeezed in panic.

"You'll stay with us, child," he said, reaching for her. "Or you can die out here by yourself."

She blinked, tripping away from him, and her head lightened. Her palms were tingling. Her muscles cooling beneath her prickled skin. A heavy blanket of air draped itself upon her. Dots danced in her line of vision. Blue. White. Warmth passed over her, and she fell into the black.

The smell of hard, cold earth filled her nose. She was wrapped, enveloped in something incredibly warm. She adjusted her head, lifting it off the leather sack pillowed beneath her cheek, and relieved the pain shooting through her neck. Her knees were drawn, her hands pulled tightly against her chest.

Avelina's mind scrambled, sorting details through the pain.

The horses. The men. Her boots. Matthias.

Matthias.

His voice. Though muffled, she recognized the deep, rolling cadence. The man seemed short on patience as his feet shuffled amidst his words. "It won't be hard to track us."

Avelina sat up, searching for him in the black of night. Blinking, she sorted the flicks of light hanging in the air like dancing fairies. Two long legs approached, and then Matthias crouched beside her.

"Princess, are you all right?"

Her mouth opened, but nothing came out of it.

Matthias frowned. "No matter. We must go."

He lifted the blanket from her—brown fur—and rolled it, walking away from her.

Avelina shifted onto her knees and stood, one leg at a time. A hand came underneath her elbow, steadying her.

"Careful, my lady." Alif said. They were the same height, and this close she realized he might be younger than she, though he well emulated the older men.

"I'm quite all right," Avelina said, drawing her elbow toward her side, but he held firm.

"I'll not see you fall again," he said, leaning in and lowering his voice. "But we'll blame that last time on Jorn." He winked at her and then his face straightened, suddenly serious. "You'll not get hurt on my watch, Princess. Come."

His hand against her back, he guided her after Matthias. She heard the horses snorting before she saw them, glistening as the night swept over their muscles like a midnight tide.

Matthias tied the rolled fur across its back, and in a swift movement he was astride the horse and reaching for her. Alif made a move to lift her, but Matthias waved him off.

"In front, so I can hold her," he said. "She's too weak, and we cannot take the chance to lose her now."

CHAPTER 8

THE CHASE

～∞～

Matthias

THEY TRAVELED THROUGH THE FLATTER woods until the first misty hints of daybreak. A heavy fog fell from the heavens, blanketing the ground in a gray cloud that spit on his cheeks as they rode. Reaching a fork in the path, they turned down the slope of the hill, working their way north. It had been a much slower journey, riding dual with the lady. The horse easily took their combined weight, keeping a smooth and even pace. The princess was smaller than he, and the horse, one of three riding beasts bought for the trip, was worth everything they had paid.

His body ached from the fight and the continued riding, but he was alert.

The princess was locked between Matthias's arms. At times, both of his hands gripped the reins; other times, if the path wasn't as level, he would slip his hand around her waist and hold her to him. She sat between his legs, her back pressed against his torso, her head fitted perfectly into the pocket of his shoulder.

At first, the closeness had been unnerving. She was tense as a board, awkward, but eventually she'd settled secure against him.

Matthias was glad she was safe and wanted to keep her that way. He also needed for her to *feel* safe with him. To trust him. To listen to him without stubborn hesitation so they could survive this trip.

Their horses moving at a leisurely pace, the group was silent, and he enjoyed the sounds of morning. Birds had begun singing to one another above them, and the familiarity of it in such an unfamiliar place tugged his heart.

Alif, who'd been trailing them at a distance, charged up beside him.

"We're being followed," he said.

"Then we get of this path," Jorn said, pulling his reins.

"Into the woods. Quickly," Matthias said.

"*Kck kck.*" Jorn tapped his horse with his foot.

They turned to the right, off the path and into the forest.

"I'd hoped they'd follow the ship," Matthias said.

"I'm sure someone did," Jorn said.

"And if they catch it?" Alif said.

"If they do, our brother will be able to talk his way out of it," Jorn said.

"How far behind, Alif?" Matthias said.

"Not far now. Only across the ridge," Alif said, his horse grunting and shaking its head. "It's so foggy; I heard them before I saw them."

"How many?" Jorn said.

"I counted twenty before I rode," Alif said.

"We knew they'd come," Matthias grumbled, tightening his arm around the princess.

They needed options. They were quickly losing advantage.

Matthias turned about. Looking. Listening. Then there it was. Water.

"The river," he said.

"I hear it," Jorn said. "Below us."

It slowed them down, but they dismounted. They couldn't afford to lose a horse. One misstep and it would be over.

Pulling the princess down, Matthias took his horse by the bit and led it down the slope. It was getting progressively steeper, and they took it at an angle, working against the thickness of the brush. The princess almost lost her footing, sliding on loose rocks, and Matthias grabbed her arm. Realizing how tight his grip was, he let go and offered her his hand.

"Thank you," she said and took it, steadying herself on the hill.

Cautiously leading their horses, picking at steps, they descended the slope. The land was fast changing.

They were further into the mountains and, he realized, their best solution.

Jorn wouldn't like it, *at all,* but Matthias could trust Jorn to do what he asked.

Matthias heard the rushing of the river, closer now. Pounding along the beds of jagged rocks, pouring over boulders, and he led them farther upriver until the water rushed. Fog poured through the edges of the forest as the trees thinned, its cloud spreading, stretching to sleep on the ground, leaving him only glimpses of the valley floor.

It would take them into the open, but the time was now. Breaking through the forest edge, they mounted their horses. Matthias pulled the princess tight against him and grabbed the reins.

"Hold his mane," Matthias said in her ear.

The horses took off, galloping directly for the river.

"The trade route?" Alif said.

"Are you mad?" Jorn yelled.

Matthias looked left and right. There. The current was fast, but it was shallow there. There was no warm sun to glisten on the peaks, but it was clear enough to see a patchwork of stones. Browns, reds, and grays, of all sizes and shapes. The water rushed above the rocks, breaking against the larger ones protruding above the water to swirl around them downriver.

"Now," he called, leading into the water. His horse whinnied but kept going. The horses splashed as their hooves tore through the water, wading, snorting in protest until they reached the other side of the river and jumped onto the shore.

There it was.

Cutting through the mountains, one kingdom to the next, the trade route united them all. It was well worn from hundreds of years and as many travelers, on foot, horse, or cart. Along the main thoroughfare, the various outposts, castles, and manors dotted along it had acted as guardians. Paying a toll tax earned a man passage, the right to travel and trade wares on it, and the protection of the men who patrolled it.

But that was before the wars.

Now, like most things, the route was a shadow of what it once was. Lawless. Hardly used except by the desperate. Leading from one wasteland to another. It was littered with groups of bandits, pouncing upon those who dared to use it. The once great houses were now crumbling ruins, giving shelter to men who hunted one another.

It was dangerous, but it was exactly what they needed, offering a faster ride and, hopefully, interference for those trailing behind them.

"Perfect." Jorn grinned, but his face fell quickly when he saw Matthias.

"Take the horses and ride," Matthias said, swinging down and reaching for the startled princess.

"We stay together," Jorn said.

The princess looked at Jorn, face flushed, but then nodded and reached for Matthias. He helped her down. She wobbled, falling back a step, but found her footing.

"The *Geisterweg*?" Alif asked as his horse came beside Matthias.

"It's the only way." Matthias quickly unstrapped his bag from behind his saddle and hoisted it around his shoulder. "They'll follow the horses."

"You've lost your mind," Jorn said, frowning. "You'll never make it."

"I will," Matthias said. "And so must you."

"But the princess," Alif said, looking down at her.

"Is mine to deal with," Matthias said. "You'll move faster without us."

Alif turned, unstrapped his satchel, and tossed it to Matthias. "Take this. She'll need it more than me."

Matthias nodded thanks and threw the strap over his other shoulder. "Find Reymund. Meet me outside Ewigsburg. By the next new moon. You know where."

"*Ja,*" Jorn said, his horse tossing its head, as restless as he was.

"Only until the next new moon. No longer," Matthias said. "If we don't make it, take the men north. You'll have your freedom one way or another. Promise me."

"You're lower than a tick on a boar's balls," Jorn said. His red face contorted, and he spit before glaring at the princess.

Matthias stepped in front of her and frowned. "Your word, brother."

Jorn shifted his hips on his horse, and the beast whinnied beneath him, stomping its front hoof at the ground. Jorn gritted his teeth, enraged, but he nodded.

Matthias handed the reins of his horse to Alif and smacked its flank. The three horses started down the path and disappeared into the mists.

Matthias turned to the princess. Her eyes were round, staring after the horses, her lips parted as if she had meant to speak but couldn't find the words.

"Come, Princess," he said, hastily grabbing her hand and pulling her into the shadows.

PART TWO
THE GEISTERWEG

AUGUST 17, 1479
NEW MOON

CHAPTER 9

UPHILL

———— ⚮ ————

Avelina

A VELINA HURRIED HER FEET ALONG, again thanking God she had her riding boots.

"You . . . you drove away the horses? I don't understand."

He didn't answer her or even acknowledge she had spoken. He only continued his maddening pace, pulling her along behind him.

I needed that horse.

She'd only meant to stay with them until they were outside of Leuceria. Let them get her beyond the border and then ride on her own. Somewhere. It didn't matter where. It only mattered the horses were riding away.

Everything was happening so fast, too fast, from the moment she'd entered the barter to this point where she was climbing an almost vertical hill. Her arm was mercilessly stretched from its socket as Matthias pulled her upward at a furious pace. Frustrated, tripping on her underskirts, she gathered them with her other hand and balled them in front of her stomach.

"Please!"

The soldier stopped at her cry. Eyebrows tight together, he studied her for a moment and released her arm. She twisted her shoulder back, easing the strain.

"We can't stop here," Matthias said.

His arm wrapped around her waist, grabbing her roughly beneath the ribs. Pulling her to his side, he restarted their climb.

Up. Farther and farther into the trees.

Her chest was heaving. Lungs prickling, a piercing pain pulled at her side, but she pushed forward. Weary. Wary of hearing the pounding of hooves behind them over the sound of their feet rustling against the earth. Her body jostled against his, knocking off his assured steps as a banner would beat against a wall through a strong storm. Innate determination pumped through her, keeping her limbs moving, pushing her to match the man's incredible stride.

She was at once inside and beside herself, fueled only by her instinct to survive. Hearing barely whimpered sounds her lungs were too tired to make. Seeing the trails of dry tears, stinging her cheeks in their descent. She was floating, carried upward, while pain rattled her shins with each thump on the uneven terrain underfoot.

Her mind raced, her thoughts jarring her mind in no particular or sensical order. Niro had planned this. The extra guards who'd whisked them away to the tunnels. Meeting Matthias's men. Whatever diversion Niro had employed had merely bought them time. Niro had gotten her out of Leuceria, but the fear and questions remained.

Had he done so to enjoy the chase? To have her slaughtered in secret?

Or had he truly meant to save her? To betray the wishes of his own son?

"Marcus."

Avelina didn't realize she'd spoken the name out loud until Matthias's fingers dug into her flesh at her waist.

Marcus would never give up so easily. His death squad followed her. She could hear them below. Their shouts. Their horses. Growing louder. Closer.

She pushed on, tripping over her own feet as the soldier pulled them into a thicket of shrubs. Thin, thorny branches struck her cheeks and pulled at her sleeves as he wrenched her forward, pulling them into the cover. He turned and, in a fluid movement, cupped her head in his hand, twisted his leg around her knee, and took them both to the ground. Covering her body with his, he pinned her beneath him. Their legs entwined, his body stiffened, his grip startled her. She was trapped. Her prayer book rammed sharply into her side; she bit her lip, stifling a squeal of distress.

The soldier raised his finger to his lips, hushing her. She nodded shakily, and he drew her head against his shoulder and cradled her, embracing her in a way she hadn't been since a babe in her mother's arms.

She heard voices now, several, at the base of the hill on the trade route.

Unable to move, she closed her eyes, and in the darkness saw Marcus's face, twisted and seething with hatred. Every day she had employed every ounce of strength to hide her fears from him. How he had terrified her, tormenting her all those years.

Had she not been under guard, he would've certainly made good on his intentions.

Marcus had his own wife. His own small son. A sweet, small, blameless cherub. In fact, after his father became regent, Marcus had married a daughter of one of the most powerful families in Leuceria. He was wildly rich, enjoying every luxury and every sin.

But it wasn't enough; he wanted her dead. He made no secret about it, and she imagined he would never be satisfied until she was. Marcus wanted the crown for himself and his children after him.

And Niro.

Though he held such disdain for her, he'd still protected her. Obsessively, while he scarily swung from one emotion to the next, for reasons she could make no sense of and dared never to question. Though she neither trusted him nor whatever motives he possessed, she could rely on his obsession—it kept her safe and it kept her pure.

His Crown Jewel.

His.

The collective sound of hooves rode off, and Matthias's rigid body softened.

"They're gone," he whispered.

She rolled, clawing at the ground to escape him. A rush of air filled her, and her stomach cramped.

Oh no.

She stumbled, trying to stand and flee, but to no avail. Bile burned her parched throat and flooded her mouth, and she lurched forward. Grabbing at her throat, she slammed onto her knees, moaning when a sharp pain tore across her skin.

It wouldn't stop. Her thoughts poured out of her in liquid form. She clutched her gurgling stomach with one hand, pawing at the ground with the other for something to hold on to and steady herself. Vomit roared through her with such force it flooded the back of her nose. No food in her belly, what water she had managed littered the leaves in front of her, streaked with yellow foam. When there was nothing left, she heaved, choking on her emptiness, spittle dripping in strings from her mouth.

Avelina's body shook, unsettled by the smell and pained from her body's rebellion.

"It's all right," Matthias said. Crouched beside her, his hand rubbed a circle on the small of her back. "Let it make its way out." His fingers brushed across her cheek and neck, pulling strands of dampened loose hair and curled them behind her ear.

Avelina lifted her arm to wipe her mouth on her sleeve, still shaking. Matthias reached in front of her with a large leaf, wiping her chin. Tossing it down, he handed her his waterskin and closed his hands around hers.

"Take some. Clean your mouth," he said, lifting it to her lips.

She took some water and swished it around, spitting what taste she could from her mouth. Her insides stung. Her cheeks burned beneath her embarrassed tears. The stench was putrid. Luckily, she'd missed soiling her skirts.

"First time?" Matthias asked, grinning.

Was he truly laughing at her?

Avelina glanced toward him and snorted, a catch of bile still stuck in her nose.

Heavens, she was a mess.

He shook his head and patted her sharply between her shoulder blades. She hacked hard and then spit again, his smack having dislodged the remaining spew.

"There," Matthias said.

Her eyebrows pushed together.

"I'm sorry," Avelina said, mortified, leaning back onto her heels. She swayed dizzily, and he caught her elbow.

"Don't be. It happens," Matthias said, looking at her sideways. "I can't imagine you've . . . exerted yourself like this before. Your body's answering your call, turning your fear into fuel. Sometimes it's too much, so your body drives it out."

Avelina grabbed his arm and inhaled, drawing air into her deflated lungs. Blood rushed to her head, and the little pinpricks of light that had started to collect dissipated.

"Not too fast, Princess," Matthias said.

Matthias shoved the waterskin back at her and she swallowed, filling the dragging emptiness in her stomach. He tied it back on his hip.

"I've hurt my knee," she said, carefully lifting it. The guilty branch next to her had torn a gash in her skin, leaving smears of blood and mud.

He tilted her back onto her bottom with her knee raised. He inspected her skin and poured water over it, cleaning it. He pulled Alif's bag from his shoulder and set it in front of him.

"It's time we rid ourselves of this dress," he said.

Her dress? Surely, he did not mean to—

Avelina looked around her. It was nothing but the same in every direction.

She could run. She should have run. She never meant to stay with him.

"Calm yourself, child," he said. "You need never fear me."

Matthias untied the top of the bag and pulled out some garments. First, a linen shirt. He ripped the sleeve and tied it around her leg, tightly covering the wound.

"There," he said, tossing her a tunic. "You can't travel in what you're wearing. Soiled or not." Matthias slung the sack back on his shoulder and turned his back from her. "I'll give you your privacy if you change yourself with haste."

He was right. In this natural mix of muted and vibrant shades of greens, browns, and creams, what little was left of her lavender silk skirts stuck out as much as his entourage had in the hall of nobles at her palace. Clumsily stripping, she pulled the scratchy tunic over her head, thankful it covered her remaining bodice and half-sleeves and underskirt. She balled the discarded dress and tapped the soldier's back with it. He packed it into the satchel.

"Your skirts, Princess. They slow your pace, and I mean to quicken it."

Avelina froze. He was right—her skirts were bulky, heavy with what hidden treasures were sewn inside them—but she had no intention of handing them over. Fixing a hard look on him, she grasped the waistline of her skirts and, careful of the seams, twisted the mound at her hip around to her stomach. She laid her hand upon it, cradling it as she would a bellied babe, and straightened her back.

Matthias lifted an eyebrow but made no protest. He reached forward, took her hand in his, and gave a light squeeze.

"Princess, I know you're tired. You're weary. Weakened and hungry," he said. "But this, now, is when it counts the most. We have no choice. We cannot stop. Hold my hand and don't let go."

Avelina nodded, ducking from his intense gaze.

"Yes," she said. "Of course."

"You've done well, Princess," Matthias said. "You can do this."

Chin low, she glanced up. His brown eyes were still locked on her. Guarded yet open. For a man of violence, a stranger, she did not fear him.

"Can I trust you, Matthias?"

The top of his cheek twitched.

"Stay with me, and I'll keep you alive." He swallowed and drew their hands closer to his chest. "I gave you my oath. I mean no harm to come to you."

They were uncomfortably close. His attention demanded hers, his commanding presence flooded the air between them, but she felt no hint of threat from the wall of a man before her.

"I believe you," she whispered.

The corners of his lips tugged. "Good."

"Avelina," she said. "Please call me by my name. I believe we've lost all rank and reason in these woods."

His eyebrows furled, and his whole demeanor changed. Matthias stepped away, dropping her hands. "You're the Daughter of Leuceria and will one day be my queen. I will call you Princess. You've been called otherwise long enough."

CHAPTER 10

THE *GEISTERWEG*

———— ∾ ————

Avelina

THEY CONTINUED WALKING, STOPPING EVERY now and again to catch their breath and take a drink. The rush of the river had long disappeared behind them and had been replaced with the sound of brush as her feet shuffled along. They had gone far enough up the steep hill that they'd crossed it and found a ridge, flatter and easier for her to navigate, though she kept to the left side of it, wary of the drop-off.

Having purged the stress coursing through her veins earlier, Avelina's nerves had greatly calmed. She pushed past her peak of exhaustion. Her body had regained its strength, its sharp pains now manageably dull. As with all things, it was about focus. Separating her feelings from the task that must be done before her, and she knew how to use that skill in order to persevere.

Matthias was only a few steps in front of her. He had long let go of her hand, no longer dragging her along. Avelina tried to step where he had stepped when she could. His legs were longer and his stride wider than hers, but she was determined to keep up.

Cresting another hill, the ridge turned, putting their backs against the sun, casting their shadows across their path. As their pace slowed, her side began to ache. She pressed it with her palm, trying to knead it away.

"We'll make camp here," Matthias said.

Thankful for rest, she leaned against a large rock, taking long breaths. Her muscles twitched and her skin, covered in sweat, shivered in the evening air. It was crisp, clear, and cool inside her lungs, the temperature having fallen sharply with the sun. She looked around her. There was nothing, but forest, thick and endless. Large tree trunks towered above them, their lower branches bare. At the top, they merged into a canopy of branches heavy with thin green needles. Tiny saplings in various heights, skinny with bursts of green, were spread like children about their parents' feet.

"Come here," Matthias said, breaking through her fog.

She turned to him.

Matthias was busy unpacking the two sacks he'd worn on his back. He spread a blanket beneath a pine and motioned for her to sit. She did so, crossing her legs before her. Wrapping her arms around the skirts balled on her lap, she pressed her mother's hidden book against her stomach. Her eyes closed, and she recited a prayer within it from memory, whispering it under her breath.

"You have to keep covered, Princess. It may be summer, but you'll freeze," Matthias said. He reached and wrapped a dark fabric around her shoulders. He unfurled a hide covered in brown fur and wrapped it over the blanket. He moved around, gathering sticks and dried hunks of grass.

"How can I help?" she asked.

"Stay where you are," Matthias said. "And stay warm."

Matthias dug out a cleared area in front of where she sat and piled his collection there, building a pyramid. He pulled a flat rock out of his bag and flicked it against another, directing sparks at the mounded kindling. She couldn't help but smile when the tiny collection of brush inflamed and the small fire steadily built.

"The men," she said. "The ones who were following us."

"What of them?"

"Will they not see a fire?"

"We're hidden well enough. And this weather helps," he said, adding some more tinder to the side of the smoking tower. "We barely made it ourselves, and they won't abandon their horses to follow us here."

Avelina watched his face, trying to decipher whether it was a flicker of unease or sadness that crossed it.

"With any luck, they're still chasing Jorn." Matthias's face grew stern. He smacked his palm on his thigh and stood, walking away into the trees.

Avelina frowned. Having been so lost in her own path, she hadn't thought about the other two men since she'd watched them ride away, but of course he had. Feeling guilty for having forgotten them, she mentally added their names to the list of those she prayed for.

Her body relaxed, her bones resting, though an ache on her foot remained. She stripped her boots and her hose, exposing the pocket of pain.

There it was. A large blister across the ball of her foot. Her finger pressed against the lump, and she drew breath sharply through her teeth, shocked at the discomfort. She shook it off and crossed her legs beneath her.

Matthias returned from gathering more wood, knelt, and dropped an armful of branches onto the ground. He broke them into pieces, building the fire until it was well aflame. He turned to her, and his face grew concerned.

"What's wrong?" he asked, eyebrows pushed together.

She startled. "Nothing."

"Something's paining you."

Avelina pushed her bare foot out from beneath her. He shifted beside her, wiping his hands on his trousers, and took her foot in his hands. His thumb pressed on the bulging blister, and he shook his head.

Avelina winced at a quick shooting pain but didn't retreat from him. His touch purposeful yet careful. Tender, even.

"I should've known those boots weren't yours," he muttered and let out an exasperated sigh. He left, disappearing into the brush behind them, and returned with a handful of flowers. Clusters of the tiniest delicate blooms with white petals atop stout stems. He handed them to her and set his satchel before them.

"We'll have to deal with this now if we mean to cover ground tomorrow." He pulled a small leather wineskin from his belt and poured a bit of the liquid over the wound. He set it aside and pulled a small axe from his belt. "I need you to sit still."

She couldn't have moved if she wanted to, her eyes remaining locked on the axe. Two hands' length, it sported a crescent blade opposite a beak-shaped hammer at the end of the wooden shaft. Dulled marks on the blade were visible as he turned it, inspecting the cutting edge in the light of the fire. Curious, she squinted and saw it clearly. An etching of a lamb.

He twisted her foot into his lap, and she leaned back on her palms to stabilize herself. She watched him curiously, proud of herself for remaining still when she felt the tip of the blade breaking through her skin. His hands made quick work of her, kneading her foot, and she bit her lip, feeling the burning release as the blister drained.

Matthias took the flowers from her lap and bit off the tiny tops. He chewed them and then gently spread the salve over her skin while the sweet scent of the crushed flower rose through the air.

How curiously normal this all seemed, sitting here with him, touching her bare skin. How easily he reached for her, again and again, without hesitation or the slightest hint of ill will. How familiar he was with her . . .

"Soldier's woundwort," he said, ripping her from her thoughts. He spat to the side and dangled a stem in front of her. "Eat some."

She hesitated, and he coaxed it to her mouth.

"The blooms and a bit of leaf. It will help with the pain. May fix your belly too."

He wrapped her foot in another piece of linen and tossed her a set of stockings from the satchel. "Put these on as well as your own. It'll help your boots fit and stave off another."

Avelina took a bite of the flower and noticed the bitterness right away. When she finished, he offered her a drink, which only washed a bit of the taste away.

"Thank you," she said.

He gave the slightest nod and set about repacking his things, only pausing briefly to add fresh sticks to the glowing pyramid before her. Reds and yellows flipped around the thin strips of brown as it slowly yet surely burned. She looked about her, curious what lay beyond them in the growing shadows.

"What is this place?" she said.

"An ancient border path."

"No," she said. "The other man called it something else."

He smirked. "*Ja,* the *Geisterweg.*"

"Doesn't that mean *'Ghost's Path'*?" she asked. "Why call it such a thing?"

He took a long pause before answering.

"There's a darkness here."

"Because of the shadows? From all the trees?"

He smirked again. "Not so much, Princess. Though they are flooded with them."

"I've never seen anything like this before."

"The mountains?"

"All of it."

"Well, I guess you wouldn't have." He sat next to her, pulling his cloak around his own shoulders, and ruffled through his bag. He pulled out a hard biscuit and handed it to her. "You need to eat."

The biscuit wasn't soft or airy like she was used to. Or flat with fresh herbs baked on top. She sniffed it, but it only smelled cold. She bit into it with care. It was heavier, much denser. Her belly growled when the first bite reached it, and she pressed on her stomach, still tender from earlier.

"They're not the best, but they keep," he said, snapping a bite off another. "I'll find you more in the morning. Today we needed to make distance. Tomorrow the same. Get your rest."

CHAPTER 11

MORNING

———— ❧ ————

Avelina

A VELINA WAS AMAZED HOW QUICKLY she had fallen asleep.

She had yet to open her eyes, still lying warmed in his blanket-and-fur cocoon against the dirt, hard-packed beneath her. She put her hands between her folded knees, relieving the pressure on her hips.

Her body was sore. Everywhere. Parts she'd never even considered before ached. From one end to the other, every muscle felt heavy. The backs of her arms. The base of her neck between her shoulder blades. Even the muscles through her buttocks. Her thighs from the horse ride. Her biceps throbbed from holding so tightly to the redheaded man one day and the horse's mane the next, when she'd ridden with Matthias.

She stretched her legs and opened her eyes. A flicker of movement in the trees beyond the fire caught her eye, and she refocused.

"Matthias?"

Two small squirrels, their coats a rich auburn with quivering bushy tails, chased each other around the base of the tree. Up, down, and around they went, chittering at one another. She leaned on her elbow and watched them.

On the other side of the trees, ribbons of warm white light crept by, capturing tiny fluttering dots in the air in their path. She blinked, her eyes adjusting further, and sat up to see more. The ribbons multiplied, all slanting toward her through the trees. She left her nest and followed them until they gathered into a bright pool. She shielded her eyes from the blinding brightness, hand against her forehead, and kept moving forward.

The trees broke apart, revealing where the forest floor abruptly disappeared at her feet. She gasped and took two quick steps back, realizing she was standing on the edge of a cliff. She eased herself to the ground, scooting backward until she felt comfortable, and crossed her legs beneath her.

The scene before her struck her speechless. Beyond the drop-off, a field of flowers tumbled happily down into the valley. Bright yellow globes, scattered between waves of bluebells and cornflowers, swayed in the open breeze. Rugged hills went in every direction, covered in shades of blended greens. At the foot of a flood of hills, a lake was centered below her, its brilliant, sparkling blue glittering like a pool of gems beneath the open sky. Beyond it, several peaks merged, and their rocky points framed the brilliant sun rising beyond them.

There was nothing. Nothing but open space and peace.

She could stay here forever. Or at least long enough to commit the scene to memory. Like so many things before that she had lost. Run the lines, the details in her mind, and hope she could see it again when she wished or needed to.

"Princess."

Avelina smiled when she heard his voice.

"I'm sorry," she said. "I shouldn't . . ."

"How is your foot?"

"Much better, thanks to you," she said, realizing it no longer bothered her.

"Here," he said, stepping behind her.

She felt a tapping on her shoulder, and from the corner of her eye she saw it was another biscuit. She took it, rubbing her finger across the crisp top.

"Join me. Please," she said, scooting to the side.

Matthias sat beside her, his knees drawn up in front of him, resting his elbows on them. She smiled at him, but he looked straight ahead.

"It's beautiful," Avelina said.

"The land?"

"Quite so."

"From here, yes."

"Why do you say that?"

"They don't call her the *Geisterweg* for nothing." He shrugged.

"But look at the rich colors. The light," she said.

He looked out and then nodded. "I guess you are right."

"It's so peaceful," she said.

"Peaceful?" he snorted. "It may have been at one point or another."

Avelina turned back to the sky. The ribbons of pink beneath the clouds had run thin and disappeared, the sun having moved on in its journey.

She frowned. "Do you mean before the wars?"

There had been so many. She'd studied them: the alliances, the rivals, the battles, leaving so many dead. Leuceria's natural borders, the vast waters before them and the great mountains at their back, and their proud and storied armies and ships had long kept their country safe. Keeping enemies at bay, protecting her homeland, ensuring unparalleled wealth of trade and discovery and culture that existed and grew for generations.

Until they didn't.

The varied armies hadn't broken through their borders and set foot in Leuceria, but the horrors spilled through nonetheless. A great evil had washed through the land and poisoned the seas until tragedy struck within the palace. Her grandfather and her uncle, neither of whom she had ever met, were gone; their untimely deaths putting her own father upon the throne.

The wars' impact on her own life was harsh and felt daily, but she wanted to understand. How far their reach was. How they started. Why they started.

All she had learned was there was no easy answer.

"The history is long here. Much longer than that. People have traveled through and settled parts of the Alps for centuries."

"But this place . . ."

"The *Geisterweg* cannot be tamed. Her path may run through the Alps to the sea, but you'll not find her route on any map. At one stretch a hand's width wide and at another an army's. She's . . . very much alive, but also a ghost."

"Still, she's nestled within such a rich, majestic place."

"*Genau*. The mountains are rich for mining. The valleys for farming. The rivers are plump for fish," Matthias said. "The land's position makes it both invaluable and almost impregnable."

"Curious that no one has claimed this path through them, then."

Matthias smirked and shook his head.

"Our king claims her—at least the northern part of her—since the wars. But she's belonged to so many before that the people here heed no one." He paused thoughtfully, then looking away. "In truth, she belongs to no one. Generations have tried to conquer her but are always shown their place. Men are fools to think mountains should bow to them."

Indeed. Avelina smiled.

"Look there," Matthias said.

Avelina followed to where he pointed across the valley to the stone peaks towering above the tree line toward the heavens. Gray stone rose until the luminescent tips of white pierced the blue sky.

"They say the light of God cannot reach here because He can no longer see it. The mountains grew so tall and the trees so thick it offended Him. The land and its people are cursed. Riddled with creatures who thrive in the dark."

Avelina sighed. "There is no shadow cast dark, or long enough, to make such a thing true."

"People believe many things." Matthias gave her an awkward smile. "They fear their God and their creatures love to meddle. Their fairies. Dwarves, dragons, and demons. Ghosts . . ." His brow wrinkled as his voice trailed off. He shook his head and straightened a leg. "*Ach*. All sorts make their home in these mountains. They'll tell you tale after tale. In verse or song if it's over an ale."

Avelina's curiosity grew. "What of the north? I heard you mention that to your men. To Jorn and Alif. What is there?"

"Many things. Many men. Rough seas. Options, *escape,* if you have no other choice."

"Was that your home?"

Matthias smirked. "I've not sat long enough in one place to call it home."

"My home lies behind us," she said quietly.

"No, Princess. Your home lies ahead. Through the mountains. There."

She looked again where he again pointed.

"Look for the tallest peak, where the tip is white against the sky."

"I see."

"Now look past it. Look for the rolling lines on either side. The gray lines. You won't see their rocks and trees, but you'll see their shadows."

Focusing, she could see a darker area then, behind the detailed ridges. Successive lines in shades of gray rose and webbed beyond them; rows of mountains appearing as bricks in a blue wall, that gradually faded, until it simply disappeared into the clear sky.

"I see them."

"Beyond those ridges and across the Rhine. Beyond the *Schwarzwald*. That's your new home. Ewigsburg."

My new home.

A new country. And a husband. A new beginning.

She'd been taught to fear this land. This land that seemed a piece of heaven. It seemed so silly now. Was anything ever truly what it seemed? Perhaps *this* was her future? What her forefathers meant for her? If this king had been an ally to her own father . . .

They sat in silence as she ate, drinking again from the waterskin, until Matthias stood, ready to move again for the day. He grunted, looking at the ground around his feet. His jawline clenched tight, set with decision.

"You're to be my queen. But for now, you'll be my wife."

Uneasy, Avelina crossed her arms in front of her. "I don't understand your intentions."

His head pulled back; his brows furrowed.

"Intentions? I have none untoward, Princess."

"Oh," she said, blushing. "You said wife, and I thought . . ."

Matthias laughed. "Not in that sense, no. There is no woman worth bedding that would cost my freedom. Should we meet anyone along the way, we will say you are my wife, and I will call you by your name. While we travel, for protection." He shook his head and his face fell. "I'm sorry if I offended you."

"You don't owe me an apology. You've been kind," she said, thinking of Marcus.

"I need you alive. For my king," he said, features turning hard. "I mean to get you to Ewigsburg, Princess. That's all.

CHAPTER 12

THE FIRST STEP

Matthias

MATTHIAS WALKED AWAY FROM HER toward the rocks. He rolled the fur and blanket, repacked the sacks, and kicked dirt on top of the burned-out fire pit.

"Right," he said, slinging the packs over his shoulders and stretching his arms. "We've got a long way to go today. So let's get on with it."

"Let's," she said, falling in step behind him.

Matthias led them through the trees, the ground slanted beneath their feet. He paused every now and again, waiting for her. Once the dry grounds ceased to crunch beneath their feet, he lifted his chin, closed his eyes, and listened. Sifting through the dawn chorus of the birds, finally he caught the low hum, barely there, carried on the breeze.

The river.

"This way," he said, adjusting their path.

"Where are we going?"

"The river. We're running low on water. The lack of a good rain's left the streams to dry out up here."

The princess was at his heels, stomping along behind him. The effort was there. She was moving along much better than yesterday but was still about as stealthy as a fawn taking its first steps. Slipping, sliding, and staggering about, even with her trusty boots.

He raised a brow, stepping over a fallen trunk. "So tell me,

Princess. . ."

"Yes?"

He'd been wanting to ask. "Your boots?"

She ran her hand beneath her nose and eyed him. "What about them?"

"Where'd you come by them?"

"It was part of my plan," she said, voice huffy.

"You had a plan?"

"Yes. To escape. I had a plan."

Matthias stopped in his tracks and grinned at her. "Good for you, Princess."

He patted her on the shoulder and immediately regretted it.

What was it about this woman that made him act without thinking?

He cocked his head to the side, nudging the two of them on. He offered her his hand, but she shook her head. Instead, she picked up the front hem of her tunic and started forward.

Matthias fell in at her side. "Tell me about it."

Avelina eyed him, her tongue tracing her top lip.

"The plan was the shoes," she said.

"And?" he said.

Her chin dropped for a moment, and then she looked on before them.

"My life was guarded," Avelina said.

"*Genau.*"

"No. You don't understand."

"I can imagine."

The crunch of their footsteps on the dry forest bed punctuated the breaths she took between words. They found a rhythm together; a slow, steady climb was working well for her, and if they maintained it, they could cover some ground today.

"How could you? Know what it was like. At all," she said.

"You confuse me with a free man."

"You seem to do as you please," Avelina said.

Matthias laughed. "In a way. *Soon.* Now, I am a servant of the king. Sworn to my duty."

"Duty," she said and chuckled. "I know a bit about that, don't I?"

Matthias watched her. Her eyes aground, she was gaining confidence as she moved. Every footstep was carefully planned and executed.

"How long have you served your king?" Avelina asked.

"Nine years."

"That's a long time."

Matthias didn't answer. He'd found a trail. He pushed a collection of low branches out of their way and held them for her to pass.

"Has it been wearisome?" Avelina asked.

"Tiring? Surely."

"Has he treated you well?"

Matthias pursed his lips. She asked so many questions. "Are you always this talkative?"

"Are you always this serious?"

He snorted.

"No. Perhaps," she said, shrugging. Her face remained tilted down, watching the narrow dirt trail in front of them. "I had no one to listen before."

Matthias's lip tugged.

This princess. Outsized boots. Remnants of her torn and soiled underskirts sticking out below Alif's tunic and the cloak he'd wrapped her in. Locks of her hair loose from the plaiting, with random grass stuck here and there on her head, replacing the circlet of jewels he'd had her remove yesterday and hid in his breast pocket.

Matthias started to reach for the grass but stopped himself, dropping his hand.

"I am a favorite."

"Of your king? That must have afforded you some nice things. Being a friend."

He ran his thumb along the underside of the ring on his finger.

"He's not my friend. I'm only favored amongst men tied to his will," Matthias said. "There's a difference."

"How did you come to be in his service?"

Matthias's nose wrinkled. "I was sold to him."

"And your brothers?"

"The same."

"What of your parents?"

Matthias did not answer her, and he wouldn't. He was surprised by how easily some responses came, but some subjects were way too heavily guarded and would remain so. She did not press the issue, and they continued walking.

"It's been thirteen years," she said. "Since my parents . . . since they were murdered."

"I am sorry," Matthias said. "For your parents."

Her back straightened. They had come to a downward slope. Arms swinging long, pumping with each quickened step, she continued talking, her phrases stuttering with each stomp. "I know what it's like. To be held to another man's will. I was a prisoner in my own home. Those vines. So beautifully painted on the walls of my room. May as well have been iron bars."

Matthias looked about, checking their surroundings. Nothing off.

She continued to push forward.

"I am. I *was* my father's heir."

"You still are, Princess."

The princess stopped in her tracks. Her eyes remained low, tracing the ground, her jawline pulling as she chewed on her words. Then, as quickly as she stopped, she turned and charged forward again.

"Every day started with a decision," she said. "Even the smallest ones. That I could make. Was *allowed* to make. Mattered. It wasn't the outcome. Well, usually." She flipped her hand in the air. "It was the simple fact it gave me power. That I could execute over my own life."

Their path flattened, and he adjusted both sacks on his shoulders.

"Would I eat that second tartlet while it was warm?" she continued. "Or save it for those long nights when I couldn't sleep? I'd wrap myself within my cloak. Lose myself in the crackling dance of the fire and savor it with a cup of wine."

The path widened, and he again took the place at her side. Avelina looked squarely at him and smiled.

"Then I made better use of them," she said.

"Of what?"

"The tartlets. I began slipping them to the guards. The ones forever by my door. Though they never, ever let me out of their sight or spoke to me, their eyes grew softer as the months of treats passed by."

Matthias smiled. Food was always a good plan and a more powerful tool than she probably even realized.

"Would I read in my east window seat? From there, on a clear day I could see the gardens. The mazes twisting and turning throughout them. I imagined running through them. Walls of lush bushes taller and thicker than men. Their trimmed branches prickling my palms while the scents of the flowers intoxicated me," she said. "Then I realized I'd *memorized* them. I knew the route I would take. Which turns led to a dead end and which would lead me to the forest. Years before I ever stepped into them . . . And what to read? My prayers? I know them by heart. Every word. Every sketch. The thin curves of the letters and lines that created them."

She paused and took a deep, thoughtful breath.

He pulled his waterskin from his waist and handed it to her.

"You see, Matthias," she said, "even if the decision was miniscule. For the smallest of details. I relished it. Because those tiny decisions would build upon one another. Like stone. Each small decision building upon another into a wall." She wiped her arm across her forehead and took a drink. "Until what once seemed like folly, an inkling of an idea, turned into an actual plan. And that plan was the wall I would scale to mount my escape."

Well then.

She drank again and handed the waterskin back to him. Straightening her posture, she gently tugged the ends of her sleeves at her wrists. Untwisted her tunic at her waist. Fixed the cloak across her shoulders and pulled her hair from her face.

Even filthy, she stood regal and refined, with an air of elegance.

He found her impressive and certainly interesting.

He had never been around a woman who spoke so much, but it wasn't lost on him that he enjoyed listening to her. Her musings. Her confessions. Her voice. Her random stories, circling around the one thing he had asked her about.

"Your boots," he said. "How did you get them?"

Her shoulders stretched, and he saw her head shake from behind.

"I stole them."

That didn't fit. "Stole?"

"There was a boy."

There was always a boy. Matthias's fists tightened, surprising him.

"I hope he didn't take advantage of you, Princess."

"No. Nothing like that."

He heard her sniffle and stepped to her side.

"I didn't even know his name," she said, her chest heaving.

"You don't have to tell me, Princess," he said, trying not to stare. Though her head hung low, he saw tears dropping from her cheeks.

"I was in the garden. With my embroidery. The flowers were so beautiful. And my guards, I'd finally bribed them with enough tartlets that I bought myself an extended afternoon outside. It was a lovely day. Until the accident."

She met his eyes, blinked away tears, and then moved forward.

"It was awful. A horse came racing, trumpeting and tearing across the garden. Eyes wild, maddened, as if he'd been kicked by the devil's own spurs. The guards ran to the stables, and I followed. There was so, *so* much screaming. So loud it chilled my bones. They were trying to help him, but there was nothing to be done. The boy's head . . ." she said, shuddering. "The gate was left wide open, and the horses, Niro's horses, were running everywhere. Everyone was chasing them. The stablemen, the grooms, *my guards*. And for the first time, no one was watching me."

Matthias waited, crossing his arms.

"I saw them. I had my basket, and it hit me I could hide them," she said, her voice cracking. "I'm a thief. I knew he was dying. I knelt and undid them and pulled them from his feet. I stole a dying boy's shoes."

They walked in silence.

"I'm impressed, Princess," Matthias said. Honestly, he was.

"Don't mock me," she whispered. "It grieves me."

"It shouldn't."

"There was nothing honorable in what I did."

"Nor dishonorable, Princess. I think it was brave of you to do so."

She stopped in front of him and turned around, placing her

hands on her hips.

Matthias placed a hand on each of her shoulders and squeezed. "There's no shame in any of it."

She shook her head. "You're wrong. There is shame. And I own it as mine."

Matthias frowned, but said no more.

A myriad of emotions passed across her face, and he stood, waiting for each to pass.

Eventually, she tucked her chin and twisted free of him. She clamped the front of her tunic in her hands and set forth, continuing their descent.

"That's about as far as it went. My plan," she said. "I just . . ."

He followed just behind her, his eyes aground, and listened.

"I didn't know how to get away or where I could go, but when I saw those boots, I knew they were my chance to run," she said. "I wanted to live. That's all."

CHAPTER 13

THANK YOU FOR YOUR SERVICE

———— ❧ ————

Avelina

IT WAS DUSK.
They had walked the line of the ridge for hours, utilizing every last bit of sunlight. The hiking had been much easier than the day before, but Avelina was beyond fatigued. A sharpness echoed from the bottom of her feet up through her legs, overworked and overtired from unfamiliar terrain. Each step was an effort, her body no more than parts, rattling against one another to work. She pressed her hands against her sides and coughed.

His hand pressed against the center of her back, barely touching her, and her eyelids fluttered and fell closed.

"You need to drink, Princess."

She smelled the leather approach her nose, and the water reached her lips.

"A little at a time," he said. "But often."

This man.

She coughed after another swallow of water and turned toward him, her eyes adjusting to the dark. Slithers of light peeked between the branches, solid strips of gold shimmering against the deep shadows within the trees.

Matthias was watching her. His face was grim. Always studying, expressive but unreadable. He stood next to her, but his thoughts were elsewhere.

Worried about his friends, perhaps? Wondering if the reward was worth the risk?

"We'll camp here," he said and set about to do so. "In the morning, we'll make for the river. We'll refill our waterskins and ourselves with fish."

She followed him off the path, pulling the cloak closer around her shoulders. It was cooler, and the thought of a fire was comforting. This time, she helped gather sticks scattered about the forest floor and handed them to him.

Matthias nodded thanks and, taking her hand, set her on a fallen log.

"Rest here," he said.

He took a drink from his waterskin and rubbed a forearm across his forehead.

Matthias's presence, and the fierce determination he seemed to assign to each task, calmed her. That look he had given her during the barter had told her the decision had been made. That she would be all right. Yes, it was in his best interest to keep her safe and deliver her to the king, but it seemed . . . different.

It was *him*.

It was an odd sensation. Trusting someone.

"Matthias. Thank you."

"Never mind it," he said, sitting and resting his back against a large rock. "You've done well, but it's time you rest."

Her bottom lip quivered, and she cleared her throat. Standing, she crossed her hands in front of her and took a step toward him.

"No," Avelina said. "I mean to thank you." She took another step toward him. "For fighting for me. For saving my life."

Matthias's knees drew up in front of him, and he propped his elbows on them.

"I will see you are properly rewarded, when I can," Avelina said. "I want to see you and your men taken care of. I can do that as queen."

Matthias's face remained twice guarded.

"I appreciate that, Princess," he said. "But we want for nothing. Only our freedom. And that's close enough now. Just over the mountains." His head fell back against the tree, and his eyes closed.

Avelina exhaled and took the final steps, her legs shaking with the renewed movement. Pulling up her skirts, she sat beside him. Her shoulder brushed against his arm and, liking the feel of his warmth, she leaned close against him.

"What you did for me. It means much more than that," Avelina said.

His hips shifted from her, and she heard him exhale slowly.

"I thought, truly, I was going to die that day." Avelina leaned her head against his shoulder. Barely at first. She couldn't explain it, but she wanted to touch him. "No man. No one. Has done what you've done. It was everything. To me." Her chest tight, she pressed her cheek against him and closed her eyes.

Falling quickly toward her dreams, she heard him muttering to her and smiled just as she drifted off to sleep.

"You have power within you, Princess. Remember that. You're a survivor. That's a hell of a thing to be in this world."

CHAPTER 14

ANY OTHER WOMAN

Matthias

I F SHE WERE ANY OTHER woman.
Matthias would've bedded her then and there.

He would've wrapped his hands around her hips and pulled her beneath him. He would've spread her on the forest floor to taste and tease every part of her before losing himself in those amber eyes as he buried himself within her a hundred ways. His gut pulled tight and his groin ached with the thought of putting his mouth on hers. His eyes closed, listening to the light rhythm of her breathing against him. *Trusting him.*

Gah. Enough. Raising his hips, he pulled the fabric bunched atop his thighs toward his knees and resettled himself a bit farther from her.

If she were any other woman. But she wasn't. That was for sure.

She was to be his queen.

She was his to keep safe and deliver to his king.

That had to be enough; it had to be everything.

Night had come; the sun had finally set on the other side of the mountain. Even on this summer eve, the temperature fell shockingly low with it. The moon, waxing and bright, taunted him, an ever-present reminder of the slowness of their pace versus the fast approach of the deadline. Only a few days until it would be full.

He had wanted to get farther today, but instead they'd made camp and would start fresh in the morning. He could tell she was done and dared not drive her to injury.

He needed to take his mind off the way she felt against him.

Think of something else.

The duel. Niro.

Matthias hadn't had time to think about it all since.

Now, watching the flames lick the frames of their small fire, with the lady asleep on his shoulder, a wave of fresh unease washed over him.

Matthias replayed it, dissecting and processing it step by step.

He had been anxious. Wanting to ensure Reymund was safely on his way home. Wanting to get through the duel. Wanting to perform the ceremony, wed the princess by proxy for his king, and leave Leuceria before anything could go wrong.

Something always did.

Of course, Marcus had had a plan. It was a clever move, thinking Barreth the soldier stood a better chance to defeat him. In a way, Matthias was glad of it. He'd much rather fight another soldier than the House of Connaire's heir. Especially since Avidius, the elder, seemed to be one of the lone honorable men left in that Great Hall. Willing to fearlessly stand against Niro and risk it all for the princess.

There had to be more to that story.

Hmpf. Someday. Someday if he had the chance, he'd kill Marcus. Marcus's raging hatred was fueled by jealousy, and once that ugly snake bit a man, its venom was impossible to withdraw.

He'd seen it on Marcus's face when the duel was won. His own roaring rush of satisfaction met by Marcus's shock hardening into a marrow-deep obsession, and then that unexpected look from the General of confidence and respect.

When Matthias's eyes had met the princess's, it felt as if time slowed. He'd bent a knee before her, out of breath and blood racing through his veins; her glossy eyes had been rounded with anticipation and hope.

His skin had burst aflame when he'd taken her hand into his sweaty palm.

He'd managed his pledge of protection, but there had been no time to complete the marriage ceremony. The crowds had pushed inward. Marcus yelling her name behind him, demanding both of their heads. The noble families flooding the ground around him as the soldiers braced against the onslaught.

His heart had thundered in his ears and he'd barely heard himself speak.

But he knew what he'd said, and he'd meant every word.

I will remain faithful to you and to my pledged word.

It was the last thing he said to her before Niro's guards grabbed them both.

Ach, that moment.

Right after his oath, still holding her hand, two guards had wrapped their arms around her and sharply torn her from him. Another pair had grabbed his arms, propelling him forward as they charged from the courtyard, through a door and down a long hallway, hurried away from the erupting crowd.

Ignoring the urge to fight, Matthias's gut had told him to follow and not dare lose her. A guard on either side of him holding his arms, he'd quickened his step, trying to not lose sight of the men carrying the princess. They'd passed through the Great Hall, wrecked from the barter, but stunning still. They'd slipped through the door Niro had entered the night before, the painted walls replaced with narrowing passageways of windowless stone, then down endless winding stairs into the bowels of the palace. Progressively darker, colder, older, along twisting corridors until they'd arrived in an ancient cavern. Massive and murky, with a handful of torches providing a circle of light, and there within it had stood Niro. Waiting for them. Arms folded in front of him, glaring at them all. Seeing the princess, he'd nodded at the guards who carried her, and they'd walked past him, disappearing into the gray-blue mists.

Matthias's cheeks had iced in the dank air. "Where are you taking her?"

"To your man. Your brother," Niro had said. "The angry one."

Crossing the distance between the two of them in pounding steps, the General had doubled in size. Matthias had straightened to look him best in the eye, though his arms were still held back, locked tightly behind him.

"The monk left on a merchant ship bound for the rivers," Niro had said. "Or so I'm told."

Matthias had stood silent.

"You think I don't know what happens on my own grounds?" Niro had snarled. He'd lifted his hand, and the guards had let go of Matthias and retreated. "Leave us."

Matthias had looked around Niro's shoulder, where the princess had vanished. A flicker of movement had let in slithers of light. Bright and clear. *Daylight.*

Only the General had stood between him and escape. Between him and her.

"I'm impressed, Sword. Barreth was a champion, though I never much cared for his person. I accounted for the crowd's reaction— and my son's—with extra guards, but Avidius . . . I did not count for the depth of his pockets nor the lengths of his interference. The man is good and no enemy of mine, only loyal to—"

"Do you mean to fight me, General?" Matthias had hissed. "Because if you do, get on with it."

Niro had snorted. "I like you, Sword. You remind me of days gone by."

Matthias had ground his teeth and trenched his heels into the ground, preparing for a fight.

"Breathe, soldier. Your men wait anon." Niro had turned, large and brooding to Matthias. "If I meant for you or her to be dead, I'd have let Marcus kill you."

Niro had turned, walking toward the exit, and Matthias had followed through the dissipating fog, the hair rising on the back of his neck. No longer on smooth stone, pebbles had crunched beneath his boots, and a rhythmic rush had grown steadily louder, swirling about them, crashing against the stone walls, as if their cavern were a hollow chamber.

"Your guards will let us leave?"

"These men are loyal to me. Once you get past them, you're on your own."

"I have a mind your son won't agree with this."

"*Hmpf.* He will send his dogs after you, no doubt. Should they find you, they will show her no mercy."

Reaching the cavern's edge, Matthias had seen a cascade of vines, some fresh and green, others brown and thicker than a man's arm, entwined and covering a slim opening in the tan stone.

Blue, brilliant and blinding, salted and shimmering, had slipped between them.

"Listen and heed my warning," Niro had said, his eyes black. "I haven't stopped you because I'm giving her one chance. *One.* I mourn my friend, but there was no turning back." His lips had pursed tight. "The queen was to be mine, but then all of our fates changed." Niro's fists had shaken at his sides as he'd stared in front of him.

Matthias had taken a step sideways toward the exit, listening but positioning himself to leave. Or fight if it came to it.

"I've taken the responsibility for their deaths and let them believe what they will." Niro's back had straightened as an air of defiance swept him. "The princess was only a babe. I had to protect her. There was nothing else to be done." Niro had paused before continuing, "They said it was a sign. Our turn to build a dynasty on the throne. But God has tormented me since. With sickness. Plagues. A heartless son."

Matthias had taken a step toward the sunlight.

Niro had hung his head. "Everything that I have done. Everything. Was for her."

"The princess?"

"All of them. My country. Her mother. And for the girl to live so my soul may be redeemed." Niro had turned a hard eye on him. "*You* are my strategy, soldier. Don't disappoint me. Go. Make sure she disappears. Make sure she never returns. Because if she does, I cannot . . . I *will not* stop Marcus. He is my son. I will cut her throat myself."

CHAPTER 15

PROTECTION

———◆◇◆———

Avelina

THE RIVER WAS WIDER HERE. They were near the shore, where larger stones peeked through the calm, crystal water to offer a tricky dry path along the bed. The center of the river rushed by, a darker blue-gray with shiny ripples from the high midday sun, disappearing into the valley behind them. Across the river, the thick cover of trees mirrored their own side. Bursts of bright lime leaves blending with olive green, blue jades, and prickly pines atop trunks of browns or whites, shading into a background of deeply hued emeralds that faded to black.

It was beautiful. Invigorating. A patchwork of color that danced on the clean, crisp air above the river, which tickled her cheeks with a splattering of chilly beads of fresh water.

"The water is clear here. Shallow," Matthias said, pointing down where the water threaded through the raised stones along the riverbed around him. "The river is flush with fish this time of year. A stray or two'll tend to lose themselves among the stones and make an easy dinner for us before the rain comes."

The rain?

The blue sky was bright and cloudless, and the sun's rays glistened against the current.

The man was mad. Or at best confused. He was also intimidating yet interesting and infuriatingly intriguing.

Several steps in front of her, Matthias was perched on a large, slanted boulder. Her eyes bore into him, studying him. His hands were on his hips, shoulders and elbows spread wide as he watched the river. He was a statuesque extension of the darkened solid rocks on which he stood, against a background of fluid and colorful movement.

"I meant to run, you know."

It had only been a passing thought, but again, for reasons Avelina couldn't place, she kept sharing things out loud. Happily, without fear, giving voice to words she would've swallowed before. As if he were her confessor, though she did not ask forgiveness. Or a friend, though she did not dare to dream it reciprocal.

Matthias glanced at her over his shoulder, and she saw a smile curve his lip.

"From me?" he said.

"Yes."

He rubbed a hand around the back of his neck. "Where to?"

"I'm not sure," she said. "Somewhere."

Avelina crouched, searching through the pebbles along the bank. Sifting through the ground with one hand, with the other she clutched her small collection close to her breast. Some were small and smooth spheres, others amorphous; she picked the ones that made her smile.

"Do you mean to still?" he said.

She paused, then reached to gather the loose tendrils of her hair that kept stubbornly blowing across her nose. She flashed a quick glance at him before returning to inspect her stones. Still feeling the weight of his eyes on her, she managed to stifle a grin.

"I haven't decided yet."

Matthias turned away and squatted on the rocks, leaning forward onto his knee for a better view. "Well then, I appreciate the warning."

There was honesty in his tone and a hint of orneriness as well.

"Of course," she said. "I . . ."

She went silent, and he peered over his shoulder at her.

"I do thank you for what you've done for me. I just can't," she said, shoulders slumping.

"What can you not do?"

Her chin fell, avoiding the question. Her forefinger dug at a gray stone with white swirls until she pulled it from the bed. Inspecting it, she rubbed a thumb across the gritty sand, turning the heart-shaped stone into the light. She frowned and shook her head, then picked at the pebbles again.

"This doesn't feel like the path I'm meant to be on," she said.

"*Ach*, well if you ran far enough north, you could book passage to one of the islands. Or east too, I guess," Matthias said, staring across the river. "Or you could get lost or die out here in the wilderness."

"You're mocking me again."

He sighed, and his shoulders slumped at an angle.

"I'm not," he said. "But I want you to weigh your options."

"Options? I didn't believe I had any."

"Make them, Princess. With what you have," he said. "But I ask, is it truly so bad to marry a king?"

"And not marry for love?"

Matthias snickered, and she felt a twinge of pain.

"You think me spoiled."

"No," he said. "I find you sincere. Thoughtful." His large chestnut eyes rounded with a softness that surprised her. "I know you're deluged with much change, but I only beg you to be cautious. Do not take for granted the safety I afford you and that which you would have at Ewigsburg. Safety and a life at least, though I will not promise you happiness there."

Her hand stilled, and she listened.

He grimaced. "I mean I will not promise you a loving husband in the king. But you will love your children, Princess. That seems to be the way of it, from what I have seen."

"Should I be lucky enough to have them," she said. "I do hope for them. At least someday."

"What is it you do want, Princess?"

"I would like to do some good."

"Then do so. Find what interests you."

"I love reading. It fuels and inspires me. Or it did until Niro closed the library."

"Then build your own. Reymund would help you. He'd enjoy that." Matthias smiled wide. "He can read and knows a bit how to write, but the man's mind is. . . unmatched among men I know. He's a living library in a way. He never forgets anything once he's learned it."

"Did the king educate him?"

Matthias scoffed and muttered as he turned from her, "No. Girault never raised a hand to better him, but he sure benefits from Reymund's expertise and reputation."

"I hope you don't think me rude," she said. "But your brother, is he well?"

"Which? Jorn? In the head, no. In the heart, yes." He smirked, picking up the sharpened stick that lay at his feet. He had found a good one, he'd told her, with a closely forked end that would do well to spear fish. He turned it in his hand, as she had seen him do with his sword. "My brother Reymund may seem a bit different, but he's a man to be respected all the same. Moreso, even. He's earned the admiration he has. He fights his own battles, but he'll never surrender to them. We all have our differences though, don't we?"

"He's lucky to have you for a brother. They both are," she said. She searched for the source of his attention and saw the flicker of movement a stone's throw ahead of him amongst the rocks.

"I count myself lucky," Matthias said, tapping his thumb against the tip of his makeshift spear. "You and Reymund have your books in common. And your God. He hasn't taken the vows. Prefers to speak to Him on his own, I think." His eyebrows scrunched together as he looked at her. "I believe the two of you will get on well."

"Reymund and I shall be friends," she said. "I would like that."

"As would he, I'm sure."

"You take care of him," she said, both a question and a statement.

Matthias shrugged. "In ways, yes. Do not worry about Reymund. Any man foolish enough to challenge him would see Jorn's temper first."

She smiled. "You take care of one another. Protect one another, as soldiers do."

Matthias gave her a stern look. "You understand what it is to be a soldier, Princess?"

"I've been around soldiers my whole life."

His head cocked to the side. "And that makes you think you understand them?"

She paused, considering.

"I admired them. Their confidence. Our soldiers were well trained and taken care of. Valued members of our society. But their training centered on technique. Skill. Weaponry. Survival. Duty and dedication to Leuceria. Not strategy or history for the foot soldiers, or much of it, so I believe."

"Did you speak to them?"

"No." Her chin fell. It hadn't been out of spite. Or some sense of superiority or rank. It was how things were. She was silent. Mute. Bound by fear, for herself and those she might mar by association. "But it didn't mean I didn't respect them."

"I'm not saying you didn't, Princess." His lips pursed, and he turned back to his task. He bent forward on a knee, dangling his fingers into the water, and then ran his hand over his face. "It's a brotherhood. We may not share the same blood in our veins, but it binds us just the same. The risk of it. For king and country, the fine men say, but it's honor really. Duty to those who stand and fight beside you."

"You are bound to them?"

"Without regret."

"You lead them, do you not?"

"They rely on me, though I often wonder how it was me who ended up at the helm and not another man. They may follow me, but I rely on them. Reymund's counsel. Jorn's loyalty. They keep me grounded, though my feet never stay in the same place long. Where they are, I am. Where our heads rest at night is home. I will never abandon them. I do this—seek this freedom—for them. To do with as they will."

"Then they are lucky men to have someone love them as you do."

"Love them?"

"Of course. Don't you? And the rest of your men?"

"I count them as friends. Family."

"Then either way, you are a rich man. To have such a thing."

Squatting down, the speared stick in his hand raised, he looked ready to strike. He relaxed when the fish turned about and away.

"I'll help," she said.

"I can take care of this," he said, keeping his back to her. He stuck the stick beneath his elbow and rubbed his hands briskly together. "Find a warm rock along the shore and rest a bit."

Avelina slipped her stones into the pocket of her tunic. She pulled her boots off one at a time and set them beside her. Bunching her tunic at her hips, she grabbed the waist of her underskirt and slid it down, stepping out of it. She carefully folded it around the hidden prayer book and set it on the rock with his satchels, not taking the chance for the skirts to get wet. She hiked the tunic to her knees and nodded.

She was doing this.

Avelina took the first step, searching for the dry spot on the closest rock, and stretched to reach it. She found another, and another, and another. One arm bundling the bottom of her tunic and the other reached wide to her side for balance, she pushed her way gingerly along. A steeper rock tricked her footing, and feeling a threatening tweak in her ankle, she shrieked and let herself fall, splashing into the water.

Matthias turned, his jaw open in shock.

"I'm fine," she said, waving him off. Clenching her teeth, she pushed upright and dug her toes into the sandy bottom. She drew in a sharpened breath, surprised how cold the water circling her calves was beneath the late-summer sun. "A bit colder than I imagined."

His wide eyes dropped to her bare legs and then jumped back to her face.

"Go back before you hurt yourself!" he said, pointing to the bank. "The water is deeper there to your left and the current stronger. One wrong step and you'll get carried away. I'll have to swim after you, and I'd rather not go backward if we can manage it. Rest before we eat."

Avelina pursed her lips and looked around her.

No, she didn't want to retreat either.

Avelina moved toward him. The initial shock of the water's chill rose on her the deeper the water became, though she began to shiver less as her body adjusted to the temperature.

"Resting won't fill my stomach," she said, giving him a saucy eye. The running waters sloshed around her legs. Each step taken slow, she made sure her foot sank securely into the sandy bed, causing her to teeter back and forth.

Matthias slid off the side of his boulder, frowning, and powered through the water toward her. Reaching her, he grabbed ahold of her arm and pulled her toward him.

"Steady now," he said, his hand moving around to the small of her back. "You won't need to know how to do all this. I can take care of you."

"What if *you* fall?" Avelina arched her back against his hand and cocked her head to look him in the eye. "Should *you* slip away, I'll need to know how to take care of us . . . or myself."

Matthias grinned. "Is that so?"

The sense of worry she'd seen when he hit the water had dissipated and washed downriver, replaced with this wide, easy smile that rushed along her chilled skin. Avelina turned, hiding the rosy warmth tickling her cheeks.

Those eyes of his had a way of pouring over her that made her uncomfortably comfortable. She peered off, concentrating on the rushing whoosh and trickling sounds about them and not on his thumb rubbing along her spine.

"Teach me, Matthias," she said, swallowing. "Or am I to leave you and carry on? You wouldn't leave me behind, would you?"

"You know I wouldn't," he said.

She took a small step back, but his hand only locked stronger on her, holding her steady. "I've had a strong education, but, well, it's not going to keep me alive. I need knowledge I can apply. And there's no shame in using one's hands as well as one's mind. I'd rather know how to and feel twice accomplished."

"You're right. There's much to learn out here that you couldn't in your library." He sighed heavily and then his eyes lifted skyward.

She turned her chin, hoping to read his expression.

Barely noticeable, she saw a drop of rain splat against his face. One more. Then another. And another, until the waters began dripping along his cheek like slanted stone.

The sky was still blue and mostly cloudless, but fresh rain began to steadily fall on them. The sunlight shimmered within the plump droplets, and she laughed, both surprised and amused.

He'd been right after all.

"Please don't think me ridiculous," she said.

"I don't," Matthias shook his head. "At all, Princess."

He slid his hand from her back and took her hand tight in his. He led her upriver, the rain picking up around them, to a set of low-hanging branches stretching out over the water. They sheltered beneath them, and she listened while he explained where a fish might look for cover among the stones and grass stalks around them.

The rain continued, with time lost to a peaceful afternoon. She laughed repeatedly and, unsuccessfully attempting to spear a fish, genuinely enjoyed herself. They hardly spoke, communicating through gestures when the noise of the world around them drowned out their voices. The river roared louder beside them, swollen with the downpour, and the once playful splatting against the branches above them developed into a thunderous rush. Resounding as if hundreds of marbles had been poured against the palace tiles, the rain cracked and smacked against the leaves in such a rush she mused how the water didn't pour past the leaves and overtake them. The sky slowed and grayed, and a fog settled upon them, laying low above the water.

Finally, having speared a fish herself to Matthias's two, Avelina bounced with glee. She held it aloft, proud and thankful for the lesson and her bounty. They traveled back to shore, hungry and triumphant.

Her skirt had fared well in the rain, only a bit dampened under the thick cover of the trees. Sitting on a low rock, she pulled her boots onto her feet and began to make easy work of the hooks. She looked at Matthias, and her smile dropped.

Knelt beside her, his body went tense. Something had made him uneasy, and she dared not move. He placed his hand against the mud, inspecting something. He raised an open palm to her and placed a single finger in front of his lips. His eyes met hers, and he shook his head slowly, and she knew she must be silent.

Frozen in place, Avelina watched him inspect the mud, scattered with shiny rocks and, in between them, indentations. Tracks. Her eyes widened when she saw them. Larger than his hand, with other smaller versions around him. Fat bottomed with five toes and claw marks above each.

Matthias moved toward her, taking her hands in his and pulling her behind him. He stood slowly, spreading his arms wide and

turning in the direction of the tracks. His back loomed in front
of her, his shoulders spread, and his arms moved slowly, fanning
like wings, as if he was trying to occupy as much space as possible.

"Stay behind me, Avelina," he said in a low whisper. "Stay
behind me and *do not run.*"

Avelina peeked around his shoulder. His arm waving up and
down in front of her face, she caught glimpses of the fog filled
riverbed in front of them.

Matthias started talking, his voice so low it rippled across the
water itself. His voice became louder. Unfamiliar words walking
across the stones. Snarling like an animal himself.

Then, through the mist, she saw them.

One at first, then two, then a third.

Animals with brownish black fur on stocky round bodies, their
feet disappearing into the shallow water. Standing in the midst of
them on two trunk-like hind legs, thick, strong, was the largest
animal she had ever seen, staring straight at them.

A bear.

She had seen its likeness carved on her great-grandfather's
cenotaph, but *this*, this enormous reality, standing right before
them, seized every last bit of air within her. Her lungs deflated;
her mouth dropped open, screeching a silent scream of terror, as
the giant took a step toward them. Snorting. The sound barreling
at them. Another step forward and it came out of the last shadow
of mist into the clear gray light.

"Stay with me, Avelina," Matthias whispered. "Do exactly as I
do."

Her heart drummed, reminding her to breathe, and she drew
long on the dense air. She nodded, although he couldn't see her
behind him, and started moving her trembling arms slowly at her
side. Matthias's heel lifted and, with a lumbering pace, set down
behind him, his muscles tense as he secured his footing. She did
the same, every measured step feeling like a year, mirroring him
without a word, determined not to get locked by her fear. Ever so
slowly, Matthias urged them back toward the cover of the trees.

The bear's head cocked to the side, sniffing at them, her large
nostrils flaring. She yawned, her large jawline splayed open wide,

pointed teeth cutting the air. Her jaw snapped shut, once, then again. She shook her neck, snorting even louder, every sound she made drowning out the rush of the river at her feet.

Her young curiously moved about her legs, tiny versions of their mother.

Matthias's voice still drummed low and loud as he moved sideways, one step at a time. His steps widened, and she took two to his one to remain behind him.

The mother slammed onto all fours and took another step toward them, growling. The threat roared through the air, and the hairs on Avelina's arms and neck stood on end. Her knees wobbly, she pushed her heels into the mud, desperate not to lose her balance.

The bear's neck elongated, jutting out her narrow head, and she again opened her strong jaw. She turned her head, showcasing her large teeth, while her three cubs laced through their mother's hind legs.

The mother turned, answering each sideways step Matthias took, shifting within her circle. Each paw defiantly slamming, her tapered legs shifted her deceptively narrow shoulders before her as her immense hindquarters lilted behind her.

They reached the forest's edge, and suddenly she charged them.

Paws thundering against the ground, the bear took several steps, clearing the distance between them in no time.

Avelina screamed in spite of herself but didn't run, firmly planted behind Matthias.

Matthias stopped, throwing his arms out and roaring his own guttural yawp back at her. His shoulders shook wildly, but he maintained his ground. Avelina didn't dare move.

The bear stopped, swinging her head about.

Man and beast stood face-to-face, protecting what was theirs.

She shook her head at him.

Huffing and snorting. Twice as wide as him, they stood eye to eye.

And then as quickly as she had charged them, she turned.

Back to her young, she called to them and they eagerly joined her side, moving to the opposite bank and disappearing into the thick brush.

"What was that?" Avelina whispered to Matthias's back as they stood watching the last cub chase its mother.

"A miracle," Matthias said. "That's what that was."

CHAPTER 16

SHELTER FROM THE STORM

Matthias

GAH. WHAT NOW?

It had to be enough for the day soon.

After the episode with the sow and her cubs, he had forced a heavy pace.

He wanted, he *needed* to get her to Ewigsburg, but he also needed to get her there in one piece.

Matthias looked around. It was pointless to turn back.

The thick canopy of the forest had provided them shelter as they'd charged for two days in almost continuous rain. The bear had claimed the riverbank and they had retreated upward, diagonal across the hills. Once an imminent threat, she had proved to be a blessing, having forced them away from the river.

From their higher vantage point, Matthias had seen smoke rising high above the slanted canopy below him. Evidence of another camp and other travelers below. Locals. Hunters. Perhaps shepherds, taking reprieve at a summer hut. Or bandits making camp. It didn't matter. Out here, it meant nothing that he was the King's Sword. That she was a princess and should be afforded respect. She was a traveler with a lone guard, and the lands they traveled were dangerous.

Best to avoid them. Whoever they were. And so they did.

It had been a miserable climb. Matthias kept them covered in the forest, where the leaves and limbs of the trees kept them mostly protected from the rain. Over the hours, the rain eventually stopped, but the state of the air about them continued to change. Thinner as they climbed higher, today it was cooler, heavier, and its dampness seeped through his bones.

They needed to make their own camp. They needed to get warm, rest, and eat, but they also needed to avoid the men and beasts who traveled along the river.

Beside him, she leaned against the tall branch of birch he'd cleaned and trimmed for her to use as a walking stick, smiling. "It's beautiful."

Matthias looked left and right. Seeing nothing but threat, he grunted.

They reached another ridge and abruptly stopped where a sharp cliff stood between them and the next peak. A ridge to their left, forcing them higher still, above the tree line, where they would be exposed, was their only way forward. The never-ending rain was creating dozens of small streams slithering through the stones beneath their feet, leaving them slippery, and some were starting to become loose. Swollen with rain, the moss had grown plump, thickly carpeting the rocks in a vivid green. Rainswept blue grasses lay slick, limply dangling downhill. Normal for a heavy rain. The larger bushes and few fallen trees, though, littered about in disarray, made him unnerved. Uprooted, tumbling, and broken, they echoed of death.

While most plants fell victim to the waters tumbling upon them, Matthias noted hardy star-shaped wool flowers still standing defiantly along the cliff's craggy crevices. Their velvety, silver white petals were fatted, thick around the yellow spikes in their center. Knowing them to be good for stomach pains, he paused, kneeling beside a growth of them. They had already used what woundwort he had carried.

"Avelina, wait," he said. He took a handful, breaking them low on the stem. Wrapping the mountain flowers within a cloth, he packed them into his knapsack. He heard stones twist beneath her heel and turned to see her peering out over the valley.

"Look," she said, reaching her hand out toward the ridges beyond. "Over there, the blue sky is so crisp. There, where the evening sun is hitting. See how it bathes the stone in spots of silver? And the trees, with rolling tops of golden green. So many rich colors. Patched together like a quilt. With so many details stitched amongst them."

Matthias's nose wrinkled, his gaze tracing to the storm they couldn't escape. Though they had a moment's reprieve, the storm followed their tracks. The sky was various shades of gray, heavy with rain, and growing especially dark.

"We need to find shelter," Matthias said, eyes narrowing at the distinct purplish-black clouds creeping over the peaks behind them. "And beat this storm."

They were running out of time. He threw the knapsack onto his back, picked one last flower, and stuffed it into his breast pocket.

Matthias led them toward an animal path cutting above the ridge. He put her in front of him, for her to set the pace, and stayed a step behind. It was flat but thin, and the rocks on either side were growing steeper. The winds were growing wilder, howling and pushing against them, whipping their faces with the icing rain. He reached his arm across his forehead to guard his eyes.

Gah. Having kept Avelina plugged with food and drink, he'd neglected himself, and his eyes were again paying for it. They'd not bothered him for days, but now they grew agitated, tired in the thin air. His drive outpacing his intake, he was growing dehydrated, as were his eyes. They were dry, a dull burn settling into his lower lids. He groaned, blinking repeatedly, desperately, until his vision's cloudiness cleared and his eyes readjusted to the dull gray light.

Matthias heard the princess squeak as she lost her footing. Rattled and heart pounding, he reached for her but missed. Her right boot slid across a stone. She slammed her hand down, catching herself from landing on her face, but her side crashed onto a large rock.

"I'm all right," she said, waving him off. She smiled at him, but the strain was evident across her cheeks. Dripping, soaked and shivering, the princess had been trying her best to keep up with him. She was determined, not one to easily surrender. But she was either going to slip again and break her neck on a rock soon or she was going to freeze.

"I've got you," Matthias shouted against the wind. He helped her stand, and she winced. He slid his arm around her waist and pulled her against him for support. She wrapped her hand around his back, and he grabbed her hand at his shoulder.

Frustrated, Matthias continued along the path. He'd pull her along again, carry her if he had to. To know she was safe.

Then there it was. Light, brighter than they'd seen in almost two days' time, ripping across the mountain side, flashing and shaking the air around them. His shoulders scrunched and the hair on his neck rose.

"*Scheiße!*" Matthias drew her tighter against him and arched his shoulders around hers. "There. Quickly."

She shuffled her sliding feet beside him.

The thunder broke, a deafening roar rumbling behind them, shaking the air.

Matthias had seen it when the lightning broke through the clouds, but he wasn't about to wait for another to confirm. The storm was still behind them, but it was too close. The path thankfully widened, and he got in step next to her, wrapping his arm around her waist.

They stumbled together across the stones until they reached the darkness he had seen. The cave entrance. It wasn't the safest place to be, but it was better than underneath the direct hammering of the storm. Water poured over it like a falling river and he thrust them through and into the darkness.

"Matthias."

"Come. Away from the edge."

Matthias pulled her along until they were away from the mouth of the cave, where the rock was dry. When lightning again struck outside, he could see they were in a chamber carved into the stone, the back corner of which fell into the deepest, darkest black. He saw no evidence of a den. Thankfully, they were alone.

"We can rest here a bit, but we cannot stay," he said.

Avelina was shivering from the cold, but he imagined the storm had shaken her as well. He set the sacks down. Weighted heavy with rain on the outside, the hides had kept the contents dry. He unrolled them and handed her a cured sausage, then licked the sticky salt from his fingers. It was their last one.

Matthias pulled her wet cloak from her, laid it out over a neighboring stone, and wrapped his fur tight around her. He rubbed her shoulders and then sat beside her.

Gah. This was not going well.

It had seemed the right decision at the time.

Their horse tiring from riding duel. And Marcus's hounds not far behind them. Jorn would cause another diversion, and he could take her, disappear into the shadows.

His gut, his bones had told him to. Downright screamed at him to.

But here in the damp, not for the first time in the past few days, he was doubting himself.

She was a mess. She was clumsy, but she was trying. She was doing downright fantastic, honestly. And she was nothing if not driven.

They could do this. He'd have to take her farther down. Once the storm passed and they rounded the cliff, they could get below the tree line again. Back toward the water. Surely, they had skirted the camps by now.

Once they had light and the rain slowed, they would go; for now, he had to keep her warm.

"You're half-frozen," Matthias said.

"Can we have a fire?"

He looked about, seeing no ventilation. "Not without choking ourselves with smoke."

He lifted the fur.

She hesitated, her eyelashes batting.

"Survival, Princess," he said. "I'll keep you warm."

Her lip pulled, and she nodded. Matthias curled himself around her and rewrapped the fur around them both. She curled into a ball, tucking her chin against her chest.

He held her through the storm until the lightning ceased, the thunder rolled away, and a steady rain was all that remained.

Matthias felt her still against him. She swallowed, and then her lips smacked open.

He leaned his head toward hers.

She sighed, exhaling heavily. She curled even tighter into herself.

"Matthias. Your king? Is he a good man?"

"Good?"

"Kind. A fair, honest man. Do his people love him?"

Matthias tilted an eyebrow. "They follow him. If that's what you mean."

"No. It isn't. It isn't the same at all."

Matthias frowned, unsure how to answer. Girault had been a great commander. The second son. Not set to inherit, he was born instead to fight, or at least lead those who did. Now he enjoyed the throne his cousin's and brother's death had left open. He was loud. Garish. Loved to laugh, to drink, and to enjoy the company of women. Many women.

But kind? Honest? Had Siegfried lived, she may have found contentment with him. Something other than what awaited her in Ewigsburg. But there was no sense belaboring what might have been with a dead man. Or hinting at a life of happiness he could never promise her.

Though he truly wished he could.

She shifted her hips toward him. "What happened to the king's wife?

"She passed from a sickness. She was a kind woman. He thought well of her."

"He has heirs?"

"A strong son, Zane."

"And the king seeks more children? You said he means to keep his bed warm?"

No. His king never had a problem with that.

"Your name brings power, prestige to his crown. The people have a long memory. Your father was known even to our people. They remember him."

She curled even closer against him, shivering less now. His arms tightened around her in response.

"Do you remember your father?" he asked.

"Do you remember yours?"

He cringed. He shouldn't have asked, but he'd wanted her talking. Not about him. Or the king. Distracted. Her mind off of the cold. The dark. And what might be crawling in it.

Matthias rested his cheek against the top of her head, and they said no more.

Finally warm. Oddly comfortable. Achingly exhausted. He let his eyes fall closed, listening to the rhythm of the rain.

CHAPTER 17

THE INEXTINGUISHABLE FIRE

Matthias

MATTHIAS WAS RUNNING.

Every time it began the same.

Legs moving furiously, straining his muscles beneath him, feet bare and slamming onto the ground. Twigs snapping. Breath ragged. In and out.

"Matthias."

He stopped at the sound of his name. Spinning. Echoing.

The princess?

No. Not Avelina.

It was *her.*

Mother.

Where? Where is she?

A labyrinth of trees.

Brown. Black. Green against green. All fading to gray.

Where is she?

Arms raised, ready, in front of him, but his hands were empty.

His palms slammed to his hips. Nothing.

His back. Nothing.

He was unarmed.

Where was his sword? His axe?

"Matthias."

There. To his right. Moving.

He thrust forward. Pushing into the mist.

His voice choked on the dense air. "I'm here!"

An empty tent. And another. Ripped curtains and empty hearths. No trace of men or beasts.

He stumbled on a large root covered by a mound of earth, and pain jolted through his knee. His palm slammed across the tree trunk, raw pain ripping through him as his skin sliced across the coarse bark. Bracing his teeth, he cried out, and spittle laced his chin.

Go man. Go.

"Matthias!"

Screaming. Voices. So many. Sharply battering his skull.

Where . . . where are they?

He ran toward them. Faster. Limping. Knee floating. Thigh screaming.

Sliding. Slippery. Grass ripping, mud seeping between his toes.

Red mud. Blood mud.

Growing darker. Stodgier.

The cries of men. One upon another. Calling. In pain. For help. From him. From anyone. Mixed voices. Ragged. Gurgling. Drowning.

He had to help. He had to get there. He had to run faster.

Run faster.

He could not fail them.

Fingers of acrid smoke curled into his nose.

Gagging him.

Fire.

Through the trees. Beyond the line. The field was roaring. Devouring itself. Sparks blasted his skin, singeing the hairs.

The shouts grew louder, shrill. Primal. Horrified.

Screaming as one voice.

Crackling of wood. Pounding roar of fire. Sizzling of greens. Roasting of flesh.

The dark wall of smoke rolled toward him. Grays and whites funneling around one another. Creeping over the blood-run ground.

Not again.

Time began to split. He was still running, pushing his body forward, sweat pouring from him, his chest set to burst, but his limbs grew hardened, his bones turning to stone against his efforts to shatter them and move forward.

Matthias bellowed in frustration. It didn't make sense. They had been right there. Right in front of him. Their voices. He had heard them.

The faster he ran, the farther away they seemed.

Was he wrong? Had he heard them wrong?

It was all his fault. He couldn't find them. He couldn't help them.

The trees began moving. Their blackened limbs stretched, bending across his path. Their amorphous shapes shifted, splintering into skeletons and filling with charred flesh. The branches broke beneath their weight, and their feet found the ground.

And the march of the dead began.

Shadowed shapes of men, women, and children. Soldiers and citizen alike. On horse and foot, they silently, slowly, sailed by. Their movements whispered; they blankly stared beyond him as they trudged by.

There.

"Father?"

No. No, no, no, no, no.

He couldn't move. Frozen. Terrified.

Air thick. Strong as steel. An iron maiden. Locking him in place.

Where are you? Eyes frantically searching side to side.

"Papa."

Wait. Wait. There.

A child. Her voice small, barely a whisper.

Sharp breaths. Chest pounding. Nerves blistering.

He had to get there.

No, no, no. Not again.

His father's voice mounted his shoulder, whispering like the devil into his ear. "You can't outrun your destiny, son."

He couldn't move. He couldn't move. He couldn't move.

Noooooooo.

The scream erupted, ripping him from his dark hell.

His hand struck the center of his chest, and spit flew from his lips.

What the hell?

Where was he?

His arms flailed about. Freed. Searching. Punching against rocks.

Pain jolted through his wrists. Grounding him.

He was awake.

His eyes opened. His hands slapped against his arms to put out the invisible flames. Sweat raced across his goose-pimpled skin, and he choked on the imagined smoke pulsing around him. Rage roared through him, and he tightly balled his fists, flexing his arms and wrapping them around his shaking legs.

He was no longer at Blutburg.

The smells . . . the screams . . . it had been so real. So loud.

He had felt it all.

The field of blood threatening to drown him.

The pillar of fire threatening to consume him.

The nightmare of his past threatening to define him.

It chased him, no matter how far he ran, leading him to his never-ending trek to put distance between them and leaving him restless.

Again, like always, it had been so real.

It was dark save the low gray light creeping into the cave. He was seated against a large stone with her beside him. Lying still, watching him with rounded, sympathetic eyes.

Embarrassed, exposed, he nestled back down, turning his back to her. Without a word, she scooted behind him and curled her body against his back. Resting her face between his shoulders, she threaded her arm beneath his, reaching around him until her hand grasped his. She held him, unfaltering, in a tight yet tender embrace.

Matthias's heart squeezed. He anchored himself against the stones and the desire to turn and take her within his arms. He was undeserving of such affection. Such trust. This moment with her. Yet he couldn't break from her and the strange comfort he felt in her arms. His hand covered hers, closing it between his. Lips trembling, he exhaled, silently begging her not to let him go, and stared forward into the night.

CHAPTER 18

TRAPPED AND TIRED

Avelina

AVELINA LAY ON TOP OF the stones, nestled inside the fur in the fetal position. She could not get warm. Her eyes clamped shut, she tried to convince her body and mind that she was, even though her teeth chattered against the wet air.

Where they nested was at least dry. The cave's mouth was soaked where water splattered against it, but the angle of the entryway kept the water from rolling toward them. They were perched upon the rock wall to stay off the dirt floor. Without an opening to act as an air vent, they had been unable to build a fire. Even if they had found dry supplies for one.

The cave was empty save for the rock formations around her. There were loose stones, shades of gray and brown, covering a limestone foundation. The porous rocks were a dull white, giving the room a sense of warmth even in the dank darkness.

Matthias had told her the cave had stood unoccupied for some time. At least by any direct threat. There were no remnants of nests or bones or animal dung. She'd thought she might see bats, like those who thrived in the Leucerian caves, but nothing of the sort. No plants that she could see either. The last vegetation she remembered were clumps of low-lying grasses and lichens above the tree line, before they were forced even higher onto a safer rock ledge.

The only sign of life was the intricate series of cobwebs built on the opposite wall and the insects spinning within them, leaving a chill of another sort reverberating on her skin.

Avelina knew they were there. Part of her hoped to see them, to at least know *where* they were. The hairs on her skin were frazzled as she imagined them. Crawling past her. On her. Biting her. The other part of her was thankful to not see them. How big they were.

A shiver ran along her spine.

"You stay on your side of the cave, and I will stay on mine," she said. Feeling silly as her voice echoed in the stillness. She looked around the ground. "All of you."

Avelina wiped her nose with the edge of the cape. The dampness in the air had given her a constant chill coupled with a nagging cough. Her throat longed for a warmed tea, a warmed anything really. A basin-like rock at the mouth of the cave collected rain, providing them with an abundance of chilled water. They had plenty to keep their thirst quenched and to make a cold meal with oats from Matthias's pack.

It wouldn't be long, though, until his pack of supplies was empty. The longer it rained, the quieter he became until he was silent and she couldn't remember the last words he had spoken. She followed his example, curling into herself, silent.

They had been here for four days. Or at least she thought so. She had lost count as the skies were hardly different between the days and the nights. Save for when the lightning struck, and even through closed eyes, the flash of white-hot light would shake and blind her.

Then the thunder came. Echoing within the cave. Crashing, screeching as though it were trying to topple the mountain itself. Or that she was close enough to God she could witness His wrath being cast below Him. They moved inward toward the pitch-black. Safer there, he had said. She shuddered, waiting until it was nothing but the solid splattering of rain against the rocks. Plopping inside puddles of muddied water.

It couldn't last much longer. She was tuckered out, the effort of their journey finally catching up to her, and she welcomed the chance to rest. Leaning into a large rock, she intermittently stretched her legs and rubbed her hands along her muscles, trying to rub out the dense cramping.

During the day, when there was at least some gray light coming into the cave and Matthias was especially restless, he had ventured into the darkness beyond them, feeling his way around, searching the black. She dared not. Whatever was back there reminded her of the Leucerian tunnels through which they had left.

No, she would stay perched where she was, not to be swallowed within the mountain.

CHAPTER 19

INTO THE DEEP

———— ❧ ————

Matthias

MATTHIAS LAID THE BACK OF his hand against her cheek. Her skin was like ice.

He pulled back the edge of the fur. She lay directly on the stones, no longer upon her blankets. He pulled her hands from where she had them tucked into her armpits. *Like ice.* He flung her underskirt up and felt the skin above her boot. *Like ice.* He pressed his fingers to her neck. Her pulse was slow. Weak. Like her breathing.

Oh no.

Matthias pulled the fur from her and spread it out on a large flat area of stone, off the dirt floor. The earth itself was almost frozen, the temperature having dropped with the continued storms. The cold stones and earth and the sweat dried on her skin were all working against her.

"Come here," Matthias said. He gently lifted her and laid her on the fur, then laid beside her. He pulled the fur around them, tightening them into their own cocoon. He wrapped his arms around her, pulling her back tight against him, and wrapped his body around hers. His hands found hers and held them in his. His thumb traced across her knuckles, warming them.

He held her to him tightly, thankful when her body warmed against his. No longer shaking, she lay peacefully in his arms. She stirred, rolling over within his arms to face him. Her head nestled into the pocket of his shoulder, and she fell asleep gripping his vest in her hand.

They could do nothing but wait for the rain to stop. To let up enough for them to safely leave. He couldn't risk the exposure to the cold and heavy rain or the slippery slopes. It was too dangerous outside. For now, he would sleep. He closed his eyes and let it all go.

The first sign was a rumbling. A great rumbling shaking on every side of him.

Matthias's eyes flew open. It was black—*pitch-black*—but he could see movement. The darkness shook around them, the very air waving before his eyes.

"Avelina," he said, shaking her. "We've got to go. Now."

She stiffened against him, then clawed at his chest when a flash of light cracked against the entrance to the cave. Blinding hot light seared through the cave, and the room quaked around them. Pebbles and rocks shook about, bouncing against one another. Another earsplitting blast broke outside above them, right on the heels of the lightning.

Himmel, Kreuz, und Sakrament!

Matthias was dumbfounded. It was just as Reymund had said. A lifetime ago.

The story of the clouds of heaven bursting open and judgment pouring down.

He could hear it. Outside. Beneath them and above them.

Rocks sliding. Crackling away from where they'd once been raised, crafted by the hands of God, and nested against the heavens. Stumbling. Slamming. Knocking against each other. And into another. And another. Crashing. Louder and louder, rushing and shaking, tumbling to the valleys below.

No, no, no.

Avelina looked at him wide-eyed, terror-stricken. She was screaming, but he couldn't hear her. The blood drained from her face while her body shook like a limp doll from the force.

"Go!" he yelled, grabbing her and thrusting her forward. His throat rasped from the strain, though he couldn't even hear his own voice. "Don't stop!"

There wasn't time. To plan. To think. They needed to get out or they would die here. The mountain shook. The floor waffled, sliding beneath their feet. They couldn't stand upright. Their feet slipped on the small rocks dancing and hopping across the cave's bottom.

Avelina was on all fours. Her hands clawing at the ground. A step behind her, he had a firm grip on her hips, lifting her. Fighting to move them forward. Trying to cover her from debris falling from the ceiling.

There was a flutter of crackling.

Slowly at first, increasing into a deafening crash.

No, no, no.

They were going the wrong way.

They had to go back. Into the caverns. Toward the tunnels.

His heart thundered in his chest, and an inhuman and urgent strength surged through his body. His hands dug into her sides, lifting her into the air, and he pulled her backward. His heart in his throat, he turned on his heels, flinging them both away from the abyss. They fell hard, his shoulder slamming against a ridged stone tower, and tumbled back into the cave.

Avelina struggled desperately against him while he dragged her backward with him, his instincts telling him not to dare stop.

A wave of sound tore across the cave, and a ragged line appeared, cutting and snapping across the rocks from one side to the other. The cave's floor split before them, as if the mountain itself had been disemboweled. Her innards spilling obscenely, helplessly. A river of mud and rocks broke away, crashing down the mountainside before their eyes.

They had to keep going.

The darkness layered upon itself, shadows pulsing through the air billowing with dirt and ash and sand and stone. Tiny particles swooshed around them. Suspended in flight, twirling about and smothering them. Prickling against his face and stinging his eyes. Pushing against their backs, it sucked the air past them at their feet, threatening to topple them over and bury them in a blanket of death.

Matthias wrapped her arm around his waist and pushed forward, both hands instinctively searching. He found the wall, trembling beneath his hands, and followed it away from the thunder behind them. He tripped and slammed onto his knees, her falling on his back. His hands felt about and found the offender.

Her walking stick. Yes. Another set of eyes.

He breathed a sigh of relief and picked it up. Tightening her arm around him, they continued forward. He coughed and closed his eyes, trusting his body's memory to lead him into the tunnels he had found the day before.

He knew they were there. He didn't know where they led, but they were there—the veins threading through the mountain—and his heart called out for his feet to find them.

Avelina was resisting. Struck by sheer terror, she screeched against him. Her chest heaved sharply while her cries were lost to the flood. His lungs raged, bursting with his own fear—the animal within him roaring, hell bent for them to survive.

He wouldn't stop. The mountain continued to crumble upon itself.

Sliding, slipping, tripping, and crawling. Banging over the rocks, pulling her behind him, they slid deep into the darkness.

CHAPTER 20

TUNNELS

Matthias

THEY'D GONE AS LONG AS he could, until Matthias's legs gave out beneath him.

He collapsed forward, and his hands scraped against the ground.

"Matthias."

He reached and squeezed her hand, still clinging his chest.

"I need to rest," he sputtered.

He coughed and gritted his teeth against the sandy dirt scraping his lungs. He turned and propped his back against the tunnel's wall.

The stone wall he leaned against was smooth. Cold and still.

Finally, thankfully, still.

They were swallowed, but they were alive.

Alive.

Lost together, somewhere in the belly of the mountain.

Overwhelmed, Matthias reached and drew her into his lap.

"Come here, love," he whispered.

His hand cradled the back of her head, pulling her tightly into his chest, and he cocooned himself around her. His lips nuzzled her hair. Gritty. Sandy. But still undeniably her.

She turned her face into his shoulder, shuddering against him.

Love.

He'd never addressed someone so.

So intimately. Affectionately.

Certainly not out loud.

Though he didn't regret using it, he knew better than to repeat it. Doubting. Hoping she hadn't heard it. He shouldn't have addressed her so, but at this moment he didn't care.

They . . . *she* . . . had almost died. Now death hung around them. Hovering. Waiting.

His heart and gut raged within him. Warring. Straining. Turning. Sickened, he gagged on a rush of spew. His nerves were shattered. Sweat. Tears poured. Draining him.

He was horror-struck. Awake in a night terror. Stupefied. Lost.

He took her hand. Lacing her fingers tightly within his own, he brought her hand to his lips and kissed her knuckles. His breathing slowed. Each breath tracing over her hand and returning, drawing her within him like she was life itself.

They sat entwined. Entombed.

Overcome with exhaustion, he drifted.

Sleep beckoned to him.

No.

They couldn't sleep.

They were without supplies. Without food. Without water.

They needed to move before they ran out of air.

Now that the moment had passed, pain radiated through his entire body. And he could smell blood. It trickled from his knees, though slowly, and soaked his trousers. It couldn't be more than a scratch. Like the ones he felt all along his arms.

Every muscle in his body ached. Tired and stretched and tested beyond reason. His shoulder was another matter. He was in agony, the intense hurt leaving him quivering and fighting the urge to scream.

Matthias leaned his head back.

He blinked. Eyes open. Eyes closed. It was endless black either way.

He sighed, trying to recoup his strength. Just another moment and then they needed to move. He concentrated on his breathing. Slow. Steady. And silent.

In the stillness, there was a noise. Beyond the ringing in his ear.

Barely there. But there.

It was a trickling. A slow, almost inaudible rush.

"Be still," Matthias said.

"I am."

"Listen." He put his finger against her lips. "Do you hear that?"

"No."

"Water."

Matthias laughed gleefully.

It was water. And it was moving. It could be a way out.

"Matthias, it's been raining for days . . ."

"No. Not above or beside us," he said. "Below us."

"But we cannot see," she whispered.

"We have to try," he said. "I've heard of these. It might be an underground stream."

Her arms wrapped tighter around him.

"You have to let me go. I won't leave you," he said, pulling her hands from him. He reached for the ground. His hands shifted through the pebbles and dirt, searching.

Finally, he found it. The staff. He breathed a sigh of relief, pulling the thick branch to him.

It was worth a try.

He'd taken the branch from a fallen birch days ago to give her extra support on the hills and ensure her footing. When they'd run low on food, he'd given her the last of the smoked meat and oats while he ate its bark. Hopefully, enough remained that he could manage a torch from it in the dark. He fingered the wood until he found bits of loose bark and began ripping it off in strips. Determined not to lose them, he held the ends in his mouth as he made more, their sweet taste making his mouth water and stomach beg for food.

Matthias felt along his hip and gave a sigh of relief, finding his axe still tied safely there. Holding the edge of the stick tight in his fist, he cut at the wood, slicing through the center of the stump. He worked the strips of bark, wrapping and twisting them around the end to make a torch.

Now for the fire.

"Hold this," he said. He found her hands and wrapped them firmly around the torch and guided her hands toward him. "But out in front of you, right here."

Matthias reached around on his knees until he found a rock. Holding it over the birch, he knocked his blade against the rock, hoping for a spark. Nothing.

Scheiße.

He dropped that rock and with the next found success. He aimed the tiny hot sparks onto the birch and then cupped his hands, blowing until they finally caught flame.

The light of the torch bounced from one wall to the other, bathing the gray walls in a soft glow. They both gasped, laughing in excited disbelief.

"There," he said. "Much better."

"I can't believe it," she said, wiping a falling tear.

She was hurt.

Matthias stepped to her and reached for her head. She was covered in a layer of dirt, as was he, with blood drying across her forehead and matted in her hair. "You're bleeding."

"It's not mine," she said, reaching her hand to his head.

A singe of pain ran across his head when she gingerly touched above his ear.

"You've a gash here," she said, concerned. "But the bleeding looks to have stopped for now."

Matthias nodded.

It didn't matter. There wasn't time even if it did.

They were alive, but they wouldn't be for long.

There were too many dangers. Too many unknowns.

And their torch, if they were lucky, might last an hour.

They needed to keep moving.

Get far enough along that if he fell, she would still have some sort of a chance.

"We don't have much time," Matthias said, taking her hand.

He turned into the black, pulling her close behind him. They were farther now than he had ventured before, shivering in the sharp coldness all around them.

There was no evidence of life around him.

But then he saw water. He could see streaks across the tunnel's ceiling. He held his torch aloft and, seeing its direction, followed it.

There was life in her veins after all. And hopefully a way out.

The tunnels continued downhill. Eerily quiet save the pebbles crunching beneath their boots. The ceiling was twice as high as him, and in most places the path was wide enough for them both to pass side by side. Masses rose from the floor in some areas, with piles of rocks in others. Large columns reached from floor to ceiling in other areas, but mostly the caverns were wide and growing deeper the farther they went. The walls rippled along on either side of them, and occasionally they passed an opening leading away into the deep.

"We follow the draft," he said. "Where the air moves, we go. If the air is stale, we don't go that way."

His foot slid, the decline getting steeper.

"Matthias, you're going too fast," she said.

"We can't slow down. We have to push forward while we still have light."

He pulled her closer, charging forward.

He shoved the torch into the opening of another tunnel.

Nothing. Don't go that way. Follow the water.

Their torch burned still, but they were racing against time.

The main tunnel led them into a cavern so large he couldn't see from one end to the other.

But there it was. Water.

Matthias charged toward its edge. The limestone around them shone against his light, reflecting it farther than he had seen before, but not far enough. What he could see was a pool of water, still and midnight blue, with no escape in sight.

His throat seized, and he stumbled.

There was no longer a draft.

There was nothing.

Nowhere to walk. No path to follow. They could only disappear into the water.

He'd led them through to the heart of the mountain.

He'd led them astray.

He'd led them here to die.

CHAPTER 21

ZIEGENGLOCKE

Avelina

"MATTHIAS?"

He didn't answer her. He'd crumpled to his knees, his body slumped back upon his ankles as he stared out into the darkness before them.

Avelina took a step forward and knelt beside him, her knee sinking into the pebbles at the water's edge. She laid a hand on his back and peered around his shoulder. His mouth hung agape, and his eyes darted spastically in every direction. The torch hung limply in his hand.

He needed time to regroup, and she couldn't fault him that.

But she knew there wasn't time to waste.

She would take the lead.

She reached forward and took the flickering torch from him. She steadied her hand on her knee, collecting herself. Her body still trembled from the unbridled fear that had been pumping through her since the first ripple of the rocks.

Breathe, Avelina.

She'd been in caves before. Not like this exactly, but the palace of Leuceria was built upon an old fortification carved deep into the earth. Lost to time and covered by generations of lush and fruitful fields and forests, they remained a foundation of strength and testament to structure. She'd been in them when she was young. Enough not to fear them. Mainly, the route in and out of the palace was a secret reserved for soldiers, and even then, only a few.

Her breathing was still heavy but calmer now. The air felt good in her lungs, though it scraped against the layer of dust speckled in her throat. Cool and clean. *Clean.* Not fresh, but not stale either.

She held the light forward to no avail. What she could see of the waters were still and faded into nothing. She steadied herself and twisted around on her ankles, the crunch of the stones loud beneath her boots.

Again, nothing before her, but she lifted her palm before her face, inspecting it. The sensation on her skin was curiously familiar, how the tiny pebbles felt rubbed between the tips of her fingers. Wiggling her fingers, the rainbow of muted yellow and brown rocks pressed into her skin glittered against the light.

Unlike the damp grays she'd been camped on for days, these were gritty.

And golden, like mustard seeds.

But damp, like granules of sand.

Like along the coasts of Leuceria, where the tide ebbed and flowed.

In and out.

God in heaven.

Avelina stood, gaining her balance and took a step away from Matthias. She held the torch out, hoping to see something. Anything. Any sign of a way out.

She took a step, and another, seeking out the same crunch beneath her boots. She turned back to check on Matthias; he hadn't moved. Still staring out over the water.

She started again, determined to check the water's periphery. Slowly, each step carefully executed, sinking slightly into the stones until the ground became increasingly steep. She turned back every few steps to check for him until he was lost to her in the darkness.

Forward, Avelina. The torch is still burning. We still have time.

The ledge grew thinner still. Angling her body, she slid her feet, as if dancing, afraid to cross them and lose her balance. Her left arm raised the torch in front of her, searching into the black, while her right palm traced along the wall behind her. Keeping her grounded. Connected. Ignoring the fear pulsing through her.

Her breath shook, rattling as she breathed in and out. Weaving and huffing, reasoning with herself to remain calm. She swallowed, pausing, and swallowed again. Lifting the light higher, convinced she saw something around the upcoming corner. A reflection.

A shimmer.

She thrust her light out again, farther, and again, a shimmer.

And a noise.

A knocking. A knocking clink. And another.

Avelina slid forward again, shaking, and then there they were.

Eyes.

Glowing, rectangular eyes. Golden, with pupils stretching from one side to the other.

They disappeared, and there it was again, the clinking. Once and then a rapid repeat, as whatever it was continued to move. It was a bell.

"Charlie. Heel."

Avelina's jaw dropped.

A voice. A whisper. But still a voice. A girl's voice.

"Hello?" Avelina said, so quietly she wasn't even sure she said it out loud.

More clinking. It was more than one bell, followed by a noise, startling, like the cries of children. But it wasn't; it was animals. Bleating.

Avelina reached the rounded corner and thrust the torch around before her.

"Hello?"

Goats. Five of them standing on a flat ledge. *Ziegenglocke* tied and clanking at their brown necks, and a white one, the smallest and closest to her, staring at her. It stepped forward, lifted its head toward the girl, and bleated loudly.

"Lukas, hush."

Avelina whipped the light at her. The girl's hand flew over her eyes, blocking the light. She couldn't have been more than ten years old. A head taller than her goats, she had the hood of her long dress covering her head, hiding everything except for her thin face.

"Sweet Jesus," Avelina gasped. She smiled, and with two fingers traced the sign of the cross on her forehead.

The girl looked at her over her raised hand, eyebrows furrowed together. She stepped toward Avelina and put a hand on a goat's head. "Are you . . . are you a spirit?"

"No. No, I'm not," Avelina said. "I don't understand. Where did you come from?"

The girl motioned behind her.

"I brought them here when the south face of the mountain fell away," she said. "To wait until the air is fit to breathe."

"You can get us out? You can get back outside?" Avelina asked.

The girl smiled.

"*Ja.* I can," she said. "Who's us?"

Us. Matthias. *Matthias.*

Avelina turned and screeched his name. Her voice echoed, as his name curved around the stones and into space. She turned to the girl and laid a hand against her breast. She smiled, as tears flooded her eyes.

"It's a miracle," Avelina whispered.

CHAPTER 22

FOLLOW ME

———— ✺ ————

Avelina

"FOLLOW ME," THE YOUNG GIRL said.
Holding the torch Avelina had given her, the young girl turned with her goats quick to her heels. She began climbing a series of rocks, using one hand to guide her, while the goats hopped from one rock to another, their *ziegenglocke* clanging about their necks.

Avelina turned and grinned at Matthias, who stood next to her, struck by shock. He hadn't said a word. He looked at the young girl, the goats, and then to Avelina. His eyes rounded, and his head shook slightly. Confused. In disbelief. Avelina wiped her hand on her skirt, reached for his hand, and squeezed it. When he squeezed back, the two of them followed the girl onto the rocks.

Avelina repeated the movements the girl made. Finding the same footing, reaching her hand for the same stones. The boulders were large with edges jutting in each direction, making the climb easier than anticipated. Following the faint path of light, the clicking of the goats' hooves, and the clinking of their bells, she made it over the top of the last large stone. There, in the top corner of the cavern, was a black hole—both entrance and *exit*— unseen from the floor below.

"Watch your head," the girl said, calling back to them.

Avelina was doing her best to stay with her. It was pitch-black everywhere but in front of her. There, the outlines of the girl and her goats glowed from the torch she carried in front of her. Their bells echoed off the walls. Loudly, at first, until they began being overwhelmed by a louder sound. A rushing sound.

Water.

Don't think, Avelina. Walk. One foot in front of the other. Don't stop.

The ground was wet, slippery beneath her feet. She walked with a hand at her forehead and kept her neck scrunched down, weary of hitting her head on the low ceiling. The tunnel was tight, and though she couldn't see them, she felt the walls just beyond her shoulders.

The goats disappeared in the girl's shadow as the tunnel closed in on them. Avelina could hear Matthias's shoulders brushing the rocks and his ragged breathing behind her.

Please, God, don't let it become any smaller.

If she would have to soon squeeze through herself, would he even be able to get out?

Don't, Avelina. Don't.

Cold droplets of water dripped from the ceiling. A few at first and then some in a stream.

They had to be close.

The water became louder and louder. Thunderous. Movement. Again.

Avelina's heart beat rapidly in her chest. Her breaths were quick and panicky in anticipation.

Avelina followed the girl around a corner and lost her breath. There was light. Dull, yet enough to show details. Shapes. Shadows. They were atop a crop of rocks, and she could see the goats, climbing down, hopping from one rock to another. Toward a floor. Of a wide, expansive cave.

Avelina climbed down, determined not to slip on the slick rocks. Her hands were shaking, and her knuckles ached. Once her last foot hit the ground, she was ankle deep in water so cold it seized her legs and her teeth chattered.

Matthias was soon next to her and put his arm around her waist. With each step, her eyes adjusted further, and she could see the origin of the deafening noise.

Extraordinary.

The dark tunnel had been replaced to her left with a torrential wall of water. The mix of fast-moving whites, blues, and grays hurtled from the edge of the ceiling and on past the lip of the cave's floor on which they stood. As tall as three, maybe four men and as wide as she remembered the hall in her palace. The water flush against the edge on their left; to the far right, a hint of light—daylight—where the girl and goats headed.

Matthias grabbed her hand, and they followed the girl. Droplets of cold water sprayed her skin the closer they came to the water's edge. There, at the far corner of this impressive cavern, was another tunnel. Narrowly cut into the rocks, it was framed on three sides with stone and the water falling over on the other. The girl slipped easily into the tunnel with her flock at her heels, and Matthias followed, pulling Avelina in behind him.

The water on their side was dissipating, thinning out into separate streams of water, revealing a river at their side. They were in a gorge. The river, flooded, swollen, and full of debris, roared with the force of a hundred cannons beside them. Slamming mud-brown waves ripped around boulders, crashing and splattering against the sides, sending shoots of spray high into the air.

There was nothing but certain death below.

Matthias hunched his body, steadily moving before her. The path running yet narrower, she withdrew her hand from his tight grasp, untwisting their arms. Her joints aching, she vised the fingers of her left hand around his shirt at his waist. Her right hand traced the rocks beside them, clawing for something to grip. Her heart beating rapidly, she leaned toward the rock wall beside them. Bootheel anchored with each step, she carefully traversed the slick, uneven stones.

When Matthias paused, Avelina stole a glance behind her. There it was—like nothing she had ever seen—the front of the waterfall, pouring the river over the cliff of white stones and into the gorge. Their path continued to twist and turn, following the angry waters. At parts, the rock walls towering above bent and reached toward each other, almost joined together as a roof.

An answer to an unspoken prayer, around another bend the walls parted and began angling down. The river widened. Large streams of gray light and mists began slipping between them. Avelina looked above them. There, at the crest of the wall, was green. Green grasses trumpeting over the edge. And then trees. Their branches reaching upward. Upward, towering above the speckled, spitting mists until they pierced through the blanket of fog and escaped into an open sky.

CHAPTER 23

ROSEMUNDE

Matthias

THEY HAD MANAGED THAT LEDGE, as the walls on either side of them dropped lower and lower, until their rocks disappeared into a hill blanketed with trees. The river had cut through the mountains, flowing downhill until it found another, pouring itself into it and merging as one. With its cliffs and thunderous rapids behind them, they could finally hear one another.

"My name is Rosemunde, but call me Rose."

"Matthias," he said, wiping his palm on his hip and holding his hand out to Avelina. "And my wife, Avelina."

Avelina looked at him wide-eyed, and then a flash of recognition crossed her face. She took his hand, cocking her head with a hint of a smile.

She remembered. Good.

Even though this girl, Rose, had saved their lives and led them out of the mountain, she was a stranger. As was whatever family they headed toward.

Avelina was right.

It had been a miracle.

Back in the first cavern, Matthias had been following along in her tracks, clinging to the thin ledge, when he'd heard her yell his name. At first unsettled, he'd heard pure joy within her shocked tone and knew he headed toward something that had given her hope. He never would've guessed it was going to be this young girl and her flock of goats, hiding within the very cavern he thought they would surely die in.

He knew of such husbandry—herds driven into the hills to take advantage of the cooler temperatures during the summer season until they were led back to the valley when the summer heat broke—but he never would've thought to see it, here, *still*, in the *Geisterweg*. His head shook side to side, dumbfounded by their luck, as the goats led them on a path, familiar to the small herd, heading downhill.

The skies were thickly overcast with low-hanging clouds. Night, and the mountain itself, was upon them. His head ached from the air pressure and the bright gray light. He shifted his jaw, swallowing, and hoped the ringing in his left ear would soon give way.

They hiked for hours.

Silently. Simply companions today, following their rescuer.

Stopping only at an offshoot stream, they cleaned their faces and hands as best they could and filled their stomachs with clean water. His body begged reprieve, to lean against a tree and catch his breath or burrow into the leaves and sleep for days. But they carried on. His feet moving beneath him, eager to add distance between them and the disabled mountain.

Avelina kept the pace well, though he noticed a wince cross her face on occasion. Her arms were crossed, as if holding herself together, and he did not reach for her. He wanted to. To feel her there. Embrace her and know this wasn't some trick in a dream. But he didn't, waiting instead for her lead.

When she was ready, she would speak. Normally when they walked, she mused over everything from the changing color of the leaves to what flowers she would plant if she were to have her own garden. He listened. Or half listened, at times. Honestly, he'd become used to the sound of her voice and took comfort in that her words were for *him*.

Today she'd been quiet, but after what they'd just been through . . . He'd tried to read her mind by the shifting of her expressions. Sometimes at war within herself, other times at peace, she chose not to share, and he chose not to ask.

"We'll have to go round," Rose said. "It'll be an extra day's walk, but there's a good place to rest nearby."

Her goats clicking close at her heels, the girl led them along. The brush became thicker around them, thorns catching on his cloak on both sides. The girl led them beneath the shelter of a rock system erupting from the ground on one side and pushing skyward at an angle until it was as tall as two men.

The trees were thick around them, protecting the north side, with a bush-laden wall of undergrowth that would alert him to anything approaching from that angle. The slanted rock overhang above them, carved out by a long since redirected river, allowed them cover in a deep-set earthen room.

Satisfied with the strength of the fire he'd built, Matthias sat back on the ground. They had a solid place to rest for the night. Across the fire, the girl and her goats rounded themselves into a pile. Nestled limbs and noses, they dozed, a rhythm of bleats and low snores, the occasional clang of a bell or shaken ear.

"Matthias?"

"Yes, Princess?"

Crumbling waves appeared where she dug the toe of her boot into the dirt before her. Her chin lolled on her knee as she chewed on her words.

"I'm not sure I'll sleep tonight."

The thought of sleep was a pleasant one. A state he eagerly sought. His body was beyond exhaustion, but he was wide awake, replaying the landslide over and over again in his mind.

"Nor I." He leaned back onto his palms and stretched his legs out in front of him, gaining release for the muscles in his calves.

He looked over at the young Rose and her goats. If the child was in shock, he hoped she had found her peaceful rest in her dreams.

"I . . ." Avelina paused, pursed her lips, and rubbed her hands over her knees.

Matthias waited. Ready to listen.

"There must stand a reason," she said. "A reason we've come through alive."

"I believe so. Or I *hope* so," Matthias said. "For one of us, at least."

Avelina fiddled again, knocking a rock around with her heel.

"Our lives. It's almost . . ." She shook her head.

Matthias's arms chilled. Prickling as the memory flooded him.

He slammed his eyelids shut against the imagery of the mountain crumbling around them and the sheer horror he'd seen on her face at that moment.

"I don't know a god as you do, Princess," he said. "But I have a mind we've been led through by . . . something. I don't believe in folly. We've come this way because we're meant to. 'Tis part of our journey."

She was watching him. Intently, innocently, as always. Could she read him? Could she see his fears, frozen in the hollows of his cheeks? The depth of his doubts. His demons. His degree of self-hate. She plied at him. Chiseling away at his walls while he desperately patched them from the other side, lest she break through and truly see him.

"Your fates, then?" she said. "If they let us survive, it wasn't by accident. No accident that the mountain swallowed us and our pasts whole, and bore us free here, on this slope?"

Toward Ewigsburg.

Where she would lay down one crown and wear another. And he was to be free.

"Is it only a game?"

He turned toward her. "A game?"

She stared into the fire, arms again crossed tight, her hands firmly gripping her elbows.

"No," he said. "That seems almost too simple."

"Isn't it, though? One I'm not allowed to play but am right in the thick of?"

"I think it's a bit more complicated," he said.

"Have you played chess, Matthias?"

"I've seen it played. Reymund, he enjoys the game. Though it is a long one," he said. "I've seen men lose too much to them. More in a sitting—fortunes—than an entire village might have in hand their whole lives."

"That is the way of it, isn't it?" she said thoughtfully. "Our birth places us on the board, and our titles name our square. Then the men sit back and move us around at their will until someone yells checkmate and a crown topples."

Matthias gave her a half-smile. "I can see how you mean."

"Where will they move you, Matthias? What part do you play?"

"I'm not so sure."

"Are you not moved from one point to the next by your master's orders?"

He grunted.

"I will be queen, as they name me, conceding one crown to wear another. Powerful in name, but limited nonetheless."

"And your king?" he said.

"I would make it a queen's game. Effortlessly move over my kingdom. Rule as my forefathers before me. As their heir. As my blood places me."

"I see," he said.

"But I can't, can I?"

He looked at her as she stared into the fire.

"Wherever I sit, I have a man's hand enclosed around me. Guiding me to his will."

"Your god?"

"No," she said with a smile. "Not Him. He gives me the strength I need, to breathe and not collapse beneath their weight."

Matthias nodded.

"No. The hand changes, as does the voice behind it and the title it calls me. Princess. Crown Jewel. Daughter of Leuceria." She looked down and her voice dropped. "The Bastard."

She picked up a stick and dragged it along the ground beside her, leaving thin lines through the loose dirt. One after another in different directions. Lines and loops. Purposeful, yet none he could recognize.

"It doesn't matter what they call me—they all treat me as pawn," she said. "Only small, stilted moves where I am laid as bait or sacrifice."

"How would you play the game?"

"I would shed their weight. And choose what I want in my life."

"You put too much weight on titles. They are too often thrown around. Given as reward. Taken as punishment," he said, shaking his head. "You may be queen, but even as a simple woman, it should be the same. Let what you do define you. Who you are and what you believe in. Your blood doesn't have to define you."

He refused to let his do so.

"You say such things," she sighed. "I hear you. And I believe you. Honestly, it's so hard. . . to be strong sometimes. To not listen to those around you. Not just Niro. Or the court. It's them: my forefathers. They call me to a purpose I cannot yet see."

"They speak to you, then? The dead?"

She wrapped her arms around her knees and pulled her legs toward her.

"I won't set you aflame at the pyre." Matthias swallowed. He knew what it meant to hear the dead. Those lost to violence. To his own sword or the swords of his enemies. To hear their screams. As they traveled lost, stuck between this world and the next. The wishes of his dead were unclear, yet they remained with him in his dreams. Every step taken with them, he felt one step further condemned.

She smirked. "They do. In a way."

"You hear their words?"

"Snippets."

"Then it is not clear what they're saying? What they want of you?"

Avelina shook her head and frowned.

"No, though I wish it were," she said. "The visions . . ."

He met her eyes, hoping to encourage her to speak more. "Dreams?"

"At times. And other times I am awake. Their grip overwhelms me."

Matthias laid a hand on her arm but removed it when she shivered.

"I'm sorry," he said.

"It's all right," she said, her body unfolding. "They don't intend to hurt me. It's more to show me. Ground me. Their hands prop me up without driving me relentlessly forward." She smiled weakly. "They are my bones, but my faith leads my soul."

Matthias shifted his hips and rolled his neck from side to side, cracking it. They sat in silence but for the popping of the fire. Around them, the forest slept.

"My forefathers, though. Only them. My mother's voice is silent," she said quietly. "I ache for her. Her words. Her guidance. Her comfort. Like nothing and no one else."

He could see how she pined for her mother, but he hoped, for both their sakes, the woman had somehow found her peace and moved on to silence.

"Is that where they lead you? To a purpose, or destiny, as queen?"

"They do." She nodded. "Though I cannot see it clearly before me. Whether the path is truly there and my foot will find support beneath it, or if I will step astray and fall into nothing."

"You seem to have two options, then—if not Leuceria, then here at Ewigsburg."

"At Ewigsburg?"

"Your purpose seems to have led you here. That you're needed here."

"But what of those I've left behind? Everything. Not the throne. The people. Those people who counted on our family, our army, for protection. For prosperity. For provision. The threads that tie me to them pull taut behind me, snapping with each step I take. I am no heir. I bring nothing but shame."

"Not you, Avelina."

"Don't I?"

"Never."

"Maybe one day I won't feel that way. The shame. The failure. The guilt."

He looked at her, watching the light dance on her sullen cheek. "There is nothing wrong with wanting a peaceful life. One of your own."

"Is that what you seek, Matthias? From this journey?"

He laughed, stretching his leg out in front of him. "I want a life of peace."

"What does peace look like for you?"

He leaned an elbow on his knee and rubbed his hand across his chin. "It's quiet."

She smiled.

"I aim to disappear into a place where no one knows me. My name. I want to grow old. Under the shaded protection of an old tree that's never borne witness to death. Sit still while the roots grow over me, cover me, and tie me to the ground. And the only noise is the sound of the settled land around me."

"I know your heart is troubled as well," she said, gently touching his arm. "You don't wake. Your joints seize while your body shakes from within. You groan and sweat and call out. You thrash about and sometimes scream."

Matthias dragged his heel toward him, leaning away from her and her testimony. "I'm sorry."

"Don't apologize. We all have our nightmares. I would lay my hand upon you as I do now and hope knowing someone was there would bring you comfort," she said. Her eyes were wet and glowing. "I pray you find peace."

He nodded, thankful for the shelter of the trees towering around them. "I will. And for my brothers."

"You are a lucky man Matthias. I hope someday to count family and friends amongst my jewels. I fear I have nothing but shame to my name."

His lips ran a thin line. "Barbarian. Monster. Murderer. Those are some of the *titles* tied to my name."

"I see," she said. "But I know you as the King's Sword. Surely, that means you are a man of good."

He scoffed. "I'm not sure I would say that."

"I do," she said. "It's like you said. You can know a man by the choices he makes. By his works and his good heart."

"Good heart," he repeated. He shook his head, scowling. "You don't know me. You don't know what I've done."

"Every man makes mistakes. Everyone," she whispered.

"And every man can be seen as either a hero or a villain; it only depends on who you ask. One man's hero is another man's terror."

"Maybe, but I believe in redemption."

Matthias clamped his mouth shut, thinking of so many. Of Niro.

Decisions, motives, results were never, ever that simplistic.

"It's as you say. To serve the purpose of others in the larger game," he said.

"Not for you. For a man who has known such violence, I see its weight on you. But I see you go gladly to it, in the name of protecting others," she said. "Will my life be one of purpose? Or will I merely be a figurehead? Polished and poised, with fancy dress and name?"

"What purpose do you wish?"

"More than to sit silently at the side of a king," she said. "Much more."

She grabbed his hand, squeezing it, and he covered her hand with his.

"We are alive, Matthias. *Alive*," she said with conviction. "There has to be more to it. More that you and I are supposed to do. *There has to be.*"

He smiled at her. For her, yes, he believed it so.

"Then don't let them define you," he said. "Any of them. Let it be suggestion. Inspiration. To travel that route or to do one better. Take their words, labels, expectations, and find a way to define them on your own terms."

"Says the man beholden to his men," she said, her lip curling.

"I choose to be. Once they are safely set, I will know my own purpose here in this life."

Avelina shifted her hips toward him. She took his wrist in her hand and lifted his arm. Ducking beneath it, she curled into his side like a cat. He welcomed her closeness, wrapping his arms around her, and pulled her closer still. She was chilled by the night air, but her cheek felt warm against his shoulder.

"What would you call yourself, Matthias?"

He swallowed the lump growing at the back of his throat and closed his eyes.

"I would call myself a free man," he said. "Before I die."

PART THREE

METZLINGEN

MID – SEPTEMBER 1479
THE LAST CRESCENT MOON

CHAPTER 24

UHRL

—◦◦◦—

Matthias

THE LAND UNDER THEIR FEET was untouched from the landslide, though brown puddles of mud were strewn across the thick grassy hill they descended. The goats were gaining speed on the flatter slope. On both sides of the girl, their ears flopped and their bells rang with every gleeful step they took toward their home.

The first remnants of civilization were clearly old, overgrown with vegetation. Unnatural piles of stone were flush with vines. They moved downward, approaching a river, with steep bluffs on their right. He could hear the water pounding below them through the trees. Younger trees grew along where a path had once been, flat and wide enough for transport to pass through.

This was older here. Much older. A land and its people clearly lost to time and on their own, even before the Long Wars.

Piles of fallen stone lay about, tumbled into an eroded ditch, evidence that a wall had once been fashioned on the man-made mound of earth behind it. The ground had been unattended long enough for new growth to appear, at least a generation of trees and brush covering the earthwork.

They continued along the path until the girl led them to an entrance point. A lone stone arch loomed over the pathway, its stones stubbornly supporting one another to an apex two men high, defiantly daring the elements to knock it over. Through it, the skeleton of a town lay broken and scattered across a great rolling valley. Remnants of a fence outlined old pastures. Where once he could picture lines of crops or herds of grazing animals, the land was overgrown and untilled. Black stained logs of charred wood stuck oddly out of the ground in places, supported by stones, showing where homes had once stood.

Fire. It was always fire. Blistering. Evocative. Both wrath and renewal, fire knew neither friend nor foe, only fuel, and its hunger was insatiable. Whether accident or deliberate attack here, the burned beams didn't say; only that it had been all consuming, as always.

Looking to the ridge, he saw what the thick trees and low clouds had hidden on their descent. Ruins. Towering into the sky, they disappeared into the dense mist, giving only a glimpse of their curves and powerful foundation. Like its village, what Matthias could see was bones, stripped bare, and only a hollow grave marker of a once great home.

Still, there was life.

Smoke rose from a single homestead at the slope of the hill. The dark and aged wooden *Heidenhaus*, with its high-pitched roof stretching over home and barn, was centered in a cluster of small outbuildings and gardens, and the girl and goats headed straight for it.

"Charlie, go find Bea," Rose said.

Charlie, the largest of the brown goats, bleated and shook his head. His floppy ears bouncing and his big belly swinging back and forth, he picked up his pace. The goats trotted along well before them, announcing their arrival with the bells clanging around their necks.

They were still at the edge of the meadow when the half-door creaked opened. A dog curved around it, followed by an older man. The dog quickly inventoried them, sniffing at the goats, before planting itself between Matthias and young Rose. The Hovawart bared its teeth with a low growl, and the long reddish-blond fur along her spine spiked.

Recognizing the notorious guard dog, Matthias stopped and placed a protective hand before Avelina. Surprised to see a favorite hunting breed of the nobles here in the mountains, he knew better than to alarm it.

"*Braver hund*, Grita." Rose praised the dog, shushing it, and ruffled its long ears.

"*Mein Schatz.*" The old man slid the knit cap from his head, exposing his silver hair, and clutched the hat to his chest. Knees bent in the way of old men, he shuffled toward Rose with a look of pure joy on his face. He fell to his knee and opened his arms wide. "My darling girl."

"*Vati.*" Rose wrapped her arms around his neck.

Meeting eyes with Matthias, the old man kissed her temple and pulled back. He smiled, wrinkles framing his pale blue eyes, and pointed a shaking hand over her shoulder. "Are these friends of yours, Rosie?"

"Yes, sir," Rose said. She took the man's hand and turned to them. "This is my papa, Uhrl."

Matthias stepped toward Uhrl to better understand him. His language was the same, but as was common amongst peasants and the lowborn soldiers of Ewigsburg, the dialect was unique and the deliverance thick.

"Not many friendly faces around here these days," Uhrl said, shakily standing back up with Rose's help.

"My name is Matthias. My wife and I are only passing through the mountains."

"I can see she had her way with the two of ye," Uhrl said, looking them both over.

Matthias looked over himself and at Avelina. They were a sight to behold. Their clothes were torn. Their skin and hair covered in a gray film of dirt and mud. Where there wasn't dirt, there was dried and caked blood. "*Genau.* We've lost everything to her but each other, it seems."

"Many a folk forget who's really in charge out there when they try to cut through her," Uhrl said. He petted Grita's head, and she settled beside his leg, keeping a sharp eye on Matthias. "If the *Geisterweg* let you through, it's because the good Lord has a plan for you."

"It was your young Rose here that led us to safety," Matthias said.

"Is that true, Rosie?" Uhrl said.

She nodded with a proud but shy smile.

"We don't want to disturb your peace here and will soon be on our way," Matthias said. "Your daughter has already done so much for us. But if you could spare us some food, perhaps a place to rest, I give you my word your generosity will be repaid tenfold."

Uhrl sighed, the corners of his lips disappearing into the wrinkles of his cheeks. He squatted and picked up the tiny white goat, Lukas. The goat laid against his forearm, legs dangling on either side, and he cradled it to his chest. His palm rubbed along the goat's neck and then scratched its chin. Lukas lolled his head, enjoying the affection.

"Peace," Uhrl said in a hushed voice, looking at the ground. He blinked and shook his head with a small scoff. "Ain't that a thing."

The brown goat, Charlie, watched Uhrl from behind Rose's legs and then trotted over when the kid's bell clinked. Planting himself in front of the old man, Charlie raised his snout and bleated loudly. He stomped his hoof, jealously knocked his head against the man's leg until the old man scratched his ear. Eyes closed, Charlie flipped his ears side to side, leaning against Uhrl's leg.

Uhrl cleared his throat and then looked Matthias straight in the eye. "Rosie's a good girl. The lady of the house will be pleased to see her home and safe."

"Apologies," Matthias said, but Uhrl held up a hand to silence him.

"You're welcome to eat, but after you're clean. Beatrix won't have you dirtying our home," Uhrl said. "Rosie'll fetch you some clean clothes. Take to the river with your wife and wash. You can rest in the ruins tonight."

CHAPTER 25

POOL OF HARMONY

~

Avelina

THE TWO OF THEM STOOD at the river's edge.

"I'll only be around the bend," Matthias said. He pointed to a thicket of trees where a small trail led down a slope to the water. "I won't be long."

"I'll be fine."

He turned and walked away.

At the edge of the water, Avelina dropped to her knees and folded her hands in prayer.

They were alive. On the other side of the mountains. Above ground. *Alive.*

She said her thanks and dropped her hands to her lap. Her body hurt in a way she had never known, having been pushed to the edge and bombarded about. Her reserves were diminished and her stomach shrunken, yet she felt renewed.

The mountain air filled her lungs and was exhilarating. Warmer now that they weren't so high, but still crisp, and clean. The roar of the river had turned into a pleasant rhythm, trickling and bubbling along its way. Birds sang above her in the trees. One chirping while another pair whistled, trilling within the billowing tree branches. The clouds were thick and low, giving the river a whimsical feel. Rich colors shone through the water, a mix of pebbles in browns, blacks, whites, and reds.

Avelina leaned forward and scooped a drink within her hands. The water was clear and colorless and deliciously cool against her

parched throat. She leaned forward again, and she was startled by
her own reflection. The last time she'd caught sight of herself was
the day of the barter, when she had dressed in her best, carefully
manicured and perfectly put together. She didn't recognize the
girl looking back at her. She was covered in a gray film of dirt and
mud, with dried blood all through her matted and knotted hair.

"Ma'am."

Rose.

Avelina hadn't even heard her approach. She looked up, and the
girl smiled. Rose lifted her bundle, showing the clothes and cake
of soap she had brought them.

"These will do," Rose said. "When you're clean, join us at the
house. Beatrix has supper for you." Rose cocked her head and
pointed toward the river. "There's a little pool there behind those
trees. The water is deeper in that spot, but calm. Makes it easier to
get your hair clean when you're needing it as bad as you."

"Thank you," Avelina said, putting a hand to her head.

"No worries, mistress," Rose said with a quick wink. "I've seen
a lot worse."

She dropped the bundle on a stump and reached her hands
toward Avelina.

"Now if you give me your clothes, or what's left of them, I can
set them to wash for you."

Avelina nodded and started with her boots, then pulled on the
sleeves of the tunic Matthias had lent her what seemed so long
ago. It was stiff, and when she moved, dust swirled and a dank
smell wafted into her nose. She coughed, choking on the stench,
and pulled it over her head. It landed on the ground with a heavy
thump.

Rose's eyebrows pushed together and her head tilted curiously,
seeing what was left of Avelina's silk sleeves. Molded to her body
like a second skin, they were muddled and ruined, merely strips of
the gown it had once been. Avelina tried to untie the strings at the
base of the sleeves, but they were stubbornly knotted and frayed.

"Let me help you," Rose said, pulling a small knife from her
belt. "We can see then what we can salvage."

Avelina held her arms out. Rose carefully and skillfully cut the
silks. First the sleeves and then the bodice, each section dropped

piece by piece to the ground. When the girl tried to cut through her underskirt, Avelina's hands shot to her hips and she stumbled forward.

"Thank you," Avelina said. "You can leave that here. I will wash them."

Rose nodded and turned back to the house. "Suit yourself."

Avelina was alone, standing naked by the river with the cake of soap in her hand.

She took the few steps to the edge, eager for the cover of the pool. Each step, her toes squishing farther into the sandy bank. The water was cool to the touch but considerably warmer than near the gorge. It crept slowly over the top of her foot, then whipped around her ankles. The water shocked her skin, pooling around her calves, until her body adjusted and she pushed farther.

Looking to her side, Avelina could see the area Rose had recommended. The water at her knees, she moved toward it. Right at the bank, it was nestled against the base of an immense tree growing from the curve of the riverbed. An overhang of thick roots grew along it, providing a living wall and bit of cover. Avelina could see the outline of the pool, where water poured over a raised boulder and then circled silkily around while the current of the river drove past and disappeared behind her.

Grabbing an offshoot of a root to steady herself, Avelina took a step in. She gasped, losing her footing as she slid down a smooth rock and into the pool to her neck. Her legs kicked furiously beneath her until they found the bottom, and she stood upright.

Ohhhhhh, this is so nice.

Avelina chuckled, dancing her feet around. Up to her shoulders, the tepid water was refreshing. She pinched her nose and dunked herself beneath, then smoothed her wet hair over her head. She made good use of her soap and cleaned her body once and then again. She lathered and scrubbed her hair thoroughly, the long, tangled locks making it quite a chore. Finished, she leaned her back against the boulder, letting the water race over her head.

Avelina closed her eyes, enjoying the peace surrounding her. The winds rustled the leaves in the large tree above her head and whispered the occasional clink of the bells when it switched direction and carried the sound across the fields. The birds still sang, their mixture of trilling tweets and singsong notes soaring in the canopy. The water whooshed past her, slapping against larger rocks that peaked above the water before tumbling downriver.

In this mountain orchestra, every noise was uniquely its own. Dancing the style and pitch and tempo and tone of each note across its ledger. Yet each only added to the next, perfectly complementary, as their ensemble blended together and their music reached deep within her soul. Moving her, fueling her, and setting her free with the comfort and beauty of their natural masterpiece.

Renewed, ready, Avelina opened her eyes. She used the root to climb out of the pool and hugged herself as the breeze kissed her damp skin. She quickened her pace to the edge from which she had come, looking for the dress Rose had brought her.

Avelina pulled the underdress on first over her head. It was loose but small on her, barely going over her hips and the sleeves ending below her elbows. She picked up the dress. It was wool and a lush, deep green, like the needles of the pine trees along the ridge. A simple design that allowed her to dress quickly. She stepped into it and shimmied it over her hips. She pulled each sleeve onto her shoulder and pulled the ties of the front bodice until it was fit as she could get it around her frame. Gathering her hair from behind her, she twisted it, wringing out the water and turned around.

Her skirts—*with all their hidden secrets*—were gone.

CHAPTER 26

BEATRIX

———❧❧———

Matthias

ABOUT TEN STEPS AHEAD OF him, Avelina stopped in her tracks. She'd been charging up the hill to the house as if something bit at her heels. Bare feet stomping through the long grass, her green skirts were fisted in her hands in front of her.

"And you are?"

This must be Beatrix. Standing before the entrance to the home. About half his height, she was twice as thick. Not round like those who may have tended toward laziness and overindulgence, but firm and strong from a life of hard living. The woman stared down her nose at Avelina and wiped her hands on her apron.

Matthias broke free of the tall grass and wildflowers rippling against his shins and onto the path. His boots crunched on the pebbles beneath his feet as he walked to Avelina's side. He put an arm around her shoulder. She looked at him with alarmed eyes.

Something was wrong.

"Ma'am," he said, giving her a respectful nod. "My name is Matthias."

The woman continued cleaning her hands and looked at him with a raised brow. "From?"

"Below the mountains."

"So you say. And she is?"

"My wife."

"I see," the lady said, wrinkling her nose. "I am Beatrix. You met my brother, Uhrl." She gestured behind her into the house. "And my Rose."

Beatrix leaned her shoulder against the wooden door frame and kicked a foot lazily over the other. She crossed her arms over her stomach.

This lady wasn't letting them in the house too easily.

"The lady? Does she have a name?" Beatrix said, cocking her head. "Or a voice of her own?"

"My name is Avelina," she said, stepping forward.

Beatrix's chin raised. "How'd you come by my Rose?"

"The mountains," Matthias said.

"The south face fell, Bea," Rose interrupted. She squeezed around from behind Beatrix and came to stand by Avelina. She pointed in the direction of the hills. "Charlie had run off again, up to Devil's Cliff. I saw it from there, Bea. The whole side of her. A river of rocks, right down her side. Swallowing everything dared get in her path."

"Criminy," Beatrix said. "Hasn't been one that big in a time. We felt it here. The ground trembled beneath our feet." She turned to Matthias. "How'd you come across my Rose, then? Were you of aid to her?"

"No. It was she who saved us," Avelina said.

"Did she?" Beatrix said.

"The girl led us out of the mountain. And then here," Matthias said.

"That's good to know," Beatrix said.

Beatrix's lips tightened, and she looked from one of them to the other.

Matthias pulled Avelina closer to his side, and she wrapped her arm back around his waist. He squeezed her arm, hoping to reassure her.

Beatrix clapped her hands and gave them a grin.

"Well. You're in time to eat," she said, turning to Rose. "Lock up your babes, Rose, before that deviling Charlie gets loose again."

"Yes, ma'am," Rose said, jogging off around the side of the house.

"Let's get something in your stomach," Beatrix said. "You both look like you're soon for the grave."

CHAPTER 27

METZLINGEN

———— ❧ ————

Matthias

MATTHIAS DUCKED HIS HEAD, PASSING through the door into the house. They'd washed their feet and left their shoes at the door and now stood in borrowed stockings on the stone floor.

The lady was proud of her home, and stepping into it, he saw why.

It was a healthy size and an impressively well-kept home.

From against the far wall, the savory smell of stew and the buttery smell of freshly baked *brötchen* wafted, seizing his attention and the walls of his empty stomach. Stationed in the center of a wall, a rounded clay-stone oven pulsed beside a fire pit built of red bricks set into the corner, where a chimney rose above a large pot hanging on an iron hanger over an open flame. Bunches of herbs hung from knobs on the beams running around the room overhead, above framed walls filled with a hardened mix of sand and hay.

Over a floor section of wide planks, a long trestle table sat between two benches along the center of the room, set with red-clay bowls, a long trencher covered with cheese, and a pot of wildflowers in the center. A double doored *schrank*, painted in dulling folkish flowers, towered beside a smaller end table, upon which Uhrl set his cap. Opposite it, a ladder led to a loft, and beneath the overhang there was a nook with a bench built along the entire wall with an iron-bound oak chest stored beneath it. Another half-door stood ajar mid-room, leading to the barn on the other half of the hill house. Grita, with a fluffy pup curled snoozing against her, lay stretched before it. She lifted her snout, eyeing him with a curved brow before settling back to rest.

The bench squealed against the planked floor as Matthias withdrew it from the table and sat across from Uhrl, checking Avelina from the corner of his eye. Avelina walked about the room. Her shoulders were pinched and her hands fidgety, but she kept flashing a polite smile at Beatrix. The older lady brought the pot over and began ladling stew into the clay bowls.

"Thank you," Matthias said when his bowl was filled. The piping broth's rich smell wafted into his nose and his mouth watered in anticipation. Following Uhrl's lead, he plucked a roll from the pile and dipped it into the hunter's stew.

Mmmmmmm. The taste of salted pork soaking the warm roll melted in his mouth. It was heartily full of cabbage and barley, with carrots and onions rounding out the flavor.

Beatrix walked around the table, handing out wooden spoons. She paused, meeting Matthias's eyes, and tilted her head at Avelina. Standing at the half-door, she stood with her hands clenched on the bottom, staring out into the fields.

"Avelina," Matthias said, standing up.

She turned to him; her cheeks still hung with worry. Her eyes darted about to each one of them and then to the table.

"I'm sorry," Avelina said, walking over to sit beside Matthias. "I was watching for Rose."

"Rose'll be around shortly," Beatrix said.

Beatrix placed a stool at the head of the table and sat upon it. Leaning forward, she took some cheese from the platter. "If you're looking for your clothes . . ."

"Yes," Avelina whispered.

"I took them." Beatrix eyebrow cocked. "To wash when you were *indisposed*. Not much worth worrying yourself over in there."

Avelina went stiff next to him.

"The only thing salvageable was the underskirt. I gave it a gentle scrub and it's hung to dry in the loft," Beatrix said, highly arching her brow. "Odd thing, full of pebbles and the like."

Avelina went to stand, but Beatrix laid a hand on hers, stopping her.

"It's fine. I didn't mind. And I was *careful* with it." Beatrix picked up a roll and placed it into Avelina's hand. Her eyes locked onto Avelina's face. "You need to eat. You're nothing but bones, and you'll need some meat on them if you mean to get with child."

"I'm sorry?" Avelina asked.

"Babe, ma'am," Beatrix said, gesturing to Avelina's waist with her spoon. "Your husband will want you pupped right away, or so I imagine."

"There's plenty of time for children," Matthias said.

"Says a man without one," Beatrix said. "When you've been around as long as we have, you know time isn't always with you." She watched him intently over her spoon. "Besides, men are always hungry for war and need sons to fight them."

Matthias looked away and over at Uhrl, who looked nowhere else but into his stew.

"How long have you been married?" Beatrix said, spreading cheese across a hunk of *brötchen*.

Matthias's jaw froze.

This is an inquisition.

"Not long," Matthias said.

The young girl appeared in the doorway, and Beatrix's attention was quickly diverted.

"Eh, eh," Beatrix quipped, pointing at the girl's shoes. Rose nodded and scraped the bottoms of them before kicking them off and hopping to an open space at the table.

Avelina cleared her throat beside him.

"You have made such a lovely home here, Beatrix," Avelina said. "Have you lived here long?"

The lady put her elbow on the table and smiled, chewing.

Well done, Avelina.

"Forty-four summers," Beatrix said. "Or thereabouts."

"Have you always been alone here?" Avelina asked. "The three of you?"

Beatrix's eyes narrowed. "Everyone else is long gone or long in the ground."

"But you stayed?"

"Our family's been working this land for generations. Were the two of us for a long while until Uhrl found young Rose a few years back and we gave the girl a home." The woman frowned, turning her spoon in her hands. "Once we're gone, well, it'll truly be the end. As we were the last of the great house."

Avelina laid a hand on the woman's wrist. "I can understand how difficult that must be for you. I am the last of my family as well."

Beatrix laid a palm on Avelina's hand and squeezed. Her eyes rounded, and she looked over at Matthias.

Her hold on Avelina was tender, but the look she drove at him was sharp and stern. This woman was head of this household, and though they were welcome to enjoy her hospitality at the moment, she clearly did not trust them and, if challenged, would not back down.

The woman's face was a shield of defiance and the stubborn strength born of a life of strife and the unending will to survive.

Just like Avelina beside her.

"It's not only the fine people in the big house that were lost—it took everybody around it," Beatrix said, her gaze never leaving Matthias. "The first time the mountain fell, it blocked the canyon pass and cut off our trade route. Our parents were young then. A group of the men disappeared into the mountains, saying they were looking for another route, and never returned. Then the wars came here to the heart of the mountains. We were kids then, younger than Rose. Our mother sent us to the hills to hide, and from there we saw them set the fires. Smoke poured into the sky, and the flames swallowed our homes. And whoever the flames didn't get . . . we lost them all. Our parents. Our brothers. Our friends. The great house was gone. All part of the cost of war and the games powerful men play. Isn't it, Matthias?"

Matthias's chest tightened and his eyes fell shut, lest the horrid smell be triggered and creep forth from his earliest memories. Her story, though decades and countries apart, was so familiar to his own. A child watching a town. Its people butchered and burned.

He hadn't realized where they were.

It was before his time. Before his wars.

A tale in passing, of the once great house, its name, people, and location lost to time.

The house at the heart of the mountains.

Metzlingen.

Uhrl cleared his throat, and Beatrix paused. His dry lips smacked, and Rose moved quickly to him to refill his drink.

"How horrifying for you both," Avelina said. "I'm so sorry."

"It's always a tragedy when a house falls," Beatrix said. Beatrix leaned forward and lifted a *brötchen* from the bowl. "Now it's gone, it's gone. The mountain, though, she remains. Ancient and immortal and all-powerful, like He who sculpted her with His own hands. She may crumble, shed her skin from time to time, but she'll never fall."

"Some folk say there's giants atop the mountains," Rose said. Piping in, her wide eyes glittered over the brim of her stew. "Frost giants. Hidden on the highest peaks. They have beards of snow and ice, and their shoes are carved from trees."

"Frost giants?" Matthias said, glad for a change in subject.

"Ruled by a frost king," she said. "And his children. They like to play with their dragons."

"Dragons?" Avelina said, tilting her head.

"*Ach,* for sure," Uhrl said. "Long-winged creatures that breathe fire." He waved his hands dramatically, imitating the beast, and Rose clapped her hands.

Rose stretched gleefully tall in her seat. "The children wish to ride them, so they chase them."

"*Ja,* they wrestle them like an ornery babe. Toppling the hills. Leaving them tumbling. People do love their tales, don't they, dear?" Uhrl snorted and winked at a grinning Rose. "They say the winged beasts' claws clatter at the stones, crushing them to pebbles, and their tails leave tracks like slithering snakes. Surely, you heard them, or saw them, on your way?"

Mouth full of soup, Matthias shook his head. He swallowed and his lip tugged, hiding a smile. "Can't say we did, Uhrl, but that doesn't mean they did not see *us*."

"*Hmpf.*" Beatrix took another bite and chewed both *brötchen* and words. Her face hardened and she wiped her mouth. "Our father never did either."

"Or at least he didn't say," Uhrl said under his breath.

"Our mother may've been taken with tales of magic and mayhem in the mountains, but our father showed us the way. The rocks are a sign. God's judgment or remedy. Either way, God settles the disputes among men that they themselves cannot."

"Ach," Uhrl said, rolling his eyes. "You're no fun, then, are you?"

"You know I speak true. The next time it fell, when our kin were in the ground, God's hand closed the last of the trade passes. Sealed our valley. Shutting us off but to those left to call it home. We've lived in peace. Rebuilt our home. There are remnants of other families, farther down along the river, dug into their own hills. Trying to live, wanting to be left alone. But not many. Not many at all anymore." She pushed back from the table and lifted her bowl. "Never you mind. Finish your stew and be off with you. I've things to do."

CHAPTER 28

ARCHES IN SPLENDOR

Avelina

AVELINA PULLED THE SLIPPING SLEEVE of her dress back onto her shoulder and wrapped the blanket Beatrix had given her tighter around her. They'd finished their meal, and she'd quickly retrieved her underskirt. The lady had handed it to her without a word, though both judgment and curiosity had simmered in her slanted eyes. Tidied and intact, without a stitch torn or secret spilled from within its folds, she'd retied it around her waist, and the weight calmed and reassured her.

After cleaning, she'd become restless, sitting so long after weeks of such a maddening pace. She'd almost felt it rude to ask, but when Beatrix suggested they explore the ruins, she'd eagerly agreed.

The door in front of her was twice her height and made of wooden planks more than twice her width. She'd read about forests of giants—trees older than generations of men—but she believed they were long gone. This wood had long since petrified, leaving it stonelike, sitting heavily in front of this once great home.

Should she knock?

Avelina reached for the iron head of a large stag, which held a snake rung in a circle and biting its tail in its mouth. It was heavy in her hand, clanking when she moved it. Feeling foolish, she placed both palms against the door and heaved it open.

She stepped through the massive threshold and into the great ruins. It was breathtaking. A monument standing as testimony to both history and possibility. A maze of stone, rising at varied heights from the ground to an open and brilliant blue sky. There was a long stone hall that looked enclosed and undisturbed to her left, and to her right the whimsical sets of stairs twisting to nowhere and partial walls without rooves leading toward the cliff.

Avelina moved forward through a labyrinth of stone until she found him at the heart. She didn't approach him at first. Quietly, she watched him.

Matthias lifted his left hand and placed his palm on the old gray stone. He began to move forward, gliding his hand along the wall. Avelina stayed several feet behind, quietly mimicking his steps. Her hand found the spot where his had lain. She followed his path, enjoying the feel of the stones passing beneath her hand.

"Hello, wife," he said, grinning at her over his shoulder.

Startled, she quickly drew her hand to her breast and felt color rising to her cheeks.

Wife.

She knew it was for appearances, with Uhrl and Rosemunde somewhere nearby, but the word, him saying it, made her stomach flutter. She looked down, hiding her warmed cheeks.

Avelina quickened her pace until she arrived at his side. They walked together among the maze of ruins, climbing through them when the walkway was blocked with debris. As he helped her over a pile of stone, her shoulder brushed across his broad chest, sending a rush through her. Every time he was near her, the lightest touch stirred something deep within her. Feelings she couldn't place resulted in the hair on her arms standing on end. Her flesh both warm and cool in the evening air.

Walking from the older gray stone foundation of the ruins, she could see where the younger part of the house had once been. Scorched walls stood as marked evidence to destruction, but there was new life and promise all around her. Felled stones littered corners in piles, with purple clusters of hanging flowers bursting from the cracks between them. Though some parts of the floor were thick with weeds or dirt, there were also places of large flat stones leading to an intricate pebble mosaic. Partially destroyed, enough remained to show the intended picture. A shepherd and his flock on these rolling hills, looking to the river below.

Agnus Dei.

"The Good Shepherd." Avelina smiled wide. She knelt and traced her fingertips over the remaining fragments. Though incomplete, the mosaic took her breath away. Each small, jagged, imperfect piece spoke flatteringly of its unique origin. Pieced together, they built a stunning, harmonious masterpiece.

"We are all puzzles, aren't we? Our pieces patched together, stronger for it," Avelina whispered, thinking out loud.

"Hmm?"

Matthias turned to her, casually crossing an arm over his chest. She smiled softly and returned to the mosaic. Avelina traced the lines of the lamb, the smoothness of the jewel-toned pieces soothing her fingertip.

"We are not weak," she said. "Like these lines, our scars don't show our mistakes. They show what we've lived through, that we've triumphed and can be better for it." She stirred to stand, and he offered her his hand, helping her upright. The touch was light, but her cheeks warmed. Looking away, she gingerly stepped around their discovery and walked past him. "There must've been something incredible here. Someone loved this place and called it their home."

Turning past the wall's end, the view was spectacular. Arches in absolute splendor defiantly towered above them. Two rows of equally spaced large columns rose from the ground on both sides of her, testimony to the greatness of the room that had once been. Built in sandstone, they were red with numerous flecks that glittered, reflecting the last light of day. At the top of the columns, the stones curved high until they joined aloft, creating the series of pointed arches framing the stars. Walking through them, she was reminded of the towering kings holding court in her chapel in Leuceria. For a moment, she felt their presence. That their eyes had found her here.

Avelina pulled Beatrix's knit blanket tighter around her shoulders. The cool breeze grew stronger as she neared the edge of the cliff. There, she could see from one end of Metzlingen to the other. The mountains that gave way to an endless view of the surrounding rolling hills. The evening sky set almost dead center of where the two rows met, as if they'd been built to house its place of slumber. A blended sky of yellow and rose clouds gathered above the edges of faraway trees and spilled into the valley and the river below. The heavens above ran from a lilac to deep purple, darkening as they weighed upon the horizon.

It was as if a rainbow, falling after the storm, had found itself suspended between heaven and earth. Finding itself favored and welcomed by both, it had decided to stay, to richly embrace this land and declare itself home.

Her father's voice rolled behind her ear in a whisper—*If stones could speak, what tales they'd weave*—and her lip tugged at the memory. Sitting on his knee, watching his finger trace inked lines. She closed her eyes, tilted her head back, and deeply inhaled, hoping to hold his voice, and the moment, a bit longer.

Exhaling, she watched Matthias, absently nudging loose debris with his foot around the base of the pillared stone.

"Will they rebuild this?" she asked.

"No, I don't believe so. It would take money and many hands. Both of which they don't have here."

"I would," she said wistfully, rubbing the chill from her arms. "I would live here and be happy."

"You belong at Ewigsburg," he said, breaking from her stare. "You'll see once we're there. It isn't Leuceria, but it will suit you all the same."

She bit her lip and turned toward the stones. "Let me pretend. Pretend this is real for a moment. That this was home. And we could stay. Tell me what we would do."

Matthias rubbed his beard and then put his hands on his hips.

"This is where the hall would be. Was, and will be again. It looks daunting. She's pretty beat down, but her bones lay strong." He looked at her, paused, and then continued. "We are positioned well. High enough. The land is good. Rich. Ripe for harvest and for any animals we keep. A solid home could be made here."

"I believe so, yes," Avelina said.

"Were it not the *Geisterweg*."

She ignored him and turned her face toward the tips of the arches.

"But the walls should remain open there." Her hand lifted toward the vast sky in front of her. "That is magnificent."

CHAPTER 29

IT IS

Matthias

"IT IS," HE SAID, HIS eyes following the loose strand of her long chestnut hair blowing gently against her cheek. "Magnificent."

The amber evening light cast her olive skin in a rich tone that drew his eyes across the line of her neck. Her moss-green blanket hung loosely off her shoulders, the cool color offsetting the golden glow shining out from behind her tightened hands. The breeze lifted her hair as she moved. She had the blanket from Beatrix wrapped around her shoulders, but it was short enough he could still see her waist. Her waist that fit perfectly against his hand. The way her rounded hips moved, swaying while she leisurely walked. Her small bosom was covered, but behind her hands, her chest rose in a gentle rhythm, the calmest he had seen since they had met.

She turned to face him. She caught the loose hair dancing around her face and tucked it behind her ear, smiling at him.

He could see it plainly.

The perfectly poised princess finally felt safe. And free. It set ablaze a warmth of comfort within his chest.

He cared for this woman.

He was in trouble. At least he wouldn't be foolish enough to act on it. Dishonor his vows. Her. Or his king. But still.

This wasn't good.

"Come. Come and eat with me," he said. "The lady Beatrix

made dinner, and then you must rest. Tomorrow we leave for Ewigsburg."

Matthias offered her the crook of his arm. She placed her hand into the space, resting it against the flexed muscle of his arm.

Matthias led her to the courtyard behind the largest remaining section of the house. A wide, empty space, he imagined it had once been full of life. Busy. Loud. Those who worked the house and land crowding around a small fire as night fell, eating and drinking their fill. They came to a doorway in a wall that only rose twice as high and then broke off, leaving what was left of a roofbeam looming above it.

Through this, they came to the standing hallway. He pushed open a door that had been left ajar, and she stepped through. His eyes adjusted to the lack of light. It was almost a finished room, closed on three sides and partially roofed with petrified wooden beams, but the fourth wall ended abruptly, as an exaggerated window or space for a terrace that was never built. On this side of the ruins, opposite the sunset, there was only gray light, falling darker before them. Through the large hole, he could see the tops of trees sloping downhill to the ravine below.

The room itself was warm and welcoming. His heart tugged, moved at the strangers' generosity. A small table stood in front of the remains of a fireplace, set with a few candles and laid with a bowl of small *brötchen*, apples, a hunk of goat cheese, and a meat pie. There were two stools beside it. A makeshift bed of straw lined with two blankets sat in another corner.

"They believe we're man and wife. I mean no offense, Princess," Matthias said.

"And I take none," she said, walking over to the table.

Matthias followed her and watched her select a *brötchen*. Avelina held it to her mouth, breathing it in before taking a bite. Her stomach growled loudly, and she tried to stifle it with her hand, laughing.

"You must be famished," he said.

"And you as well," she said, nodding for him to join her.

Sitting down, he took one for himself. The outside was crisp, the inside soft and tasting of butter. So much better than the hard and flavorless biscuits they'd lived off of for days.

Matthias watched her as she ate, not taking anything further for himself but a drink from one of the large mugs. He handed her a mug, and her lips found the edge quickly. Her eyes opened wide, and she grinned.

"You like the wine?" he said.

"Very much."

"I believe they grow the grapes here. A small harvest, I'm sure, but enough for them."

"Lovely. It's rather good."

"So were the *brötchen*."

"Quite," Avelina said, looking off to the side. She shook her head, as if to dislodge a thought, and drank long from her mug of wine.

He watched her, waiting.

"I could help them," she said.

"Who?"

"Beatrix. Uhrl."

"I don't think they're looking for it."

"If the land is suited for growth, they could have more. Vineyards. With all varieties of wine. They'd have their pick and plenty of it, and the rest they could trade or sell for profit. There's money to be made here, if it would help them."

Matthias smirked.

"It's a nice thought, but like the eyes of God, the king's don't linger here," Matthias said. "And they won't. Metzlingen is a name lost to time, and the king doesn't know anything stands here. As long as Ewigsburg is at peace, he wouldn't send resources here. Men are back to their fields and their families and making money. That's a good thing."

"I only meant if it would please them. And the king. I can help with the planning. How to build them. The structuring. Rows on terraces, built so the vines grow brilliantly under the most sun, and the fruits grow strong and plentiful. You see, Niro, he didn't speak to me much. Or care for my presence. But he ensured two things—that I was guarded and that I was educated. I had a tutor at one time, many years ago. When she passed on, she wasn't replaced. I spent most of my time on my own. Studying."

She paused for a drink, then set the mug aside, preening, and continued. "Leuceria's library was full of everything my father could find—scrolls, parchment, music. Old maps. I enjoyed reading histories. Learning languages. Your German. Latin. Italian. Flemish. Some French, Spanish, and English. It brought the world closer to me and brought me happiness." Her nose twitched, and she batted her eyelashes. "Words . . . they simply make sense to me. Much more than people do."

He rubbed his hand across his mouth, watching her eyes glisten.

"I turned to my father's drawings. Some of his own and others, years older. Plans for buildings, for the grounds and gardens, and for the city. For the vineyards. Oh, the way the lines moved across the parchment. The script. The notes. The letters and lines danced, one along the other. Curving or straight. The angles. The sharp edges. Everything coming together beautifully. Complicated, yet clean and clever." Her hands had been dancing across the table as she talked until she brought a hand to her mouth. Her fingertips barely touching her lips, a sly smile spread behind them. "Might I tell you a secret?"

Matthias raised an eyebrow and gave a slight nod.

"I have them with me."

"What?"

"The parchments."

Matthias leaned forward. "From the library?"

"I only have a few. Pieces of them really. The vineyard parchments. My father's notes in his own hand. I found them. I hid them and I *saved* them," she said. Her cheeks bright red, a combination of her confession and the wine loosening her tongue.

Matthias smiled and took a long sip of wine out of his own mug. It *was* quite good.

"Would you like to see them?" she said.

Matthias laid his elbow on the small table, leaning in toward her, and poured more wine into her mug, which she eagerly raised to her lips.

"Someday," he said.

Her eyes flickered again, and the corners of her mouth curled.

He cut small slivers off a hunk of cheese and pushed the plate in her direction. "You'll have to eat more to match that wine."

She locked onto his gaze and sipped on her drink.

"I have them here," she said, her features suddenly firm. "I didn't steal them. They were *my father's*. And his father's. And his father's, and on before that. Now they are *mine*."

"Tell me about your father," Matthias said.

"I don't remember much of him," Avelina said. "I was young when he died."

"I'm sorry."

"I wish he'd died in the war," she said. "At least then there'd be honor in his death."

"*Hmpf.* I've never subscribed to that idea," Matthias said.

"An honorable death?"

"Many do." He shrugged. "It matters to me more how a man lives."

She looked at him through the flickering light of the candles and then hung her head. Reaching her hand, she lifted the side of the dress Beatrix had given her to her hip, exposing her underskirt. She stood, took the table knife, and then carefully cut along the seam. Reaching within a fold, she pulled out a small satchel and set it on the table in front of him.

"I know he loved my mother. Very much," she said, standing over him. "I know that much to be true." She coughed, clearing her throat, once and again, then turned the knife handle toward him. "Open it. With care, please."

He nodded and took the blade from her. The satchel's contents were wrapped tightly in leather and tied closed with threads of numerous colors. He began cutting them one by one at their highest point, mindful of the effort.

"Do you think me a bastard, Matthias?"

Matthias eyed her. She stood, one arm tight across her waist and the other lifting her mug. Her cheeks had fallen sullen. Half from drink, half from their talk, he expected.

"Whether you have his blood or not, you have his name," he said.

She stared at him blankly.

"Jorn would say there's nothing wrong with being a bastard," Matthias said, winking at her. She didn't grin. "Your father, the king, didn't think you were. He named you his heir at your birth, did he not?"

Avelina inhaled and looked away from him, biting her lip. "Yes, he did, because I am. I know I am his daughter."

Having unwrapped the warped leather and the waxed linen below, there was one last piece of fabric left to remove. Whatever this was, she had carried it with her across the mountains from her home. Like the boots, she had had the forethought to bind it and sew it away, hidden in her skirts before the barter. Had she not escaped and been sent to the gallows, these were the things so important to her in life that she'd meant to have them with her at death.

She may as well have stood naked before him, presenting him with such secrets.

His chest tightened and he paused, waiting.

For permission to look.

For permission not to.

Matthias heard her sniffle. Even with the little light they had, he could see the tears she quickly wiped away from each eye. She sat back upon her stool and straightened her shoulders.

"Open it," she said, nodding at him.

Matthias inhaled and pulled back the last of the cover.

He was struck speechless.

He had never seen anything like it. He had seen parchments. Scrolls. He had seen a scribe at work when he was younger. Long ago. Even a binding, but nothing such as this.

This was no ordinary book of prayers.

This was a treasure binding.

This was a crown's—*a kingdom's*—worth of jewels.

Sapphires. Emeralds. Diamonds and pearls.

The brilliant gems of several shapes and colors glittered within the candlelight. Fastened around the Crucifixion hammered in gold at the center, there was hardly a space left between them.

"It was my mother's."

Again, she wiped her eyes, though he caught a glimpse of a soft smile.

"Her book of hours," she whispered. "Her own prayers tucked inside."

Smaller than his hand, the book was thick with pages. Both bound within and others, folded and slipped between them, pushing out against the clasps. Avelina fumbled with the clasps, unclipping them, and the stretched, half-broken binding poured open. Her fingers shook, selecting a small, frayed card with a sketch of a lamb. "See. My mother's hand. *Agnus Dei, qui tollis peccata mundi: miserere nobis.*"

Matthias reached forward and placed a gentle palm on her forearm.

"Dona nobis pacem." Eyelashes batting, she tucked the lamb back into place, continuing to whisper the prayer as she flipped through more of the vellum pages. "Have mercy upon us…grant us peace." Each illuminated page was painted from corner to corner with vivid color, meticulous drawings, and lettering surrounded by intricate bordering. And in between those pages, she fingered scraps of paper with scrolling notes or larger pieces folded, browning and cracking at the seams.

"And my father's," she said, sniffling. "Parts of his vineyard notes. Others. Folded inside. Written in his hand."

Avelina pointed to them, pushing them toward him, but he dared not touch.

Such skill it had taken to create such a thing. Such riches she had stored within. Like the mosaic they had seen earlier, it was a mastery of work. Immeasurably personal. And valuable.

"Do not show this to the king," he said, covering it back up. "To anyone."

She hung her head low, eyes closed. Her arms crossed around her at her waist.

"The things. The things they say about her." A whimper, and another, her chest heaved as she sought breath. It caught, tearing through her throat, as if the cry had been trapped there for years. Several times she tried to stop, to speak, but could not. She buried her face in her hands and wept.

Matthias's heart ached as if he'd been kicked in the chest. "Let it all out."

"I'm sorry," she said, weeping through her hands.

"Don't be, love. It's all right to not be all right."

Her shoulders shuddered, and she continued to sob. "I've failed them."

"No, you haven't. The last thing you are, Avelina, is a failure. You are young, but you're a pillar of quiet strength," he said. "With your whole life ahead of you."

She didn't respond, and he pulled his stool closer to hers. Closer, to let her know he was there. That she was not alone. Elbows on his knees, he leaned toward her to speak. "What you are is grieving. Grief doesn't make one weak. 'Tis born of love. Friendship. Family. Brotherhood. Once you grieve, you can find your peace."

Matthias used a single finger to raise her chin.

Her eyes met his. Unencumbered, she sputtered. Defiance and sorrow mixed on her face. Rivers of tears marked her cheeks, dripping from her chin. "My mother. She was *not* what they said she was."

"None of that matters here, Princess."

His chest tightened further, and he reached a hand along her cheek, brushing the tears away lightly with his thumb. Her wet eyes rounded and closed. He knew he shouldn't have. He had touched her, held her, many times over the past few days, but purposefully. For support. For safety. For warmth. He withdrew his hand and sat back on his stool, crossing his arms tight in front of him.

"It matters to me. They were lies. Horrible lies," she said. "Someday I will know. Everything. The whole and honest truth."

"Yes, Princess," he said, nodding.

Though knowing even as much as he knew of the situation, he wasn't sure she would ever know the truth. Or truly want to.

"You don't believe me," she said, eyes reading his thoughts.

"It's not that, Princess."

"Someday everyone will know the truth."

"Do you mean to avenge them? Fight for your crown?"

"God willing, someday. My blood demands it. And if this king was my father's ally, would he not help me to avenge him? Wouldn't he support my claim?"

Her tears had slowed. She sat tall again and took another long drink from her mug.

The poor princess didn't know what she wanted. Torn between two kingdoms, tied to duty on both sides. Would she ever even have the autonomy to choose?

"You'd need more than an army behind you. The General is old, failing as a politician, but don't be a fool and discount him in battle. Even if the nobles rallied around you, you'd have to be smart. Strategic. Win before the battle even starts. Once you're on his ground, thick in the theater of war, you're playing to his strengths. Where the General has never been beaten."

"Am I to forget what was taken from me?"

"No," he said. "But wait until the timing is right."

"How would I know when the timing is right?"

"I cannot answer that." He shrugged. "But I can tell you this. If you spend the entirety of your life looking back, you'll be stuck there. Stuck in the misery and pain behind you. Look for what went wrong and figure out how to use it. Use it to move forward. To be smarter in your decisions. To avoid pain as you can in the future, for yourself and for others. That's what a wise man does."

Having poured herself more wine, she crossed her legs and looked at him over the rim.

"Hmm. A wise *man*."

"I meant—"

"I was the heir. The *first* celebrated female heir," she said. "That throne is my birthright. They may have called me hateful names, but my father named me the Daughter of Leuceria."

"Those nobles came to barter for you, no matter what they called you," Matthias said. "Should you choose to fight for the throne one day, I'd expect some of those Houses to stand with you. But not all."

"If I'd been born a man, maybe none of this would've happened."

"No," he said, staring directly at her. "Because he would've killed you when he killed your parents."

"How would you know?"

"Because I do," he said. "And it's what most would've done."

She frowned. Her brows wrinkled.

"If you mean to take over a kingdom, you eliminate the entire dynasty," he said.

"But I'm alive."

"I intend to keep you that way."

Her head tilted to the side, and she lifted her mug to toast him.

"Then let us both hope and pray our paths lead to freedom. To glory and to peace."

"*Genau,*" he said, smiling.

He needed to change the subject.

"Your grandfather," Matthias said. "Why the Bear? What was the story there?"

"You've heard of him?"

Matthias nodded yes, and she stared off for a bit.

"The Bear," she said. "After seeing her in the mountains, I don't understand why they called him that. No man is that big."

"You'd be surprised at the size of some men," he scoffed. "I'd wager it wasn't the size of the man, it was the instinct they named him for. If that sow had thought us a threat, she would've torn us down to protect her cubs. Like a man, a good man, *or* woman, should do to protect their own."

Matthias shifted on his stool. He tightened a fist around the mug and drank from it, watching her.

The corner of her mouth turned down, and her chin dropped. Her hand found the table edge, and she swayed clumsily in her stool. "I'm sorry."

"You have nothing to be sorry for," Matthias said, exhaling sharply. "I should have stopped you. You're a slight thing, and I watched you drink when you should've eaten."

"No, no. I'm fine," she said. "I'm just cold."

"I'm sure a bit, but you're also drunk."

Matthias set his mug aside and swiftly moved around the table until he stood in front of her. He put out his hand for her, waiting. Her palm was sweating when it found his, and she rose slowly, wobbling a bit on her way up. He laughed, the other hand catching her waist as he pulled her steady. *Too much wine. Too fast.*

"I'm not drunk," she said, trying to take a small step back from him, her arms drawing to the center of her chest. Her bottom lip quivered, and her eyes glazed over. Her stupor had almost put her to sleep. "Or maybe I am."

Her knee gave, and she stumbled within his grip. She laughed heartily and tapped him on the shoulder.

"Are you trying to dance with me, soldier?"

"Heavens, no," he snorted.

"Perhaps another time."

"Perhaps." Matthias lifted her left arm and placed it around his neck, then scooped her into his arms. He carried her body, heavy with drink, and sat her on the bed. Taking a knee, he untied the new waterskin Uhrl had gifted him from his waist and put it to her lips.

"Drink."

"I'm good."

"Drink."

"No more wine."

"It's water, Avelina. From the spring. Drink."

Her eyebrows raised, and she took a drink. It trailed on her chin, and she wiped it away with her sleeve and drank again. She sputtered, then swallowed more. When she had drunk it dry, he guided her down onto the blankets. She curled her legs into her stomach, nestling, and closed her eyes.

"Matthias."

"Avelina."

"Please stay with me."

Avelina laid her hand atop his, and with that, she fell asleep.

Her breathing was deep and rhythmic, and he laughed when a snort rattled from her. Matthias brushed several locks of hair off of her face, gathering them behind her head, where the rest of her curls lay in a twirling heap behind her. She rolled onto her back, her legs stretched back out from where they had been balled against her stomach.

She was beautiful. And innocent.

Matthias looked at her, smiling, and then frowned, seeing her shoulder exposed from her clumsily shifted gown. The curve of her breast. Peeking at him above the disheveled neckline, rising and falling in the waning candlelight. He wiped his hand across his mouth and reached for her sleeve. He tried to pull it and cover her back up, but it wouldn't budge, twisted around her arm. His eyes moved across her calves, along the inside of her knee and up the supple skin of her thighs to the point where her skirts lay bunched around her.

He wanted her to rest. He didn't want to disturb her. But the longer she lay in disarray, exposed and vulnerable, the more protective he felt over her.

Some men would still take her as she lies there. His fists clenched guardedly, at the thought of such evil. Moving swiftly to her, he twisted her skirts down across her legs and tried to pull at her sleeve. It wouldn't give under her drunken weight, so he removed his own shirt. Placing it gently over her chest and under her chin, he tucked it around her shoulders.

She need not fear him. Ever. He said that he would protect her, and he meant it.

Even from the ache that raged in his loins whenever he looked at her.

He scanned the room, mapping it before pinching the candle flames between his fingers.

This would do for now. He could sleep once they arrived safely at Ewigsburg.

He combined what was left in their mugs into one to enjoy a last drink and walked to the wall opening. His eyes slowly adjusted to the dark, only slips of pale light from the last crescent moon, waning and almost lost amongst the stars.

Tomorrow was the new moon. The deadline he'd given Jorn.

A month they had traveled, with still far to go.

He sighed, dread and hope warring within him, and leaned against the stone wall. He would drive them on. He had to. He was already late to meet Jorn. Even if his brothers gave him a few extra days, the king's patience would grow thin.

In all honesty, the closer they came to Ewigsburg, the greater a sense of unease grew within him. Doubting the king's sincerity. His commitment to this plan. Disavowing his mistress. Turning his back on her growing babe. Marrying his nephew's intended.

Gah. Matthias wiped his hand down his face. Exhausted in every way, he was confusing things. Allowing feelings for her— that he could no longer deny—to cloud his thoughts.

He had to stop this. Caring for her. There was no future there. Only heartache.

Hopefully, there was still time. A chance he hadn't failed them all. His options were limited, but he would never give up. Perhaps he could offer to buy a horse from Uhrl.

What would a simple man like that desire? Coin?

Even if the elder had no need of coin, surely there was something he could promise them to ease their life and work here. Once she was set at Ewigsburg, he would return here with payment for a horse. Hopefully much more to repay their care and kindness as well.

No. Not hopefully, but certainly.

He would make sure to repay them and with much.

Matthias took a slow sip of wine and sorted through the noises carried on the curling night breeze. An owl. Fox, a pair of them. Horses, behind him, on the far end of the house. The river. The forest in front of him was dense, ancient. Bits of pale light cut through the canopy, offering a rough sketch of the floor some distance below. There was nothing to scale the wall unless it was carried here. This room was a good choice. Safe. For her. Them.

Matthias finished the wine in one last gulp. The corner of his mouth curled as he picked up another light noise from behind him. *Snoring.*

CHAPTER 30

JUST ONCE

Avelina

OH. HER HEAD.

Avelina pinched her eyes tightly, trying to thwart the glow of the new day. Her hand rose to her face. She lazily brushed at the strands of hair draping across her nose and sneezed as the scent of hay and summer wool danced into her nostrils. Covering her mouth with what she thought was the blanket, his scent flooded her nose and poured through her. Stretching her limbs lazily like a purring cat, she rolled on her side, blinking above the shirt still clutched at her lips, and her eyes adjusted to the golden light warmly creeping into the room.

She saw him. Seated on the floor beside her where she lay on the edge of the small bed, with his back against the wall. His body—his shirtless body—looked tired. His broad shoulders were rounded inward, with his elbows propped on his bent knees.

She had seen him like this before.

Bare.

The clean lines of muscle that cut across him. Hard and cut as the stones holding up the room around them. The scar that ran the length of his left arm. The flick of his pulse on his neck. The rhythmic rise and fall of his chest. The glimpse of his stomach just beyond the slope of his leg. His body at work even when at rest.

Yes, she had seen him.

Bare.

But never like this.

She unabashedly drank in the sight of him. All of him. Every detail, though familiar, was new. Her eyes danced over him, following along his skin, and she imagined the tips of her fingers, barely a whisper, moving over him. Down along the scar until she could entwine her fingers in his. Feel her hand stretch to meet his. Or crawl into his lap, where he could pull her in, wrap his arms around her. Where she could burrow her head against his chest.

Matthias's head lolled to the side. He was watching her with an easy smile.

"Good morning." The corner of his lip tugged, and he pulled his hand across his mouth. When his hand dropped, his soft smile had erupted into a full grin. "How's your head?"

There it was. That smile. The one that stretched along that square jaw until it reached and lit his eyes. Eyes she could swim in.

"It's all right," she said softly.

His eyebrows furled, and she laughed.

"It hurts, honestly," she admitted.

Matthias scooted and knelt at the edge of the bed, reaching his hand to her. For a moment, it hung motionless in the air above her, and then his fingertips began rubbing, ever so gently, across her hairline.

Ohhh. That feels good.

Avelina leaned her head toward him, and his large hand spread across her forehead. His fingers felt rough against her skin, but so very welcome. His touch deepened and settled at her temples. His fingertips massaged into them, rubbing deeper in a circle until a strange relief waded through the fog as the pockets of pain burst free and subsided.

"Better?" he said.

"Much. Thank you."

Avelina needed to touch him. Wanted to. In a way she couldn't explain.

Heart tripping in her breast, she reached forward and was surprised when he took her hand within both of his. He sighed and tenderly leaned his forehead against hers, though a darker intensity replaced his easy smile as their close breaths danced between them. His thumb glided back and forth sweetly on her wrist, the light touch of his rough skin rippling currents up her arm, into her chest, and down along her legs until her toes curled under his gentle touch.

There were so many things that she wanted to say to him.

So many things.

The two of them were alone here, for now, until they set out for Ewigsburg. Where she would lose him.

She told herself she should be ashamed. Ashamed of how she felt for this man. For what she wanted from this man.

That her feelings were wrong. Sinful. Forbidden.

But instead it felt honest. And good. And somehow easy.

His eyes. Those deep brown eyes of his. Searching hers. Locked there, boring into her soul. No longer tracing liquidly over her open neck, where she had felt them the day before. Watching her bosom rising with each breath. Oh, how her cheeks had warmed under his gaze.

It was that his eyes—he—*saw her*, as she was.

Totally, truly, fractured and flawed, herself, and yet he held her still.

Avelina laid her hand against his stubbled cheek, her thumb beside his parted lips.

All she wanted was him. To hold her, touch her, like he had so many times. But this was different. A yearning. A desperate need. Driving her in a way she didn't recognize, from the deepest and most secret parts of her soul.

Avelina reached around his ear and trembled, but determined, she leaned forward, and her lips found his. A moment of gentleness, their wine-stained lips brushed against one another and then pulled apart. Their eyes locked between them. Nose to nose. Breathing ragged. His mouth twisted into a smile, which quickly disappeared.

His fingers spread through her hair, cupping the back of her head, and he pulled her toward him. His lips pressed against her cheek, and she felt his breath on her ear. A heat she had never known poured along her skin. She purred; her body turning liquid, melting then and there.

He said her name, and her eyes closed.

"Are you sure?" he said.

Her brows wrinkled and she nodded.

"Say it," he said.

Avelina's heart pounded until it burst, opening every secret she had to him.

She was his.

"Kiss me, Matthias."

The next moment hung in the air like an hour.

Her eyelids fluttered open when his lips brushed against her cheek and then pulled away. Straightening his back tall, Matthias locked his eyes on hers and pulled her toward him. At the edge of the bed, she draped a leg on either side of him, shuddering when he reached behind her and scooted her hips closer to him. She felt him, pressed between her thighs and lost her breath.

"Say it again."

He caressed her—at her jawline, then lacing through her curls and caressing the soft skin of her neck—and she felt she could crumble right there before him. His body. His hands. His lips. An unfamiliar urging mounted deep within her, and the quizzical sensation left her trembling. Her arms. Her legs. Her lips. Her insides screaming, but she managed to speak.

"Please."

He kissed her. Again, soft at first. She whimpered, parting her lips, and he dove into her. His lips hungrily found hers, and his grip on her tightened. Her hands traced over his bare shoulders and around his neck, pulling him toward her. It was all new, but she followed his lead, her tongue dancing with his. Tasting him. Trusting him.

His hands traced along her back. His hips thrust forward against her, and she pulled her face away from his. Breathing rapidly, mouths parted, they stared at one another.

His hands firmly on her hips, he watched her, eyes rounded, as she fumbled with the ribbons tying her bodice closed. The stubborn knots wouldn't give way, though the tops of her breasts peeked above the loosened neckline.

"Matthias."

Frustrated, Avelina whispered his name, and he grinned and took her into his arms. One across her back and the other found her bottom. Lifting her farther back into the bed, he was on top of her.

Kissing her. Gently, then fiercely. Teasing and tasting her.

She met his pace, clinging to him, giving him everything she had. She lifted her hips, and he burrowed between her legs, driving himself against her eager frame. Her cheek pressed against the base of his neck, and she arched into him.

A hot, excited tear slid down her cheek. And another.

She was ready.

"Matthias."

She moaned, stuttering as she cried out for him.

"I'm yours."

He stopped. Suddenly.

His body jerked. His every muscle tightened.

She pawed at him, though he stilled against her.

She kissed his neck, pulling herself closer still to whisper in his ear.

"I'm yours."

His face collapsed into her shoulder.

"I'm sorry," Matthias whispered.

"You have nothing to be sorry for," Avelina said, exhaling sharply. "I want this."

He pushed his arms straight on either side of her and lifted his head. His eyes closed, and the line of his lips drew tight. "We can't."

She shook her head at him. Reached her hand toward his face, but he caught her wrist and pulled it away. A sharp pain ripped through her chest, and she sniffled.

"I can't."

"I may be a virgin, but I know what *that* means," Avelina said. Her leg wrapped around his, she lifted her hips against him, and he exhaled, his body shaking. He groaned and pulled back from her sharply, leaving her rejected body frozen in place.

Turning awkwardly, he moved clumsily off the bed. After a few steps, he stood with his back to her and ran both of his hands over his head, squeezing the back of his neck.

"I want to be with you."

He didn't answer her. She could've counted his muscles as one by one they grew tight, his body hardening to stone.

"I don't understand." Her throat squeezed. "Do you not want

me, Matthias?"

His hands found his hips. "You belong to my king."

Avelina shuddered. The air between them grew colder, settling against her naked shoulders. His shirt lay crumpled beside her hip from the night before, and she covered herself with it. "I belong to no one."

"I won you, to be his bride."

Avelina swallowed, trying to clear a path for words, *for anything*, to fight the heaviness breathing into the room, absorbing her sense of freedom, and pushing them apart.

"We have not taken our vows."

"No. But you soon will. And I will not sour another man's wife."

Another man's wife. Avelina's eyes fluttered closed. Please, no. Not back to duty. She didn't want duty. She wanted love. She wanted Matthias.

"I will be his. One day. And I will be a good and true wife to him," she said breathlessly, desperately. "But today I choose you. I want to be with you."

"We cannot be together, Avelina."

"Please don't push me away," she said.

His head hung in front of him.

"Matthias. *Matthias.*"

Again, he didn't answer.

"Matthias, I love you."

He strode to the other side of the room and slammed his fists against the wall. She followed him, her bare feet smacking against the stone floor. Stopping a few steps behind him, she dared not reach for him.

Everything had changed so quickly. Everything. The sharp pain in her chest grew more intense, squeezing the bottom of her throat. "Did you not hear me? Matthias, I love you."

Matthias turned to her, his shoulders pulled back and his arms bent at his sides. His bottom lip pulsed, looking at her, but then he shook his head. "You cannot love a man like me."

"Don't say that." The sharp pain in her chest amplified, squeezing her heart in a clamp. "*I love you.* I'll say it again. However long it takes until you believe me."

Matthias turned his head sharply away, looking everywhere but at her.

"This is my choice; I want this. I want *you*." Avelina took a small step, reaching her hand toward his chest. "When you are long gone, I will have this memory. Always."

"I will not ruin you," he said, withdrawing forcefully. "And I will not betray my king. Hell, woman, if he found out . . . And what if you were to get with child?"

"Then take me away. We can run. Away from all of this."

His face fell. For a moment, she thought he would speak, but then he frowned. He balled his fists, and his bent arms trembled.

"Avelina, I gave my oath."

"You did. *To me*. To protect *me*."

"And that's what I'm doing. I'm protecting you and your honor."

"You're breaking my heart," Avelina whispered. Taking a step back from him, she wrapped her arms tightly around her own waist, bracing herself against the pain of his rejection. Her knee smarted, and she stumbled but caught herself and turned to the bed and sat down.

He paced before the quiet fireplace, his heavy steps smacking against the stone floor.

"I'm a fool." Her lips quivered. Fresh tears fell along the lines of her cheeks, where moments ago they had run from joy. "You don't want me."

"Not want you?" Matthias scoffed. His hand grabbed at his temple, squeezing. One hand planted on his hip, the other waved at her as he began to speak. "Your voice has been singing in my head since we met. Telling your stories and asking your endless questions. Or the way your lip curves when you smile. The way your hair smells when you move by me is singed in my thoughts. I want to burn everything about you into my mind so it never leaves me. How perfectly your body fits against mine when I hold you in my arms. How your hand feels when your fingers are laced within mine. The sounds you make when you sleep . . ."

He crossed to her and took a knee in front of her.

"*Of course I want you.* I've dreamt about taking you to my bed. How it would feel to bury myself within you, but only if you were *mine. Ach*, Avelina, if you were *mine* and *mine alone*." He took her hands within his and gently squeezed them. "I've wanted you from the day we met. I want you now. I will want you tomorrow. And the day after that. But I *cannot* have you. I will not dishonor you."

His words hung like stars. Frantic, she pulled through the fog, trying to piece them clearly together and hold them and imprint them on her heart. Her voice broke as her chest caved in with heartache. "I would rather you loved me."

He rested his forehead on her hands and sighed heavily. He squeezed her hands and kissed her knuckles as he let go. He retrieved his wrinkled shirt from where it lay beside her, put it on, and turned toward the door.

"Matthias, don't leave me."

He paused for a moment with his hand on the door's iron latch.

"I do love you, Avelina. And that is why I cannot stay."

And he left.

CHAPTER 31

IN THE WILD

Matthias

MATTHIAS'S MUSCLES WERE BURNING. FROM the lack of sleep. From the frustration binding his loins. From the steep climb following the young girl to the pasture.

He had wanted to leave Metzlingen early. Much earlier than they would now. After she had had plenty of sleep and was well rested, he was going to push them hard today. Get on the road, cover a lot of ground, and try to finish this task.

But he was a fool.

He had feelings for her. Feelings that were foreign to him. Confusing. Overwhelming. He tried to tell himself it was simple—he had saved her life, she was beautiful, it was natural to want to bed her—but there was nothing normal about how he felt about her. He tried to deny it. Stifle the feelings. Ignore them, because eventually they would be at Ewigsburg. She would belong to his king.

But then last night. And this morning happened.

She had kissed him, and he'd felt it. She wanted him as badly as he wanted her.

And by the heavens, did he want her.

And he had almost lost control.

Until she'd said those words.

I'm yours.

Even before he'd let himself admit it, he'd known. Before he dared to admit how he felt and dared to believe she might feel the same.

Then he'd hurt her. He'd seen it on her face. He'd heard it in her voice. He knew he had broken her heart.

Rotting hell.

He had even used those words because it was true. He did. He loved her.

Matthias tightened his grip on his walking stick. He slammed it against the hard earth, propelling himself higher on the climb, following Rose's path. She was moving quickly, faster than he could think this morning.

"Rose," he called after her. She didn't look back.

Rotting hell.

The girl was on a mission. She was missing a few goats from her flock—Charlie specifically—and she was hell bent to find them. If they'd followed their floppy-eared leader, the goats were dispersed across the ridge.

"Quick trip up. Quick trip down. My Uhrl's knees can't take that ridge anymore," Beatrix had said, slapping the walking stick into his hand. "Take the girl. Grita will find the goats and herd them home. There's another storm brewing, and I won't lose my Rose again in those hills."

This climb wasn't going to be easy on his knees either.

"Matthias!"

Matthias looked up. He saw her cresting the hill with her small black-and-blond pup, Liesl, hopping at her heels.

He heard the screaming of animals.

The kind that could only mean one thing.

Scheiße.

"Rose!" Matthias charged up the remaining section of the hill after her and onto the ridge. They'd found her goats all right. And complete chaos. "Rose!"

The girl, screaming, raised stick in hand, was charging a lynx.

The lynx startled, standing over its small kill. Its stance shifted defensively. The lynx's body became rigid, locking its thick legs to stand its ground.

As if fired from a cannon, Grita shot forward. Barking feverishly, her legs catapulted her across the open ridge as the lynx lashed at Rose. Ears back and yellow eyes wide, it screamed, teeth snarling, and arched its back.

Horrified, Matthias sprinted after Rose. Arms pumping at his sides, his boots slammed beneath him. "Rose, no!"

Before him, Grita barreled close to the ground toward Rose, determined to defend her. A few steps shy of the lynx, Grita crossed into Rose's path and intercepted it. Her legs locking, Grita anchored herself before the wild cat.

Both animals snarled at one another. Like a soldier on the battlefield, the dog raged its war cry. Ferocious barks roared from her gut as strings of spittle flew from her bare teeth. The lynx responded in kind, piercing the air with its wicked high-pitched scream. About the same size, evenly matched, and cornered on the ridge, it would be a fight to the death.

"No, child. *No!*"

Matthias finally had Rose within a few steps of the fight. Grabbing her around the waist, he tossed her aside and away from the carcass, where the predator had been feasting on its kill. Bit through the neck, the smell of fresh blood surrounded it. Torn, loose strips of flesh dangled around the small goat's thigh bone. A young kid bellowed beside it, while another hopped away startled. The puppy yelped madly after its mother, who had fully engaged the lynx.

When the lynx raised a large paw, the dog lunged. Their two bodies tangled together. Golden fur flashing against the reddish-gray summer coat of the lynx, they growled and thrashed.

Matthias bellowed loudly, rushing the animals. The lynx was trying to strike the dog's neck, but Grita avoided the deadly blow. They wrestled noisily, tumbling across the ground. In a quick move, the lynx twisted, swiping at the dog. Its paw cut across Grita's stomach, and the dog let out a piercing shriek. Stumbling, the lynx struggled, aiming to sink its teeth into the dog's neck.

Matthias launched himself onto the lynx. Taking it by surprise, he ripped it from the poor dog. The animal twisted beneath him, and Matthias screamed when its sharp claws ripped his skin.

"Rotting hell!" Matthias raised his axe and slammed it against the lynx's neck. Missing it with the blade, the handle knocked the lynx back. It jolted and mewled. Matthias raised the blade to again charge the cat, but the cat turned. Hissing at him, it scrambled, retreating, and then took off into the trees.

Matthias's heart fell from his throat.

It was done.

He rolled back onto his hip to check on Rose and took in the spectacle around him. Blood was spattered about the ground. A few goats stood, scared bone straight, while others ran, scattered in circles, their bells clinking on their necks. Rose was safely curled on the ground with her pup. It yowled in her arms, its tiny black nose slamming against her chin while it tried to wiggle free of her grasp.

"*Shhhh,* babe, *shhhh,*" Rose said, stroking its fluffy fur.

Because of its mother. Like all living creatures, it wanted its mother.

The poor dog lay whimpering and torn against the bloodied ground.

He crawled to the dog and gently laid a hand on her neck. Her ear was torn, and her fur was mangled with blood and mud. Blood dripped from her mouth, and her breathing was haggard as she pulled whistling breaths across her dark lips.

"You gave that boy a hell of a fight," Matthias whispered, petting her gently behind her ear. "Brave, *brave* girl, protecting your flock. Protecting your Rose. You've done well, love."

Death was never easy.

Matthias pulled another blade from his boot, ready to shove it through her ribs to put the animal out of her misery, but he hesitated when her brown eyes turned toward him. He looked closer at her wounds. She was torn but miraculously intact.

Grita was badly hurt, but if they moved fast, she might be saved.

The dog had proven itself invaluable for the family and had surely earned the chance. He removed his shirt and ripped the shredded sleeve into two strips. Holding them in his teeth, he packed the remaining shirt against the dog's wound. He dressed her ear and then turned to his own arm.

Rotting hell, his flesh burned like a thousand suns. Lines of blood trailed from where the cat's claws had ripped the backside of his upper arm. He began wrapping the wound.

"Rose, I need you to tie this around my arm." Matthias said. "Rose, help me."

Sniffling, Rose knotted the linen. "We cannot leave Grita here. Please. *Please.*"

"I know, child, I don't intend to." He hoisted the dog into his arms, turning her as best he could to keep pressure on her wound. Hopefully, her goats would follow or find their own way home; it couldn't be helped now.

They began the trek toward the homestead, keeping the sharp cliff as a guide on their left. Though the girl was agile as an ibex on the rocky cliffs, his own steps were unsteady. Unable to see past the large dog, he stepped blindly, feeling his way down the embankment. Sliding on needles and loose rocks as the ground grew steeper, he began using the trees as a guide, smacking his bare arms against their trunks to break his fall, trashing his body.

Rott. Ing. Hell.

He kept on going. Fast as they could. Twigs snapping beneath his feet. Bells clinking randomly around them. The dog roughly breathing in his arms. Rose cooing at her babe.

Amidst all the other chaos, another sound drifted toward him.

Slowly, curiously. Then surely, and the hairs on his forearms stood on end.

The thundering of hooves. Many of them.

The telltale rhythm of men in pursuit.

The lynx had been one thing, but this was another danger altogether.

"Get down," Matthias said, crouching. Rose was quickly on her knees at his side. Her eyes flew wide, and she curled into a fetal position around the pup, pushing it against her chest. *"Don't. Move."* Laying the dog beside her, Matthias crawled forward on his stomach to where the ground dropped sharply over the valley.

Peering below, his breath seized and Avelina's face flashed before him.

There, on the field, a group of riders headed toward Metzlingen.

A trio leading a group of men-at-arms wearing the crest and colors of Leuceria.

Marcus's assassins.

God's bones.

Avelina.

He'd left her there to die.

CHAPTER 32

BURIED SECRETS

———∾∾———

Avelina

BEATRIX LIFTED HER APRON AND, bundling it in her hands, picked up the warm kettle from the corner fire. She brought it to the table and poured piping liquid into the mugs beside Avelina.

"That'll warm you up," Beatrix said, nodding to the sweet-smelling drink. "It can be right cold in the mornings round here."

"Thank you," Avelina said.

After returning the kettle, Beatrix pulled a stool over and sat right in front of Avelina, scooting toward her until their knees touched. The woman's scrunched face studied her.

Avelina picked up the mug between both hands and blew slowly across the top of swirling steam. She sipped from her cup, the warm liquid soothing her from the middle out. Avelina looked around the room, pausing when she saw a plate of rolls on the table. Her stomach turned from too much wine the night before, and the smell of the buttery *brötchen* made her salivate.

"Hungry?"

Avelina smiled. "Yes, please."

Beatrix leaned over the table and drug the plate toward them, offering one to Avelina. They were still warm. Taking a bite, Avelina closed her eyes and savored it.

"I sent the man to the mountains."

Avelina opened her eyes.

Her head leaning against her hand, with her elbow propped on the table's edge, Beatrix continued to watch her intently. She took another sip of her own mug and wrinkled her nose.

"We meant to leave this morning," Avelina said.

"Rose needed help with the goats, and it's too steep a climb for Uhrl. With his leg bothering him so. Seems another of her kids has gone missing."

"Oh no."

"And I meant to talk to you. Alone."

Avelina took another sip of her drink and licked her lips.

"Rose favors you. And for her sake, I let you into my home." Beatrix wrung her hands and leaned toward her. "No woman has hands like yours that's seen a day of work in her life. Or has *secrets* sewn into her skirts either. You're not who you say you are. Either of you."

"I am his wife," Avelina said, lowering her eyes.

Beatrix snorted.

"The hell you are. It doesn't become you to lie, lady. You might be carrying a flame for the man, but you're not his wife. I'll know whose lady he's taken."

Avelina's face dropped. "You don't understand."

"I'm listening," Beatrix said. "Has he hurt ye?"

"Matthias?"

Beatrix's nose scrunched, and she wrapped her clammy hands around Avelina's. "Has he taken advantage of you? Had his way with you?"

Avelina choked, trying to forget his rejection an hour before. "Heavens, no."

Beatrix leaned back and put her thick elbow on the table's edge. She bit her bottom lip and chuckled. "So you say, then. Good man."

"He's been kind to me." Avelina squirmed, feeling exposed.

Beatrix looked her deep in the eyes, grinning, the wrinkles around her mouth becoming more pronounced. "Well then, who is the man to you? And you to him? Your secret's safe here."

Uhrl hurried into the house, his right shoulder drooping as his limp was aggravated by his quickened pace. Beatrix was right on her feet and closed the half-door behind him.

"Riders," he said, coughing.

"How many?" Beatrix said. She glanced at Avelina and to the table set for five. She grabbed two of the cups and tossed them into the firepit. They broke against the stone back, what little ale there was sizzling, and the pieces disappeared behind the fire.

"I didn't wait to count," he said. "Josef leading at the front, with many others behind."

Avelina was on her feet. Beatrix briefly touched Avelina's shoulder as she slipped to the window, looking around the open shutter.

"Blast that man. You're right. Three at a pace, coming through the meadow, and a blur of horse legs behind them," Beatrix said.

Avelina's pulse quickened, a vein throbbing in her neck. "Marcus. He's come for me."

Beatrix grabbed her by the wrist and began pulling her to the center of the room.

"Let me go," Avelina said. Digging in her heels, she wrenched her arm.

Uhrl had pushed the table aside and was lifting two of the floorboards.

"Christ, child, we don't mean to hurt you," Beatrix said, grabbing Avelina's other wrist. "In with you. Under the boards."

Uhrl beckoned Avelina, and she swiftly climbed into the hole. Beatrix was at Avelina's side, helping her scoot flat into the shallow dugout. Lined with root vegetables, there was just enough room for her to lie in the ground betwixt them.

"You too," Uhrl said.

"I will not, you old bird," Beatrix said, smacking him away. "They know me. And you. They'll kill her."

Uhrl hurriedly placed the boards over her, tight so only a sliver of light shown through a crack. Beatrix's face hung over her as Uhrl fashioned the last board into place. "Silence, child. Make a sound and we're all to meet the good Lord today."

Avelina grimaced, shaking against the cold earth as she heard the table pushed back into place above her.

Pressed tightly on all sides, Avelina's hand flew to cover her mouth, afraid she would whimper in fear. She was locked in place. As good as buried alive. Again.

She heard the door open and the shuffling steps of Beatrix and Uhrl as they exited the house. Her hearing was muffled, but the pounding of the horses reverberated through the ground as they neared the house.

Avelina strained to hear voices. Beatrix was easy. There were men. Many, but muffled. She closed her eyes and listened for Marcus. Waiting. Breathe bated.

The wooden door scraped against the floorboards, and a heavier pair of feet entered the house. Then another. Then another.

"Where's the girl?" a deep, gravelly voice said, walking the length of the room above her.

"She's not here, Josef." Beatrix. By the door.

"Where is she?"

"Off somewhere," Beatrix said.

"That's too bad." A second man. He sounded younger. Near Beatrix. Not moving.

The deep-voiced man. Beatrix had called him Josef. His steps continued until they were over her head, at the table directly above her.

Who were these men?

"I'd wager she took downriver," Beatrix said. "With her goats. To Orion's place."

The goats. They were looking for Rose.

"Then why did I see them in the yard?"

The second man moved to the table, pulling a chair back and sitting himself upon it. Dust fell through the slither between the floorboards, and Avelina closed her eyes against it.

"Not all of them," Beatrix said. "She probably chased that favorite of hers."

Now her feet, lighter than the men, walked toward the fire. The scraping of the pot.

"You know she's only a child," Beatrix said. "And the girl is simple." She walked back toward the table and two plates landed atop it. "You know she gets lost sometimes when she goes a-ways downriver."

The other man sat and scooted the bench beneath him. "Is the dog with her, then, Bea? These men might be interested in a good tracking dog."

"*Hmpf.* You don't see her here, do you? You've already taken her mate from us," Beatrix said. "Will you eat? All of you?"

"You've got a lot of questions today, Beatrix," Josef said.

Their shadows cast over her, Avelina dared not move.

"Just a lot in my mind," Beatrix said. Her feet shuffled to the open door. "Those men. Who are they that ride with you?"

"Mercenaries," Josef said.

"They won't hurt my Uhrl, will they?" Beatrix's tone remained even. If the old woman had any fear of these men before her, her voice didn't show it. When Beatrix spoke of Uhrl, though, Avelina heard a twinge.

"They have no reason to," the second man said.

"You know them that well, Iban? Do you?" Beatrix asked. "That you trust them?"

"No, and I don't want to know them either," Iban said.

"Get them off my land," Beatrix said.

"They paid us coin to show them through the pass," Iban said. "Been a long time since we've had any."

"Whoever they're looking for is worth a fortune to them," Josef said. "That's for sure."

"Enough to betray your own kind?" Beatrix said. "Shame on you both."

The first man's bench scooted.

"You seen something, Bea?" Josef said, voice dropped so low it sent a shiver scraping over Avelina's skin. Chair pushed back, he walked to the door.

Beatrix scoffed. "All I seen is strangers riding on my land. I don't like strangers on my land. I thought I paid you two to keep them off of it."

The second man stood and walked to them.

"And you know I don't trust strangers around my Rose," she said firmly.

"I don't like them here either," Iban said.

"Then be smart about it," Beatrix said. "Keep your coin and take them toward the lowlands."

"There's none left in the lowlands," Josef said.

"*Genau*," Beatrix said. "Cross the river. It'll be an easy ride for them and keep them away from any of the poor souls hidden in these hills." She paused. "Our people have suffered enough from all sides."

Silence hung between the three of them.

Avelina heard hooves again as whoever else was outside rode about. Searching.

"Beatrix," Josef said. "Don't ever keep anything from me."

"Why would I? We have an arrangement, you and I."

"We do," Josef said. "And I want to honor it."

"Then choose a side."

There was another long silence.

"If you ever lie to me or hide anything from me, I'll burn this house to the ground around you. I'll kill your man. And I'll let Iban take the girl."

"Don't threaten me," Beatrix said. "I know well enough what will happen. But if you expect me to keep my word, then I'll have you keep yours." The door scraped across the floor. "Now get those men off my land."

CHAPTER 33

HASTENED PROMISES

———— ⌘ ————

Avelina

"WHERE IS MY LADY?"
Matthias. Matthias!

Avelina twisted her arms up, pressing her palms against the floorboards above her. Nothing. Nothing would move. She banged her hands.

"Matthias."

Still frozen in fear, she tried to scream his name. She only squeaked.

She was buried alive, for the second time in so many days.

But this time, she was trapped in what felt like a shallow grave.

Perhaps it was her time after all.

"What have you done, you beast?" Beatrix said.

Avelina banged her hands and opened her mouth to let the guttural scream break free. Dust and dirt poured into her mouth, gagging her, and she turned her head to the side. The grit tore against the back of her throat.

"She's not your lady," Beatrix hissed.

They were shouting at one another above her. Elbows dug into the dirt at her sides, Avelina pushed hard against the boards. She pressed with everything she could summon, biceps screaming against the weight above her. Tears burned as they poured from her eyes, pooling in the cold earth against her cheek. Ready to pull her under. Swallow her.

She coughed. Choking. Shaking. Slamming her palms against

the boards.

Her nerves at once frozen and on fire, panic fully set in. Like stones piled upon her chest, the weight consumed her, caving her ribs in, and forcing the air from her lungs.

She couldn't breathe. She was wheezing. Heart pounding. Dizziness. Spinning. Whirling.

Death had found her here.

Running his fingers along her. Caressing her. Seductively whispering in her ear as his fingers closed around her throat and squeezed.

Like her father before her, she would disappear. Buried. Unmarked. Lost to the earth. Ultimately ending her dynasty.

No. NO.

Matthias.

She kept repeating his name. He was there. So close.

Her fingernails dug into the boards.

She would claw her way to him if she had to.

Like an animal desperate to survive.

A splinter pierced under her nail, and she screamed.

Skin prickling. Tingling. Warm. Scraping noises above her. Ripping. Voices.

"Heaven's ghost." His voice. Right above her. His bearlike hands clamping around her wrists. Pulling her from her grave.

Body upright, the dirt in her lungs shifted. Avelina retched, mud twisting within her. She coughed and heaved and turned her body. Her stomach contracted, and vomit lurched through her throat. She choked on the mixture pouring from her, coughing and snorting when it stuck in her nose.

"I told you she was fine," Beatrix said. "Merely put her underground with the turnips. Works well enough when we aim to hide our Rose."

Matthias's large hand wiped across her face while the other held her upright.

"I've got you."

Matthias.

Her eyes readjusted and sorted through the blurry images.

She was alive. She was on her knees on the floor, his arms wrapped around her, and she welcomed them. He pulled her onto his lap, cradling her. One arm strongly around her back, the other palm holding the back of her head against him.

"I thought I lost you," he whispered. His lips pressed against her forehead, and his grip tightened around her as he squeezed her against his bare chest.

"I saved her life, which is more than you plan to do," Beatrix hissed. "Whoever this Marcus is, sending that kind of crew after the two of you. You've crossed the wrong man, Matthias. Stealing the lady's heart is only going to send her to the grave."

"Woman. Don't test me," Matthias said, stroking Avelina's cheek with his thumb.

Beatrix's face was a mix of pride and fury and defiance. Hovering over the herding dog spread across her table, her hands nimbly made work of a needle against its torso. Covered in blood, it was alive, if barely; its side rising and falling slowly yet steadily in shallow breaths. "If you hadn't saved my Rose . . ."

Young Rose was curled into a chair at the table's end. Her face was buried against the whimpering pup, swaddled and clutched in her lap, while she slowly petted the injured dog's snout with two gentle fingers.

The old man shuffled beside Avelina and held out his hand, giving her a weak smile. "Come, lady. Warm yourself by the fire. Have a drink. And get right."

Matthias's grip on Avelina loosened when she put her hand into Uhrl's. Propping his other hand into her elbow, Uhrl helped her rise and settle onto a bench he'd scooted beside the fire pit, where the bricks pulsed from the embers within.

"Here now." Uhrl placed a blanket around her shoulders. After feeding the flames a fresh log, he settled beside her and handed her a clay mug. She took a sip, and a toasty spiced wine hit her lips. Hard on her throat at first, it coated it and warmed her from the inside out.

Avelina's eyes continued to adjust. It was later in the day. The light glowing around the drawn shutters had dulled, and what slim shadows there were grew longer across the floorboards. Propped against the wall, Matthias grimaced, holding the tie on his arm. Streaks of dried blood ran from beneath it.

"Sit and let me tend your wound, soldier." Beatrix's eyes narrowed at him and the axe at his side. She crossed her arms, still staring down the man towering over her. Even rising on her toes, she was two heads shorter than him. "And you'll tell us everything. Who you are and what you plan to do."

Matthias dragged himself to the table and sat as instructed. "The less you know, the better you are for it."

Beatrix wiped her hands on her apron and unwrapped Matthias's wound. Her lips pursed as she inspected the darkening gashes. "*Hmpf.* Making friends, I see."

"My name . . ." Avelina cleared her throat. She owed the lady an answer, and why was she hiding anyway? "I am Princess Avelina of Leuceria."

"Leuceria?" Uhrl said, his stubbled chin trembling. His bushy brows cinched as he blew across the top of his own mug of piping drink. "You're a long way from home, my dear."

Beatrix lifted a small wicker container and slowly poured liquid from its glass neck onto Matthias's arm, dousing the wound. Avelina heard him suck air through his teeth even from across the room. Beatrix prepped another needle and line, as she'd done to sew the dog's stomach, and took hold of Matthias. Avelina shuddered on his behalf and dug her heels into the floorboard.

"Matthias . . ." Avelina paused and straightened her back. "The King's Sword is charged with bringing me safely through to the capital. I'm to be the wife of the king."

Beatrix snorted. "We have no king here."

Uhrl's knee bounced and tapped against hers. "Which king?"

"Yours," Avelina said. "King Girault."

Uhrl's eyebrow raised. "At Ewigsburg? That's a-ways from here."

"*Of all the men* . . . I don't care whose wife you're supposed to be," Beatrix said. "You've fallen for the Sword."

"You are mistaken." Avelina averted her eyes, knowing her denial pained and pointless.

"*Ach,* there's more than one way to be felled by a sword," Beatrix said, frowning and digging her needle digging into his flesh. "And *you*, you ox. Taking her to that man who calls himself a king. He doesn't deserve her. And she deserves more than what he'll make of her. You neither protect her from him or her heart from you."

"You know nothing." Matthias grumbled. "I do my duty, and

so does she."

"Bea. Please," Uhrl said. "Tend to the wound and leave the man be."

They sat in silence while she finished.

The fire spit and hissed beside them until it collapsed upon itself. Uhrl rose to tend it, readjusting the embers with an iron poker. Collecting them beneath the pot dangling on the trifold, he then ladled himself a mug of warmed wine. He moved to the window and pushed the shutter open, letting in a whoosh of evening air.

Beatrix retrieved a folded shirt from a chest and brought it to Matthias.

"The least I could do for you saving Uhrl's dog." Waving off Matthias's thanks, Beatrix laid a hand on Rose's shoulder and cast an eye on Avelina. "But I'll speak true. I could've given you to those men. Easily. But I didn't. It wasn't for you I did it. It was for the girl." Lines welled around Beatrix mouth. "You'll be taking her with you."

Avelina swallowed and glanced at Uhrl, whose back remained to them all.

"For your care and your hospitality, you have my thanks, truly, but I cannot take a child with me," Matthias said. "With these riders about, it's not safe."

"She's not safe here," Beatrix said. "It won't be long until one of these men takes her, like they did to her mother and her kin. Uhrl found her, and we took her in and kept her safe as best we could. Take her. Find her work. With this one."

"I would like that," Avelina said, getting to her feet. "Matthias, she did help us. If what Beatrix says is true, we cannot leave her to that fate."

"We don't have the time," he said, exasperated.

"Beatrix, Uhrl," Avelina said, ignoring his protest. "You have my word. Young Rose will come with me, into my household. I will take care of her."

"Avelina, you cannot make such promises," Matthias said.

The sharpness of his tone sent a storm of emotions through Avelina, boiling her blood. "I do not make them lightly."

Matthias ran a hand across his forehead and pinched his temples.

"You have nothing to give. Nothing," Matthias said, his face dark and severe. "This is no game you can win."

"Game?" Avelina said, shocked.

"The danger is that you think you have power. And at Ewigsburg," he said, shaking his head. "How many titles have you had Avelina? What have they brought you?"

"Don't, Matthias. *Don't*."

"What will being queen bring you?" Matthias said.

"How am I to know?" Avelina said, putting her hands on her hips. "You tell me nothing of my future. Only that you could not promise me happiness."

Matthias shook his fists and growled.

"What would you have of me?" Avelina asked.

He spun on his heel and marched toward her. Chest heaving, he craned his neck and loomed above her. "I *cannot* have you, can I?"

She felt the color slip from her face.

"You made that clear," she spat at him, her voice so hard that it hurt her jaw. "But you'll have the freedom my title earns for you."

"Your titles," Matthias said, scowling.

Avelina leaned in, refusing to back down. "What would you have me do? Forsake my forefathers? My duty? Or should I throw my titles away to suit you? Which one? Which one bothers you the most? When you call me *your queen* or when you call me *his*? Tell me."

Matthias fell back a step and turned his head from her.

Avelina stomped her foot. "Or do you see me as all men do? Only in how I can suit your needs?"

"Heavens, no, woman, and you know that," he said, stricken.

"I told you who I was. Whose I wanted to be. And you turned away from me," Avelina said. "I made that choice, and you've reminded me that I don't have one."

His eyes rounded, and the corners of his lips fell. He stared blankly above her, refusing to meet her stare.

Avelina saw movement out of the corner of her eye. She had almost forgotten they weren't alone.

"I pray you both to listen," Uhrl said, still staring out toward the pasture. "I believe you intend to do what is right. You may have started upon another path, but it is no accident the mountains brought you here. There's a reason you warm yourselves at my hearth." After a thoughtful drink, he set his mug aside and turned to them. "You're still a long way from the city. I'll give you my cart and horses if you help my Rose."

Beatrix's skin paled. "You're mad."

Uhrl lifted both palms, waving her off.

Beatrix crossed to him and tapped a finger against his chest. "You mean to kill yourself with work, you old bat?"

Uhrl put a calm hand on her shoulder and, slanting his head to the side, looked her in the eye. "Sister, don't argue with me."

Beatrix scrunched her face and hard lines ran under her eyes. "They'll know what we've done. And they won't take kindly to it. Josef has made his threats plain and often."

"He has, I know. We're soon for the grave either way, and then what?" He turned to Matthias, his weathered face drawn and voice hoarse. "There is no other option. It tears my heart to send her away, but I'd sooner be dead than miss the chance to give her a better life."

Hanging her head, Beatrix tapped her fingers across her forehead. "You're right, brother."

Avelina swallowed and turned to the girl. Still sitting in her chair, she had curled into herself. Knees drawn toward her chest, her slippered feet dangling over the chair's edge. She twirled the pup's ear, now asleep in her arms. A line of tears rolled from her rounded eyes. Her small mouth lay open, but she looked to dare not speak. Avelina's stomach fell at seeing her weep, and she took a step toward Uhrl, hopeful to help. "I can pay you. You could buy ten carts and more horses to work."

"Lady, I thank you, but they'd be stolen soon after you brought them here," Beatrix said. "There's no law here. Those men travel between homesteads, sucking us dry, and act like they're helping us. They'll kill us as soon as the day comes it suits them."

Matthias exhaled and turned to Uhrl. "It would get us there quicker to meet my men. I'll have it brought back to you and then some. The king would reward your helping his betrothed."

Betrothed.

Even without infliction, the word still dealt a blow to her chest.

This was it. They may have well been strangers. Even with all they'd shared. Even standing so close to him his scent curled around her, making her feverish for him. He was gone. His walls reframed and rebuilding around him, and with every passing second, she begged her heart to erect her own.

Beatrix stepped between Avelina and Matthias, breaking the tension.

"You'll come back, then?" Beatrix snapped at Matthias. "Your king will allow it?"

"I'm a man of my word," Matthias said.

"I want to believe you, Matthias; I do. We've not known many just men out here. Men have marched through these mountains my whole life. The only thing that changes is the standard they carry and which direction they're going."

"I'm sorry," Avelina whispered. "That you had to live like that."

"We're a borderland, lady. They fight over us, but nobody fights for us." Beatrix crossed her arms. "Well, I'll get to packing you out. But maybe as a service to me, when you deliver this lady to your king, you can deliver a message?"

"Surely," Matthias said.

"If he thinks to tax us. Take our food and harvest like he's tilled the ground himself. To take our men away to build his castles when they could be here trying to rebuild our homes. To take our sons away to fight his wars, one battle after another. Fighting for *nothing*. Nothing that *matters*. Leaving our daughters to toil alone and defend themselves and their children," Beatrix said. "We've had our fill of false men. One generation to the next, it's always the same. If he will not be a righteous and true king, if he won't support and protect us, then he can leave us the hell alone. We do not need the crown."

CHAPTER 34

HORSES. A CART. A PRINCESS. A GIRL, A KID, AND A PUP

Avelina

THEY'D BEEN TRAVELING FOR THREE days.
Horses. A cart. A princess. A girl, a kid, and a pup.
We might as well raise a flag and bring a band along.

Avelina had understood when Matthias protested. She knew he wasn't angry. He was afraid. Anxious. Irritated to the point he had stopped talking to her. Instead of traveling quietly through the shadows, they now rode openly on the roads. Easily seen. Easily attacked. Their pace, at least, had quickened.

Avelina had watched the hours pass away in fields of grain, winding rivers, and rolling mountains. Unable to sleep, she watched the movement of black-on-black passing before her, trying to make out anything in the layers of shadows. Burrowed in the cart beneath blankets, Avelina wrapped her arms around Rose's shoulders.

Avelina was happy to help her. Take her to safety. Provide her a home. Avelina was thankful she would have a companion, though she grieved Rose the loss of her home. There was a genuine love and care for the girl there, and Avelina hoped to offer her the same.

Matthias would soon leave. He was ready to find his men. To gain his freedom. And, she believed now, to be rid of her.

It's so dark here. One moment gray and the next a glorious blue. Misty streams of pale light had started to poke sideways through the tree trunks, stretching thinly until they disappeared into the forest floor. The rhythmic turning of the well-worn wooden wheels on the dirt road had lulled her into a trance until she caught the chirping of a few birds high above her.

Morning. The denseness of the forest began to thin as they reached the edge, and their path broke free of the huddled trees. The orange crest of the sun was visible at the horizon, spilling warmth as its blanket unfurled over rolling hills. Fields thick with golden grains alternated with green fields glistening with dew or littered with animals, clusters of slate rooftops mixed between them in the distance. Passing closer to the larger homesteads and farms, unfamiliar scents—such as the foul manure freshly fertilizing the fields—caught on the wind and invaded her nose. She wrinkled her nose at the strong scent, as she settled back within the cart.

The cart had moved along steadily over the king's lands without incident. The ride peaceful, she welcomed the new scenery. They had traveled along the river, twisting about at times to follow it as it roared downstream from them. Occasionally, she saw men along the river with their sons, drawing in fish from the clear waters. The sounds of the rushing waters shifting around scattered pockets of stone made for a pleasant mixture with the sounds of the carriage rattling along on the path.

This leg of the journey had been much calmer, but Avelina was still anxious here at the end of it. Piecing together the images of the various stone castles and fortresses they had passed on the way, nestled into valleys or along riverbanks or atop rolling hills, she imagined what awaited her at Ewigsburg. Her new home. A new life. There was a satisfaction in that, now that the excitement of their passage through the mountains had waned. A satisfaction, but not excitement. That would come later. Hopefully.

Avelina looked down at her hands. She'd been rubbing a small section of the linen between her fingers. Taking the far corners, she pulled the skirt taut and re-draped it over her legs. It wasn't as fancy as her old silks, without embroidery, pearls, or lace sewn into it. But it fit well, and it was clean. She was tidied and feeling a sense of the familiar beckoning her closer.

Shifting on her bottom, a clump of jewels pressed hard into her thigh. Her lip tugged, guessing which they might be. Surely, she had lost some along the way. That any had survived this trip, secured by her amateur stitches, seemed a small triumph. That she had some part of her past with her, of a home she might never see again, seemed a small gift. That she had her mother's books and her father's tattered notes, rewrapped and buried within Alif's knapsack beside her, seemed a small miracle.

Do not show this to the king. To anyone.

Matthias's words of warning whispered at her ear, and she pulled the knapsack closer, tucking it out of sight beneath a blanket. Sighing, she leaned over the side of the cart, hoping to lose herself—and her thoughts of him—to a better view.

The midmorning air still clung with dew. Inhaling it deeply, she felt cleansed; exhaling, her breath, mixing with the brisk air, tickled her lips and stirred the sensation of his kiss. Her fingertips rose and touched her lips. Remembering. His lips on hers, the warmth, the friction, the taste. The longing she'd felt, then lingering disappointment when he'd left her.

The carriage jolted, tipping at an angle, and both girls grabbed at the wall to steady themselves. Pulled forward quickly, again they were rolling along. Avelina squeezed her hands together in her lap and smiled at Rose, hoping her cheeks weren't as red as they felt.

Rose watched her, twirling her small fingers through the pup's black-and-white spotted ear. "I bet you're excited to meet the king."

"I am," Avelina said, though her stomach fell a bit.

"He's old. Like Beatrix."

Avelina wasn't sure whether to laugh or cringe.

"Older than the two of us, surely. Especially if he already has his own child. A son, I believe." Avelina looked away, eager to change the subject. "I will appreciate your companionship and your honesty. It will be more than helpful as I get settled and learn more."

"We'll stay with you, right, ma'am?" Rose said, pulling her babes tighter to her. It was at least the tenth time Rose had asked her, desperate for the reassurance. "You don't mean to send us away?"

"You'll live with me," Avelina said. Leaning forward, she placed her hand on Rose's and squeezed. "*I promise.*"

The girl gave a weak smile and then looked away.

Avelina blinked, looking away as well. She hated to admit it, but she was worried about the king's reaction to Rose and the pair of animals resting on her legs, whose heads the young girl affectionately scratched. She trusted the girl and wanted her close, and on her own staff preferably.

Rose was pleasant. Beatrix had referred to her several times as "simple," though Avelina believed that had been to divert the man who searched for her. *That Iban.* They may live simply, but both Beatrix and young Rose were clever.

Though Rose had mutely cried the first day of their travel, she had become quite animated on the second. Avelina was glad for it. She could see that Rose enjoyed conversation and was eager to learn. Eager to share what she knew. While nestled together, Rose acted as guide, pointing out places and telling stories as they rode. Names of villages no bigger than a collection of small structures. The type of fish that were pulled from each river (and the one that curiously swam upstream each year). Birthplaces and homesteads of powerful and influential families whose names she'd never come across in her studies.

The young girl's mind was impressive. She retained information with as much enthusiasm as she had for caring for her young kid and pup. Avelina appreciated that, and she would do what she could to encourage her studies. Perhaps even adopt her father's dreams as her own by building a great library or a school or even a university. She could teach Rose to read. Maybe they could find a sunny hill where Liesl and Lukas could play while the two of them could sit each afternoon.

That would be lovely.

Avelina pulled herself back from the side of the cart and rested her back against the side. She closed her eyes and stretched. She was again without a proper night's sleep. The stifling pressure of seeing her new home weighed on her, and the sharp discomfort mounted in the small of her back with each jarring turn of the wheels beneath them. They had been traveling with brief stops for the horses, but today Matthias said they would push on.

Today was the day.

Today was the day she would meet the king.

Seated above her, driving the horses, Matthias had his back toward her and hers to him. The longer they'd traveled, the less they'd spoken, and the more her heart had sunk within her. She well knew her feelings for him. She had made them plain enough when she'd humiliated herself.

The thought of it still made her heart ache, but she was determined to move on. It was their secret, and she knew he wouldn't share it. He would do her that honor.

Her feelings, and his for her, were forbidden. Forbidden feelings that must be forgotten.

Though she trusted him. Enjoyed his company. Yearned for his touch. Simply wanted to hear his voice. She was not to be his. She must dismiss it as folly. The folly of a young lady fallen for the man who rescued her, who did not know any better. She resigned herself to her fated role and the king he had won her for to begin with.

They turned around a bend, and Avelina saw Rose's eyes light.

"Ewigsburg, ma'am," Rose said. "We're here."

CHAPTER 35

KING'S PARK

Matthias

H E COULD HEAR IT BEFORE he saw it.
King's Park.

There was no mistaking that sound. As they crested the hills after the lower village, the rumble rolled into them. A throng of voices, all together cheering, thundering across the field. The king was a madman for a show, thriving on the attention and adoration of his people, and the building offered him another stage. The pageantry had grown; the recognition had spread across borders, calling men, and their coin, forth. What the city put in, it made back through sales, causing both the city's economy and the king's reputation to flourish. Alliances were made on those seats.

It was smart, it was strategic, and it was spectacular.

The oblong stadium rose high above the southwest city wall. Built where the forest had been cleared decades ago for melees of old, the stadium was encased within an extension of the southwest city wall. The king had chosen to abandon the melee long ago and funnel the expense into the building of his stadium. Boasting two great spectator stone towers, with the king's seat positioned for the best view, four tiered wooden stories stretched between them for the citizens' use.

Near the city square, it was always busy. The building was a chameleon, morphing to serve the king's current mood or obsession. Trade shows. Markets. Theater. Sport. Census. But there was only one event that fueled the crowd so, that brought them to their feet and caused the roaring wave booming toward them.

The king's favorite—the tournament.

The hairs on his forearm rose.

"Matthias."

Her voice startled him. He glanced back at Avelina. Her hands gripping the side rim of the cart, she stretched over the side, peeking ahead of them.

"What is that noise?" she said.

"Tournament," he said, turning back toward the road. He tapped the reins, urging the horses forward. They were almost there.

He should have anticipated a tournament. A celebration of the battle won. The harvest was well underway. The closer they'd come to the city, the more the roads had filled with people. Either traveling to the capital for market or for sport. Even though a tournament meant safe passage for the participants across borders—or should—there were always others with malicious intentions drawn to such crowds. There was theft. Cutpurses. Random bouts of drunken idiocy. But there was also mayhem. Violence. Abductions. Some seeking ransom opportunities and others . . . only seeking the opportunity.

They needed to pass these last few acres without drawing attention to themselves. The closer they came however, the more restless his passengers seemed to become. Whenever he'd think they'd finally settled, he'd again hear them. Shuffling about in the cart behind him. From one side to the other. From the back to the front. The ladies, talking endlessly and occasionally laughing. The puppy, yelping loudly and hungrily whining. Today though, that kid goat of theirs . . . *Lukas* . . . seemed to be set just behind Matthias's shoulder, nudging him, and ceaselessly bleating.

"Settle, ladies," he said. "I have no intention of stopping to chase another goat should it *fall* out."

Matthias turned an eye on the kid. One ear flopped comically backwards; the tiny goat tilted its small, white head. Lukas's tail wagged, watching him, and Matthias rolled his eyes.

"*Ach then, wee one,*" he grumbled, turning forward once more.

"Matthias. *Matthias.*" Young Rose this time. "Have you been to the tournament?"

"Yes," he said. "Many times."

"Matthias?" Young Rose said, tapping his back. "Can we go?"

He didn't answer. His anticipation of their arrival had grown with each turn of the wheels below him. Now that they were here, his nerves rattled. His stomach soured, churning from the chaos and uncertainty that awaited them.

Jorn. And young Alif. Had they made it here? Had they outrun the Leucerian assassins, or had he sent them forward only to die alone?

And Reymund. The rest of his men with him. Had they found safe passage? Or had they been lost or delayed? Or had his own delay caused them to lose hope and flee?

Like a battlefield, tents were littered across the fields, creeping up to the city walls as the population of the city would have doubled. Tripled for the larger events. Rooms within the city would be bulging. The castle would be filled to capacity. Its suites would house the highest-ranking visitors, while their entourages littered the halls and undercroft. The workers would be spinning. The wine and ale and food would be flowing to support the bellies of those crowds. The soldiers would have been called in as extra security. Tradesmen would line the streets with wares for the spectators to buy. The king's stables would be full.

And the king. The king would be entertaining. He would be occupied. Hopefully jovial. Hopefully ready to welcome the princess seated quietly behind him. And ready to keep his word.

Matthias exhaled, eager to expel the gnawing sense of dread mounting within.

"Have courage, ladies," he said to them as much as to himself. "We're almost there."

PART FOUR
EWIGSBURG

END OF SEPTEMBER 1479
FIRST QUARTER MOON

CHAPTER 36

EWIGSBURG

Avelina

MOVING TO THE OTHER SIDE of the cart, Avelina could see their destination at last.

Ewigsburg was easily the most impressive castle Avelina had seen on their journey. Reaching high above a craggy cliff wall, it dwarfed the fortresses they had passed along the way to get here. Ewigsburg's size and beauty couldn't rival the grand palace of her own—there simply was nothing like Leuceria—but the way it sat on the cliffs, towers reaching into the clouds on this warm morning, commanding the lands as far as the horizons, took her breath away. It rose out of the white stone, without evidence of a sharply set end or beginning, mount and castle blended as one, as if it had been pulled forth, stretched toward the heavens, from the very hands of God himself.

Defenses sat strategically on lower cliffs. Rings of walls from the base to protect it and the city nestled on the hills below it, layering protection against any army of men daring to attempt to reach the heart of the castle. The base and slant of the mount were thick with trees that grew steadily until towers began poking through in concentric circles along the west ridge. Halfway up the mount, the angled slant stopped, turning into a steep cliff on the east side, the castle starting upon the edge of it. The castle, and its city on the hill, stood well protected.

The path to the gate twisted and turned like a snake as they crept closer to the side of the mountain. The roads became congested with travelers headed in both directions. The air was thick with noise, booming from within the city. Reaching the first wall, they were met by a towering gatehouse. It was one of several entrances in a great stone wall that stretched from one side of the cliff to as far as she could see, disappearing around the bend. Men called from above the wall, and Matthias pulled the horses to a stop.

"Stay down," he said over his shoulder and hopped from the seat.

His low tone rattled her, and Avelina pulled Rose to her side. The two of them scrunched into the cart, listening to the sound of Matthias's steps across the pebbled road. A bit of muffled conversation swiftly changed to excited guffaws and laughter. Words she couldn't understand, but the knot in her gut loosened.

They were here. Finally.

A horn blew, twice and long. There was a loud clattering of iron, followed by a rattling of chains. The gates were opening. The cart shook, and the wheels started moving beneath them. Avelina looked up, looking for Matthias, not having heard him climb back onto the cart, but he wasn't there. Peeking over the wooden rail, she saw him in front of the horse, guiding it on foot through the gates.

Avelina turned back around when she felt Rose's arms tightly link around her waist. The girl's cheek dug into Avelina's shoulder. Rose was shivering, and Avelina laid her hand on top of the girl's head. Surely, being in a city would be intimidating for a girl that had grown up in the mountains. So much noise. So many smells. So much change.

Avelina's eyes darted around her as they passed through the thick walls. A footpath was to their right, leading crowds of people to a separate inspection station swarming with guards. Men-at-arms stood ready on both sides, some in red-and-gray tunics covering their mail, safeguarding the gate. A few men held the collars of large dogs. One with thick gray legs barked at their horse feverishly while the others paced back and forth with their masters.

They rode slowly through an open court towards the second gate. Walls three stories high surrounded them on either side. Dotted with arrow slits, she noted guards in each, armed and ready to rain hell down upon them. After passing through a second gate, they turned quickly off the main path and onto an alleyway along the inside of the city wall. The ground changed beneath them. The clicking of the cobblestones was replaced with the rutting of the wheels against dirt. Avelina hunkered down and waited for them to stop.

CHAPTER 37

ROOM AT THE INN

Matthias

"COME, PRINCESS," MATTHIAS SAID. "YOU'RE home." He unlocked the hinge on the back of the cart. It swung down hard with a clang, and a cloud of dust rose from the hay his crew were crowded upon. They were there in a line, wrapped within a blanket, nestled against the back of the cart, staring blankly at him. The princess, arms draped protectively around her new ward. The nuzzled pup, its paw stretched over young Rose. The goat, ear flicking in its sleep.

Matthias squeezed the bridge of his nose and then, hands on his hips, stretched his back.

Enough riding. Time to get her ready for the king.

A voice called to him from the alehouse doorway, and Matthias grinned.

Reymund.

Reymund waved his arm wildly above his head and began making his way toward him. The smile on his face warmed Matthias's heart. His brother looked rested, happy, and was moving well with his cane. This was a good day for Reymund.

Stretched tall and thin, Reymund was walking more upright with his cane. His chest not so curved into itself today under crooked shoulders. His hips were still tilted, but not as sharply, leaving only his one leg slightly bent. Matthias jogged to him and wrapped Reymund in a tight embrace, lifting him from the ground.

"*Ach* man, I'm so glad to see you," Matthias said. He put Reymund back down and held both shoulders warmly. "So very glad."

"And I you, Matthias. The waters were calm, and I was well looked after. My voyage was easy and uneventful yet entertaining," Reymund said, smiling. "Better to arrive early and see to what must be done. There is much to do here, my brother." His smile dropped, and he grabbed Matthias's arm. "But after a moment's reprieve." Reymund looked around Matthias's shoulder. "The princess?"

Matthias rested a hand on his hip and cocked his head toward the lot in the cart. "I have her."

At the cart, Reymund handed his cane to Matthias and grasped the side, peering into the back. His eyebrows furrowed, and he rubbed his balding head. "And a few stowaways, I see."

Matthias shrugged his shoulders, and Reymund laughed.

"Should I even ask?"

"Not today, brother," Matthias said, shaking his head.

Reymund put his hand on his chest, smiled, and bowed deeply to the princess. "Princess Avelina. My dearest lady, I bid you welcome. My name is Reymund."

Avelina straightened her shoulders. Her eyelashes fluttered, and a solemn change washed over her face.

"Thank you," she said, tipping her head to him in return. "I remember you. Delighted to see you again, sir."

"My lady," Reymund said, gesturing toward the alehouse. "I have fresh clothes for you, as well as a maid to attend you. Your companions will be taken care of."

"Thank you, Reymund," Avelina said with a small smile. She took a deep breath, exhaled, and climbed toward the rear of the cart.

"Aren't you a sight, you arse!"

Jorn.

Matthias turned to see Jorn, grinning with arms stretched wide, walking toward him.

"Brother." Matthias laughed and embraced Jorn in a tight hug.

"I was starting to fear we lost you," Jorn said. Jorn slammed the mug he was holding against Matthias's back and stepped away.

He took a drink, and ale poured down both sides of his beard. He wiped it with his sleeve.

"Alif?"

"*Ach,* the boy is fine," Jorn said, waving his hand dismissively. "Not for lack of trying to get himself killed."

Jorn turned an eye on the princess, walking with her hand tucked within Reymund's arm toward the alehouse.

"Never again, brother," Jorn said. He laid a hand on Matthias's shoulder and gave him a stern look. "Where you go, I go."

"Understood," Matthias said.

Rose hopped off the edge of the cart, one of her babes tucked tightly beneath each arm. All three faces stared at Jorn curiously and then turned to Matthias, waiting.

"What's this, then?" Jorn asked, gesturing to the girl.

"They're with the princess."

Jorn raised an eyebrow at him.

"*Ach,*" Jorn snickered. "I left you on one side of a mountain alone with the princess, and you stumble down the other, a month later, with a barn on wheels?"

"Another time, brother," Matthias said, shaking his head. "I'm not one for stories today."

Jorn's face fell, and he lifted his mug toward the alehouse door. "*Ja.* Well. Come rest and eat, brother, because I've got a hell of one to tell you."

CHAPTER 38

OATH-BREAKER

—∞—

Matthias

MATTHIAS'S STOMACH DROPPED. "A SON?"

"A healthy boy," Reymund said.

Matthias rubbed his thumb across the rim of his clay mug. No wonder there was a tournament. The king would celebrate this news. A full cradle. And a *son*.

"Oh, you wait," Jorn said. "There's more."

Matthias looked at him over his ale, ran his tongue over his teeth, and set the mug down.

Jorn was avoiding his gaze. Chin tilted down, his green eyes were dull, staring at the ring he spun in circles on the table. His red locks hung loose over his shoulders blending into his beard. Almost covering the shaken look that twisted the end of his mouth.

Something was wrong. Very wrong.

Not getting his attention, Matthias looked to the wooden stairs across the room. Avelina was up there, preparing for the ride through the city. To the castle. And the king.

Alif, sitting guard across the bottom step, met his look with a drawn face.

Matthias frowned. He was broken down. His arm, though healing, hurt like hell. He was filthy, weary, and not one for bad news. He leaned forward on the table, looking back and forth between his brothers. "What is it?"

Still not looking at him, Jorn flicked his ring again and set it spinning in front of them. His nose wrinkled with a sharp inhale.

"Your king is an arse," Jorn said.

"That's not news," Matthias said. He laid a palm on the table and turned to Reymund. "Reymund?"

Reymund laid his hand on Matthias's wrist. "The king . . ."

"What's he done?" Matthias said.

"He's taken a wife," Reymund said.

Matthias's heart stopped in his chest. "What?"

"He's married another," Reymund said.

"He didn't," Matthias said as a flood of warmth rolled through his biceps. "Jorn?"

Jorn's head kicked back, and he rolled his neck around, still not looking at Matthias.

"It's true," Jorn said. "I had Alif ride to the wall and speak to the men."

Matthias put a hand across his mouth and exhaled slowly. He leaned back in his chair and pushed his palms down the length of his thighs.

"Who?" Matthias said.

"His mistress," Jorn said.

"Lilith? Eger's wife?" Matthias said.

"Duke Eger's dead," Reymund said.

"No." Matthias shook his head, stunned.

"Three weeks now," Jorn said. He crossed his arms and turned to Matthias. "Little more than convenient. She birthed the babe upon the army's return. Eger died. The king took her as his wife. The tournament to celebrate *the new prince* was announced. All within a matter of days."

"Girault couldn't have been so brazen," Matthias said.

"Mind your words," Reymund said, leaning in. "This room is friendly, but there may be others about."

"Your king always hated Eger," Jorn said, lowering his voice. "Those two were like dogs growing up, trying to piss on the same stump and only hitting each other's legs. Both with a claim to the crown that your king took after the wars."

"But this," Matthias said.

"The crown was never good enough, Matthias," Jorn said. "That snake's goal has always been to take everything Eger had. Everything. And humiliate him, taking Eger's wife as his mistress.

Leaving Eger only with daughters."

"The Duchess Lilith was a young mother then," Reymund said, frowning. His shoulders twitched. "The king had already brought her daughters here as his wards."

"*Ja*, she was. And I do not blame the woman for following her daughters to court," Jorn said, nodding his head to Reymund. Jorn leaned back against his chair and resumed spinning his ring. It ran a small line across the surface, light flicking from the metal until it slowed and the ring fell onto its side. "Like most of the daughters of the great houses, the lady's been a puppet to the men around her. Caught in their never-ending rivalries."

"Seems like a theme," Matthias muttered under his breath.

"Now that your king's finally got a son off of her, and Eger *dies*, he marries Lilith," Jorn said. "He gets everything. Your king finally wins."

Matthias slammed his fists on the table. Once and again.

"That rotting . . ." Matthias said.

"I told you not to trust him," Jorn said. "The man shits in his hand and then asks you to shake on it. He's nothing but a—"

"That doesn't help, Jorn," Reymund said.

"No. It doesn't. But our brother needs to watch who he's loyal to," Jorn said.

"Your meaning?" Matthias growled.

"The man doesn't deserve your allegiance. He never has," Jorn said.

"We gave him our oaths, Jorn. Long ago," Matthias said.

"You did. I didn't say a word," Jorn said.

Matthias groaned and covered his face with his hands.

"Now he sends you off on this mission. You nearly get yourself killed. You've done what you were asked to do, and we're no better off for it. He promised us our freedom, but we're not free," Jorn said. He pointed above them. "Your princess is stuck here. And we've somehow inherited a ward and her pets. More mouths to feed without a pot between us to—"

"There has to be an explanation," Matthias said.

"It's simple. Your king's betrayed you. Again. And expects you to heel," Jorn said. "He's betrayed you. Her. All of us. Cast off like bones to crows."

Matthias groaned, rubbing his temples. His leg tapped furiously beneath him, knocking against the table leg.

"The man is only loyal to himself. We all know it," Jorn said.

"*That rotting* . . . I'll kill him."

Jorn smacked the table, shook his fist, and pointed at Matthias. "Now *that's* what I said." He leaned back against his chair and crossed his arms in front of him, smiling.

Matthias pushed the plates in front of him away. He no longer could stomach the smell of the pies, though he hadn't eaten since Metzlingen. He propped both elbows on the table and leaned his mouth against his fists.

Girault had done it again.

That arse. That total and completely selfish arse.

Matthias had seen him do it before. Break an oath to men. Or if not break it, bend it to his new will. And craft a good enough excuse that made people believe it was all in their best interests. Or their idea. Or their choice.

But what did this mean for them? They were supposed to be free. Finished.

The king had left a tangled web of oaths dangling behind him. By breaking one thread, were they all to fall? One after another? Girault's word to marry the princess. His pledge to honor Prince Siegfried's word. Matthias's own word. To keep Avelina safe. To his men that they'd be free. All they had to do was ride up the hill and deliver the princess.

Avelina.

His gut bottomed out when he thought of her.

"Matthias?" Reymund said. "We must devise a plan."

Matthias side-eyed him.

"I say we ride," Jorn said. "Go and don't look back."

"Where?" Matthias asked, holding his palm up. He shook his head and leaned back, staring at the thatched roof above him.

"North. To Hamburg," Jorn said. "We have friends there who can help us reach the sea."

"And do what with the princess?" Reymund asked.

"Take her with us," Jorn said.

Matthias turned to Jorn, who nodded at him.

"The king sent us to Leuceria in his name and with his chest of gold. He's paid plenty of coin for her, and he's expecting her," Reymund said. "He'd have us followed until he caught us. Heaven only knows what would become of her."

"Then we give her to him," Jorn said, tapping the ring he held between his fingers twice on the table. "We leave her at the gates and go."

"I will not," Matthias said.

"Not what, brother?" Jorn said. "Leave her?"

"It might be our best option, Matthias," Reymund said.

"I will not abandon her now," Matthias said.

Jorn and Reymund looked at Matthias and then each other.

"No, Matthias," Avelina said, her voice breaking through the tension in the room. Matthias stood, his chair scraping loudly against the floor, and turned to the steps. She stood there, hand on the railing, a few steps above a wide-eyed Alif. "You will leave me at the gate and go. I will find my way."

"Avelina," Matthias said. "I won't have it."

She tucked her hair behind her ear and pulled the blanket wrapped around her shoulders tighter around her.

"Yes, you will," she said.

"Avelina . . ." He took a step toward her, but she stiffened, and he stopped.

"Just because another man proves false doesn't mean that you should do the same. You go back on your word once, and it becomes worthless. I will not let that happen to you after what you have brought me through," she said, lifting her chin high. "My path has changed, but it doesn't mean that yours must do the same. I will not see misfortune befall you, any of you, because of me. It's my choice. But tomorrow. If I'm not to be somebody's wife, there's no reason to make haste. I'll take one more night. For me."

Avelina gathered her skirt, turned, and disappeared back up the stairs.

"She's right. Another day won't matter," Reymund said.

"He's right, brother," Jorn said. "Let her rest. Heaven only knows what waits for her there."

Matthias stared at the empty stairs, wanting to follow her but knowing he couldn't. Grabbing the back of his chair, he withstood the urge to slam it against the table. He sighed, leaving it, and turned his back to them all. He needed to be alone. "Tomorrow we will ride into the city. At dawn."

CHAPTER 39

THINGS WE DO NOT SEE

———— ✺ ————

Avelina

AVELINA WOKE LYING ON HER stomach. Startled, her
hands flew out in front of her. She grabbed the blanket in
her fists and grounded herself. *Where am I?* On a bed. In the inn.

Remembering, panting, Avelina blindly patted before her,
frantically searching. Her finger struck the point of the needle
she'd borrowed from the innkeeper. Pawing at the string attached,
she found her skirt bunched against the wall.

Thank God. Avelina's fingers traced the fresh stitches, calming
her. She had carefully resewn her book at the waist and fallen over
asleep while finishing the task. Her left leg dangled off the edge
of the bed. She pulled her foot toward her, rubbing it between her
hands, trying to get the blood flowing and stop the awful tingling.

Her eyes began adjusting. It was dark except for the candle next
to the bed. A puddle of wax was left now, with only a tiny lip
holding the flame aloft. The window shutters were closed, but she
could still hear the shuffling and voices of those left awake in the
city alley below her. Pulling herself along the bed, she opened a
shutter slightly and peeked through. Night had surely fallen; the
only outside light from a lantern lit on the corner of the alehouse.

How long had she slept? It couldn't have been long.

Avelina rubbed the sleep from her eyes and then laid a hand on
her growling stomach. She hadn't eaten when they arrived. She
had gone for a moment's reprieve and then happened upon the
conversation. She gritted her teeth. This was certainly not what

she had been expecting. And it certainly wasn't Matthias's fault.

It had happened. It would be what it would be. She would deal with it in the morning.

Right now, she simply wanted to eat.

Avelina turned and placed her feet on the floor. She slipped her fingers through the ring on the candle holder and pushed to stand. Her left foot still tingling, she misjudged her gait and her knee faltered. She almost fell, flinging hot wax onto her right hand.

Owwwwwwww!

She shrieked and dropped the candle holder to the floor. Burning pain ripped across her knuckles, as the liquified wax scalded her hand. Crying out, she batted at the wax with her other hand and tried wiping it on her skirts. In a few moments, it cooled and crusted onto her skin.

She fumbled in the dark until she found the throw at the end of her bed. Cradling her hand against her breast, she wrapped the small blanket around her shoulder as best she could. Her free hand followed the wall until she found the wide beams that framed the door. She opened it and stepped into the narrow hallway. She headed toward the stairs that were thankfully cast in a glow from lanterns below.

Where was Matthias?

Avelina would find him, but as quietly as possible. The tables at the bottom floor were mostly empty except for the table across the room near the fireplace. Where Matthias had sat hours before.

She heard them before she could see them.

Beastlike grunting.

The joining of flesh.

Rhythmically together.

Sounds she had never heard before, but she knew.

She knew and her heart fluttered.

She felt to flee. Embarrassed, but still determined, she moved forward. Her back against the wall, Avelina slid slowly down the stairs, staring at them.

The couple were locked in full embrace, lost in one another. The woman's back was toward Avelina. She straddled the man's chair, on top of him with her dress bunched around her waist, writhing against him. Lit by the light of the fire, her body cast a shadow over the man's face.

Once at the bottom of the stairs, she could see his tall black boots. Familiar black boots. And his hands, *familiar, large hands*, with a firm grip on her bare arse.

No. No, it couldn't possibly be him.

But wasn't it?

Avelina's mouth opened, and his name dropped from her lips. "Matthias?"

How could he do such a thing?

Her throat clenched in shock. Her stomach rolled with disgust, as her heart twisted and tore and bottomed out.

She needed to run.

"I'm . . ." Avelina said, mortified. "I'm sorry."

Avelina lifted the corner of her throw, covered her mouth, and rushed through the front door of the alehouse. Her bare feet froze on the cold, hard earth, and she stood on her tiptoes, hopping between them.

Avelina bit her lip, trying to forget what she had just witnessed. How cruel it felt. How careless. How awful a feeling it was to see him with another.

She looked about, the reality of her present situation sinking in.

What was she thinking? Where was she even going?

She dared not go back through that room, but she had to do something.

It was eerily still. Avelina's eyes darted about. *Where was everyone? Where was Rose?* She'd seen no sign of her. Of anyone, *but Matthias.*

No, Avelina. No.

She scolded herself, needing to get and stay on task.

The stone wall towered in front of her with a steep, narrow staircase rising into the black. She looked left and right, where lanterns lit the intersection of the dirt alley and the cobblestone street.

A crude mix of smells swarmed around her, tickling through the throw still covering her nose. Damp stone, spoiled food, and waste, animal and human, mixed with mud. Stronger toward her right, so she turned to her left, anxious to escape them. A murmur at first, reaching the edge of the alehouse, she heard a chorus of voices, raucous and deep. She turned left around the slanted corner beam of the alehouse and saw a courtyard with stables tucked beside it. Still smelling of beast, but not as putrid. The area was open, with groups of men clustered around fires, laughing and drinking into the dark night.

Please be here.

Rose. Or any of them. But especially him. Especially Matthias.

She searched their faces one-by-one, hopeful, yet nervous.

And that was where she found him, at least one of them.

There was no mistaking that red head of hair.

She tiptoed closer, keeping herself hidden, and peeked around a beam. She saw Reymund seated on the bound haystack beside Jorn. Reymund was singing, with a *scheitholt* across his lap. The instrument was thin-necked with a wider boxed bottom settled on his right knee. Beside him, Jorn's hand cupped the base of the instrument, holding it steady. Reymund's elbows shook as he played and sang, but he did so quite well. His left fingers deftly hopped to the notes, while his right hand dragged a small bow across the strings. The rich sound droned as the men joined in a chorus around him, bellowing notes and whoops and cheers.

Feeling like an intruder staring from the shadows, Avelina waited for his song to finish and then darted across the courtyard without meeting any of the stares of the men around her. A young man near Jorn stood and stared at her.

It was Alif. He lifted his mug toward her, and Jorn turned around, eyes wide.

Jorn was quickly on his feet and grabbed her elbow with his free hand. His speech somewhat slurred, his green eyes lit wild from the roaring fire. "Woman, are you mad? What are you doing out here?"

"I'm . . ." she said, looking around. All eyes were on her. She shook her head side to side, not sure what to say.

"Hell, woman," Jorn said. "If you were anywhere but *here* with *our men*." He gritted his teeth and shook his head, stepping over the bale of hay he'd been sat upon. He took off the cloak from his own shoulders and wrapped it around her, pulling it tightly. Looking her over, his eyes rounded at her feet. He stared at her widemouthed. "Runnin' bare legged in your nightdress. Are you trying to catch your death?"

"Is the princess all right?" Alif called from across the fire.

Her jaw fell open, searching for a reasonable excuse. "I'm hungry."

Jorn snorted and called to Alif, "She's fine, runt, just looking for some drink."

Jorn wrapped his arm around the back of her shoulders and turned her toward the house.

"Come now, to the kitchen, then," Jorn said. "You don't belong out here with these sots."

Avelina looked about. A few pairs of dark eyes met hers. "Are these men not your friends?"

Jorn snorted. "*Ja,* they are, but that doesn't mean they should be yours," he said, nudging her forward. "Eyes on each step, my lady or you'll be ankle deep in horse shit."

They moved to the other side of the courtyard, and Jorn opened a small door.

There he was.

Sitting in front of a fire, staring at the floor. Matthias's head was laid heavily against his fist, elbow propped on one knee, the other hand firmly clutching a large mug. It hadn't been him in the front room after all. Or had he finished, left whoever that was to retire here? Her stomach flipped, both elated to see him and disgusted with the thought of him holding another woman.

"Look who I found," Jorn said, stepping into the room. Avelina stepped after him but slammed her toes against the stone threshold. The sound of bones snapping rattled the air.

Owwwwwwwwwwwww!

She shrieked, crying out, stumbling, and grabbing at her aching foot.

"*Ach,* no," Jorn said. Still holding her shoulders, he'd kept her from falling onto her face. "I should've told you to watch your step in."

Matthias turned, quickly on his feet, and took the few steps toward her. He reached for her, and she shifted her weight back from him, surprising herself.

"Don't touch me," she snapped. Sharp pain tore through her foot.

Matthias's hands withdrew, palms open, and he stepped back from her. He looked at Jorn and nodded toward the chair he'd come from.

Avelina shuddered, and she bit her lip.

Jorn helped her hop over to the chair and sat her in it.

"I think I broke my foot," she said.

"*Ach,* only a scratch," Jorn said. He rubbed his hand over his head and looked at Matthias. "I'll go to the kitchen. Fetch you something, if you're still wanting to eat, Princess?"

Avelina shook her head, then nodded, her stomach still crying as well. "Yes, please."

Jorn left, and Matthias crouched in front of her. Close enough she should've felt his warmth, but the room was icy around her.

"Let me see," Matthias said.

"No, thank you."

"Avelina."

"Don't touch me." Glaring at him, she reached to rub her foot. It pulsed with pain and, regretting touching it, she quickly covered her mouth to stifle her wails.

Matthias stared at the wax coating her hand, met her eyes, and then shook his head.

"You're having a hell of a night, it seems."

"And so are you, apparently," she said, seething.

His eyebrows pressed together, and his jaw shifted.

"Fine, you're on your own, then," he said, standing to stretch.

I'm always on my own.

Avelina pursed her lips and tried to push to stand. Putting weight on her toes only caused them to throb even more. She tried to manage a few steps, with her arms moving wildly, trying to find balance. He was quickly at her side, grabbing her elbow.

"You need to sit," Matthias said, putting another arm around her waist. She hobbled with his support back to the chair. He threw a few logs onto the embers that burned low in the fireplace and started to walk away.

"Do you mean to leave me here?" Avelina asked, looking at the floor.

"You don't seem to want me here."

She wiped a tear from her cheek, hoping to hide it from him.

"You left me," she said. "Again."

"I've been here the whole time," Matthias said.

"Not with me you haven't."

"What?"

"It's not right," she whispered, her heart low in her chest. "It's not right."

"What's not right?"

"All of it," Avelina said.

"Yes, I know," Matthias said. "But we'll figure it out."

Matthias looked around the room and scooted a small table, set with a jug and two mugs, to her side. Avelina frowned as he poured them each a mug.

"It's almost dawn. Haven't you already had enough to drink?" She spat the words at him, surprising herself.

"Drink it," Matthias said, lifting a mug to her. "You could use a drink."

"No," Avelina said, pushing his hand away.

"*I* could use *you* having a drink," Matthias snipped at her.

"You're no gentleman, Matthias."

"And you, Avelina, are not behaving like a lady."

"What?"

"You're acting like a spoiled child," Matthias said.

Avelina was seething. Is that what he thought? She was a child?

"Treat me like a woman and I will not act like a child," she said defiantly.

The line of his jaw hardened.

"I will treat you with respect. And I expect the same from you." Matthias pulled a chair opposite from her and sat directly in front of her. He patted his lap. "Give me your foot."

He patted his leg again, and she reluctantly pushed her foot out in front of her. Scooting forward to the edge of his seat, Matthias lifted it gently by the heel and laid it on his thigh. She grimaced as his fingers felt along the bones in her foot and then to her toes. Pain shot through her two toes when he touched them, and she whimpered. He nodded and gently set her foot back down.

"Well, you didn't break your foot. Maybe only these toes. You're lucky," Matthias said. He walked to another table and then returned to the chair, carefully placing her foot on his thigh. She gasped and bit her lip when he started cleaning her foot with a chilly, wet rag. When finished, he began wrapping her foot with another dry one.

Avelina took a long drink from her mug, watching him over the rim intently. Her toes continued to throb, but the binding alleviated some of the pain right away.

"I'm sorry," Avelina whispered, remembering her manners. "I was unkind."

He smiled out of the right side of his mouth.

"You're hurt. It's all right," he said, smirking. "I've been there."

Matthias pointed at her other foot, and she set it forward. Lifting it by the heel, he set it on his knee and washed it as well. His hands wrapped around her feet, and his thumbs ran along the inside of the soles. She had forgotten how cold her feet were until they warmed under his touch.

"I don't understand you," Avelina said, turning her head to the side. She couldn't look at him. The longer he touched her, the more her chest ached. Both thankful and broken.

"What is there to understand?"

"Everything. You," Avelina said. "Why her and not me."

His thumbs dug deeper into her feet, and her whole body settled into her chair. That, and the drink, she suspected, setting her body more at ease. Her mind, though, couldn't shake the look the lady had given her, that mocking look, and the *sounds* . . . the sounds of them together.

"I don't know what you mean," he said, turning his hands around her ankles and lightly tugging her toward him.

Avelina twisted her hips back in her chair, retreating, but he didn't let go. His fingers continued methodically crushing the pinpricks in her cold skin, leaving each spot tingling with heat.

She covered her mouth with the edge of her cloak and forced a cough into it, trying to clear the lump in her throat. "I saw you."

His hands stopped moving.

Avelina turned to him. His face was closed. He only looked drained, slumped in his seat. He shrugged his shoulders and then started on her feet again.

"Well, on that, I did not have much choice in the matter," Matthias said.

His eyes were moving about now. The more intently she looked at him, the more he avoided her gaze.

Really, then? Is that the way of it?

Avelina pulled Jorn's cloak and blanketed herself, then tucked her hands tight against her ribs. "You sure sounded like you were enjoying yourself."

He pinched the bridge of his nose and sighed.

"*Ach,* woman, you're speaking in circles. No man here would dare touch you. They know who you are and that you're under my protection." He reached for his own drink. "The young one, Rose, is another story. She wasn't going to leave her babes. And I didn't trust her to stay put, though you were the one out running around in your bedclothes."

"Rose?"

Matthias pointed to a small door off to the side. "They're in there. And I've been here."

"But I saw you," Avelina said. "Your hands."

"These?" Matthias said and raised both of his hands.

His hands. Familiar. Strong. Large like a bear claw.

Wearing the ring. His gold ring. And she knew she had been mistaken.

She hung her head. "I thought I saw something else. I was mistaken."

Matthias sighed and leaned against the back of his chair. She started to pull her ankles back, but he grabbed her feet and held them there.

"Forgive me. I shouldn't have spoken to you in such a way."

"Nor I you." He sighed heavily. "You've had a lot on your mind, Princess. And it's going to be a long day. We'll sit a while."

They sat quietly, the popping and crackling of the fire beside him replacing their words while the tip of his thumb again lightly traced the bottoms of her feet.

Jorn brought a meat pie, silently placing it on the table, and left them.

Avelina nibbled on the flaky crust, studying Matthias. He was still. No tightness rippled along his jaw. His cheeks had fallen. His eyes dropped to the floor beside them, unfocused. His breathing was calm. His chest rising and falling steadily, as if he was peacefully asleep.

She had spent so much time with him. And today it would all be over.

"Tell me a story," Avelina said.

"About what?" he said, pinching the bridge of his nose.

"I don't know," she said. "Start at the beginning."

"There's nothing to tell."

"Tell me about your childhood. Where you come from."

He said nothing.

"Matthias."

Matthias stopped rubbing her feet and straightened himself in his chair. He took a long drink from his mug and refilled both of theirs.

"Your brothers?"

"What about them?"

"When did you meet them?"

His face darkened. He lifted his knee, and she withdrew her feet from his lap. Spreading his legs in front of her, Matthias curved his back like a cat and leaned in toward her. His head was cocked to the side with his jaw squared.

Avelina hoped he would reach out for her. She still yearned for him. His attention. His devotion. Now, even more. She couldn't deny it. But the way he looked at her—the hopeless harshness deeply lined in his face—anchored a weight deep into her chest. Like the one sewn there years before, that she thought she'd finally removed.

She averted her eyes from his, lest he see her sorrow.

"We could have run," she whispered.

"Perhaps should have," he muttered. "But the world has grown too small and the reach of men too long. Can you not see the danger?"

"I'd have taken the chance," she said. "For you."

"You don't know the world of which you speak. And it's all that I've ever known," Matthias said. "You cannot outrun a bounty placed on you and what men will do when there is one. Or what men will do when they've been crossed." His cheeks hung so heavy his jaw looked to break. "This. This I know better than most. I will not feed you to the wolves."

She nodded, biting her lip.

"I'm sorry, Avelina. I've always been honest with you . . ."

"And I with you."

"I cannot save you from them all."

"I'm not asking you to save me."

His lips pressed into a thin line, and his head rattled back and forth. "I can't be any more than I am. Or change who I am. And you. I can't . . . I can't live with more loss. Or more regrets."

"I regret nothing but that we could've been together," she said.

He turned away and closed his eyes. "I didn't ever mean, or want, to hurt you."

"I know," she whispered, managing a weak smile. "And neither did I."

CHAPTER 40

LIKE A QUEEN

———— ❧ ————

Matthias

"TRUCE?"

Matthias walked up beside Avelina. Sitting on the edge of the chair, her back was painfully straight. She'd been tended to by the maid, she was freshly clean, and she wore a new blue dress that Reymund had seen bought for her. At the sound of his voice, her shoulder blades moved toward one another tightly and then fell loosely. Relaxed.

"Truce," she answered.

She turned her face toward him enough that he caught the profile of a soft smile. A grin spread across his own face.

"Are you ready?"

"Soon," Avelina said.

"What do you need?"

Avelina lifted her hand, which held several blue ribbons, and motioned toward her hair. "I've never done it myself."

Matthias took a ribbon from her hand.

Matthias lifted her hair back from her temples and tied it at the crown of her head. He took another ribbon and held it between his teeth. He separated her long hair into three sections and began loosely plaiting it.

When he finished with the braid, Matthias secured the ribbon around the bottom. It wasn't nearly as intricately designed, tight and neat, as those worn in the castles, but even in its simplicity she looked lovely.

He pulled the bit of cloth from his breast pocket, where he had hidden her circlet so many nights before. He unwrapped it, finding a lone wool-flower from the mountain crumpled beside the jewels and his *gulden*. Its leaves and stalk were dry, sucked thin of their moisture. Though the center yellow bulbs had withered and browned, the silver-white petals remained, softly fanning about.

Ach. So the little star of the mountain had made it through with them after all.

He started to show her the flower but stopped himself. He sighed, running his thumb over it before gently tugging the circlet from beneath. He refolded the cloth and tucked it safely back into his pocket. Straightening the jewels, he placed the circlet across the line of her hair at her forehead and tied it beneath her braid at the nape of her neck.

"There," he said, placing his hands on her shoulders.

"Thank you, Matthias."

Avelina squeezed his hand. He promptly withdrew and crossed his arms.

"I wish . . ." He paused and cleared his throat. "I wish I could give you better."

"I'll be fine," she whispered. "This dress is lovely, and I've been well tended to."

Avelina stood and turned to him.

Somewhere in the hour lost between their fireside chat, with her scolding him while he tended her wounds, to this moment, she had aged. Grown in a way he couldn't place. Shadows of the woman he had seen on the mountain cliffs remained, but here, again before him, stood the princess.

Avelina straightened her dress at the waist, smoothed it across her stomach, and clasped her hands in front of her. Its blue color, warm and crisp like the sky, set her skin and eyes aglow, even in this barely lit room. Her shoulders were drawn and set back, her chin raised proudly.

Moment by moment, she looked more like the princess he had seen that first night at the barter. And less like his Avelina. Her body reworked itself, molding her into a perfect picture of regality, standing in this dank, filthy alehouse in an alley by the city wall.

An inkling of shame ran through the back of his throat, twisting at his jaw.

Had he ruined her somehow, her chances here? To have been so free with her? Spoken to her so casually? Not treated her as she deserved to be?

Or had he condemned her by not arriving fast enough? Should they have taken the road? Would they have beaten the birth? Would she still have wed the king?

Had he failed her after all? Saved her life only to bring her here? And for what?

Matthias immediately regretted having plaited her hair. Though it was gathered behind her, it draped across her bare shoulders, drawing attention to the line of her neck. The memory of the taste of her skin hit his tongue, and he took a step back, lest he reach for her.

He felt a fool in front of her, having dared to touch her. A line squeezed from his throat through his gut, remembering every time he had done so, so freely. Without thinking, grabbing her hand, instinctually, as if it was meant to be in his own.

He took another step back. Squared himself.

It had been to protect her. Help her.

Hadn't it?

Avelina took a step toward him, and the hair on his neck rose.

It was as if the woman was fire herself.

Light he was drawn to. A beacon in the dark world he had been born to.

Warmth he could cling to. And find both comfort and peace.

Both death and rebirth. She was his end and his beginning.

Now that they were here in Ewigsburg—and he had turned her away—their journey was over.

It had to be.

For the sake of his word to a king that had broken his.

For the sake of his word and the freedom owed to his brothers.

For the sake of his word to protect this woman, even from himself.

The truth hit him deep in his gut, and the shockwave roared through his limbs, crushing every bone.

Avelina was no longer his.

She had never been his and would never be.

Matthias ground his teeth. He swallowed the boulder blocking his throat. He took to his knee in front of her and hung his head.

"Princess Avelina," he said, clearing another quickly growing lump. "If I . . ."

There was so much he wanted to say, but the words were caged, his ribs locking them in his chest.

"Matthias."

His eyes closed tight when she said his name.

"It has been an honor, Princess."

"I know that I'm no longer to be a queen," Avelina said. "But you've made me feel like one. I thank you."

He didn't move, keeping his gaze locked on the floor at her feet, noting the pointed slippers that stuck out at the bottom of her dress. There were no worn, broken boots. No intention to run.

"We should go," she said.

Standing erect, he nodded to her. He offered her his elbow, remembering her toes, but she did not accept. She meant to walk on her own. *Rightly so.*

Matthias followed her through the front door and into the morning sun.

His men were there waiting. Six men lined the dirt alley, as Reymund was already at the castle. All size and age. Armed, dressed, and ready. Standing tall. Focused and at attention. Still the motley crew, rough and hardened as ever, but a more honorable set of friends he had never known.

"Brothers," Matthias said, stopping at Avelina's side. "I present Princess Avelina Elisabeth, Daughter of Leuceria."

Following Jorn's lead, the men bowed their heads to her, and she returned their show of respect with a slow and graceful curtsy. Matthias's lip tugged at the genuine display of reverence from both sides.

"Princess Avelina. These are my men. Learn their faces and know them by the black cords they wear on their wrists. You can trust any man who wears one to be honorable and at your service."

The men scattered and climbed onto their own horses. They would ride strong through the streets of Ewigsburg to the king's gate. He wanted to set the stage. He wanted the people to see her. To see her riding with him and know that she was someone who should be revered.

Matthias approached his horse and greeted him. Brom snorted at him as he scratched his neck. The second horse, a steady mare, was saddled and standing patiently beside Matthias's much larger stallion. Matthias smiled and turned to Avelina behind him. She stood stiffly with her hands clasped in front of her.

"The cart?" she asked.

"It does not suit you to arrive like that," he replied, grabbing the reins of the mare and walking it toward her. No matter what Girault's intentions were now, she would arrive in as much splendor as he could manage for her. She deserved that.

When he saw her take a step back, he paused. "First time alone?"

A bit smaller than Brom, the mare was still heads taller than Avelina. The large black eyes blinked at Avelina, her head low. Avelina gently laid her hand on the mare's neck and nodded. "It's been a while."

"She's sweet by nature. She'll stay with mine. And the men will be on all sides of you." Matthias bent a knee and patted his thigh. "Hop on up."

Avelina put her foot on Matthias's thigh and her hand on his shoulder. He lifted her onto the saddle, and she grabbed the horse's reins tightly, eyes wide.

"Sit tall. I will lead you to the castle." He climbed on top of Brom beside her. "Avelina . . . Princess."

She cocked her head toward him.

"Once we arrive at the castle, we may not again have a chance to speak," he said with weighted chin. "I need you to promise me something."

Her amber eyes widened, and he caught a glimpse of the trepidation in the whites of her eyes. Her chin bobbed ever so slightly, and he knew he had her attention.

"Whatever happens here . . ." He trailed off, looking at his hands. He gripped Brom's reins in his fists and squeezed until his knuckles turned white. Matthias leaned, guiding Brom closer to the side of Avelina's horse, and lowered his voice. "You may not see it yourself, but you have strength inside of you. At your core, you're a fighter. I have seen you look death in the eye and not back down. I've seen it time and time again. Remember that. Remember who are you. Whose daughter you are. Don't ever forget. No one can take that from you."

Her eyelashes fluttered. Her lips parted but quickly pressed into a line, silencing whatever thought had been there.

"They won't understand you, and they will see your silence as a threat. They'll try to contain you, diminish you, mold you into an instrument to suit their own ambitions. Don't let their words weight your wings, convince you that you're unable to soar." His words were heavy, and his jaw ached as they passed through, but he was determined for her to hear them. "I can see you, Princess, the woman before me. Be brave and hold true to who you are. I daresay that you have not begun to even dream of all that you can accomplish. Once you are ready, *truly ready*, you will rise above it all."

Matthias laid his hand on his heart and, closing his eyes tight, bowed his chin to his chest. He rose, and their eyes locked on one another.

Her lips pulled into a soft smile that still managed to reach her eyes. She inhaled deeply and reset her shoulders. "Thank you, Matthias. Truly. For everything."

Her chin trembled and his soul emptied, save the heart thudding within his hollow chest.

He thought for a moment to turn around.

Her horse would follow his. They could run. Fast, far, and forever . . .

Brom shifted beneath him as Jorn arrived at his side. Avelina turned away from him as one of his men rode up on each side of her, the rest falling in behind.

The moment was gone.

CHAPTER 41

MAN AND BEAST

———✦———

Matthias

"*KCK. KCK.*" Matthias nudged Brom with his heel, and the large animal shook its head about, neighed, and started to trot forward. It was early still, the crispness of the morning hanging low on the stones beneath them, but the mount and he were both full of energy.

Considering man and beast were used to sleeping in the wild, or on a cot in a tent, or at best a night in a flea-ridden bed at a tavern, their days at the castle were always interesting. Markedly uncomfortable. And uncomfortably rewarding.

Matthias was irritated and restless. He was glad, though, to have his horse back and to see him well. Brom was in good health and happy to move freely.

Brom—scarred, stubborn, and built like he'd been carved out of stone—had taken well to the tending of the stablemen. His freshly shod and clean hooves pounded onto the cobblestones with a stark force, reverberating a warning to clear a path before him. He was a gorgeous creature, black coat stretched over taut muscles that shook a lesser man's nerves to stand next to him. He had scars across his chest and on his forelegs, evidence of his fearlessness when charging into battle underneath his master. His mane was black and long; his only color being what reflected in his wildly bright, black eyes. Matthias patted his neck as they began their march through the streets of Ewigsburg, and the horse snorted in reply.

Matthias—scarred, stubborn, and built like he'd been carved out of stone—never felt well shut within the city walls. Born into the darkness of war, he'd lived in the forests, camps, and then the farm until in the king's service. Huddled in the trenches with the army, things like bathing, soaps and perfumes, clean or even fresh clothes, were a seldom thought about luxury. At the castle, when he'd accompanied Prince Siegfried, they'd groomed him to look the part, but he'd always felt like a fraud. He'd accepted gifts bestowed on him with all respect due his king, more on behalf of and to share with his men, but today he was done.

It had to end today.

Matthias owed that to them. They were owed their freedom. The dignity of controlling, and living, their own lives.

"Matthias?"

Jolted from his thoughts, Matthias shook his head, sighed, and reached a fist over to strike the arm of the man riding on his right. Jorn laughed, jerking his arm out of the way in time, leaving Matthias to miss his mark.

"Bastard," Matthias laughed.

Matthias grimaced and shifted on his saddle. He had been so lost in his own head; he hadn't noticed the looks on the faces of those on the streets. Those out and about, starting their morning, parted and pushed to the streets' sides by their large horses. Matthias gave no greeting to anyone, though he was familiar or friendly with several they passed, only driving forward on their mission.

"Are you ready for this? I sent Alif ahead to the guardhouse this morning, so they know you're coming with *her*," Jorn said, cocking his head toward the towers looming closer above them. "'Course he road like hell to come back and ride with us. Think he's got a softness for her."

Matthias glanced over his shoulder to where the princess rode in the center of their group, his men surrounding her should there be any misstep. From anyone.

Matthias nodded his thanks.

"Reymund too," Jorn said. "He's long at the castle to put them to task."

"He rode?"

Matthias frowned. It wasn't that Reymund couldn't ride, it was more that he shouldn't, at least for that long a period of time on such roads. His body wouldn't allow for it.

"*Ja*, he rode," Jorn said. "He'll be fine. That daft man doesn't know how to *not* do something, even if he shouldn't. Kind of like another arse I know who keeps getting himself into trouble."

"Piss off, Jorn," Matthias said, to which Jorn roared with laughter.

"And *you*, Sword," he laughed. "If I can't bedevil my own brother, then who can I?"

He winked at Matthias and waved a signal to their group of horsed men. They rode farther uphill and onto the flatter but narrower roads.

"Are you going to make me ask, then?" Jorn said, breaking the silence.

"Ask?"

"What's she like?"

Matthias turned a stern face on Jorn's quizzical gaze. "What do you mean?"

"Not in bed, you fool," Jorn said with surprising forcefulness. "Unless . . ."

"Mind your tongue, Jorn," Matthias growled.

Jorn smirked and cocked his head. "Something's changed, brother."

Matthias shifted again in his saddle, ignoring him.

"The lady herself. What's she like? Have you spoken with her?"

Matthias snorted and said, "Yes, a bit."

"And?"

"She's kind," Matthias said.

"And?" Jorn coaxed.

"Beautiful, then."

"Even a blind man with an empty sac sees that," Jorn said.

"Right." Matthias smirked. "She does like to talk much."

"*Hmpf.* I didn't expect that."

"Sometimes she's as windy as a flock of starlings, other times as mute as a fawn."

"Well, so are you most times," Jorn said, shrugging his shoulders. "Especially with women. Besides paying for your ale, your sup, or your bed, when the hell did you ever speak to one?"

"I've never paid to bed one."

Jorn snorted almost as loud as Matthias's horse. "*Ja*. Me neither."

Matthias rolled his eyes.

"She's different," he said.

He looked forward, avoiding Jorn's sly grin. Jorn was pleased with himself, having caught Matthias off guard. His brother looked like the barn cat holding its fresh kill.

Matthias dismissed the noise of the world around him, and her face drifted back into his mind. Those eyes. The lightness of her hand in his. The softness of her skin. Her breath brushing against his ear. The hunger in her voice. The woman had grabbed ahold of him stronger, tighter, and deeper than any other he'd ever lain with.

Might I tell you a secret?

Her words that night came whispering to him through the bustling, crowded streets.

Arousal stirred low within him, and he gripped Brom's reins tighter, adjusting himself.

Purpose and shame, duty and regret raged against each other within him.

Matthias wanted to turn around and race her away from here. Somewhere safe. He would post men on every corner. Thwart every last evil he'd raised his sword against and leave her untouched and unblemished.

Perfectly herself. *And happy.*

Man, and devil, at war within him, wanted to make her his. Treasure and protect her. But also strip her down, devour her, and bury himself deep within her until she screamed his name.

"Well, of course she is," Jorn said.

"She's what?" Matthias said.

"Different," Jorn said. "She is a true lady. Not some filthy doxy hanging around the battle camp for coin."

"Hell, Jorn, yes." He ran a hand over his face.

Jorn wasn't finished with him. "I bet you she knows how to read. They usually do. Those royal ones are educated. I bet she can read and write."

"Yes. She can."

"That'll be useful. A skill that can help her," Jorn said. "Will be nice to know someone besides Reymund who can."

"True," Matthias said.

Jorn hesitated before asking, "Does she smell nice?"

Matthias groaned and rolled his eyes.

"She looks like she does." Jorn shrugged.

Honestly, she does. Like the king's roses when they catch on a warm breeze.

Matthias turned his head around to look at the lady behind him before quickly righting himself. He nudged Brom forward, needing a bit faster pace to try and outrun his thoughts.

CHAPTER 42

DELIVERED TO THE KING

Avelina

THE RIDE HAD TAKEN LONGER than she had anticipated, and Avelina had taken the opportunity to drink in the details of her new home. Their entourage kept to a wider street of stone that seemed to be the main thoroughfare for the city. Alleyways turned off occasionally to the left and right, while most of the larger buildings were pressed together against the street. Structures of thick wooden beams and plaster rose several stories high, some with each successive floor jutted out over the street. On the upper floors, their shutters were held open by iron prongs, while at the street their planked doors were open at the storefront. Decoratively carved and painted signs advertised the wares and specialties within.

The closer they came to the center of the city, the more bustling it became. They passed within view of the square in front of a towering church and the stadium beyond it. The clicking of their horses' hooves against stone was overtaken by the roar of commerce. A farmer's market was underway from one end to the other, the large open area littered with stalls of animals and produce. Peddlers shouted their wares, displaying items she didn't recognize. Dogs were barking near sheep and goats huddled within gated enclosures. The competing odors from the animals were stiflingly unpleasant, and her eyes blinked against the stench. A loud clang rang out above her, and she tilted her head to the sky. The church bells were ringing, bonging high in the tower, marking the hour, and Avelina warmed at the deep, familiar sound.

Once past the square, they continued to drive forward, the road slanting gradually upward beneath them. Their pace had remained steady since the start, but the farther along they got, the more attention being paid them had slowed their progress. Avelina watched Matthias, at first aloof, then variedly greeting people along the way, with great curiosity. His quiet command, his friendliness, and his ease amongst the people, was interesting and heartwarming to watch.

This man, who didn't want to lead, clearly had a way of connecting with people and they with him. Matthias and his men were well recognized and received by the townsfolk, and the more he accepted the greetings, the more frequently others paid their respects. Several men on their own greeted Matthias and approached his horse. Jorn, at his side, received the same. The men would grab each other by the forearms, looking directly into each other's eyes while they spoke and laughed. A few families watched from their front stoops, and Matthias tipped his head to them and waved at the small children.

Friendly yet inquisitive faces turned to her, but none spoke or called to her. At first nervous, she set a pleasant smile on her face, nodding back at the few who nodded at her. She was used to being presented officially at court, but having never been allowed out of the castle and amongst her own people in Leuceria, this was all so new. She had such a mixture of confused feelings that she found herself lost in the whirlwind of it all.

The road continued to rise, though less steeply now, flanked by trees on both sides. They had passed around the last edge of the city and through another gatehouse leading to the main gates of the castle, where circular defensive towers sat between the trees, poised to intercept upon anyone who breeched this far.

Avelina took a long breath as their horses turned at the crest of the hill. Jorn, who had been rather talkative beside her this last turn, clamped his mouth shut, as they passed through the last gate and entered the courtyard of the great castle of Ewigsburg. The horses slowed to a stop, their rhythmic clopping turning sporadic and then ceasing altogether.

It was still, save the sound of flags whipping in the wind, and the silent yet thunderous crash of the eyes of the new court boring into her.

The courtyard was full of smartly dressed men and women, all staring at her.

Waiting.

Matthias and Jorn both lifted a leg over their horse's backs, turned, and slid to the ground. Once their boots were on the ground, the rest of the men followed their lead. A tall, bald man who had ridden silently next to her the entire time took control of organizing their horses. Once they began to clear, she saw Matthias walking toward her.

Avelina held out her hand. Matthias grabbed it firmly and steadied her as she turned. Letting go, he reached for her, took her by the waist, and helped her down. Back on the ground, she winced at the pain that shot through her foot, but she found her legs quickly, standing tall.

"My dearest lady! Princess Avelina Elisabeth of Leuceria."

The low voice boomed across the courtyard.

"The king," Matthias whispered.

Avelina turned in the direction from which it came and, without even trying to place it, dropped her eyes. Placing her injured foot behind her, she lowered into a deep and dignified curtsy. Matthias dropped to his knee next to her, and together they waited.

Footsteps crunched in front of her and then stopped.

"You are most welcome at Ewigsburg, my dear," King Girault said.

A large hand covered in rings was held out before her, and she placed her fingers into it and was guided back upright. King Girault towered in front of her. As tall as Matthias, though his chest and stomach were twice as round.

"Forgive me if I startled you, Princess Avelina," King Girault said. "It isn't every day we have such a fine lady come here. And on such an occasion, it's only right I greet you myself."

"Of course, Your Grace," Avelina said.

"What a journey you've had," the king said. Tightening his grip, he drew her a step toward him. "I trust my man was good to you. Treated you kindly." He turned to Matthias and winked. "Well done, Sword."

Matthias stood and said, "Thank you, sire."

"I know we have a lot to discuss, but there is much to do. Your timing is . . . pleasing," the king said. "Why don't you get your men settled and then join me for a drink?"

"Thank you, sire," Matthias said. He turned to her but did not meet her eyes. He bowed his head low. "Princess."

With that, Matthias turned on his heel and was gone.

His full attention on her, King Girault's commanding smile split his silver mustache and full beard. His worn and scarred face and plump belly told a story of years of both hard and comfortable living. Flanked by tightly stitched smile lines, his aged blue eyes were kind and attractive but twinkled with a mix of playfulness and mischief she recognized quickly.

Reading a man's eyes had always been a good indication of a man's motives toward her. Many were honest enough to give fair warning of foul play, even if the rest of their intentions were well masked, but something in the king's eyes sparked alarms within her.

There was something there, lingering behind that twinkle.

The hair on her arms rose, her instincts telling her to immediately be on guard. Having grown up with Dolion and Marcus, she knew well how to recognize the range from salacity to seething hate.

This was much trickier. Confusing. Conflicting.

Something she'd never seen before. Or couldn't place.

Something was wrong here. Very wrong.

Her heart quickened, and she wondered if she'd just been winked at by the devil.

"It isn't every day I bear witness to such a prize," King Girault said. "The Jewel in his Crown. That's what Niro calls you."

Avelina regained her poise while he circled her. Close enough to hear his ragged breath. Smell the ale on him. He inspected her. Openly, in front of everyone in the courtyard, as if she were an animal at market on sale.

He stopped in front of her. Centered, his chest right before her face. Where she could see nothing but the three jeweled golden chains that were laid across his red tunic a mere hand's width from her.

The king grabbed her chin, and her heart froze. Rough fingertips brushed her cheek, then along the curve of her neck, where he pulled a lock of her hair toward him. He rubbed it between his fingers, then pulled along the length until he laid it at her breast.

"The man is treacherous, but Niro definitely is no fool," he said, snickering.

His fingers lingered there at her breast, searching until his knuckles found her nipple, ripe against her thin dress in the whipping winds circling the courtyard. She startled and he smirked, tilting his head toward hers, and teased it between his knuckles.

Avelina dug her heels into the ground, begging her body not to shake in front of him.

"I see why you caused me such a headache," he said. "And cost me a fortune, I might add." He bent his neck, looking into her eyes. "I take none of this arrangement lightly, Princess. Out of respect for your father—"

"I have little memory of him, Your Grace," Avelina interrupted him.

She knew it was daring. And rude. But it worked, and the king removed his hand. The king took a step back and set his hand on his hip. When he again spoke, his tone had changed.

"You wouldn't, would you? You were only a babe then," King Girault said. "Your father was clever and the very best of men. His death, a tragedy, affected us all. Affected everything, I daresay."

Avelina took a step back and ducked her chin, waylaid by the inappropriate intimacy of his touch and the mention of her father.

The very best of men.

Avelina folded the words inside her where she kept her secrets.

"'Tis an honor, to save his only daughter. To see you like this. You are radiant. And I am a *very* fortunate man," King Girault said, regarding her intently.

Avelina swallowed the stone wedged in her throat and pushed the edges of her lips into a modest smile.

"Thank you, Your Grace."

King Girault placed her hand within the crook of his arm and patted it. He turned and smiled to those packing the courtyard, all watching them stone-faced.

"Shall we?" he asked, and they started across the courtyard.

Shaped like a beaver's tail, the castle hugged the edge of the rounded end of the courtyard, rising stories high into the sky. It was incredible. While the outside and lower tiers of the castle were functionally defensive, the inside was intimately structured—like a rose, with a stiff skin covered in thorns to protect its detailed and delicate beauty. Decorative embellishments traced her lines as embroidery would a dress. Towers thrust tall to the heavens, covered with intricate patterns of iron windows filled with colored glass. Terraces hugged the corners, with boxes along their rails stuffed and overflowing with hanging red and purple flowers.

King Girault led her across the courtyard and up a flight of stairs into the castle. The two of them walked the length of a slowly rising corridor of carved, ancient limestone. The floor was covered in a deep red carpet threaded with green vines leading them forward. On her right side, tall open windows lined the walls, providing a view over the city and rolling hills below. In between them, soldiers stood at attention as their king strode by.

Through another corridor, they came to an open wooden door, and entered a bright chamber. The room was comfortable, full of carved oak furniture set with red cushions. She averted her eyes from the large canopy bed anchoring the room to a credenza along another wall. Beneath a series of intricate green tapestries, the cabinet stretched long, overflowing with a fresh feast and a centerpiece of purple and white flowers.

"I hope they bring you happiness." King Girault nodded to the blooms.

The colors of Leuceria's crest. The sight and smell were warm and intoxicating. Their fragrance danced on the breeze coming in through the slanted windows.

"They are lovely," Avelina said. "And thoughtful."

Avelina was teetering as her nerves soared. They were alone, and his touch still tingled at her breast. Anxious, she pulled at her reserves of strength to remain poised.

The smell of warm *brötchen* curled into her, and hunger tore through her eager stomach. She covered her belly with one hand, begging it not to cry out. When the king turned from her, she crossed to the credenza and laid a hand beside the vase to steady herself. Her toes were throbbing inside her slipper from the walk, and she lifted her foot beneath her dress to alleviate the mounting pressure.

"These were Lilith's—the Queen's—rooms before we married," the king said, circling the periphery of the room. He ran his fingers along the carved arm of a wide chair and cocked his head toward her with a satisfied smile. He stopped midway behind it and spread his hands across the back, leaning forward.

Feeling his eyes openly tracing her body, Avelina averted her own over his shoulder and stared at the tapestry behind him. All the same shades of green, the stories continued from one to the next. It was a hunting scene. Groups of men on horse, stitched as large as she, riding through the countryside, their herds of dogs driving stag and boar from one tapestry to the next.

"I never did meet your mother. I long heard tales of her beauty, and seeing you, I believe it." The king crossed his arms and looked down his nose at her. His smile faded, but his eyes . . .

Simmering and seductive.

Sparkling and smoldering.

Darkly beautiful and dangerously bold.

She felt trapped by them. Locked on.

Like she was the prey, and he, the diamond-eyed dragon luring her in.

Avelina's skin crawled. Her heart thumped loudly in her ears.

"I have things that I must attend to now, unfortunately." King Girault smacked the back of the couch and strode to the door. Stopping, he turned and presented her a small bow. "There's a new dress for you in your wardrobe. A gift for you to wear to the banquet tonight celebrating the opening of the tournament. I hear you are a pious woman, Princess Avelina. You may make use of my private oratory. Perhaps you could say a prayer for both of our souls and then adjourn to the Summer Hall for tea. The ladies of the court are most keen to see you. Enjoy your time, but make sure to rest. I would like you," he paused and bit his lip, "ready."

CHAPTER 43

CONFRONTATION AND
OTHER WORDS UNSAID

———❦———

Matthias

"YOU REQUESTED AN AUDIENCE?" KING Girault said. Matthias stepped through the door into his king's apartment.

"You requested a princess?" Matthias returned.

"Ha!" King Girault laughed, and the grapes he was eating spit onto his chin. He took a linen and wiped his face. He motioned for Matthias to sit and then pulled a bunch of grapes onto his wooden plate. "Glad to have you back, son." He winked at Matthias. "Go on, then. Speak your mind."

Son.

The moniker ground through Matthias's bones every time the king said it. Making him remember his own father—a man he had long distanced himself from, denied and tried to forget.

Matthias sat at the corner beside the king. Placing his elbows on the table, he pressed the tips of his fingers together and rested his mouth upon them.

"I've done what you asked," Matthias said.

King Girault glanced at him, chewing open-mouthed and lips smacking. "You heard about Duke Eger?"

"Fell to his death? I did."

"The timing was convenient," the king said, cocking his head and snorting.

"Sounds so."

The king raised an eyebrow at him. "Zane's gone north in my stead to review Eger's accounts." He licked his fingers and pushed the plate away from him.

"Zane is at Hilzarion?"

"He should return soon to report. His wife remains here, now that she's lying-in, swollen with his own heir. A boy, he's sure of it," the king said, pleased. "Zane will take control of Hilzarion, as Eger died without a son to inherit. Isn't that a sad thing in this world we live in?"

Matthias rubbed his thumb across his nose. No doubt the king was thrilled to absorb Eger's lands and his great fortress at the northern border.

"Eger's wife hadn't lived with him for years," Matthias said.

King Girault snickered.

"Also convenient, having Lilith here at my pleasure. Can't provide your husband an heir if you're being sarded by the king, can you?" He winked at Matthias. "Now that she's borne me a live babe, and *a son* at that, the time had come."

"To have Eger killed?"

King Girault slammed his fist on the table, and his eyes rounded. "'Twas a sign from God himself."

Matthias ground his teeth.

"She's borne for me before. Four. No, six babes. But *maids*. All lost." He shrugged. "She's immensely pleased with herself now. And the lady's earned my respect."

"And with Eger gone . . ."

"A widow." The king grinned. "A wealthy one at that. She's earned her crown."

Matthias sighed, rubbing his hands together.

"And all that Duke Eger had. The wife. The land. The men. The money. The son he sought but could never have. All of it is now *mine*."

Matthias tapped his foot beneath the table. He should've expected this. Been prepared. King Girault's hatred for Duke Eger had been long and deeply seeded, though a one-sided rivalry.

"Come now, you know I couldn't let my chance slip away. Or for another to crawl forth and lay claim to that fortune," King Girault said, looking long down his nose at Matthias.

"And the princess? What becomes of her?" Matthias asked.

The corners of the king's lips fell, and his nose wrinkled. Instead of answering, he reached for his mug. Finding it empty, he flicked his fingers at a servant. The king's mug was promptly refilled with wine, along with the empty one that sat before Matthias.

"She's mine as well." He shrugged and reached for a plate of meat. He leaned over it and pulled a leg from the cooked bird.

Matthias reached for his mug, thinking to take a drink, but stopped. He ran his thumb along the lip and swallowed. "You said you would marry her."

"So I did," the king said with a greasy grin.

He pulled the skin off the leg and plopped in into his mouth.

"I fought for you," Matthias said.

"Wasn't the first time." King Girault looked over the bone at Matthias as he took another bite. "Circumstances changed."

"Did they, then?"

"And I understood there to be no proxy ceremony, so no vow has been broken."

Matthias's hand balled into a fist.

"She'll have a home here," the king said. "With me."

Matthias pressed his heel to the floor, trying to settle his leg. "How?"

Flesh dripped from the king's mouth while he chewed, watching Matthias.

"What are your intentions?" Matthias asked.

"Ha! My intentions?"

"Toward the princess."

"You seem rather interested, son."

"I am."

King Girault tossed the bone onto the table and licked his thumb.

"*That* in itself I find interesting," he said, tearing the other leg free.

Matthias grimaced, looking across the table. "I gave her your word and gave her *mine. My word.* That means something to me."

"I know it does, son. But it was never my intention to marry the girl."

Matthias's palms spread on the table in front of him. He shifted his feet beneath his chair, fighting his rising annoyance. "Then why did you send me? With an offer of marriage?"

"To save her life. I owed her father a life debt. Now it's paid in full." King Girault cocked his head again, watching Matthias. He pushed his elbows forward onto the table and tapped the legbone toward Matthias. "She is a pretty young thing. Maybe I can get a son off her too." He chortled. "At least I'll enjoy trying."

Seething inside, Matthias efforted a blank face. "You mean to keep her as a mistress?"

"I paid for her in gold, didn't I?" the king said. "A sum of it."

"You'd dishonor her?" Matthias said.

"She'll live. Here. Well. Like Lilith before her," the king said, lifting a brow. "Nothing wrong with having another womb to fill, and she looks ripe for a bedding to me."

Matthias's jaw smarted, and he exhaled slowly.

"I could sell her perhaps. Or offer her as a prize for the tournament if she bores me. Maybe. There's something . . . I don't know, powerful? Satisfying?" His eyes rolled around, and his cheeks grew bright red over his beard, clearly pleased with himself. He smacked the table with an open palm and stared at Matthias. "Ha! It feels downright deliciously devilish to claim the Daughter of Leuceria as your mistress."

Rotting hell.

Matthias averted his eyes, worried the king would see them aflame with anger. Matthias pushed his arms back from the table and grabbed the arms of the chair. Every muscle in his body raged with the urge to throttle the old man's neck and snap it in his hands. His heel tapped even faster beneath the table.

"What of your promise?" Matthias said. "You gave me your word."

King Girault coughed, wiped his nose, and took another drink. "So I did."

"Did you never intend to honor that promise either?" Matthias said, leaning forward. "*You, your men, will be free.* Those were your words to me."

The king side-eyed him and licked his lips. "And I meant them."

The doors to the king's chamber opened, and Duchess Lilith, now queen, entered the room. Hands set in front of her and her chin high, she glided across the floor to them. Matthias rose from his chair, gave her a nod, and turned back to his king.

"Matthias, have you paid respect to your new queen?" the king said, tilting his head toward her.

"Congratulations on the birth of a healthy son, sire," Matthias said, formally bowing to his king. "May he grow as strong and wise as his father and brother before him." Matthias turned to the queen and dropped his chin. "How fortunate that you have been safely delivered, my lady."

The queen sneered at him. She still had a sense of her beauty about her that had driven the king mad with lust for her years ago. The king had indeed treasured her and spoiled her with everything his coin could afford, but the years spent as a court spectacle had not been kind to her. No amount of face paint or jewels could soften the quiet anguish on her face. Ignored by so many, but plainly evident to Matthias. Stress lines set at her taut lips and at her bright blue eyes, brimming with her reserve of calculated patience.

"You have my sympathies on the death of your husband," Matthias added, widening his stance. "Duke Eger was a good man."

She ever so slightly wavered for a moment but recovered, pulling her shoulders back and standing firm.

Matthias hadn't really ever considered her. How she felt all these years as the mistress of a king. The daughter of a great house. The wife of another. This great lady's life bent to the will of the king.

She wore a crown, but at what cost?

"I will not have her in your bed," Queen Lilith said, turning a hard eye on the king.

"She will be no more to me than a plaything," King Girault said.

"You have no need for a mistress," Queen Lilith said.

"Says the lady who was mine?" King Girault said, raising his eyebrows. "You saw no problem with it when you were my mistress."

The king snickered and leaned across the arm of his chair. He held an open hand to her, and she went to him. She slid her hand into his, and he kissed her fingers without taking his eyes from her face.

"You're right. I never complained," Queen Lilith said, giving him a strained smile.

The king raised an eyebrow at her. He wrapped his arm around her hips and pulled her toward him.

"I have given you a son, and I will give you more. I have always kept your bed full and warm." The queen placed a hand on the king's chin. "She vexes me. She is nothing but—"

"She is a lady by all merits," Matthias snarled at her, and she shot him a look. Her eyes became as drawn as a sleeping cat's. Though a full head shorter than Matthias, she raised her chin to stare him down.

"Did you think Girault would put me aside for some foreign tart? Keep me as mistress and put a crown on some harlot's head?" the queen asked, tousling the king's bearded chin.

"I see the crown on your head has given you reason to believe your opinion matters." King Girault grinned at her.

Queen Lilith turned white. Her hand froze at his chin while his hand found hers and closed around her wrist.

"Your belly is the only reason that crown sits there," King Girault said and kissed the inside of her wrist. "Don't give me reason to take the head it sits upon—you know I adore you. Watch your tongue, madame, or I'll be forced to replace you with someone who will mind their place."

King Girault slammed his mug on the table and let go of her. He leaned back in his chair, lacing his fingers over his stomach, and sucked air through his teeth.

"Your men, Matthias. They are free to leave. As are you," the king said.

Matthias's gut dropped, and he bowed his head. "Thank you, sire."

"Though my new queen has plans for you to consider," he said, lifting a thick brow. "Don't be so quick to leave, Matthias. Listen to her offer. She's a sly one."

The queen turned to Matthias. Her folded hands squeezed tightly together. "I want you to remain in the king's service."

"I am a free man," Matthias said. "You heard it yourself."

"You are, but like my king said, circumstances changed," she said.

Of course she'd been listening.

"You know I don't favor you, but now that I have a son, I have need of you. *We* have need of you. I want my son to grow up in a land that is safe. And it is safer with you and your men here, beside my king."

"There are plenty of men here in the king's service," Matthias said.

"There are," she said.

"And you have the Duke Eger's men now. You have no need for me," Matthias said.

"I do have his men," King Girault said. "But they will remain on Eger's lands and keep them profitable and loyal to me."

"I want my son protected," Queen Lilith said sharply. "I ask you this, as your queen and as a mother."

"And as a free man," Matthias said, "I decline."

Her lips pursed. "I will reward your efforts."

"I desire nothing," Matthias said.

"You will have a bride." King Girault arched his brow.

"I have no want for a wife," Matthias said.

Queen Lilith took a step toward him. Though her chin was raised, her eyes were set hard on the floor, avoiding his.

"My eldest daughter," she said, "is yours."

Matthias turned to King Girault, who lifted an open palm and smiled wide.

"Wasn't my idea," the king snorted. "But it's a good one."

"You have no money. No prospects. Nowhere to go. For reasons beyond me, my king favors and trusts you. Bend the knee to my husband. Stay in the king's service, in my service, and you may marry my Helene."

"You'd marry your daughter, a lady from the House of Eger, to a simple man? To me?"

"At least consider it." King Girault tilted his head with a smile. "Stay through dinner. Your men can have a meal, a drink, and find someone to bed. Then leave in the morning, if you so choose."

CHAPTER 44

WHERE LOYALTIES LIE

—⁂—

Matthias

MATTHIAS STORMED THROUGH THE KING'S doors. The guards on either side of him flinched but righted themselves with their backs against the wall.

Jorn was waiting. Back leaned against the wall, with one foot casually rested in front of the other, Jorn's arms were crossed loosely at his chest. He lifted a palm and cocked his head to the side with a mischievous grin. Saying plenty without speaking a word.

Matthias snarled and balled his hands into fists at his sides. Jorn fell in step behind him. They turned for the stairs, circling down the tightly spun stones. They entered the armory and walked through the wide hallway. Lines of forged iron were propped, orderly and ready, against the dank walls, reflecting the light of the torches that lit the underground passage.

A few soldiers glanced their way, but most were mid-shift change, and paid them no mind, eager for rest and reprieve in the barracks. Matthias kept moving until another smaller set of stairs spilled him outside toward the stables. Dirt pounding beneath his boots, he walked toward them, Jorn still at his heels.

"That rotting bastard," Matthias seethed.

Under the cover of the stables, Matthias paced back and forth. He ran a hand through his hair, shoulders heaving.

Matthias wanted to ride. Ride until he couldn't feel anything, couldn't think anymore. Matthias found his stallion, greeting him by petting the bridge of his nose. The horse snorted, nudging his head. Brom's black eyes blinked hello, and Matthias laid his forehead against the horse, petting its shoulder. "Brom. You ready for a run boy?"

"What's it going to be, brother?" Jorn asked.

"Raise the men and ready our horses," Matthias said.

"He means to honor his word, then?"

Matthias grimaced. He turned and rubbed his hand across his eyes and nodded.

"We're free?" Jorn's eyebrow raised.

Free.

The word hung in the air between them, heavy, bloated, and surreal.

His brother stood wide-eyed, hesitant, and waiting on his answer.

Matthias put his hands on his hips and gave a small nod.

They were, weren't they, then?

"*Ja,* brother." Matthias half-smiled. "We leave for Hamburg within the day."

Jorn put his palms together and pressed his pointer fingers against his lips. He closed his eyes and took in a slow breath. His eyes opened wide, and he grinned. "*Excellent!* I've grown tired of eating and drinking from the king's purse anyway."

Matthias laughed.

"Pottage and berries it is, then," Matthias said.

Matthias grabbed a comb, scratched Brom behind the ear, and started to groom his shimmering hair. He craved silence, but he knew Jorn would not leave. Instead, Jorn paced, shuffled hay with his boots, waiting behind Matthias for his attention. Matthias rested his hand on Brom's hip and turned to Jorn.

"Speak your mind or leave me be," Matthias said.

Jorn stopped moving and exhaled loudly.

"The princess. Will she ride with you? Or does he plan her to stay?"

Matthias scowled at him, his jaw twitching. "Don't."

"I only ask for your orders, brother."

Matthias clenched his fist tighter around the comb and returned to his task.

"What's your king to do with her?" Jorn said.

"She's no longer our concern."

"Really? After all of that?"

Matthias shot Jorn a hard look over his shoulder. "Girault's honored his word. We are free men."

Jorn nodded, moving closer.

Matthias laid a hand on Brom's back and looked at the ground, avoiding him.

"We cannot let him forget it, then," Jorn said, lowering his voice. "Either of them."

Matthias shook his head. He might as well be out with it; Jorn wasn't leaving him alone. Matthias turned, tossed the comb into the grooming bucket, and walked across the stable. He leaned his back against a thick beam and crossed his arms.

"They bid me to bend the knee," Matthias said.

Jorn scoffed. "That didn't take long. I knew he would."

Matthias grunted. "They want the new prince protected."

"Are you to play nursemaid?"

Matthias snorted and rubbed his jawline. Restless, he strode back to Brom and ran his hand along his long back. The animal shifted on its hooves, as if he too stood in need of a run.

"They offered me a wife," Matthias said. "As payment."

"God's bones," Jorn said, shocked. "They've lost their senses."

"Genau."

Jorn laughed heartily. "Was he serious?"

"He taunts me," Matthias sighed.

"So you say. He is a man child." Jorn spat. "Playing with you."

Matthias shrugged his shoulders. That definitely wasn't a point he would argue against. Not today.

"Who'd he offer you?" Jorn asked.

"Helene."

"Eger's daughter?"

"Ja."

"She's a right pretty maid," Jorn said, leaning forward.

"She is," Matthias said.

Jorn crossed his arms and leaned his shoulder against a beam. "And the princess? What's to happen to her?"

Matthias pursed his lips.

"Do not tell me you do not care," Jorn said. "I've seen the way you look at her."

"I didn't say that." Matthias looked to the ground and rubbed his temples. "It's been a long day."

"It has," Jorn said. "But that snake's done something to her to set you on fire. Your jaw's set to break in two if you chew any harder."

Steadying his hands on Brom, Matthias hung his head between them. "Damn it, Jorn."

"I mean no offense, brother. I only intend to protect what's yours."

Matthias exhaled, trying to expel the tightness in his chest. "She's not mine."

"Isn't she?" Jorn said, walking to Matthias's side. "You need only say the word, brother. I'll protect you from that vile king of yours if I must."

Matthias hung his head, frustrated. "I don't need protection from the king."

"Yes. You do," Jorn said. "And so does she." Jorn crossed his arms and widened his stance. "You're loyal to a fault. To men who don't deserve it. You forget he was a warrior before that pretty crown sat on his head. He killed many a man to get it, and he'll kill anyone to keep it."

"We've killed men for less."

Jorn shook his head. "Your cock's clouding your mind, and he knows it. You think he offered you a wife for no reason?"

"It was the queen's idea."

"Ha! That snake? Oh, she'll play that card she's been dealt all right, making you feel sorry for her, but she's always got a full deck hidden behind it at the ready," Jorn said. "She's a right awful sort. Always has been. The two of them together are infinitely worse."

"That's treason, Jorn."

"If your sword isn't loyal to the crown, they see you as a threat. You know that."

Matthias laid his hand on Jorn's shoulder. "Brother. Lower your voice. Mind your tongue that it doesn't cost you your head."

Jorn's eyes flickered with the underlying rage that was always there, simmering, waiting, framed by his flaming red hair.

Matthias swallowed. "King Girault's kept his word. He's

rewarded our service, as he said. We are free men."

"And the girl?" Jorn raised an eyebrow.

Matthias scoffed and took a step back. He raised his palms in the air, submitting. Lacing his fingers together, he cupped the back of his neck.

"Gah." Matthias threw his head back, twisted at the waist, trying to shake the nervous energy pulsing through him.

They'd done what they set out to do.

It should have felt exhilarating, but everything about it felt wrong.

He crouched with his head in his hands and his heart in his throat. "What have I done, Jorn? What have I done?"

Jorn knelt beside him and rested a hand on Matthias's shoulder.

"Your duty, brother," Jorn said. "Tonight you go to the dinner. You find her. And you say your good-byes." He grunted and spat. "Enough of this place. We leave tomorrow at first light. Quickly and quietly. The greater the distance we make from here, the better, though not soon enough, I'm afraid. This place is poison."

CHAPTER 45

FORKED TONGUES

Avelina

HAVING OFFERED HER LAST PRAYERS, Avelina rose from the prayer stool. She paused, enjoying the winged altarpiece before her. Rather grand for a private chapel, it was perfectly placed within. From the tall glass windows beside her, ribbons of warm honeyed light cascaded across its open panels, enriching the scenes from Christ's life painted upon them. On the center shrine, the relief of the Ascension shone brightly against a blue background as the sunlight set the golden accents painted upon the carved wooden figures aglow. Exquisitely carved, it stood testimony to the gifts bestowed on man and of God.

Ready to leave the king's oratory, Avelina turned and saw a lady, about her own age and with a cherubic face, standing just inside the doors.

"The colors. They're lovely, aren't they?" The lady smiled. Her voice was pleasant. Light. Large brown eyes sat wide in her small face. Her blond hair was tightly plaited behind her neck and woven with a robin's egg-blue ribbon that matched her dress. She was lovely in a delicate way. A child of extensive fortune, based on the richness of detail sewn on her dress. "The windows remain, but as the hours change, their beauty focuses themselves upon a different part of the chapel. On the altar, as you see now. Other times they cast their colors across the chapel floor. Sometimes they act as a mirror, simply reflecting the flames from the candelabra beside them. My favorite is when the sunlight comes at such an angle they paint the ceiling in rainbows, pulling the heavens inside."

"Lit from both sides," Avelina said, smiling.

"Precisely." The lady's chin tilted, satisfied. She held out an open hand to Avelina. "My name is Wilhelmina. I'm to be your guide as you settle into your new home here at Ewigsburg. Come, Princess Avelina, it's time for tea."

Avelina had delayed long enough. She placed her fingers in the lady's palm. Wilhelmina tucked their bound hands to her side, and they walked together through the chapel door and down the hallway until they reached the arched entrance of the Summer Hall. Avelina took each step purposefully, though lightly to relieve the throbbing in her still tender foot, daring not to wince before the increasingly gathered crowds.

Bright and long, the room was bustling from one end to the other. The high walls were painted from floor to ceiling in intricate details. Thick branches twisted up from the floor on a soft yellow background. Clusters of rich green leaves framed crests and portraits of people and scenes from their lives. Giant columns rose on either side to an arched ceiling, where beams crossed the sky, threading through and supporting one another like a thick forest canopy. At equidistant spots along the wall, bowed windows rose high above sets of window seats bathed in sunlight.

Wilhelmina led her across the room to an empty window seat. Some of the women strolling around the room paused as they walked by to openly stare. Bored—or disappointed—they fluttered on. Their voices chirping, their conversations animated, they were like groups of birds hopping around a pile of seeds.

"Here we are," Wilhelmina said. "This is perfect. Do sit, Princess. I'll have some refreshment brought round."

Spreading her skirt wide, Avelina settled onto the burgundy cushion and tucked her feet beneath her. She chose not to meet any of their prodding stares with her own, instead keeping her face plain and pleasant. She was not new to the games of court; she had played them her entire life. She was a survivor, only wildly out of practice.

If she needed to pass the time, Avelina knew to keep her mind, as always, otherwise occupied. She concentrated on the large vase of overflowing flowers set on a wooden table with three carved legs.

The vase itself looked spun by hand, with thin ascending ringlets barely visible beneath the glaze work upon it. Thin gray details were painted along the curved neck, where the low-lying flowers dripped from its lip. All shades of white. Several shapes and sizes. Avelina surveyed them one by one, trying to extract and sort their individual scents from the flowery mix sailing through the air.

Avelina found and focused on the hydrangeas. A trio of woody branches held the bunches of delicate yet simple white flowers aloft. Their smell was sweet and heady against the spiced honey notes of the roses, in a nook whose undercurrent was of sun-warmed stone.

Wilhelmina returned and set a pewter plate of finger foods on a small table and folded her limbs into the chair beside Avelina. Slight and unsteady even off her legs, the girl seemed thankful for a place to nestle. Well versed in etiquette, judging from her manners and poise, there was still a vulnerability to her, an unease in the way she straightened her back in her seat. Like at any moment she might collapse into herself.

"Eat. Please." Wilhelmina handed her a small glass of white wine and motioned to the plate. "This day will be long, and you'll need your strength."

Avelina smiled politely and ate a piece of rolled meat. Richly flavored with marbled fat, it melted on her tongue. After another bite, she took a sip of the wine. A bit sweeter than she was used to, with hints of apricots and apples, it paired well with the salty flavor of the smoked meats.

"Do you like it?" Wilhelmina asked.

"It's delicious," Avelina said, enjoying the lingering taste. "It's fruity. Light."

"Quite so," Wilhelmina said. "It's a Riesling from the Neckar region. Where my mother was born."

They smiled at one another and let some time pass in silence.

The pewter plate between them was stacked with meats and tiny tartlets and her cup kept full of wine, but Avelina couldn't stomach much more of it. She pursed her lips behind a folded handkerchief, stifling the small moan rising in her throat.

This dress. From the king, it was luxurious and the finest thing she'd ever been gifted. A silk brocade of the deepest green, its sleeves and skirts were decorated in a pattern of pomegranates and thistles stitched in glittering golden thread, leaving every movement of the fabric to sparkle like a rolling wave under a full moon. It was exquisite, and she was grateful, but she'd been tied into it like a babe swaddled by a nervous mother. Avelina swung her knees to the opposite side, hoping the shift might relieve the pressure in her gut, but to no avail. She sat rigidly upright on the edge of her cushioned chair, equally uncomfortable and exhausted, and lost herself again in the flowers.

"She's here," Wilhelmina said.

Avelina looked in the direction of Wilhelmina's stare, and her breath caught.

There was no mistaking it. Queen Lilith had arrived.

The woman was beautiful. *Strikingly* beautiful. A vision in varied shades of gold, from her skin to her honeyed blond hair to the richly cut dress accentuating her figure, she was crisp and clean and curvaceous, as if she were a goddess molded on earth. She arched her shoulders back, drawing all eyes to her and the golden flower pendant she proudly wore at her breast. Beset with an immense emerald in the center and dripping with pearls, it folded out in layers of jeweled petals onto a bed of green leaves. A showpiece for this event.

Satisfied, the queen slid into the hall.

A snake in a bonnet.

Those were the words she'd heard Jorn use to describe the queen. She'd thought them crass until she saw the queen move, when Jorn's words of warning reverberated within her memory. The very last leg of their ascent to the castle, Jorn had fallen back beside her, muttering rather harshly about the woman.

Though Jorn's language had been colorful, his message was now clearly received. This queen was an actress who clearly knew how to play her audience and send what message she willed to the courtiers. One shoulder flirtatiously dropped, the curve of her neck curled to the court as if to a lover, beckoning them seductively to only tease them with a taste at arm's length. Her loose and forked tongue tickled the ears of the elite. Nastiness dripped from one side, cloaked in a silky cadence aching to own the authority in the room, while compliments and pleasantries rolled off the other in a sweet purr.

Queen Lilith appeared beside them, and with a nod of her head, several chairs were set in a semicircle around Wilhelmina and Avelina. The queen curled herself into the chair beside Wilhelmina and squeezed the young woman's knee. She elongated her neck and then set her chin with the style and grace of a swan.

For the briefest of moments and just as quickly corrected, the queen's beautiful features flashed severe. Face like a hawk, her beady eyes and thin eyebrows pulled tightly over her beaked nose. She stared sharply at Wilhelmina before turning to Avelina with an exaggerated sigh and stilted, fake smile.

"I see you've met my daughter."

Avelina's throat squeezed in surprise. "I've recently had the pleasure. She's lovely."

"Hmpf." Queen Lilith waved her hand about, gathering the attention of her minions, who settled into the chairs around them.

"You ladies know King Girault requested that I take this lady, Avelina, into my service."

"Mother, she is a princess," Wilhelmina whispered, not looking at her.

The queen stopped. Lips pert, she rolled her eyes so hard her head rolled with them.

"Wilhelmina, you have such a trusting, innocent heart." Queen Lilith turned back to her ready audience. She covered her mouth to whisper, and her eyebrows lifted high. "The good king pitied the lady, you see, and had her rescued. She was to be *executed.*" The ladies gasped, and she waved her hand, fanning their flames. "Yes! She's no longer welcome in Leuceria, as the child is a *bastard.* Hers is such a tawdry, sad, and scandalous story."

"Mother," Wilhelmina whispered, her chin low.

"The king trusts me to give the girl an opportunity to avoid her shame. How could I refuse my king and husband?" Queen Lilith said.

Wilhelmina laid her hand on her mother's and interrupted her. "Avelina, tell us about Leuceria."

The queen's eyes flicked down, where she removed her hand from beneath her daughter's and placed it prominently on her ribbon-ridged décolletage. "Of course, you come from such an interesting place. And have had such a long and strange journey."

"I'd like to hear how Leuceria and Ewigsburg compare. I've lived here so long I've almost forgotten everything beyond these walls," Wilhelmina said.

"You *are* a bit unworldly, my dear," Queen Lilith said, her nose wrinkled. "Well, I can tell you about the palace, as I've heard the full report from Master Reymund."

"The crippled man?" one of the ladies, a brunette said, before covering her lips.

"The same. He is a bit of an oddity, but he does prove trustworthy in his reports to my king." The queen lifted her brows and chin, as though her own words were noisome.

The line of Avelina's lips grew thinner, but she expertly readjusted into an empty expression. This woman had games written all over her. Dangerous games. Avelina had dealt with enough people like this in her life, but usually it was the men who positioned themselves around Niro's feet like dogs, begging for scraps of power.

Women, in more ways than one, were different here.

"I hear the Leucerian palace is nice, but not grand, *majestic*, like Ewigsburg. It's seated in a valley outside the city. Poorly decorated. Painted in golden tricks." The queen twisted her head side to side. Loudly enunciating the words and flicking letters, and the ladies were held by every syllable, leaning forward in their chairs, not to miss a single detail or any intended slight. "Statues everywhere you look, and of *nobody* in particular. Some rather shocking, barely dressed. Rather vulgar." She nodded to the small crowd before rolling a shoulder back and draping herself against her cushioned chair arm. "In Ewigsburg, a man must make a name for himself to have his likeness carved. Or be from a great family to have his portrait painted." Her tone belittling, she waved her hand dismissively, sighing. "Simply too ostentatious for my taste."

Mute, Avelina was determined to seem agreeable. She demurely set her hands in her lap, watching the other ladies. Their eyes followed the queen as if entranced and occasionally to Avelina with a mix of curiosity and apprehension. Avelina knew that look—they watched her, waiting to see how she faired and whom she favored before they decided to align themselves with her or secure the best seats to watch her downfall. Except Wilhelmina, who kept her eyes aground.

Wilhelmina scooted forward in her seat and leaned toward Avelina. "My lady mother speaks the truth. The palace is different, but the gardens—I've heard they're extraordinary. Mirrored works of art that wrap around the entire palace."

Avelina smiled at Wilhelmina, thankful for the compliment. The palace gardens were just that—living masterpieces, planned, planted, and meticulously maintained. Some sections generations old; others, her mother had developed.

Wilhelmina stood. She offered a deep curtsy to the queen.

"Forgive me, Lady Mother," Wilhelmina said. "I promised Avelina that I would show her the good king's gardens. The sun is lowing, and you always say the colors are richest and best appreciated in the golden hour."

"I would love that." The invitation was a surprise but welcome. Both the company and the lack of a proper night's sleep prickled through Avelina's limbs, making her most eager to move. "If the queen allows it, of course."

"You've already had such a long journey," Queen Lilith said. Her pasted smile faltered; her cheeks shaded red with warning.

"Just a quick turn about, Mother, and then our prayers." Wilhelmina slipped her arm through Avelina's. "Please, Mother. I hate to miss it, and I hate to walk alone."

After presenting another curtsy to the queen, Wilhelmina turned and gently pulled Avelina with her.

"A moment, Avelina," Queen Lilith said, standing. Eyes twinkling, unnerving, she opened her arms wide. Avelina stepped forward, and the queen placed a hand on each of her shoulders.

Now with full attention, the queen's head gracefully turned to Avelina's, leaning toward her in a move that spoke not only of familiarity, but of fondness. A devilish red smile drew across the queen's face, as if delivering some darkly delicious secrets meant for Avelina alone. "Little fool. Do not think you can destroy the house that I have built."

Avelina pulled against her, but the queen wrapped her arms around Avelina and pulled her in tight, as if embracing a close friend.

"You think I survived this long in this castle only because I let that old man bury himself between my thighs?" Every word sharp as a dagger, the queen whispered into Avelina's ear. "I cannot stop the king from keeping you as his mistress. But one day, when I have my chance, I will finish you. I will find everything you care about. Everyone. And destroy them. I promise you: if you should breed before then, I will strangle your children at your breast."

Squeezing Avelina's shoulders once more, the queen let her go.

Her blood running cold, Avelina steadied herself.

Watching her with a raised brow, the queen sighed heavily. She unfolded her taut muscles, molded a serene smile on her face, and recast herself into a woman of grace, melting back into her luxurious chair.

Avelina backed away from the queen and eagerly followed Wilhelmina from the room.

The two ladies walked side by side into the hallway in silence.

This place. These people. Everything, every moment, felt both a move forward and step back. At once, a piece of clarity added to the puzzle, revealing more of her future within this place, each vapid incident proving only to strip away another bit of her hopes, sucking her dry and speechless. Avelina was being baptized into her new life here and had no choice but to put her best foot forward and keep her steps in sync with the other ladies serving this queen if she were to survive this place.

Another palace, another charade. Another decorative prison.

Avelina stretched her back, alternating between one flat foot and the other weighted on its heel. She enjoyed the slow and steady pace as they walked in silence. Little by little, the stale air of the halls was replaced with a freshly perfumed and earthy breeze.

They stepped out onto a long veranda that wrapped around the curves of the castle. Flags flapped, snapping above them on the towers reaching toward the first stars peeping through the evening sky. To one end, over a cliff's edge, Avelina saw low rolling fields, waves of green shimmering golden in the sun's kiss. From here, the clusters of small buildings looked like pebbles, patched between farms and fields. To the other side, Avelina saw the promised gardens. Symmetrical patterns twisted along the grounds of the walled space, with pathways cut between them. Shades of rich red bled into crisp whites, blooming heavily on the twisted greens below them. It was lovely but held nothing against the blended fingers of pinks and purples and oranges beyond it, laying the sun to rest in the arms of the horizon.

"I love it here in the open air." Wilhelmina's voice broke through her rambling thoughts, reminding Avelina of her companion. It was soothing in its sincerity, the assuredness with which she spoke. "It's beautiful, is it not?"

"It's impressive," Avelina said.

"It's never been taken. Not in all the wars. The Rock—that's what we call the castle—stands strong as the Lord himself."

"A fitting choice," Avelina said.

Avelina turned again toward the horizon. Here, sitting atop the mountain cliff, with the height the castle afforded, the day's clear sky offered her an almost endless and breathtaking view. Following the river, desperately hopeful, she found her lines—the *Geisterweg*. Disappearing into the muted gray, Metzlingen was hauntingly weaved between the heavily draped lines of dusk and the blurred edge of the king's land.

"We should get back. I knew you needed the air, but the king will arrive soon," Wilhelmina said, turning squarely to Avelina with a sigh. "Forgive my frankness, but . . . be careful with Mother."

"I don't understand," Avelina said, though she knew very well she did.

Wilhelmina squeezed her elbow, pulling Avelina in closer.

"Mother was recently widowed, and though she had to hide it, the loss of my father devastated her," Wilhelmina said.

"I see," Avelina said. "I'm sorry for the loss of your father. I am told he was a good man."

"Yes, thank you. I know you have long mourned your parents. Both father and mother."

"Death is never easy. On anyone."

"True," Wilhelmina said. "But thankfully there is reason to celebrate now. Her marriage and the birth of my brother, the new prince. Both have given Mother position and security. All things Mother has plans to feverishly protect. Many plans."

"Plans?" Avelina raised her eyebrows, both interested in the queen's plans and how loose the girl's tongue was with her mother's secrets. Maybe Wilhelmina had overindulged in the spiced wine as well. The large kegs had certainly been flowing for hours.

"Well, first, for the King's Sword," Wilhelmina said.

"Matthias?" Avelina stopped abruptly and turned to study Wilhelmina's face. "But he's earned his freedom. And means to leave."

The corners of Wilhelmina's lips flittered.

"Mother says he has no means or will of his own. A boar who mindlessly takes his coin, but he *does* love his king." Wilhelmina nudged Avelina along, squeezing her hand. "Mother also says no *woman* here is ever free. So why should a man be? The king wants Matthias to stay, which is why he will wed Helene."

"What?" Avelina blinked. Another development chiseling away at her hopes, this news drove its crack deeply right through the heart of her.

It couldn't be true. Not her Matthias.

Hers.

He wasn't, though, was he?

"My elder sister, Helene. The king offers her to Matthias in marriage," Wilhelmina said. "He isn't noble by birth, but the king believes he's the best there is to safeguard the new prince."

"But his freedom," Avelina said.

"The king rewards his favorites, and a betrothal to my sister is a great reward indeed," Wilhelmina said. "No man could refuse her. The daughter of Duke Eger, the stepdaughter to the king. Now that Matthias has returned, I know it to be true. It is a sign, a blessing. God smiles on him for sure."

CHAPTER 46

THE VIEW FROM ON HIGH

Matthias

MATTHIAS ENTERED THE BACK OF the Great Hall and paused. A habit long instilled in him, he mentally mapped the room. Marked where his men stood. Noted their allies. Any potential threat. Weapons he could use or could be used against him. A plan of attack. A plan to withdraw. A plan to escape.

The feast was well underway. The hall was bustling, bursting with conversation and laughter. The king had spared no expense, and the court took full advantage of all of it. The richest families throughout the kingdom and visiting nobles were there, all vying for the same place around the king. Where they could be seen. Earn favor. Make alliances. Measure one another. Measure their new queen against the foreign princess.

Barrels of wine and kegs of ale poured freely from the front corners of the room, where tables overflowed with platters brought from the kitchens below. Maids brought them around to the tables, stuffed with nobles from one end to the other, loudly enjoying the king's banquet. Two large *schwein* were hoisted on spikes. Smaller roasted suckling pigs surrounded a stuffed swan centerpiece. *Brötchen* and cheeses in woven baskets were placed between plates of duck and rabbit. Matthias's favorite, the venison pies, were piled high on the table's end next to bowls of bright apples.

The smells that usually watered his mouth made his stomach sour. His last meal had been at the tavern, and since then he'd had no appetite.

A drink, though. He could suffer a few of those.

A trio of musicians played on the far side of the room, two plucking at their lutes, another pulling a bow across a psaltery. A group of jugglers and acrobats were collecting their wares, having finished entertaining the king. The new queen sat in all her glory at the king's side, as she had for years, though now she sat taller, wearing her crown.

Avelina sat to the king's right as a favored guest. A sign of respect. Deep respect. But also a sign to the court that she was with him. Was *his*.

King Girault met Matthias's stare from across the hall and held it. With no intention of approaching the king, Matthias gave him a slight nod and remained rooted where he stood. Message received, the king smirked. He planted his hands on the edge of his throne and stood. He slapped himself on the chest and opened his arms wide, demanding attention.

"A dance!" he yelled, and the room erupted into cheers. The king turned to his queen, offering her a hand, and led her to the center of the open floor.

Avelina remained in her seat. Sitting still, staring off above the crowd of heads.

She hadn't seen him yet. Or had she, yet she refused to look his way?

Matthias walked toward the stairs against the wall. Taking them two at a time, he reached the balcony. Three of his men—Michel, Harock, and Lars—sat tightly around a corner table. Their backs toward the court, they were enjoying their ale and a game of cards and dice. Boone was nowhere to be seen. No doubt he'd already found himself a woman, and good on him.

Matthias had been glad to see them again. He hadn't known them as long as his brothers, but they were family all the same. He patted Lars's thick shoulder in greeting when he walked by, and the large bald man grunted, not looking up from his game. Matthias grinned. There was a good mix of coin and conversation between them, and he was happy for their ease.

Matthias continued to his usual table, right at the front center of the balcony, where he had the best view over the entire hall. Jorn slid a large stein over to him and nodded. The ale's foam slopped over the top as Matthias eagerly picked it up.

"Brother," Jorn said, clanking his own stein against Matthias's.

"Thanks." Matthias took a thirstful swallow and closed his eyes. *There* it was. The heavy and familiar dark ale of Ewigsburg.

He savored the soured, smoky taste—once he got past the smell—quenching the hell out of his thirst and filling his empty stomach. Though not a spiced winter cider nor a sweet southern wine, it could still knock a grown man on his arse and help him forget his name, if that was his purpose in drink.

And if Matthias was honest with himself, tonight that may have been it.

"Whoa, brother," Jorn said, nodding at Matthias's stein. "A bit easier on that drink. It's been a while. Nobody's trying to take it from you."

"I'm fine," Matthias said, taking another drink.

"So you say." Jorn raised an eyebrow.

Matthias peered onto the floor below, where the king danced with his new bride. The music was bright and gay, and the court cheered around them. Once they were done, a few members of the court formed a line on either side of them to join in while the rest crowded the edge of the floor.

That was when she joined in.

The king turned to Avelina and opened his hand, and she stepped into the line of ladies. The music continued, and the dancers began twirling one another, spinning and kicking their feet. It was dark but for the walls of candles, and he watched, searching for glimpses of her as she moved in and out of their best light, her long brown braid bouncing behind her.

"She looks well," Jorn said.

Matthias scoffed, side-eyeing him. "So do you, brother."

Jorn smiled ear to ear.

The man was clearly set to bed a woman tonight. Or he already had, as someone had tended to him. Jorn's clothes were fresh. His hair was pulled back off his face, and the curls sat thick, combed, at his shoulders. The beard that wrapped around his rock-hard jaw was clean and tamed. The stench of the road was gone.

"Take a seat," Jorn said. "Stay a while."

Matthias stepped over the bench to sit beside Jorn and leaned his elbows onto the table. His fingers traced the line of his trimmed beard, and his mouth settled against his knuckles.

"Lady Helene is here," Jorn said, wiping his thumb over the lip of his stein.

Matthias exhaled. There was no way to avoid the topic. "And?"

"Arrived for the tournament," Jorn said.

"She's only a child." Matthias grunted.

"A child? She's a year older than your princess. And eager to be married, I hear." Jorn grinned and poured ale down his throat.

Matthias shook his head, dismissing him, and took another drink. "Then let them find her a prince of the *Hochadel*. If not the upper nobility, then a baron."

"The men are hearing different. Eger's man, Ulrich, has given warning of the king's intentions," Jorn said, eyeing him.

"It's not happening," Matthias said.

"That's not what the underground is saying," Jorn said. His fingers drummed against the table. "No matter what slippery story these fine people tell you, you can usually count on the maids to know the real one."

"Spending some time in the kitchens, are you?"

Jorn grinned. "A man has to eat."

Matthias snorted.

"Let them say what they will." Matthias surveyed the nobles below, dressed richly, colorfully, and laden with chains of jewels. Their knights strutted as well, hoping to catch a lady's attention. Their favor and adoration, and sponsorship purse, were all great prizes to earn. "Eger was a great man, and his daughters should be taken care of."

"Pity Eger didn't see to arrange it before his death," Jorn said.

Matthias grimaced. Duke Eger had been a powerful man, one of the most respected at court, but even his authority had been limited and threatened by the crown. "Now it's on the king to find her a suitable husband amongst these men."

"*Ach*, well for her sake, we'll hope it's a good match. 'Tis a sad truth she's only another innocent caught in the king's schemes." Jorn's nose wrinkled. He lifted his stein and gestured toward the dance floor. "I don't trust them. Bunch of walking arses with ears. Dressed in diamonds and speaking in circles. Riddles. Never in truths." He took another drink and sucked air through his teeth. "Look at them, watching your princess. Circling her like prey."

Jorn was right. The nobility, men and women alike, made no effort to hide their curiosity toward Avelina. Staring openly at her. Pointing at her. Huddling around her.

"With Eger gone, they'll be vying for position with the king and his new queen. Where that leaves your princess, I don't know," Jorn said.

Matthias's grip tightened around the handle of his stein.

"I told you," Matthias grumbled. "Girault plans to keep her."

"That is what he said, isn't it?" Jorn said flippantly. "I'll be back. Hands off my ale."

Jorn tapped his palm on the table, stood, and stumbled away.

Matthias narrowed his eyes, moving from one noble to the next.

He knew their guards. Those who defended their great houses, lands, and people. He judged them by the standards to which they kept their households. If their soldiers were ill equipped or their people starving while they ate and drank their money away, then Jorn was right and they were no better than the shit they scraped off their shoes by the doorway.

A burp rose from his sloshing stomach, and Matthias covered his mouth with his fist. Exhaling, he leaned forward and propped his forehead against his hands.

"I didn't want any of this," he said, squeezing his eyes tightly shut.

A hand gripped his shoulder, and a body twisted heavily down into Jorn's empty seat. "I daresay this isn't what the princess hoped for either."

Matthias reached his hand out blindly, smacking the man square in the chest, and felt the familiar wooden cross.

"Where've you been?" Matthias said, a grin spreading across his face. His back straightened, and he stretched his legs out, relaxing in Reymund's company.

"Around," Reymund said, wrapping his hands around his thigh and pulling at his stubborn leg. "Listening. Learning. As hard as I am to miss, people take my presence for granted. The lot of them confuse my mind to be as broken and worthless as my body."

"Nothing about you is broken or worthless, brother."

Matthias reached and assisted, feeling the muscle in Reymund's leg spasm against his hand. Nodding thanks, Reymund propped himself onto the table edge for stability.

"Their words, not mine," Reymund said with his crooked smile. "Still, I think I'll forego another dance this evening."

Matthias rubbed his hand across the short brown hair atop Reymund's head. Grabbing him by the back of the neck, he squeezed gently and smiled. "Missed you, brother."

Jorn stormed up behind them and planted his hands on Reymund.

"You rascal, I was only gone for a piss." He grinned, jostling Reymund's slender shoulders. He found a stool and pulled it over to join them.

Matthias finished his ale and gestured at a maid along the wall. She returned with three heavy steins in each hand and set them on the table in front of them.

"Thank you." Matthias handed her a coin.

"Eat something, brother," Reymund said, pushing a plate of *bratwurst* and *brötchen* in front of Matthias.

"I intend to drink my supper." Matthias took a freshly filled ale and slid one of the others to each of his brothers. Reymund shook his head and tucked his hands into his sleeves.

"What've you learned?" Jorn asked, leaning toward Reymund.

"It's complicated. With the young prince, there are many plans afoot. But that's a story for another time. When you fools haven't been drinking so much."

The three of them fell silent.

Matthias stared blankly at the table and finished his ale. He lost himself, mindlessly tracing the grain of the wood until the lines became blurry, growing fat and fuzzy. He blinked and looked about their collection of empty steins and full plates. Seeing Reymund hadn't touched his ale, Matthias retrieved it for himself.

"What are you two chattering on about?" Matthias said, turning to them.

"The king's plans," Reymund said. "If you don't want to find yourself cornered by them, you have to always be a step ahead of them."

"Is that so?" Matthias said, taking another drink. "I, for one, no longer care for the king's plans."

"Yes, you do. And you should." Reymund shifted his elbow along the edge of the table toward Matthias and lowered his voice. "The king means to call upon you on the morrow. Matthias, you *must* keep your wits clear." Glancing at the ale in Matthias's hand, Reymund laid a hand on his arm. "The only thing you'll find at the bottom of that stein . . ."

"Is another." Matthias pulled his arm from beneath Reymund's hand and swallowed another drink.

"Or a burned arse after you spend the night shitting fire," Jorn said with an arched eyebrow.

Matthias laughed, then quickly cringed. He wiped his sleeve across his face, cleaning the stray dribble of ale around his mouth. "It's no matter. The king will be sadly disappointed. If he means to call upon us tomorrow, we will already be gone. I mean to leave early."

"No, Matthias, before dawn. *After the bedding*," Reymund said.

Matthias's throat tightened, choking his words. "The princess?"

Reymund's chin dropped. "The king means to make a show of taking the princess to his bed. Especially given the expanded audience in attendance."

Matthias slammed his stein on the table.

That unbelievable—

"The king is determined for you to stay," Reymund said.

Matthias stared into his ale and sneered. "He can think as he likes. I will not bend the knee, nor will I marry Helene. What would I even do with a wife?"

"*Uhhh.* Hump," Jorn snorted.

Matthias lifted his mug but set it back without a drink.

"Must you always—" Matthias stopped short. He grabbed the edge of the table with his free hand and clenched his eyelids shut, hoping to push the wave of drunkenness away. The music and ale thumped furiously through his veins, battering his skull.

Gah. That had come fast. Too fast. He reached for a *brötchen* and took a hearty bite.

"Jorn's right," Reymund said. "Lady Helene is meant to keep you loyal. And she's exquisite. A gift."

Matthias looked at him, puzzled. "That doesn't explain why *me*.

There's plenty of men here who seek her favor. Any number who would marry her."

"It's all quite calculated." Reymund leaned forward and put a hand on Matthias's forearm. "You are the King's Sword. They want your steadfast support and your sword behind the new prince. You must remember that the boy was born out of wedlock, though quickly claimed and named legitimate when the king married Duchess Lilith. The queen's now strengthening her son's claim and using Helene as payment and her womb as the building block. Any sons you have, their swords would also be in service to the new prince."

"That woman's slyer than a starving fox," Jorn hissed. "I wouldn't trust the fruit she dangled in front of you, even if you picked it off the branch yourself."

"I've had too much ale for this," Matthias said, rubbing his temples.

Jorn's lip tugged, and he raised his stein. "*Alles gut*, brother. *Prosit*. To freedom."

They toasted. Matthias turned back around, drinking until he finished the ale and set the stein clumsily on his thigh. This time, he did not reach for another.

Matthias's hand curled and uncurled at his side as he looked back out over the dance floor.

Searching for her.

He found Helene. Her braided blond hair hanging below her veil to the waist of her copper gown, she swayed through the crowd. A reflection of her mother in her younger years, though with the easy and amiable presence her father had possessed.

She really was beautiful.

But Matthias looked past Helene, searching for Avelina.

He found her, following the route of stolen glances and gossip that hungrily moved through the crowd toward the princess.

In the midst of them, Avelina glided across the dance floor like a flower adrift on a stream. Out of place. Floating, twirling, delicately on top. Powerless against the force of the water. Any moment to hit a rock and be swallowed by the current and disappear below the surface into the darkness.

"Enough," Matthias said.

Laying his palms flat on the table, he pushed himself to stand. His knee jarred and he pulled his hips up, stretching his body to his full height. His bloated stomach soured, and he drew a breath deep into his lungs, and another, aiming to settle his drunken nerves.

"Brother . . ." Jorn's stool squealed sharply as he stood and stepped toward him.

Matthias held a hand up to Jorn, stopping him.

He had to do this, and it had to be now.

"I am a free man. I go to say good-bye."

CHAPTER 47

TAKE MY HAND

—◆◆◆—

Avelina

ONE. TWO. THREE AND . . .
Perfectly on count, Avelina stepped toward the king, mimicking the ladies lined on either side of her. She raised her hand and pressed her fingertips against the king's palm, the two of them gliding in circles.

After the queen retired for the evening, the king had moved her to first position. Avelina was trained well enough to follow the king's lead, and the moves for the dances themselves, though strange and more stilted than what she'd learned in her country, were uncomplicated. Rising on the ball of her foot, stepping lightly, another twirl. Each step another count following the seductive call of the musician's strings. Rising and falling, folding herself into the score, she could escape, at least momentarily, on each note that carried through the air.

Avelina's body longed for a break, and when the bows drew long across the strings, signaling the end of the dance, she tilted her head in thanks at the musicians, then drew her skirts wide and curtsied to the king.

"Thank you, Your Grace."

Avelina straightened her tired legs, begged her apologies, and withdrew.

The longer the day crawled by, the more uncomfortable her new dress became and the more restricted she felt within it. Its ties remained taut and tight. Cinched across her stomach, bloated from food and drink after scarcely eating for weeks, she felt like her insides were squeezed together and displaced into already crowded cavities. She longed to strip herself of it, unfold her limbs, and fill her lungs until they burst.

Eager to leave the dance floor, Avelina searched for a way to break through the throngs of courtiers.

"My apologies," she said, dropping her chin to a cluster of smartly dressed men.

Outfitted in striking patterns in shades of rich reds, brilliant blues, and bright greens, the younger men sported doublets, embroidered in gold and embellished with pearls, over their hose. Others were wrapped in belts of gold, wearing long cloaks lined with fur, some boldly in all black. Jeweled caps covered their hair, chin to shoulder length, and they wore layers of jeweled chains about their necks or clipped at their shoulders with broaches.

Their bodies were amassed at the edge of the dance floor, like weeds at a garden's boundary. Looming, twisting into one another, eager to see and be seen by the king. Rooted together, the pointed hats on their heads bobbed in air made thick with the breath of too many people. Laughing, roaring, raising their mugs for drink, their eyes openly traced over her.

None of them moved, and Avelina searched for an escape. Seeing a small crevice to slide through, she stepped between them and was swallowed in their midst. Their bodies pressing against her, she was knocked about, bombarded, as if she were a pebble in the middle of a rockslide.

Avelina felt a slender hand wrap around her wrist and guide her through the swarm of men. It was Wilhelmina. She laid her other hand on top of Avelina's and squeezed. "You looked like you might be swallowed in there."

"You are kind," Avelina said, smiling. "Thank you."

Wilhelmina tilted her head behind her. "Come. We can find a bit of sanctuary over here."

They stepped away toward an outer wall. Avelina steadied herself with a hand on the wall and lifted her aching foot. Closing her eyes, she counted her breaths like she had done on the dance floor.

Inhale, one . . . two. Exhale, three . . . four.

"Are you all right?"

Avelina dropped her foot, fixing her posture, and batted her eyelashes to refocus through the haze of exhaustion. "I am, thank you."

Wilhelmina gave her a half-smile and nodded toward an open seat.

"Perfect," Avelina said, her cheeks simmering from exertion.

Wilhelmina slipped a hand through Avelina's elbow, locking their arms, and led them to a pair of window seats. Bathed in silver moonlight, the crescent-shaped halves were built on opposing sides of the towering bay window and comfortably laid with velvet cushions and pillows. They settled into a quiet corner against the glass panes. Wilhelmina stretched her back and leaned her shoulders against the wall. Her eyes squeezed tightly closed and her lips parted, a slow exhale sliding across them.

"My lady," Avelina said. Wilhelmina looked smaller, and the scarlet of the gown that swallowed her gave a blue undertone to her already pale skin. Avelina felt a tug of concern at her appearance. "Are *you* all right?"

Wilhelmina lightly covered her face, and her eyes fluttered open behind her fingers.

"I'm so sorry. Please don't take me for a fool," she said. "It's all lovely. The music, the banquet, the people." Wilhelmina's mouth pulled to the side. "My mother, and my sister, *adore* this. It fuels them, but not me. I become desperate to retreat to a quieter place. It makes me so very tired."

"Honestly, the crowds wear me out too." Avelina said with a small laugh. "One can appreciate the beauty that surrounds us while craving a bit of peace. Sometimes a soul merely craves simplicity."

Wilhelmina smiled, her cheeks dimpling, and leaned her head toward Avelina.

"Yes, a bit of peace," Wilhelmina said, then turned her glazed eyes back to the dance floor. "I'm grateful for your company. It's nice to have a friend beside me." Wilhelmina cleared her throat, and her mouth twisted into a frown. "Though I fear there is another reason I have sought you out."

Avelina's shoulders tightened. She twisted her body farther onto the seat, took a goblet off the tray presented to them by a servant, and took a sip of the wine.

And waited.

Avelina surveyed the room. Candelabras fully lit were all around the periphery, and the glow of their overflowing fruit caught in everything, reflecting warm hues that danced on the windows and jewels that hung obscenely around everyone's necks. It gave a homey warmth to the stone walls that otherwise rose darkly, ominous and cold.

Dancers still moved, gliding and winding across the tiled floors. Watching them, she was grateful to disappear within her corner's shadow. Though the hours had waned, the crowds had remained, circling around their king. The king erupted with laughter; his wrinkled, rounded cheeks became as reddened as his shirt. The men roared, lifting their steins high, finishing each other's sentences, and their circle continued to grow.

Avelina took another drink, eager to indulge in the slippery promise of something familiar. Its flavor was sweet, delicious, rolling easily over her tongue. The wine went down quickly, and the bottom of the glass welcomed her with the warm embrace of escape.

Wilhelmina finally cleared her throat and looked to her hands. "It's Mother. She means to ensure you understand your place here and that you don't dare stray from it. To me, she says, 'If you mean to please her, you will find yourself a hole, and put yourself in it to be forgotten.'"

Avelina bowed her chin. "I know my place."

"I believe you, Princess. I believe you mean no quarrel or to cause discord, but . . ." Wilhelmina paused, straining a swallow. "You must realize what she has gone through. Mother, like yourself, was born to greatness but now is only bent on survival. In a better world, the two of you may have been friends, or at least allies. But not here. Here there is too much for Mother to lose. I understand and I pity her, but I pity not her methods to ensure you heed her warnings."

Avelina blinked, listening, wanting to look away, but she didn't dare. Any comparisons between them—one former mistress, one future—though possibly accurate, were certainly unwelcome. The queen herself had made that perfectly clear. Yes, she understood, but one word stuck out as a warning to her.

"Methods?"

"I overheard her." Wilhelmina looked pained and leaned toward Avelina's shoulder. "Mother means to send you a message by cutting down *the thing* you brought with you."

Thing?

"I brought nothing with me," Avelina said.

"The girl," Wilhelmina said. "With the goat and mutt."

Oh no, not young Rose. Avelina was prepared for her own fate, but no, not this. She had hoped to talk to the king herself and secure—no, *plead* for Rose's place with her, or somewhere close to her, before sending word for her at the inn. *How had the queen even known?*

"There is no one," Avelina said, startled but steady.

Avelina studied Wilhelmina's face, looking for a sign. A sign of something slippery or sinister behind the innocence. She was the queen's daughter after all, and had laid her threats plainly at Avelina's ear, but still, there was something about Wilhelmina that gave Avelina great pause and drew her in, wanting to trust that Wilhelmina meant her no harm.

Avelina's heart squeezed, and she looked away.

There must be something she could do. But what?

Her lips trembling, Avelina searched the balcony for Matthias. While dancing, she had caught sight of him there, overlooking the hall, but had lost him. Perhaps if she could find him again. She continued to search to no avail. There was no sign of him.

Her heart fell even further and the tears she'd been stifling with it. Grief-stricken, she turned from the crowd to hide them, only to find Wilhelmina brimming with her own tears, watching her.

"Oh, dear Avelina, I am so very sorry." Wilhelmina grasped Avelina's hand and squeezed it. "I will pray for your friend."

CHAPTER 48

THE DANCE

~~~

Matthias

MATTHIAS LEANED FORWARD, EYE ON his mark. His arms pumped at his sides. Each step sure in his stride. He cut around the back of the room, against the wall, where it was less crowded. Those who were in his way and saw him coming stepped aside.

When Matthias reached the window, he balled his fist, crossed his arm across his abdomen, and kneeled before her. He steadied himself and waited with his chin low, staring at the bottom of her skirts.

"Matthias."

She and her lady companion rose from their bench seat, staring open-mouthed at him. Her voice was almost swallowed by the shocked silence of the people standing around them. Matthias peeked and saw the edge of her lips curled into a smile.

"Princess Avelina." He stood and took a step toward her.

Matthias caught a flicker in the corner of Avelina's mouth as her smile dropped and then was swiftly replaced with another. A deeper one that lit her eyes.

His hands were restless at his sides, wanting to touch her. To reach his arm around her waist, run his fingers along her back, and pull her body in closer to his. The thought of touching her purposefully, intimately, made his stomach flip like a virgin's.

Matthias couldn't wait any longer.

He reached for her, taking the tips of her fingers into his. He lifted her fingers and, keeping his eyes locked on hers, gently kissed her hand. He didn't let go right away; instead, his thumb lightly rubbed across her knuckles.

"How good it is to see you," Avelina said.

Her breasts heaved within the tight gown. Her lips trembled, and he could see the slight reflection of water around the edges of her eyes. He noted the thin, irritated red veins in the whites of her eyes. He'd seen that before. Evidence of her tears.

"Princess, I'm not much for dancing."

"Yes, Matthias. I remember."

"I might be made the fool," he said, swallowing. "But I am soon to leave Ewigsburg."

Her chin waivered, and her stance fell a bit off balance.

"I believe I owe you a dance," he said. "If you'll have me."

Avelina glanced at her companion and turned back to him. A wistful smile flickered across her face, and she nodded. "I would like that."

They turned to the dance floor and made their way through the crowd. It was against protocol for a soldier to be here amongst them. Especially for him to approach a noble like this. But nobody said a word.

Matthias leaned in close to her ear.

There it was again, the scent of roses.

"I have to admit, I don't know the steps," he said.

Avelina whispered. "Neither do I."

The admission made him smile.

"Aren't we a pair?" Matthias said, moving in front of her.

He stood still, his pulse racing. He had no idea what to do.

Avelina held up her right palm and stepped toward him. Nodding at him encouragingly, her cheeks rising pink. Matthias stepped forward and met her hand with his own, their shaking fingers tapping against one another. He noticed a hint of sweat between their hands and shook his wrists.

"Might I tell you a secret?"

He grinned sheepishly. "Of course."

Her eyelashes fluttered, ready to spill the secret.

"Listen to the music. Find the rhythm and lean into it." She took another step closer to him. "Imagine it as another duel. Watch your surroundings, your peers, the movements, until you can anticipate them. Until it is almost natural," Avelina said. "You're a warrior. A dance cannot get the best of you."

He smiled.

"We'll give it our best try. Just this once."

"For you," he said. "Yes."

The music started, and the dancers moved with it. Stepping and turning about, Matthias saw the king standing at the opposite end of the floor, glaring at him.

No. Not now. Just a few more moments.

Matthias felt Avelina's hand grab his other hand. He turned to her when she placed it above the bend of her waist.

"There," she said.

Avelina smiled, and they began to move. Their hands barely touched, but the friction between them pulsed through him. As she turned into the music, the loose bits of her hair toppled over her shoulders bounced with the steps.

She was right. Anticipate. Respond. He kept his eyes locked on hers, whichever direction they turned. Twirling her late and awkwardly, but she smiled, floating along with him, so it didn't seem to matter.

She was beautiful.

Those eyes. They held nothing back. They held on him like he was the only man in the room. They held a sense of peace. Trust. Slivers of gold flickered in the amber against the deep green dress that rolled over her curves. Gold piled upon emeralds; she was a dancing treasure.

She was exquisite. Perfect. And for this moment, she was his.

The music changed into a slower, simpler tempo, and the couples began twirling around them on the floor. The court seemed to shrink, both sexes openly watching her. Trained masks were fixed upon their faces, but he knew how to recognize a predator. There was no admiration. No simple curiosity. This was the place of plotting and piracy and a king who meant only to humiliate and abuse her.

His chest tightened. Jorn was right. This place was poison.

He needed to get her out of here. Now.

She must have sensed it. Her brows furrowed, and she stopped.

He stepped close to her, dropping his lips close to her ear. A tendril of her soft hair swept across his nose, and he sighed.

"Avelina."

"Yes." She stepped closer and her hand curled around the back of his shoulder.

His own hand slid across her back, edging her closer to him. Where their palms had barely touched, he wrapped his hand around hers and drew it to his chest. His chin rested against her, and he closed his eyes.

"I hear you are to be married," she whispered.

Matthias squeezed her hand. "No. My men and I leave at first light."

He felt her shudder against him.

"The king? Then he's granted your freedom?"

"He gave his release."

"I'm so glad of it," she said. A whimper escaped her. "I thought—"

"Others make their own plans, but we'll stay no longer," he said, clearing his throat. "I've only come here tonight to say good-bye."

Her chin lifted, and he bent his neck, pressing his cheek against hers as they moved.

Her hand shook within his. "You were right."

Matthias snorted. "Actually, I've been dead wrong about a lot of things lately."

"No," she said with a slight shake of her head. "About giving my word."

Matthias sighed and shifted, breathing her in.

"You warned me not to make promises that I would be unable to keep," she said, her voice cracking.

"It's all right."

"No, it's not," she said, voice shaking. "I thought I could help. I wanted to help her, like you helped me."

Young Rose. He hadn't even given her a thought since they got to the castle.

"Where is she?" he asked.

"I don't know," Avelina said. "You must take her with you. Far away from here. Please, Matthias. She's not safe here. Promise me you'll take care of her."

"I'll find her." His lips pressed against her temple. "I promise."

They turned the next few steps in silence. Though the speed of the music increased, they kept their own tempo.

She raised her chin, turning into him with her lips close to his ear. "We're almost at the end."

"There will be another," he said, squeezing her hand tighter. "The night is still young."

His head was spinning. From the ale. From the dance. From his heart breaking within his chest.

"I've failed you, Avelina. Forgive me."

Avelina drew her face back. Her nose twitched, and she blinked furiously.

"You're free," she said, giving him a weak smile. "I want nothing more for you. And you owe me nothing."

Avelina pulled back from him, let go of his hand, and curtsied. The music had ended.

His drunken limbs sinking heavily, Matthias dug his heels into the floor.

No. It wasn't time. He wasn't ready.

"Well, wasn't that something?" a voice said.

The king.

Gritting his teeth, Matthias turned his head. The music had stopped, the dancers withdrawing to the sides and front gallery of the hall, while the king strolled toward him. He pulled at the end of his sleeves, straightening his shirt, grinning at Matthias.

"I knew you could fight, son," he said. "But I never knew you could dance."

Now at his side, King Girault gazed at Avelina, still hovering in a curtsy.

"Rise, lady," King Girault said, snickering. "I believe the Sword is finished with you."

"As you wish, my king," she said.

Avelina stood tall but kept her eyes low. She took a step back to the edge of the dance floor, slipping into the cover of a shadow. Even out of the direct light of the candles, he could see the tears reflected in her eyes. She fought them, winning, and they did not fall.

Perfectly poised, everything about her hardened until she was a strong, striking, hollowed, and painted shell.

"I trust you and your men have enjoyed the feast," the king said, his eyes broadly lit and opened wide. He laid a hand on Matthias's shoulder.

"Most generous of you," Matthias said.

The king's head tilted to the left. He stepped back and rubbed his hands together, surveying the room.

Matthias lifted his hand.

"As was this honor," Matthias said, looking at the golden sword that circled his finger. The ring he had earned but never wanted. That had taken him to Leuceria, *to her,* and ultimately to the freedom he'd been promised.

Nothing was easy in this life. Nothing. But Matthias was done. Done with their plans for him. The games they played with others' lives.

Matthias twisted the gold ring until it slid from his finger and held it out to the king. The king's smile dropped quickly into a hard frown.

"This isn't what you want, son," King Girault said.

"I'm not a man made for such fine things." Matthias bowed his head, keeping the ring aloft, waiting. "You raised me too high, sire."

"You earned it. You know I reward loyalty, son."

"I do. And I appreciate your faith in me, sire. Truly," Matthias said. "But it is time for me to find my own path."

King Girault exhaled loudly and plucked the ring from Matthias's fingers.

The king looked at him, over at Avelina, and then cocked his head to the side. The air lay thick between them—the two men standing as son and surrogate father, or as rivals, bucks ready to lock horns over the prize.

"Why don't you go have another ale? Eat and drink until you're sick, and then have some more. We'll discuss this later," the king said, waving at him dismissively.

King Girault turned to Avelina. "Say good night to your Sword, young princess. It's time for us to retire."

Matthias's cheeks grew cold, and he wiped his hand down his face.

Curse him. Curse him to hell.

Avelina's eyes alone moved, meeting Matthias's for a moment, and then again ran aground.

The king folded his hands in front of his stomach and took a few steps back.

"Come, Princess," he said. He sneered at Matthias, tossing the ring up and catching it in his hand. "In the morning, then." He winked, turning on his heel. The court bowed lowed to him as he passed through them and walked out of the hall.

Avelina avoided Matthias's stare and laced her fingers at her waist. She straightened her shoulders, setting them back, and lifted her chin.

"Good-bye."

Matthias barely heard the whisper when she walked by him, but the word rammed his chest like an axe. He stumbled a step back, and his mouth dropped open.

No. No, no, no.

Matthias ran a sweaty hand over the top of his head and grabbed the back of his neck, watching her leave, following in the wake left by the king.

"Brother."

Jorn was at his shoulder.

Matthias's chest caved in, his heart twisted and torn. He gawked after her. Desperate to memorize every detail about her. Her voice. Her touch. Her words. The way she laughed. How she looked. How she moved.

And then he saw it. The strain at her hips. She was fighting, trying to mask a limp.

Her toes.

His body tensed, seeing her pain.

"No, brother," Jorn said, putting a hand on his shoulder. "Don't."

Matthias rolled his shoulder, and Jorn's hand gave way.

Protocol be damned.

Matthias cleared the distance behind Avelina in six giant steps and put his arm through the crook of her elbow, startling her.

"What are you doing?" she whispered.

He felt her muscles tighten beside him. He lifted his shoulder so she could lean her weight on him, and they continued the length of the room to the doors.

Soldiers stood on either side of it, guarding the entrance, watching them. It wasn't the main hallway of the castle—well-lit, warm, and well-traveled—but another, carved within the limestone. Cold and dank, it eerily glowed in the light of the torches that lined its walls. This was the king's private hallway that led him from one bedchamber to another.

Avelina twisted her arm from his. Her chin dropped, only for a moment, and then reset.

She wouldn't look at him.

Matthias lightly laid a hand on her shoulder and charged around to stand directly in front of her, his back between her and the guards. He lifted her chin with a single finger.

Her eyes darted to the right, and her breath quickened.

"Avelina."

Matthias took her face in both hands.

Shocked gasps erupted all around him.

He was a fool.

Driven to the cliff's edge, he was teetering, falling.

So he might as well jump.

Matthias tilted his head and pressed his lips against hers. Lips slightly parted. Light at first and then heavier. Her mouth sweet and soft, like her skin.

He held her there, cherishing the moment.

That in this moment, she was his.

Her hands closed around his wrists, and she pulled her mouth away from his.

He stood frozen in shock, watching her eyes darting about his face until she pushed him sharply away.

"How dare you."

She stepped around him and followed after the king.

CHAPTER 49

MADAME FLORA

———

Avelina

INSIDE THE TUNNEL AND OUT of sight of the court, Avelina covered her mouth with one hand as the other reached forward into the darkness. Her lips tingled from his hungry kiss. She rubbed the back of her hand across them, desperate to erase the sensation. To erase him, before the love she bore for him landed her on her knees in despair.

She'd been so happy to see him. Overjoyed. Foolishly hoping for a moment that he had come back for her. That he meant to take her away from this.

But that. That was not fair.

Matthias had been drunk. Very much so, like most in the great hall. The point in most nights where the laughter grew loudest, boundaries were crossed, and chivalry died. The point in her past that she had avoided at all costs, excusing herself to the protection of her locked rooms. Hiding from those who tried to break through her doors.

Avelina had smelled the ale on him before she'd even touched him. He'd been unsteady on his feet, his sour breath circling her as they danced, yet she cleaved to him still. A good man, normally so grounded and set in his ways, made a fool by too much drink.

She shook her head, sadness and regret layering themselves upon her shoulders, and moved forward.

"I've got you."

A woman stepped out of a shadow from against the wall and

took Avelina's arm in both hands. This was a lady—exquisitely dressed and decorated in fine jewels—not a servant. Startled at first, Avelina was quickly thankful for the kind gesture and company.

And not to be alone.

She was devastated, physically and mentally, and her night was still not over.

Avelina had hoped to be drunk herself. To be drunk and let it all be easier.

But she wasn't.

She remained herself and well aware of what was to come.

Now that the hour was upon her, her fears only enhanced her senses, rolling them in nauseous offense. She had eaten early and then only nibbled at the endless supper dishes, thrown by the richness of the courses, the foreign flavors and mixed odors of the meats. The wine, one glass after another toward the desired end, only left her sickened, sloshing and swirling sweet within her belly.

They arrived at her chamber. The lady lit the fireplace, then moved around the room lighting others. Seeing her table still overflowing with food, Avelina sat beside it and devoured a fig tart that remained from her luncheon.

"Good girl," the lady said in the buttery-smooth French accent. "That will soak up the wine."

Embarrassed, Avelina wiped a crumb from her lip but continued to eat.

"My name is Madame Flora."

Madame Flora gave her a sweet smile. Her snow-white hair, threaded with silver, was pulled tightly back from her forehead, accentuating her features. Chiseled features, sharply angled toward a slim chin, she stretched her neck and straightened her slender shoulders. Plain and unremarkable in appearance, Madame Flora was waiflike, with skin the same oatmeal color as her finely stitched dress. She seemed faded, as if purposefully subdued.

Avelina nodded a quiet assent.

"I'm here to help you," Madame Flora said, folding her hands in front of her. "When you're ready, my dear."

Avelina sat her biscuit on the table and stood.

"Thank you. For your kindness."

Madame Flora directed her to a corner table.

Avelina stood beside it, and the lady disappeared behind her, unhooking the ties of her dress one by one. She softly sang in French while her nimble fingers worked along Avelina's back. The relief was immediate, growing with each ribbon's release.

Avelina looked over her shoulder at Madame Flora. Her voice was extraordinary. Perfectly on pitch. Smooth as silk. Rich in tone. A true gift that calmed Avelina's nerves significantly.

"I was once a member of the late queen's household," Madame Flora said.

"Here?"

"Yes," Madame Flora said. "Queen Isabella."

Loosened, Avelina's dress slid off her shoulders and hung at her elbows. Madame Flora reached around, untying the ribbons on each sleeve. Bit by bit, the weight of the dress released. Avelina inhaled happily. Her lungs and skin welcoming the cool night air.

"She was a wonderful, kind lady," Madame Flora said. "We were quite young when we arrived here from France. We lived here together, in the court, until she wed the king. Those years were full of friendship. And love. I was heartbroken when she died."

"What happened to her?"

"The poor dove caught the sickness birthing her second son. The babe was with the angels within a day, and my queen never recovered. I daresay the king didn't either."

"So horribly sad for them all," Avelina said. "And for you as well."

"She was very dear to me," Madam Flora said.

Madame Flora pulled the sleeves from Avelina's arms and slid the dress down over her hips. Madame Flora gasped. "What happened to you? Did someone hurt you?"

The bruises. Though a week old and faded to a yellowing brown, they were still there, testifying to the peril of their journey. Avelina's hands went to cover her breasts, feeling naked in her underskirt.

"No. The mountains . . ." Avelina said and then was at a loss. How could she even begin to explain what happened to them? Any of it?

When the lady's hands moved to the tie at her skirt, Avelina remembered the pockets, her mother's prayer book, and quickly grabbed the waist.

"It's all right, Princess," Madame Flora said.

Avelina let go, and Madame Flora loosened the back of the cloth, unwrapping it from her. Madame Flora raised her skirts in front of her and then showed her where she laid them with her dress inside a tall cupboard. The lady removed her slippers one by one, pausing over Avelina's foot, where her latest injury was bruised purple and swollen.

"You've had a rough journey, my dear," Madame Flora said. She stood and smiled weakly at Avelina.

Standing stripped, bare in every way, Avelina began shaking.

The harder she fought it, the more her body betrayed her.

"It'll be all right. It will all be all right," Madame Flora said. She picked up the swan-neck jug on the table and poured its contents into the basin beside it. She folded a cloth, soaked it into the liquid, and wrung it. Madame Flora began singing again and bathed Avelina where she stood with rose water.

"Come, dear." Madame Flora took Avelina gently by the hand. She led her to a cushioned stool and sat her upon it, bare bottomed. "I know nothing is working out the way that you hoped." Madame Flora began removing pins from Avelina's hair. "I daresay it hasn't for a long time."

Avelina's lip quivered as hot tears burned her eyes. She straightened her back, trying to cover her breasts with one arm while covering the fold between her legs with the other. Her damp and perfumed skin chilled in the night air, leaving her goose pimpled and her nipples ripe. The lady had left no part of her unclean, working in meticulous detail to prepare her for the king.

"May I ask you a question, my dear?"

"Yes," Avelina said.

Another pin dragged across her scalp, leaving a brown curl draped in front of her face. One by one, pins clinked against a pewter plate on the table.

"I know it doesn't seem so now, but it can be simple. When you think of tomorrow. And the day after. What do you want it to look like?"

"I don't think I have much choice in the matter."

"And why is that?"

"Because . . ."

"Of the king? And his queen?"

Avelina sucked in a steady breath and batted her eyes, determined to push off the impending tears. "Because . . ."

Why? Because. *Because.*

She didn't have much choice, if any. Her heart had played tricks on her, letting her believe that there was . . . that there could have been . . . something wonderful ahead of her. That she would have purpose. That her destiny would be more than that of another daughter of royal blood. But no. This, *this* was it.

"I am no one," she said, her voice strained as she forced each word through her chest and past the anguish within it. "I am a daughter born to a house that needed a son. An inconvenience. A disappointment. A pretender to my throne." She swallowed, and pain ripped through to her ribs. "I am a fool. A fool who dared to lose herself in a dream."

Another pin clinked, and the tightness across the top of her head eased a bit more.

"Is that so?" Madame Flora said.

Avelina's heart tugged, and she hugged herself tighter.

"Your mother—"

"My mother?" Avelina asked. A hot tear broke free and dripped from her chin onto her thigh. "My mother is long gone."

The lady's fingers paused.

"What did your mother call you?"

"My mother only ever called me by my name. Avelina."

"And who is she? This Avelina?" Madame Flora asked, taking out the last pin. "Who does she want to be? What does she want? What makes her happy? Who does she love? You define that. Not the position you hold or the names others call you."

The last pin clinked, and Madame Flora's hands pushed through her hair, massaging along her scalp, setting her long hair over her shoulders.

"I . . . I don't know. It is of no matter. Those names have defined me for so long I don't even know where they end and I begin," Avelina said. Tears streamed down her cheeks, one at a time, each following the path of the first. "I've lived inside a box for so long. Sitting in wait as others decided what it all meant . . . that I have no idea."

Madame Flora picked up a carved ivory comb and began slowly tracing its wide teeth through Avelina's locks.

"I understand. I do," Madame Flora said. "Too often titles are shackles when they could be the instrument of service. The power to act responsibly, with genuine care and a chance to do good. Other times they are abused. Therein lies one of the problems. Look at Lilith."

"The queen? You know her?"

"More than half of my life. I was here when Lilith first arrived," Madame Flora said. She spoke slowly, like her brushed strokes. "You see, I remained here for a time after Isabella's death. Though I would never dare replace her, the king and I became close and found some comfort in our shared grief."

"The king?" Avelina said.

"For a time, yes, until . . . When the king brought her here, Lilith became lost. Then she became angry. That anger became determination. She was driven. Wildly. For power. Influence. To escape ridicule and earn respect. To earn favor and a place of honor beside the king. She sacrificed much, but to her credit, her position became an official one. 'The King's Mistress.' And it's always been about titles for her. Whose daughter she was and the title that came with it. Whose wife she was and the title that came with it." Madame Flora cleared her throat. "Things grew dark in those days, and I was returned to France."

Avelina shivered. Squeezing her thighs together, she crossed her ankles beneath her.

Madame Flora continued. "The one position Lilith never cared for was being a *mother* to poor Helene and Wilhelmina because the title brought her nothing. Nothing, until she bore the young prince. At once, she became widow, queen, and mother to an heir."

"What of her daughters?"

"Helene is determined to make her proud, so she seeks a good marriage and a future. I would not dare to imagine what she thought of the king's plan to marry her to a soldier."

"And Wilhelmina?"

"Wilhelmina is another matter," Madame Flora said. "Lilith hasn't put her forward the way she has Helene."

"But why?"

Madame Flora sighed.

"Because she isn't a reflection of her mother and her mother's desires. Lilith thinks her kind temperament means Wilhelmina's simple, but the young lady has found her peace walking within her faith."

"Would she not send her to an abbey?"

"Lilith refuses. Though Lilith thinks Wilhelmina is weak, I'm sure someday she will find a use for her. Wilhelmina is one you may count as an ally here. Remember that," Madame Flora said. She set a palm on Avelina's shoulder, barely touching her, and leaned to Avelina's ear. "Until you decide what it is you want for your own life."

Avelina whimpered, and the lady gently squeezed her shoulder.

Madame Flora laid the comb beside her. Reaching her hands toward Avelina's face, she gathered her hair and laid it down her back. "Tell me, love."

Avelina cleared her throat and wiped the last fallen tear from her cheek.

Avelina knew what she wanted.

It was a thousand things, but she could only find two words—*to run*. Run until she found freedom. But sitting here, naked on this stool, it had never felt so far away.

Avelina remained silent, and Madame Flora took ahold of her hand.

Madame Flora led Avelina toward the bed. Its imposing headboard was centered against the far wall. Elaborately carved along every stretch of wood with four thick posts rising at the corners of the large base and supporting a canopy of painted beams connecting one to the other. With its heavily decorated curtains drawn and tied at the sides, it reminded her of a puppet theater for children. Her stomach lurched, thinking of the role she was to play.

The lady pulled the bedding back, and Avelina climbed onto the sheets, sliding beneath the cold smoothness that felt like ice against her bare skin. Madame Flora pulled the sheet over her and tucked it around her shoulders.

"Relax your nerves, my dear one," Madame Flora said and then paused. She gingerly brushed her fingers across Avelina's cheek, pursing her lips. "I wish . . ."

"I bid you leave me," Avelina said, shocked at her own words, but she meant them. Another moment of kindness and she would break.

Madame Flora nodded and looked away from her. "If . . . when the king comes, it will be over quickly. And you will be all right."

"Yes," Avelina said, disappointed in the harshness of her own voice. "Thank you. I know."

Avelina watched Madame Flora walk toward the door. She wanted to beg her to stay as much as she ached for her to leave. "Madame Flora?"

She turned to Avelina, waiting.

"Will I see you again?"

Madame Flora's head hung to the floor, and then she righted it, her eyelashes fluttering. "No, my dear. I should think not."

"But why?"

"In truth," she said. "I am returned to Ewigsburg at the king's behest, but it is for the celebration, not for my services. The queen would never approve."

"I don't understand."

Madame Flora sighed.

"I came to you, my dear, because you deserve to be treated with dignity. Promise after promise to you has been broken," Madame Flora said. "I saw your broken heart, though you were held in the arms of one who loves you." She gave another weak but tender smile. "Sometimes a soul needs reminding that it is of value. That it is cherished and is not alone. Everyone deserves a bit of kindness, love, especially on nights like these. Good night, dear Avelina."

CHAPTER 50

WAITING

———— ✺ ————

Avelina

THE KIND AND GENTLE LADY was gone. As suddenly as she had appeared, Madame Flora departed, and a hollow silence filled her space.

Avelina pulled the sheets tight to her chin, desperate for cover.

Her mind was racing. Thoughts branched off of one another, heading in every direction. Her mind tried to follow and sort through everything, hoping to make sense of any of it.

Avelina had so many questions.

The most immediate of which hung over her, weighting her to the mattress.

She had lied to Madame Flora—she didn't know what to expect here—and what she'd really wanted to say was *please don't leave.*

There was no joy here. No excitement. Only an overwhelming dread as fear cradled her bare body.

Like most well-born daughters, Avelina was expected to share a stranger's bed.

To let the smooth-tongued devil named duty seduce her while its tricky hands plied open her thighs.

Was this what she was fated to? Trading one prison for another?

Without mother to comfort her. Or governess to advise her. Or friend to share tips and tricks. The secrets told, one woman to another, of what lay in store. The knowledge within Eve's apple had never been passed to her, and she lay famished, addled, shivering in the anticipation and dread of the unknown.

She only knew what she had felt for Matthias. *With* him. That insatiable desire had felt *good*. And *honest*. It had fueled her, awakening parts within her, feelings, needs that were unfamiliar and exhilarating. Made her brave enough. Confident enough. Careless enough to reach for him. To want him. To feel safe, and happy, within his arms.

Her eyelashes fluttered against one another, tearing apart the memory of his face above hers. She couldn't think of him anymore, or she would break.

No, Avelina. No more of this.

He is gone.

Her eyes fell closed, and Avelina lay perfectly still.

Save for the rising and falling of her chest, Avelina had half convinced herself the king wouldn't even see her there. That her body would disappear underneath the sheet and the stuffed mattress would swallow her. Or the king was drunk enough he would simply stumble into bed without a glance in her direction. Or drunk enough he'd forget his intentions. Forget he'd said he was coming for her and instead go to bed his wife.

That wasn't much to ask—for a man to only bed his wife and forsake all others.

Avelina exhaled slowly.

No. That was folly.

It would be soon. The king would come to her. Pull back the sheet and expose her. He would see her nakedness. He would climb into the bed next to her. And . . .

She stretched her legs farther down the bed. She needed to remain poised, so she sought mindless distraction.

Her eyes adjusted to the dark like a cat.

Any other night the wine would've lulled her to sleep. Tonight it heightened her senses. She became aware of every detail about her. The mattress cradling her back, offering support and releasing the tension built from so many uncomfortable nights traveling. The wind outside, sharply piercing the air, whistling and whipping around the curved stone towers.

The sizzle of the fire. The moments between each crackle and spit. The lines of the stones in the wall. The candles, flickering and casting strings of light onto the hanging tapestries behind them.

She focused, trying to place the creatures and decipher the words stitched upon them until the lights dimmed. The candles burned out, and the shadows grew darker. Longer. Pulling her attention with them to the one place she dare not look.

Avelina's attention finally settled upon the door. The shadows surrounded its thick wooden beams, swallowing them, turning the intricate iron hinges that decorated it into fingers, pointing toward the large iron clasp.

She waited.

No. Please, no.

Each breath intensified. Terrified it would soon open. Each moment drawn long, becoming another stone stacked as torture upon her aching chest. Crushing her in anticipation. Thinking she saw it move, her chest heaved once a bit too hard, and she cracked wide open.

A whimper escaped her, and hot tears again began to fall. She quickly reached her hands up from beneath the sheet and wiped them away.

Heaven forbid the king come in now and find her weeping like a child.

But then again, she no longer cared.

A wail pierced the silence when Avelina let herself admit the truth.

The woman's kind nature had awakened a longing she'd fought hell and earth to quiet. Her armor split, and her bones were crushed beneath the blow. Each limb shattered, splintering and tearing her open. The ache was so desperate, so innate a part of her, that she barely recognized it, having been buried so deep within her bones. A primal need. Instinctual. Honest. And raw, riding the marrow seeping through and staining the sheets about her.

Her mother.

She wanted her mother.

Desperately.

The child within her aching to feel her warmth. Her affection. Her love.

The woman within her needing her assurance. Her guidance. Her acceptance.

And love.

What did your mother call you?

Nothing. Nothing, now and for years. All these long years. She could hear her father, the cadence of his voice still in her dreams. Her forefather's voices drummed through her at times until they controlled the rhythm of her pulse.

Her mother remained silent. Battered and broken. Stilled.

Mama. Please, Mama.

She ached for her voice.

She ached so very, very much for her.

A simple word from her. To tell Avelina what to do. To tell Avelina she would be all right.

In her mother's resounding silence, Avelina had always tried to do right. She'd been perfect for years. She'd never set a foot wrong, doing everything right to survive in Leuceria. Where she had lived her entire life bent to another's will. Waiting, afraid, to see what their moods would be that day. And she had survived. Building up solid walls and lowering expectations to protect herself. She never gave up hope that one day she would have a chance, and one day she would be all right.

But then again, had Avelina been lost to her own vanity? Had they ever spoken to her at all, or had she invented their voices, their words? Orchestrated it all in her mind and created her own significance? Daring to think she was meant for something, that her life had some greater purpose? Thinking she mattered, that she had a part to play besides being moved by the will of others and to meet their end?

Where had it all led?

Here. Here, to this.

Avelina placed a hand across her heart, hoping to ease the strain in her throat.

It can't end like this.

Surely. This couldn't be what became of her.

With frantic breaths, she looked side to side. The room was full of eyes. Stitched and painted, they stood witness to the truth she needed to acknowledge.

She was alone.

Her mother was long gone. Her father. Her line. All gone.

Niro and his questionable yet reassuringly steadfast presence was gone.

Matthias . . . Matthias was gone.

Avelina had loved him, and though he had never been hers, she would add his name to her list of lost things.

Matthias had saved her life. For that, she would forever be grateful. He'd realized his dream and taken care of his men. She would allow herself to grieve him but take great comfort knowing he would be free.

Avelina coughed, choking on her thick tears, and wiped her face with the sheet. She'd stifled them for so long she could no longer bear it. For the first time in years, she embraced the tears pouring from her broken heart. There was no hiding her pain, nor did she wish to anymore.

She called out, but there was no answer.

The emptiness consumed her.

Never had her faith wavered so.

In all her years, it had been the rock she stood upon. The hope she cleaved to. The presence that sustained her, bringing light to her darkness. But had she prayed for the wrong thing? Had she offended God? Angered Him? Had He turned his back on her? Or could He not reach her here?

Avelina rolled to her side, gathered her knees to her chest, and sobbed, lost to grief. She needed to let it out, free herself of the enormity of it all, and then hope to heal and begin again.

Eventually.

But lying in wait, shivering and naked in silence, she had never felt so alone.

CHAPTER 51

DECISIONS

———∽∽∽———

Matthias

M ATTHIAS WAS JOLTED AWAKE AS his jaw slid off his fist. *Scheiße.*

He blindly waved through his mind's fog. He remembered leaning his forehead against his fists when, though seated, the floor had waffled beneath his feet, and then the black wave had come. Rolling. Inviting. Beckoning. Curling its finger and calling him forth. He breathed in hard, the cool air and taste of old ale jarring along his throat.

Where am I? What time is it?

Matthias rubbed his eyes. He was still in the Great Hall. His eyes adjusted to the blue light creeping in through the tall windows. Tiny flames of yellow still dotted the room, though the majority of the candles had been snuffed out. Food platters were splayed across the tables. Dotted with crushed candied fruits, they were piled high with the bones of beasts stripped bare and forgotten. The merry and annoying band had retired. Their tunes replaced by servants shuffling quietly amongst those who, like him, hadn't found their beds. By one corner, a few men remained. Huddled in their seats in the predawn hours, their heads and bodies slumped together as they pulled at the last of their mugs.

He had passed out at the table. Not for the first time in his life, but he hadn't meant to drink so much. Or maybe he had. Either way, they were meant to leave soon. Beside him, Jorn snored heavily. Boots crossed on the table, his long torso was crumpled into his chair and his cape drawn over his head. Reymund was nowhere to be seen. Nor was the king. Or Avelina.

Matthias stood, knocking over his chair, but he caught it before it fell to the ground.

Hell, he was still half-drunk. Or half-asleep.

He stumbled along, sliding his hand along the wall for support, heading toward the king's hidden garderobe.

Oh hell, what is that?

The putrid stench ripped through his nose and turned his stomach. Matthias stepped wide to avoid the offensive recess in the wall. He slammed into someone and heard water splash onto the stones.

"Sorry," Matthias said, looking behind him.

"Sword," the smaller man said, lifting his bucket. He leaned into the vomit-bathed stones and tossed what water he had left against them. The remaining hot water hit the inside of the cavern, warming the dried bile, and breathed new life into last night's excess.

Foul. Matthias wrinkled his nose and shook his head, stepping over the feathers left limp on the ground that had tickled throats to make room for more courses. *Such a waste.*

Matthias found the privy, pushing past another wide-eyed servant. His hand steadied on the slanted stone above his head in the cramped quarters as he centered himself above the open hole, the sound of his relief smacking loudly onto the yard some two floors beneath him.

"Sword?" a voice whispered from behind him. "The king asked for you the moment you woke."

Matthias nodded and tied the flaps of his breeches together. He followed the man—a head shorter, several years younger, and much steadier—down a long hall. Guards stood on either side of the heavy door. Seeing him, one leaned and turned the iron latch, opening the door.

Matthias entered the room and took only a few steps inside without looking anywhere but at the wall in front of him.

Why had he come up here? Why hadn't he turned and left?

"Matthias," the king said. "Come here. Sit with me by the fire."

Matthias pressed his lips and turned. There was the king, in his robes, seated in front of his fire. He gestured to the chair opposite him, and Matthias stumbled to it as gracefully as he could muster.

"*Ach*, can you not smell yourself?" The king waved a hand in front of his face and laughed. His other hand clutched the top of a jeweled goblet, stained at the rim with evidence of long hours of wine. "You smell like you rolled around on a floor covered in ale and piss."

"Apologies," Matthias said, stifling a burp. He laid his elbows on the arms of the chair and stretched his palms on his thighs. Nervous energy, anger, and disgust warred within him but became lost, drowning in the ale still swimming in his veins and oozing from his pores.

"You're a fool, Matthias."

King Girault curled forward and planted his elbows on his knees. His eyes reflected the light of the fire, spitting into the frigid morning hours between them. He looked tired but settled in the shoulders the way a man was once he'd spilled his seed.

Matthias's stomach rattled. "And you, sire, are an arse."

King Girault gaped at Matthias. His open hand rubbed his silver beard, and he started laughing. Hard. He smacked his knee and leaned back into the corner of his chair.

"And you're still drunk," he said, tipping his goblet at him. "All right, then."

The king shook his head and turned to refill his goblet from the pitcher on the rickety table beside him. The furniture here in the king's quarters was severely lacking in comparison to everything elsewhere in Ewigsburg. The king spent his money where it could be seen, strategically, *like the gold he spent on the princess.*

His cup full, King Girault turned and took a long drink.

"We need to talk, son." He cleared his throat and bore his eyes into Matthias.

"There's nothing left to say."

"Ha!" the king said, laughing. "There's a good bit, son. We need to talk about your freedom."

Matthias turned a hard eye on him. "You gave your word."

"I did. I did," the king said, waving a shushing hand at Matthias. "And there's Helene." He grinned and tilted his cup. "And your trip to Leuceria."

"Reymund's already given report."

"Promptly and passionately, as always, and appreciated," the king said, pointing at him. "That man of yours doesn't know how to fail at anything, that's for sure."

"Reymund is brilliant. True and thorough. Which is why I know there is no more I can tell you," Matthias said, trying to stand.

"Son, sit your arse down," the king snarled. "You may have earned your freedom, but you have not been dismissed. Do not forget to whom you speak."

Matthias sat back into his chair and spread his elbows over the rails. Sticking a bootheel out in front of him, he settled his head against the high back of the chair and closed his eyes. The room spun, and he quickly reopened them, jutting his chin and breathing hard to center himself.

"First, Helene. After all I've done. All that I've given you," the king said. "The lady came here for *you* last night."

"I did not ask her to."

"And that *foolishness* on the dance floor. In front of everyone here at court, when Helene is your intended bride."

"I have no intention to marry."

"You made the Lady Helene look a fool. *My* stepdaughter. Hell, *Eger's* daughter. You humiliated her, and you undermined me."

Matthias grimaced, thinking the blame lay elsewhere. He spoke without even thinking. "And the princess?"

"What about her?" King Girault said.

"You humiliate her, and your queen, and question me?" Matthias said. He paused, chewing on his words. "Is the princess here, then? With you?"

"With me?" The king snickered and took another drink.

They stared down their noses at one another.

The king leaned sideways, draping himself over the arm of his chair, and stretched out his leg. "I was young once. A great swordsman, like you."

"I remember, sire."

"The weight of that iron in my hand. That fire than burns in your veins. Rushes heavy from your chest down into your cock when the fight's coming. That moment. That death blow. That flood of relief rushing through you when you know you're still alive and you *know you've won.*" The king's hand swung about while he spoke. He sighed and looked squarely at Matthias. "Son, I miss that."

"Which part?"

"All of it," King Girault said. "How many men have I killed to keep my throne? To keep others on theirs? And you, Matthias, toppled a dynasty simply by making a man *bleed.*" He smacked his palm against the chair. "You're a kingmaker, Matthias, do you realize that? More than that. You set up the *next* dynasty. You're the reason Niro has the throne. The General. Ha! The man, the *legend,* who could do no wrong. Never lost a battle. Not *one.* But for all that, the very man who murdered his best friend—the last of those great Leucerian kings—couldn't bring himself to kill a little girl. His obsession with that girl cost him the control of his own court. And almost cost him the kingdom. But you, Matthias, you're the reason. You're the reason Niro will finally be able to crown his son."

Matthias felt sick and covered his mouth with his hand.

"You. You have no idea, son. I've never known a man who knew himself so well yet didn't recognize what he *could* be."

"You think too much of me, sire. Always have," Matthias said.

"Nonsense. Though if you pull a stunt again like you did last night, I may reconsider."

Matthias nodded and exhaled slowly.

This was all starting off very badly.

The king glowered at him, eyebrows and forehead creased over his sharp eyes, but his mouth was pulled to one side in contradictory pity.

"Reymund filled me in on Leuceria. I'm interested in what happened *after* Reymund got on the boat. Tell me about my borders."

Matthias's brain smarted across the top of his skull. He was too hungover for meaningful conversation. He rolled his head around, hoping to loosen his neck. He rested his elbows on the chair arms and laced his fingers together loosely in front of him, studying the lines of the king's face. It was evident the king hadn't slept.

"The *Geisterweg?*" Matthias said.

"Then you did indeed take that path? With the princess?" King

Girault said, rubbing his beard.

"*Ja.*"

The king snickered. "That must've been something, dragging a woman across the mountains."

"You underestimate her," Matthias said, looking away.

"I see," the king said, shifting in his chair. "But why that route? Why not use the lowlands?"

"The boy. Marcus sent his men after her."

"I'm not surprised. Doubt it will be the last time."

Matthias sighed. "We needed to separate. Jorn and Alif took the trade route; we took to the hills."

King Girault steadied his elbow on the arm of the chair and leaned his temple against his fist. "And?"

"They're the same as they've always been. And always will be," Matthias said. "The rivers run wild and strong. The mountains are high and difficult to navigate. Dangerous for any number of reasons. The land itself. The animals. There's nothing but ruins, shadows of another time."

"The trade routes? I didn't think they were still navigable."

"With the Houses gone, they're wild. Without the gatehouses along them to collect tax and keep watch over them, there's nowhere to find sanctuary along them anymore. Any man fool enough to use them risks his wares, his coin, or his life."

"I see."

Matthias remembered Beatrix. "There's no law there. And there won't be."

"Why not?"

"Because the reach of war is far and wide. The battles may not have been fought there, but the wars destroyed those mountains. Most of the men were called into your service at one time or another. You took the men who worked the land, and the farms went under when their herds died. You took the men who guarded the roads, and the towers crumbled without protection. Without protection, the women who couldn't fight were ravaged while raiders took or killed their children. There are two types of people remaining in those hills—the families who are dug in, with nowhere else to go, and the cowards who take advantage of them."

The king rubbed his thumb along his bottom lip.

"You've given me a lot to think about, son," King Girault said. He planted his palms on the edge of his chair. "But first, I need more wine."

The king stood and walked to a side table. He picked up another pitcher and brought it back to the chair with him. He sat and raised his goblet to toast. When Matthias showed his empty hands, the king refilled his own goblet and handed it to Matthias. With a wink, the king toasted Matthias with the pitcher and then drank from its side.

"I wasn't born a king. I was the second son. Born to swing my sword and spill my seed," King Girault said, grinning. "They say second sons are a curse to a throne, but my father saw me as an asset. Your firstborn takes your throne while the second secures it. My father. Oh, if he only knew. That I would be king and our family would rise so. And my sons . . ."

Matthias gritted his teeth and shifted in his seat.

"Your sons will come to be great men, sire."

"They will. Both of them," the king said. "You know, Matthias. My father. Like his father, and his, and so forth. He trained me hard. I still remember my first wooden sword. Watching. Learning. To defend myself. To fight. To kill. I drilled until my knees gave out and my hands bled."

"As did I," Matthias muttered.

"*Ach*, the stories my father told. Of the old men. The families. The politics. Territories. All the maps. The kingdoms that rose and fell. So much plodding history."

"Sounds tedious."

"You have no idea." King Girault laughed. "I hated those maps." His pitcher empty, the king tossed it aside. "I didn't have to, but I studied. And I always listened. Which made all the difference when my brother died and I became heir to my House."

"God rest his soul," Matthias said.

He knew the king grieved his brother. Almost as much as he liked to rattle on.

"The wars came. Houses fell. One after another after another." His hand rubbed across his gray hair. "My crown's not long been on my head, but I earned it." Girault's face scrunched, his nose wrinkling as he spoke. "These families, or what's left of them, whose ancestors are buried one on top of another, will seize any opportunity. *Any.* To take my power. My lands. To take what is *mine* and will belong to my sons after me."

The king leaned his elbows onto his knees, rolling his hands back and forth between them. He pointed his hands at Matthias and shook them.

"What happened in Leuceria can happen here. I need your sword."

Matthias shook his head.

"Hear me, Matthias," the king said, scooting forward. "My boy, Zane, has grown into a fine lad, a strong heir. And now, after all these years, I finally have another boy. My family is stronger, my kingdom is stronger, but a swaddled babe is of no present use to my Zane. You, Matthias. You can help him; you can help them both."

Matthias swallowed, turning his head. He liked Zane, he did, but he couldn't do this.

"You always asked me 'why you.' The answer is simple. Because you don't want it," the king said. "The title. Everything that comes with it. But you're my man. I know where your loyalties lie and trust you to do my will. To fight and keep what's mine."

"I cannot stay," Matthias said, tapping his chest with a splayed palm.

"You can. And I can make it worth your while. I'll make you an *edler*," King Girault said. "A low-ranking title, but it comes with privilege."

"I will not trade my freedom for a title."

"You would be *Edler* of the border lands and hold the fiefdom in my name. The heritable land would be yours in exchange for your allegiance and service. You said yourself there's no law there. The people need help. I need your help."

"The border lands are untamable," Matthias said. "Generations have been trying to bring that land to heel, and every one of them has been crushed by those mountains."

"But you, Matthias. You and your men—"

"I will not behold my men to you," Matthias said, standing. "They are free, as am I." He strode to the window and sat upon the stone seat. Reaching through the crossed iron bars, he pushed the wooden shutter ajar and drew in the crisp air, hoping to clear his throttled head.

"But the girl Helene," King Girault said. "Better you marry her, someone I trust, than someone else."

"It is not my place to find her a mate," Matthias said. "It was Eger's, and now it is yours. You can easily find her a good husband."

King Girault sighed loudly. "Any other family here, it would give them a sense of power over the others here at court. Keeping them in their place is precisely what keeps order."

Matthias put his hand on his hip and looked at the king over his shoulder. "I am not the solution to every problem you cause."

The king rolled his eyes and threw his hand toward Matthias. "Take the land *and* the girl. Make a home there along my border."

"At Metzlingen?"

"*Metzlingen?*" The king's face dropped. "*You found Metzlingen?*"

"What's left of it," Matthias said, crossing his arms.

"On my word, I don't believe it," King Girault said. "'The house at the heart of the mountains' stands after all." The king leaned back and traced his beard with his fingers. "Rebuild the old house, Matthias. Make something of it for yourself. For your men. Make the land manageable. Safe and profitable. If you strengthen my borders, you strengthen my entire kingdom."

The door opened, and a commanding figure strode into the chamber. Shoulders back, head erect, the young man moved purposefully through the shadows. Entering the light of the fire, he nodded to them both.

"Ah, Maximilian," King Girault said. "I see the predawn hours steal your rest as well?"

Startled by the archduke, Matthias leaned forward to rise.

"Please," Archduke Maximilian said, shaking a head and raising a palm to Matthias. "I've invaded your private chamber and conversation to sit with you as a friend." He scooted the chair Matthias had left vacant beside the king and settled into it.

"I'd offer wine, but I fear we are out," King Girault said. "I can call for more."

"We'll drink later to champions and peace," Archduke Maximilian said. "I come with news. The Leucerian guard arrived not long ago."

Matthias balked. *The assassins.* It couldn't be anyone else.

The archduke propped his elbows at the edge of his chair arms and pressed the tips of his fingers together. His chin dropped, and he arched a brow. "I've met with their leader, Amis, the heir of the House of Connaire. There is a lust for blood married to an anger and humiliation I've not seen in a long time. They demand the princess's immediate release."

"Ha!" King Girault said. "Demand, do they?"

"Death is all that awaits her in Leuceria," Matthias spat.

The archduke landed a piercing gaze on Matthias, and the corner of his lip fell. "They purport they were wronged by your negotiations and broken betrothal to their princess. They accuse you of treating she who was to be your queen with degradation. Though they, not the law, never recognized her as such within her own kingdom."

"Words." King Girault rolled his eyes. "They forget I paid a large sum of gold for her."

"That was presented as a gift," Matthias said.

"Was it?" King Girault said, grinning. "I also have possession of her, so I would argue she is mine to deal with as I see fit."

"This is the first opportunity in years to negotiate with Leuceria. The General may sit on the throne, but it would be unwise to make an enemy of the House of Connaire. You cannot make those who hold such power look a fool without consequence," the archduke said. "To maintain peace and the alliance your man procured, I acted as mediator and negotiated terms on your behalf."

"You did, then?" King Girault said.

"You were otherwise occupied," Archduke Maximilian said. "The situation was tenuous but is now resolved."

"Good man."

"The Leucerians cannot enter the tournament at this late juncture, so I have offered them a Feat of Arms. They may put forth their own champion to duel for her hand," Archduke Maximilian said.

"Ha! It will cause a riot. They will fight harder to win her and love me for offering the chance to win such a prize," the king said. "A fine way to broker peace."

Matthias's foot tapped beneath him, and he rubbed his hand across his mouth.

Was it this easy for them? To treat her as nothing. Simply hand her to the winner as they would a golden feather. And possibly to her own countrymen, who meant her harm. Matthias looked back and forth between the two men. His stark features set in stone, the archduke stared at him.

After a few moments, the archduke's nose twitched and he nodded, a decision made, resting back into his chair. "Forgive me, but how do I know your face?"

"I was at Guinegate," Matthias said. "Near you on the field with the late Prince Siegfried. I have fought for my king and for you many times."

Archduke Maximilian's eyes went wide. He looked to King Girault and then back to Matthias. "*Ah, Matthias.* The foot soldier who brought you the princess."

"I fulfilled my mission to my king," Matthias said.

"A king is lucky to have so faithful a servant," Archduke Maximilian said. "I'm sure you have rewarded him justly."

"Matthias has earned his freedom," King Girault said. "Though I bid him bend the knee to me. I have offered him the fiefdom of Metzlingen."

"*Metzlingen?*" The archduke's mouth hung agape. "It's true, then? The mountain house stands?"

"Enough of it," King Girault said. "I've offered him the hand of Eger's daughter, but my man seems not to be swayed."

The archduke leaned forward, putting his elbows on his knees. His face severe, he continued to study Matthias. "The Lady Helene is a fine woman and deserves an exceptional match herself. I suggest placing her hand for the tournament prize. You'll have two champions today. The first from the tournament and the second from the Feat of Arms. It will make Eger's knights happy to see his daughter recognized so and to find a good match. It will solve your problem with the Leucerians."

Matthias crossed his arms across his stomach. The archduke was clever.

"I cannot argue those points," King Girault said, rubbing his chin.

"I saw you with her. The princess, this last night," the archduke said, still watching Matthias with a hawk's eye. "I wonder, soldier, if given the chance, would you fight for her hand yourself?"

"The tournament has already begun, and rules are finite," King Girault said. "Only nobles can enter the tournament."

"Easily solved. You thrust one title upon your man to send him to the barter; you can thrust the other upon his shoulders as quickly should he agree to it." The archduke leaned back into his chair with a satisfied expression. "You offer this man a position of honor, which I believe his actions have shown to be well earned. If he would agree to the Feat of Arms, I will provide his armor and sponsor him."

"You would do this?" King Girault asked, cocking his head with a grin.

Matthias closed his eyes and hung his head. His heart pounded in his chest. The longer the king rattled on, the clearer his own idea became. He was either roaring drunk or a hapless fool, but he'd never forgive himself if he wasn't certain of it.

"I'll do it, but on two conditions," Matthias said.

"Name them," King Girault said.

Matthias met the king's eyes. "My men are free; I alone bend the knee."

King Girault rubbed his beard and raised a hand, relenting. "Done. And?"

Matthias balled his fist in front of his mouth and exhaled. "If I win—if she is to be mine—you will *truly* bless a betrothal to Avelina. Say you will, and I will bend the knee."

Silently, the king walked to the fire and laid his hand on the large stone mantel. He picked up a fire iron and rearranged the logs. Their smoldering carcasses split open, red-hot embers falling across stones.

"Today, then," King Girault said. He turned to Matthias and nodded. "You'll bend the knee, and I'll vest you as *Edler* of Metzlingen." His lip curled wickedly. "But you must defeat the Leucerian. *If* you win her, you'll marry your princess."

Matthias's heart stopped in his chest. Floored by what he had done.

"But later. Right now, I'm tired and wish to rest," King Girault said. He rubbed his reddened eyes with a fist and then gestured toward the door. "I'll pray you at least get a son off of her. A strong heir, so I can sleep well at night knowing my sons will have a friend."

CHAPTER 52

TELLING HIS BROTHERS

———❧———

Matthias

"I KNEW I'D FIND YOU HERE," Jorn said as he walked into the stables. "Getting your arse flogged this morning, eh?"

Matthias was sitting on a crate, holding a mug of warm mead between his hands. He took a long draw, hoping the warmth of the liquid would settle his stomach, turning from too much ale and not enough sleep.

"I've had better whippings," Matthias said.

Jorn snickered and grabbed another crate from the pile by the wall. He flipped it over and sat beside Matthias. Both men leaned forward, settling their elbows on their knees.

"Alif?

"Gone after the girl. I sent him straightaway after the princess' warning. He's to wait with Rose at the alehouse. Or leave at the first sign of threat."

"Good," Matthias said.

Thank heavens at least that was settled.

"Reymund?"

"At prayers. He'll be limping along shortly," Jorn said.

Matthias's neck cracked, as he rolled it side to side, only half listening.

"You're not going to tell me to piss off, then?"

Matthias blew the air out of his lungs. "For what?"

Jorn chewed on his response. "You always call me on harassing our brother, but not this morning?"

Matthias smirked and rubbed his temples.

"Then I'll be the one to tell you to piss off, brother," Jorn said, frowning. "What have you gone and done?"

"We'll wait for Reymund. It only concerns me, but it's for you both to hear."

Jorn leaned in and narrowed his eyes.

"Only concerns you, you say?" Jorn turned and spit on the ground. "*You arse.* If it concerns you, it concerns all of us. Or have I been a loyal brother to you for nothing all these years?"

Matthias scoffed and leaned back.

"Whatever he's offered you will never truly be yours. You know that, don't you?" Jorn said. "You know I speak the truth. Your king would offer you the moon to fight his endless wars."

"You're of a mind today," Matthias said, avoiding Jorn's piercing glare. "We were fighting well before we came into his army, and we'll be fighting long after."

"*Genau,* but now we will bleed for *ourselves,*" Jorn said. "Not for *him.* With what little we carry. Without house or name to give us rank or armor or respite. All the while watching the favored sons grow richer around us."

Matthias groaned. "Favored sons?"

"His knights," Jorn said. "Wearing their painted armor, flying their coats of arms."

Matthias turned to Jorn, frowning. "Those men are warriors and fight all the same."

"You're right. I don't mean to disparage them. Some of them are good men, truly," Jorn said, lifting a palm. "Though I daresay for all their finery and wealth and talk of chivalry, I've met none who could compare to the man here beside me."

Matthias shook his head and turned to protest but found Jorn's finger pointed in his face.

"Hear me, brother. Your king could've had you bend a knee at any time and knighted you, *honored you,* as you've long deserved. But he didn't. *Ja,* we've fought beside them and seen some fall, but we've also seen them spared. Ransomed from the field of battle. Had that been you or I, we would've been left to bleed the ground and feed the crows." His shoulders shook, and he grunted. "I mean you no offense, brother. Hell, I mean them no offense either.

I know there are good men amongst them. They cannot choose what House they are born to any more than you or I. Names have power. They're either our catapult or our noose."

Jorn's words rang raw but true, and Matthias's cheek tugged. Names either thrust you forward or ripped the ground from beneath your feet, which was why they'd both dropped their own so long ago. "We're not them, Jorn. We're merely men. There's no shame in that."

"I never said there was." Jorn ran his palms down his face and stared ahead. "I . . . I'm angry. And I'm tired. I'm so rotting tired of seeing my brothers treated thus. Torn and trampled afoot while mocked by those in power. Brother, stop and think. You're his weapon—*his Sword*—even so, you're expendable. Sending you on this mission, after this princess . . . When the prince fell, he could've sent anyone in his stead, yet he chose you. Someone he wasn't afraid to lose. The king has no loyalty to you. He's only loyal to his purse."

Matthias stood and moved across the stable, keeping his back to Jorn. "I hear you. I do, but that's over now. Your service to the crown is over."

"Mine? But not yours?" Jorn snipped. "That man was never going to let you walk away. I knew he would find a way to make us stay."

"Not us, brother. Only me," Matthias said. "I would never have agreed to it otherwise."

Matthias noted the low dragging sound playing against the shuffling of hay from Jorn's stomping pace. He turned to see Reymund at the entrance, watching them both.

Reymund winked at Matthias, and a slow grin spread over his face.

"You can't possibly think that I'll be the coward who runs away?" Reymund asked, gesturing toward Jorn with his cane.

"What?" Jorn said, throwing his hands wide. "You too?"

"You didn't crack a joke at my expense for once," Reymund said, grinning and tapping his chest. "Me? Running?"

"Piss off, Reymund," Jorn spat.

"That's more like it." Reymund smiled, turning back to Matthias. "Tell me, brother. Will it be the Lady Helene?"

"No," Matthias said. "She is to be given to the tournament champion as bride."

"And the princess?" Reymund asked.

"Avelina will be mine," Matthias said, hanging his thumbs on his belt. "If I win her."

"*Win* her?" Jorn scoffed.

"I've accepted a challenge to a Feat of Arms," Matthias said.

"*God's bones,*" Jorn said, rubbing his hand across his beard.

"Against the Leucerians?" Reymund said.

Matthias crossed his arms. "Yes. With the archduke's sponsorship."

"The archduke's?" Jorn said. "Not your king's?"

"Impressive, brother." Reymund walked toward Matthias. Once beside him, he patted Matthias on the shoulder. "It's a laudable move on Maximilian's part. I've always told you both: Fools compete. Friends empower."

Matthias laid his own hand on Reymund's and squeezed.

Glancing over his shoulder, Reymund raised his voice. "With you taking a wife, that leaves me in charge of our baby brother here."

Jorn threw his arm up. "You're taking his side?"

Reymund chortled, tried to hide it, and only smiled wider.

"You two are as thick as a frozen cowpie. Do you not understand? It's only *if* you survive the arena. Men have been grievously injured in there. Killed." Jorn put his hands on his hips and paced around the dirt floor. "What's he promised? What's the man *rewarded* you with?"

"Metzlingen," Matthias said, crossing his arms over his chest.

"*What?*" Jorn said. "At the foot of the *Geisterweg*?"

"The very same," Matthias said.

"It is a huge challenge," Reymund said. "Not only a gift, it's also a job, and one no one in their right mind would agree to."

"You've gone plain mad, brother." Jorn threw his hands in the air. "An impossible place to secure and defend. Lawless, dangerous area. Those people don't want to be ruled; they merely hope to survive." He pointed at Matthias. "Those were your words. Not mine."

"You're free, brother. Both of you. All of you," Matthias said.

"I'm telling you to go."

Jorn spun on his heels and growled at him. "And I'm telling you to piss off."

"You're so eloquent, Jorn," Reymund said.

Jorn shook his fists and let out an angry groan. Brom, standing in his stall beside Jorn, snorted and nudged his large head toward him.

"You're allowed to be angry," Matthias said, his chest tight. He knew Jorn would be. Jorn trusted few in this world, but those he did he was both stubbornly and ferociously loyal to. Those who lost his favor rarely renewed it.

"Of course I am." Jorn said. "The princess is the reason for all of this." He hit the back of his hand against Matthias's chest. "You've taken up this mantel and written the rest of our life stories as one of servitude to that snake. Don't pretend you did this for us. You chose *her*, your princess. Over all of us. *Own that.*"

Jorn was furious. He crouched and put his face within his hands and groaned.

"I had no choice," Matthias said.

"My. Arse," Jorn said. "Do you really think he didn't have this planned all along? He knew he had you from the moment we got here. And if not then, that stunt you pulled last night was enough to show the entire court you're in love with her. Hell, my chest even ached, watching you. And Reymund was crying."

"It's true," Reymund said. "I was moved."

Matthias ran his hand over his head and exhaled forcefully. "What kind of man would I be if I left her to the Leucerians? Betrayed the oath I made to her and walked away?"

"A *free* man," Jorn said. "You gave him exactly what he wanted."

"I didn't save her life to watch her become someone's harlot or be handed to those who would soon slit her throat," Matthias growled. "I retained your freedom. None of you are beholden to me."

"Don't be a fool. He knows we'd never leave you. Where you go, I go—remember? Until the day we die, brother. But I will not chain myself to a crown or pledge myself to some pretender; I will die a *free* man." Jorn turned to Reymund and put his hands on his hips. "Why aren't you angry?"

"It's simple. Our brother had no good option, yet he picked the best one," Reymund said. He turned to Matthias. "The men will have a home. A place to lay their heads. Build their own fortunes and, if they choose, their own families. In return, the people of the Metzlingen will have an *edler* who will promise protection. Ensure their security as they work the land and serve their king." He turned to Jorn. "The orphan princess, who you're so eager to walk away from and leave at the mercy of men you cannot stand, will have a home too. A husband who loves her. And she'll retain the dignity that never should've been in question."

Matthias took a step back from them both. They were listening. At least Reymund was.

But this talk of love . . .

It was true. The knowledge clung to the bottom of his throat, squeezing him. Choking him while he tried to bury it within his bones.

He loved her, but he wouldn't keep her.

He would set her free.

"I'm not trying to walk away from her." Jorn sighed and hung his head.

"Our brother bends the knee for all of us, including the princess," Reymund said. "He's committed himself to a life of servitude to the king. The land. The people on it. The title, the responsibility that comes with it. You, brother, can leave. Disappear and never have to deal with any of this again. Or you can choose to stay."

Jorn turned away from them both.

His balance shaky, Reymund looked up to Matthias. His deep brown eyes shone with emotion. "I know this wasn't an easy decision, and I can see how heavily it weighs on you. I commend your bravery to take this on."

Reymund walked to the crates and eased himself upon them. He tapped the empty one beside him with his cane. Jorn grunted and sat beside him. Reymund leaned his shoulder against Jorn's and adjusted his hips. His face looked strained but then relaxed as he straightened a leg out.

"Do you remember the day you found me, Jorn?" Reymund said.

Matthias's knee jolted, almost causing him to stumble where he stood, hearing Reymund's words. They never spoke of it—for good reason—and like Blutburg, it was a subject long buried. Matthias steadied himself, trying his best to block the scene reemerging in his mind.

"Of course I remember." Jorn hung his head, looking away from him. He picked up a strand of hay and began stripping it into thin threads with his fingers. "Though I'd hoped you'd forgotten."

"I was a boy then, but it's not hard to remember the first time someone tries to kill you, is it?" Reymund said. "Especially when it's your own father."

Jorn smirked. "No, I guess it's not."

"Tell me then," Reymund said. "When you found me, with my hands and legs bound and the farmer's knee upon my back, what did you do?"

"We didn't let the arse drown you." Jorn frowned. Just boys themselves, Matthias had charged the farmer, knocking him from his son, and kept the man from Reymund while Jorn cut his bindings and freed him. Matthias had carried Reymund's limp body up the riverbank on his shoulders and, by a miracle, they'd found he was alive.

"No, you didn't," Reymund said. "You saved my life."

"*Ja,*" Jorn said, tossing his last torn piece of hay. He sorted through the strands closest in front of him and picked up another long one. He inspected it and then started stripping it.

"Then what?" Reymund said.

"We took you to *Kloster* Maulbronn. To *Bruder* Klaus."

"And?" Reymund said.

"Worked your father's fields," Jorn said. "For a place to rest our head and the occasional coin."

"But it wasn't that simple, was it?" Reymund asked.

Jorn kept his head turned, avoiding Reymund. "Nothing ever is."

"And that's the truth of it. The two of you were on your own journey, yet when you found me, you changed your course. It was no chance that the very day, *the very moment*, the farmer had chosen to end my life, was the same one you walked into it."

Matthias crossed his arms, watching and listening to them both. There'd been nothing simple about it, except for the ease with which they made decisions to save one another. In those early years, when Matthias had saved both their lives and they, in turn, his, their brotherhood was born.

"Do you regret it, brother?" Reymund asked. "Saving my life?"

Jorn turned on him. His green eyes flickered as he shook his head. "Never a moment in my life."

Reymund put his palm on Jorn's cheek and smiled.

"And I will thank you for it every moment of mine," Reymund said. "I beg you to give our brother the same courtesy. Let Matthias make this sacrifice, born in the name of love, and do so without regret."

Matthias leaned his back against a thick beam and slid down it until seated on the ground beside his brothers.

"Matthias, you've protected me since we were boys. From the hands of a mother who believed me a devil. You gave my father, in his broken and desperate hour, a reason to let me live," Reymund said. "You—and you, Jorn—have treated me as an equal, as a brother."

"Why would we not?" Jorn said. He coughed, then harder, clearing his throat. "You're a better man than I am any day, brother."

Matthias's heart swelled at the rare glimpse of spoken compassion from Jorn. For all his fire and faults and fury, Jorn was fiercely protective of Reymund, as he was of no one else.

"Both of you have given your lives in service so that I would have one. Over and over again," Reymund said. "Matthias, you always find a way. Putting me, and Jorn, and your men first." He grabbed Matthias's hand. "I am thankful for you. For your belief that my life is worth living. For being my champion and convincing others, like the king, that I have a voice. That I have something to contribute, even if I cannot hold a sword."

Reymund shook in agitation, overstimulated, and Matthias took to a knee in front of him. He folded Reymund's hand within his own and steadied his shoulder with a light hand.

Reymund flashed a smile and continued speaking. "Somewhere on our path is greatness, but also simplicity. You are the reason I am alive. I will never question your loyalty to me. Or the direction you see fit to lead. Because I know, on the days I cannot walk beside you, you, and my God, will carry me."

Matthias wrapped his arms around Reymund's shoulders. He clutched Reymund's head to his chest, hugging him. He kissed the top of Reymund's head and blinked away tears. "You know I love you, brother."

"It doesn't bother me where I lay my head at night," Reymund said. "In time, we will know our true purpose there. Ours, and my own. I look forward to it. I will go with you to Metzlingen."

"Thank you," Matthias said, pulling back from him. He leaned back on his ankle, with one knee in the air, sitting in front of his brothers. Jorn still wouldn't meet his eye.

"We won't have any money, but we will have each other, and that's what matters. The land gives us purpose. This family is what makes us rich," Reymund said, pointing around at them all. "We will be all right. *Vires acquirit eundo.* We will gather strength as we go."

"Every man will have his choice," Matthias said, clearing his throat. "To leave, now, or years from now, if you wake up and feel caged. I won't force you to stay. I won't ask you to bend the knee. With every breath in my body, I will ensure that freedom. That your will and your life is your own. But if you choose to come with me, you will have a home at Metzlingen. The doors of Metzlingen will always be open to you."

They sat in silence.

"I do not seek greatness, brothers," Matthias said. "I never have. Power. Titles. Reward. It was all my father sought, and it ruined him. Drove him mad with fever for blood and gold." He shook his head. "I have only ever meant to—"

"Titles have never made a man great, Matthias," Reymund said, smiling and gripping the cross at his chest. "A great man is simply a good man, brother. An extension of my Lord, though they may never see it as such. The monks saw that in you and chose your name accordingly. One who brings hope. Who lends a hand to the fallen. Embraces the sinner. Gives ear to the outcast. Value to the lonely. Peace to the tortured soul. A good man makes mistakes but in the end, in the shadows of anonymity, will do what is right."

Matthias hung his head.

His brother's words were almost too much. It all was almost too much.

"Please understand. I could not walk away," Matthias said. "I meant my vow to her, as I have always meant to keep them to you, brother."

Jorn snorted and shook his head, then finally turned to meet Matthias's gaze. He sighed and half-smiled, pulling a knee up in front of him.

"Brother, I knew you wouldn't leave her side from the moment you fell to your knees in front of her in Leuceria. Even if it meant you were going to stay here and shovel shit in the stables," Jorn said. "I knew. I knew you weren't going to leave her, even if you chained yourself to your king."

Matthias freed the words waylaying his heart. "I love her, Jorn."

"I know you do, brother," Jorn said. He stood and offered his hand to Reymund to stand. Reymund took it and the three men stood, looking from one to the other. Jorn looked away but grabbed Matthias and wrapped his arm tight around Matthias's neck.

"I love you, brother," Jorn said, hugging Matthias and patting him on the back. "And I will never abandon you. I am your man, always. Where you go, I go."

"Go to the archduke and prepare. Jorn and I will go talk to the men," Reymund said. "Go and win your bride."

PART FIVE
THE ARENA

END OF SEPTEMBER 1479
WAXING BLOOD MOON

CHAPTER 53

PLACEHOLDER

———— ❧ ————

Avelina

*T*HWACK.

Startled awake from the sudden sound, Avelina gasped, kicking at the blanket wrapped tight around her legs. Her crusted eyes tore open, and she blinked until she could see. See, *and confirm*, it hadn't been a dream.

Avelina had wept until the first light of dawn, when her depleted frame fell into a light sleep. Her eyes burned with fatigue. Her throat ached. Her marrow sucked dry, she felt brittle. A hollowed shell.

Drained yet unbroken. Alone and untouched.

"Apologies, mistress." The first of a pair of maids said from across the room, picking up the platter that had fallen onto the floor. With the briefest bob of a curtsy, she scurried out of the room without a glance at Avelina. The second maid, with a slight frown, folded her hands in front of her apron.

Wishing desperately for a drink, Avelina rose. She wrapped the sheet around herself and walked to the buffet. She found her pitchers empty and plates bare.

"The queen has ordered a fast today. You are to pray for God's protection and blessing for the joust," the maid said, watching her.

And for my own forgiveness, no doubt.

Avelina nodded, intending to, though the idea of prayer seemed so intangible this morning. She remained silent and followed along as directed. Passing up the king's extravagant dress for the simpler blue dress gifted from Reymund, she was led to the end of a parade of carriages below the courtyard. The two ladies before her spoke Flemish, and though Avelina understood their language, she chose to shut out their words and not engage with them.

A hand reached into the crook of her elbow, and Avelina turned to see Wilhelmina.

"I'm glad to have found you," Wilhelmina said. "We will ride together."

"I'd like that," Avelina said, thankful for a kind face.

Tucked into their carriage, Wilhelmina took Avelina's hand within her own. They rode in silence, winding down through the hills and streets of the city. As the chaos and colorful crowds and celebrations around them grew the closer they came to King's Park, Avelina felt increasingly invisible and thankful for it. And, especially after Madame Flora's assurance, she was ever so thankful for the calm and steady, thoughtful presence of Wilhelmina beside her.

Sometimes words weren't needed.

Sometimes being there was enough.

And this blossoming friendship, allowing herself to trust and become vulnerable, seemed worth the risk.

Their carriage pulled to a halt once they reached the marketplace, and they stepped out onto the cobblestones. The city buzzed beside them. Much larger than what she'd seen on their approach to the city, this market's wooden stalls and raised tents lined the square farther than she could see. People were everywhere, eating and drinking in a flurry of movement. Their voices tumbled over one another, bartering their goods and raising their steins. Smells were potent, overlapping. The stall closest to her was piled with baked treats, and when their fresh smell reached her, her empty stomach rolled, remembering Beatrix's buttered *brötchen*.

Above their heads, the immense buildings towered over the market. On one end, the large church of white stone commanded the square, its twin towers reaching high toward the heavens. Opposite, a bit beyond where the buildings of exposed timber and painted plaster crowded around the square, was the tournament pavilion. The structure was massive. There were two main gates of stone at opposite ends of the oblong complex, reaching four stories high. Curved wooden spectator levels rose above its foundation, arching between them, supported by a series of smaller stone towers.

The tournament had yet to begin, but already the walls rattled. The collective voices of those within it poured from it, rushing along the streets of the city. The air pulsed with a fervor and excitement she had never witnessed, goosing her flesh.

"They've been arriving for two weeks. Princes, nobles, knights, tradesmen, spectators, and opportunists alike. The festivities began two days ago, when they presented their arms and credentials to the king," Wilhelmina said.

"We saw the encampment as we approached the city. It was impressive."

They fell in at the rear of the procession of court and visiting ladies. It was a short walk across the cobblestones to the stadium, but their pace was exceedingly slow, as the queen was greeted enthusiastically by the market crowd.

"It's expanded with more tents and pavilions every day. Though this will be much smaller in comparison, having the battles just past. Still, the promise of fame and reward and honor and spectacle and notoriety will draw them here. Even the French, though not as many in number," Wilhelmina said.

A child pushed round Avelina's skirts, squealing as she dashed toward a gathering of children a few steps before them. Her mother quick on her heels, the babe excitedly clapped her hands, wiggling for a better view. Stepping closer, Avelina saw the source of her attention and slowed her progress, finding herself equally curious. A lady in a red costume with a matching feather mask had pushed a puppeteer's cart into the open area, and children excitedly crowded around her, waiting in anticipation of the show to start.

The cart itself was deep, with four tall beams stretched from its corners, and covered with a canopy. A multitude of strings fell from beneath the canopy into the cart's bed. The lady began carefully manipulating a set of sticks within the canopy, and a small wooden head peeked over the edge of the cart-bed, delighting the children. The lady sang as the marionette, a skeleton of carved and painted wood, danced from her strings, teasing the audience with jokes and playing a series of mimicking games. When the puppet tired, it nestled down within the cart to sleep, and Avelina and Wilhelmina applauded with the children.

The show over, Wilhelmina again led them forward. Avelina's head turned toward the market, lured by the smell of something familiar, and caught sight of the source between two crowds of people. Her coastal roots were right—fish smoking over hot coals and hunks of hickory wood—and her mouth watered. The fish were lined, some smoking whole with blackening scales and others fileted, displaying their meat, pink and plump, dripping fat onto the charring bed of firewood. Their view gone as quickly as it had appeared, she longed to see what other treasures there were to discover in the heart of the market.

Wilhelmina continued as they slowly approached the stadium gate. "The tournament brings glory to the city—and profit. It's been a year of plentiful harvest, so even more people flock to the city from miles around. The city is overflowing. The inns and stables are full, and their visitors' colors hang from their quarters. The townspeople are happy to display them and decorate the city. They'll string them together over the streets to lead to the square and dance long beneath them each night. The vintners. The bakers. The butchers. The armorers. All hard at work and hard at play. The kegs are flowing. Food is abundant. Trade is strong. The castle may host the balls and grand feasts, but this is a celebration for all. It is both market and festival to them. The city drinks and dances and doesn't sleep for a week until they have a champion. And then they must celebrate *that*, of course."

"Sounds wonderful." Avelina looked up at the web of festive flags. Fabric triangles zigzagged back and forth across the street on lines stretched from one building to the next. Large banners stitched and painted with the various coats of arms were strung along the outside lip of the stadium. Going on and on, they were an explosion of color and pattern and finery.

Passing another pair of stalls, Avelina noticed a mass of woodwork. Carved wooden bowls and the like were piled high on one. The next overflowed with trinkets and toys and the hands of children reaching for them. Another was loaded with baskets, convenient for carrying the hearty displays of assorted vegetables at the next.

"King Girault is passionate about the tournaments and holds them often, but this is the first Mother will officially perform the ceremonies. We are merely ornaments. We do not speak. Not today," Wilhelmina said. She side-eyed Avelina and whispered, "Especially not today."

Avelina swallowed and gave a slight nod. A group of townspeople hovered around the stone gates, waving, watching from behind the spears of the king's guard.

"Look how they cheer for their queen," Wilhelmina said warmly. "The people are happy. There is much to celebrate, especially with the new prince. Their cradles, tables, and pockets have been blessed this year."

They entered the stone gates of the stadium. Avelina caught a glimpse of the empty field below, surrounded by the stories of spectator seating.

"The noblemen and their knights display their helmets here for the queen's inspection," Wilhelmina whispered.

Avelina's lips fell open, surprised by the sight before her. Centered in the large room was a rectangular display that rose to waist height. For each participant, alternating standard and fork-tailed pennons hung above a decorated helmet. Smaller versions of the detailed banners outside, they signaled the allegiance of he who would wear the armor beneath it. Each helmet suspended on its own carved pedestal, they floated in a line waiting for the queen's blessing.

The viewing aisle narrow, Wilhelmina let go of Avelina's arm and stepped before her. Avelina was last in the line of women following behind the queen like well-dressed sheep. She appreciated the slow pace, the pain in her toes having subsided to a manageable ache, and the time to look at the helmets.

They were all works of art, masterpieces of metalwork, yet each a testament to whom they belonged. Some were intricately detailed with patterns highlighting the metal's curves. Others were embellished with gold, richly decorated with detailed metalwork. Some with large plumes of feathers. Some with horns, curling like rams or devils, beautifully wicked and intimidating. Another had simpler golden wings suspended in flight, while another sported a carved head of a falcon. Besides the helmets themselves, their pedestals were decorated, wrapped in ribbons and boas and the occasional jewel. It was a display of wealth and mastery, hinting at rivalries that would no doubt be amplified on the field.

They ground to a halt, and Avelina caught a glimpse of the queen. Animatedly engaged in conversation, she laughed and nodded her approval. She was dressed grandly today, but Avelina could see purple circles beneath the powder at her eyes. The queen had not slept well either. Avelina withdrew, wanting to avoid her gaze at all cost.

Avelina diverted her attention to looking at the helmet beside her. She glanced upward to the pennon and found only a solid black flag. Tucked into the corner was the plainest helmet she had seen. Dented, its design was simple. Well crafted, but not distinct. No gold. No décor. Only a thin line where the wearer could see out. And for the audience to see in.

"A placeholder, ma'am," a voice said.

"I'm sorry?" Avelina said, peeking around the helmet, where she found a boy. Perhaps a squire, who could be no older than young Rose. He was small but stood proudly behind the helmet.

"Holding the position of a contestant yet announced," he said.

Avelina nodded her thanks and turned, but her eyes drifted back to the helmet.

Perhaps a royal riding in disguise. Cloaked in his iron, if this knight so wished, he could hide. Another noble face lost in a line of many. The anonymous rider.

Riding before the crowds. Boisterous. In the hundreds. Perhaps thousands.

Hidden from them all.

Could she do the same?

Her heart sputtered at the thought, coming back to life.

There had to be a way. Somehow. There would be plenty of distraction, leaving heads turned and attention otherwise occupied. There *had* to be an opportunity to slip into the crowd and disappear. They were near the city walls. There would be horses everywhere. She would leave here and run. Run far enough away that none of it mattered and no one knew who she was. Where she could disappear, shameless, nameless, and simply be.

Like the mountains. Where for the first time in her life, she had felt free.

Untethered. Weightless. Yet anchored.

She would have it again—that freedom she had tasted. Where her decisions were her own. Her body was her own. Her life was her own.

That was what she wanted.

She would survive. *She* would disappear. *She* would determine her own destiny.

CHAPTER 54

"DUTY BEFORE SELF. HONOR ABOVE ALL."

Matthias

MATTHIAS ENTERED THE THRONE ROOM. The room went silent around him, the court watching him curiously, this favorite of the king. He balled his fist, crossing his arm across his abdomen, kneeled, and bowed low to the throne and the man who sat upon it. The move was awkward for him in this tailored and much longer coat made heavy with the chain of jewels—his tested, solid clothes having been replaced with these new, symbolic things. He steadied himself and waited with his chin low.

Curse this man and his pageantry.

His well-worn but young hands in front of him, he twisted the ring around his finger. He had meant to be rid of it, but again it sat on his finger.

The King's Sword. And soon to be *Edler* of Metzlingen.

Renewed oaths. Titles. Lands. Responsibilities . . . and a bride. *Hopefully.*

King Girault waited. Matthias knew the king had seen him. Matthias was expected and on time after all, but the man was going to make him wait.

"Matthias," King Girault said after several long moments. "Come forth."

Matthias rose and, chest proud, walked the red-and-gold carpet that led along the center of the room to the throne. Keeping his face forward, Matthias swept his eyes left and right through the assembled crowd. His men were here, along the wall, behind the members of the court. His heart swelled to see them. Jorn even offered a slight bob of the head as Matthias passed by.

At the foot of the throne, Matthias stopped.

The man couldn't help himself. The king sat on his throne, grinning and knee tapping with unbridled excitement, no doubt pleased with the bargain that was struck.

"On your knees, soldier," King Girault said, standing.

Matthias took a knee, and the king walked to his side.

Puffing up like a rooster in the yard, the king began to loudly address the gathered court.

"Matthias, who served me faithfully for so many years as soldier and as my Sword, comes today to pay homage and to swear fealty to his rightful king. You all bear witness to his oath and to the rewards I bestow on those most loyal to me."

The king stood in front of Matthias.

Clasping his hands together, Matthias stretched his arms toward the king with his head bowed. The king took Matthias's hands within his own.

Determined for an unwavering voice, Matthias tightened his core, focusing his will. He knew the words by heart and the weight of each of them.

"I, Matthias, of my own free will, make you, King Girault of Ewigsburg, this pledge. I am your man. My sword, my service, and my life are yours."

The king patted Matthias's hands in his.

"I, King Girault of Ewigsburg, accept your homage."

The king let go of his hands and turned to a servant beside him. He was handed a sword and, turning back to Matthias, held it across both of his palms. Matthias looked at the blade. Newly forged. Meticulously crafted. Engraved toward the hilt with a cross and the soldier's oath—*Duty before self. Honor above all.*

Matthias laid his hands on the blade and closed his eyes.

"On my honor, I pledge my service and my allegiance to the crown. Never to cause harm or raise men or sword against you. I will protect your lands in the name of the crown. I will remain faithful in my homage to you and to my pledged word."

"I, King Girault of Ewigsburg, accept your oath of fealty."

King Girault took a step back and laid the blade against his shoulder.

"In honor of your renewed pledge and service, I confer on you the title of *Edler* of Metzlingen and my lands of the same name. I confer all hereditary privilege to you and yours. You will serve as my representative and in my stead."

The king tapped his shoulders with the sword and stood back.

"Rise and claim your new name—Matthias von Metzlingen, King's Sword and *Edler* of Metzlingen."

CHAPTER 55

SYMBOLS OF FRIENDSHIP AND AFFECTION

Matthias

MATTHIAS STOOD BEFORE THE TENT of the archduke. He exhaled slowly, urging his feet to break from the ground and move forward. One weighted with the possibilities this opportunity provided, the other weighted with the enormity of the changes within the past few hours.

He squeezed his eyes shut. His temples still throbbed from the excess of alcohol he had so readily consumed the night before. His hope then had been to drown his regrets. To dull his senses until he no longer ached when he thought of her. Now he needed those senses. A clear mind. His strength. And not to get knocked off, or fall off, another man's horse.

"Matthias von Metzlingen."

Matthias opened his eyes and saw the archduke before him.

"Archduke," Matthias said, bowing his chest to him. He followed him into the tent.

The armor was laid out, piece by piece, with squires waiting to dress him.

"You do me a great service, one I am not sure I can repay or that I deserve," Matthias said.

The archduke smirked. "For a man of no consequence and, until this morning, no name, you have quite a reputation. I heard whispers of the tale of the lowly soldier crossing the mountains for the good princess. I travel here for a tournament to celebrate the birth of my ally's son, to hear they had arrived after traversing the mountains, on foot no less."

"I did not face that challenge alone."

"No, you didn't." The archduke raised a hand, and the squires came forth. They stripped Matthias to his arming garments and, at his feet, began to put on the armor.

Lifting his heel, Matthias marveled at how the small, riveted plates of the sabatons they attached over his shoes moved, easily sliding over one another.

The archduke circled him, as the squires continued piece by piece. "The princess must be an extraordinary woman. Strong. Loved by our God and meant for a higher purpose, to have been led safely through."

"She is," Matthias said. He lifted his arms, allowing the squires on either side of him to finish buckling the cuisses into place around his thighs and hips.

Maximilian nodded. "Losing her parents so young left her vulnerable, without the advantages and wisdom of age to be able to resist and fight for what was hers, as my own virtuous wife did at her father's death. To have been treated in her own country as she was and met here like this by your king is a disgrace. Mary and I would see her safe, with someone who would care for her with the respect she deserves, and protect her, as I have done for my own dear wife."

The quilted gambeson tied tight around his torso, Matthias was fitted into the cuirass. The large breast and back plates were belted at the sides and secured at his waist. A wash of excitement moved across his skin with each strap tightened and stud fastened.

"Your name was unknown to me, but in the little time since we met, you've shown me who you are. You are a man of honor, as you kept your word to your king. A man of substance, strength, to have made such a journey and conquered those mountains. I daresay you have purpose as well. I saw you dance with her, and I knew. This is not about power to you. Or ambition. You love her, do you not? And your brothers. You bartered your own service for their release, did you not?"

Matthias shifted. "They have earned the reward as much as I."

"You do much in the service of others," the archduke said. "What do you wish for yourself?"

His arm defenses complete and pauldrons attached at the shoulder, Matthias boosted his chin to allow the squire to place the bevor at his neck. Almost in full armor, Matthias thought his answer ironic and hesitated. "A life of peace."

"Peace?" the archduke said, turning back toward him.

"Truly," Matthias said. "To no longer see the world burn around me."

"Igitur qui desiderat pacem, praeparet bellum," the archduke said. "It only makes sense; if we mean to avoid war, we *must* be strong. A man is born and follows the path set for him, and then he dies. Few men manage to change that path, but when they do, they do not change who they truly are, only the ground upon which they tread. I am born, divined by God himself, to someday be king to all Germans and an emperor." The archduke lifted his hand and made a fist. "Though I was born to rule, Matthias, I too know what it's like to want. To starve. To fear. To be a rightly placed artillery shot or thrust of a spear away from death. Nothing is guaranteed, even for a prince of God. So I say to you, if this is to be our last moment, then let it be honorable. If this is to be our last step, then let it be purposeful. If this is to be our last fight, then let it be won."

"Hear, hear," Matthias said.

Maximilian took the sallet from the squire and held it in his hands before Matthias. He inspected the helmet, his eyebrows pushed together, and then met Matthias's eye. "I like to see men rise. Good men. I like to thank those who are loyal to me and support them as I can. Likewise, when I am made emperor, I would have your support and friendship. Yours and that of the princess."

"You have it," Matthias said.

The squire stood before him, holding the concave shield he would use for the joust. Matthias's eyes traced the lines of the finely crafted shield. Wooden, with iron reinforcements, covered with painted leather, with a cutaway where he would rest a couched lance. A blunted lance for the *gestech*, this "joust of peace" of the nobility, *for* the nobility, into which his new position granted him entry.

The second squire pulled the long cuffs of the gauntlets over his wrists, and each finger became housed in its own series of lames. Even the sliding plates at each finger allowed him to easily move. Though measured and custom made for another of the archduke's knights, the armor snugly fit his frame, as if it had been created for him.

He had long had his own armor and helmet, fielded from battles and bought with coin over the years, but he had never worn anything such as this. It was magnificent. Matthias balled his fists and shook his head, thinking of the worn-through gloves he had so proudly patched so many times before. "You give too much."

"You've earned your opportunity. I've given you the tools. Should you win your princess, I will again seek you out and offer you a jewel to use as a wedding ring."

Matthias opened his mouth to protest, but the archduke raised his hand, silencing him.

"I bid you. My wife has sent a token to the good princess as a show of affection and our friendship. At one time, I sent my own wife a ring to cement our betrothal. A gold ring set with a diamond to symbolize my intentions and my protection. Seems so long ago now," the archduke said with a smile. "The ring sent for the princess is meant as a symbol of our friendship, but should you triumph, let it serve as her wedding band—one fit for the Daughter of Leuceria. Let it be a symbol of the love between you and the promise of a better future."

Matthias swallowed the ball of emotion at the back of his throat. Thrusting dagger and his axe lastly tied one to each side, Matthias took the shield and the hand-and-a-half sword. His chin jutted out, working to form the right words of thanks.

The archduke grinned and smacked his shoulder.

"Enough. You are ready. We go." He spun on his heel and strode out of the tent.

Matthias moved into place behind him.

"Do not be afraid to test the armor. My armorers are master craftsman. It fits you well, as I expected. You are well protected, but remember, he who thinks himself invincible digs his own grave. Even in the most superior armor, there are always the smallest and deadliest points of vulnerability. Cover your heel or fall like Achilles. I'll pray for you, Matthias von Metzlingen, *my friend*. This is your moment. Do not waste it."

CHAPTER 56

A FEAT OF ARMS

Matthias

THE REINS OF THE FIERCE horse held secure within his gauntlet and armor moving fluidly with him as he walked, Matthias emerged from the darkness of the tunnel into the majesty of King's Park.

He was completely, absolutely, utterly awestruck.

Matthias rolled his shoulders back and looked around at the crowd. The stadium swarmed with all sorts of folk, jammed into their boxes and tiered seats. His gaze traveled up the stories, searching for, where years ago, the brothers had watched their first tournament. He'd hoisted Reymund onto his back and, one flight after another, climbed the narrow wooden stairs until they'd reached the highest level. Reymund had dangled his legs over the floor's edge, his arms propped across the wide bottom railing, while he and Jorn had stood on either side of him. Hoping for a thinner crowd, the brothers found they had the best view. From their corner, they could see the entire grounds. It quickly became their favored spot.

They'd been entranced by the plays, with extravagant costumes and comical dialogue and tumbling acrobats. Cheered when the beating of the drums signaled the beginning of the parade and called out to the mounted nobles, their knights and retinue, as they rode into the stadium beneath their banners. Dressed in their finery and eager to impress with their skill. Their elaborate armor striking works of art in themselves, they embellished still with

feathers and characters on their helmets. Their shields bore their
coats of arms. Each man's charger wore a covering almost reaching
the ground at their hooves; some simple, yet in the richest of colors
and décor, others as detailed and storied as a woven tapestry. Each
complete ensemble a testimony to their status and the glory their
House.

They'd watched them line the fields. Salute their king. Listened
to their heralds proclaiming their contestant's heritage. Speak of
their character and praise their exploits. Strike the shields hanging
on the column to accept their chosen challenges. Every blow and
event recorded to amplify their renown and reputation.

It had been a show from start to finish, both gloriously
entertaining and gut-wrenching. The building had quaked as the
stomping of the crowd vibrated along the stands and into his calves.
Hundreds of spectators shouting as one. Seeping into his veins.
They'd screamed for the knights, celebrating their prowess. Every
blow of a sword. The screeching of armor and splintering of lances.
They'd watched some blown from their horses, grossly crushed
and injured, as the field of martial elites narrowed, garnering pride
and glory unto themselves, their House, and their country, until
finally a champion was called.

To the children, they'd been Titans. Heroes to so many.

Seemed so long ago. Sitting here now, staring up at the same
tiered seats, surrounded by so many, he realized he had never felt
so out of place. *So alone.*

He'd fought many battles. Many. On horse or on foot. With
all sorts of weapons. But he'd never trained for this nobleman's
sport. This felt so different, leaving him both eager and on edge.
Wearing another man's armor. Seated on another man's horse.
Holding another man's weapon in his hands. Being called by
another name. A noble name. It felt so surreal. Wrong, as if he'd
trespassed upon another's fortune. As if he were a thief. A fraud.

Was he?

Matthias tapped his elbow to his waist, checking on his battle-
axe. It was there, as it always was. Had been since he'd been gifted
it. He snorted, thinking of *Bruder* Klaus. The monk who'd tutored
Reymund, counseled Jorn, and tolerated him. The monk who'd
listened, somehow knew his words, confessions left unsaid.

Matthias didn't know God as Reymund did, but still, this monk . . . The monk knew this. Knew *him*.

When they parted, *Bruder* Klaus had given him a name, a weapon, and his blessing, saying, "*Gesegnet ist der Löwe, der dem Lamm dient und die Herde tapfer verteidigt. Wer die Dunkelheit trägt, um anderen Hoffnung zu bringen.*"

Matthias exhaled and shifted in his low saddle, remembering. *Blessed is the lion who serves the lamb and bravely defends the flock. He who bears the darkness to bring others hope.*

A message. Heavy for a boy too early made a man. He tried not to think of it often, or interpret the weight of those words, hoping to at least do good with the gift given one so unworthy. The axe at his hip had been weapon, tool, *and comfort* to him since.

Staring blankly, Matthias realized the folk standing there were waving their arms, calling to him. In return, he raised his lance, and they clapped excitedly. He turned back to the field. It was midday, and a champion had just been called. The stadium rattled; crowds of supporters clambered over one another in the stands for a better position to see. Fellow knights and their squires raised their arms, their voices bellowing with praise. A German prince had won the day, and with that, the hand of the Lady Helene.

To his right, Matthias recognized a few of Eger's knights. He doubted their wounds were yet healed, the pain of Eger's death fresh, but they seemed pleased, raucously cheering when the prince grandly bent his knee to their lady. As was Matthias. It was a good match. One worthy of Eger's daughter.

The presentation over, the field cleared before him, and the workers began to clear the grounds and scatter fresh straw.

It had come to this.

This second duel.

It was time.

Finally, the Leucerians emerged from the tunnel opposite him. His opponent climbed onto a horse at the other end of the grounds and turned to face Matthias.

Marcus's dog.

As desperate as Matthias was to save her, Marcus had been to kill her. Trailing them from Leuceria. Chasing them through the mountains. Nearly finding her at Metzlingen. Here, now, their champion stood across from him. Ready to fight for her.

There was no room left for error. If he lost this, she was lost to him. If he lost to this competitor, she was lost to the world.

Matthias's breaths were short. Halted at the iron covering his face, they echoed around him. He batted his eyelids. The sun high and bright above him and the grounds well lit, he concentrated through the horizontal slit that offered him his only line of vision.

Matthias's horse pawed at the ground beneath him and snorted.

"Easy. Easy now," he said.

Matthias was directed to ride forward to the center before the king. Matthias looked past him into the crowd. His eyes darted from person to person, hoping to find her. For a moment to see her face.

The Leucerian was soon beside him. Dressed in full armor.

The horns blew loud, silencing the crowd, as King Girault stepped forward to the rail of his box to speak. "It is with joy that I tell you another challenge has been set this day. Amis, the heir of the House of Connaire, from the Kingdom of Leuceria, has challenged, Matthias von Metzlingen, Kingdom of Ewigsburg, to a Feat of Arms."

Matthias squeezed the reins in his hand. When the crowd cheered the king, he leaned toward the Leucerian. "I already fought a soldier from the House of Connaire."

"Barreth is not of my house," Amis said. "And I have no interest in avenging him."

Matthias scoffed. "I know you. Son of Avidius. Your father talked of honor, but I saw you. Cowering behind your father in the Leucerian court. Letting a hired man fight your battle."

Avidius's son laughed and turned toward him. "The House of Connaire does not cower. There is more than one way to win a war."

The horns blasted again, quieting the crowd for the king to speak.

"According to the rules laid out in the Chapter of Arms, the participants must agree to the terms of combat and number of blows for this duel," the king continued. "There will be two courses with weapons of war. On horse with lance. Three rounds. On foot with sword. There will be no points per strike, as in the

tournament; the man who grounds his opponent will be nar.
the champion. Should the winner be the House of Connaire, th
will have earned the right to return Princess Avelina to Leuceria
Should the winner be the House of Metzlingen, the *edler* will earn
the right to her hand."

Matthias strained forward, still searching for her.

"You betrayed your word, *Sword*. Or should I call you *edler*.
Bringing her to your king to be his harlot," Amis hissed. "How
you rise while you let the Daughter of Leuceria fall."

Matthias seethed.

King Girault's voice boomed above them. "What say you,
Connaire? What say you, Metzlingen?"

"My father thought you were a man of honor." The Leucerian
spat, hoisting his lance to the king. "You put her on her back to
stand on her shoulders."

Matthias's shoulders heaved. He raised his lance and turned to
Amis.

"And you mean to put her in the grave," Matthias growled.
"Crawl back to Leuceria. Tell Marcus his assassins have failed."

The Leucerian scoffed. "Marcus's assassins?"

"Any of his men left in my lands will be hunted for the dogs
they are."

"The House of Connaire does not ride for Marcus," Amis said,
shifting in his saddle. "Those beasts have been dealt with. Their
bodies rot in a ditch not much south of here. The Leucerians here
answer to me."

"She cannot go back to Leuceria," Matthias said.

"It was your king who betrayed the agreement and brought us
here. I am here for my father. He would not see her live a life of
shame. As your king's harlot. Or as yours."

"You know nothing of me," Matthias growled. "You demand
her release. To kill her? Imprison her? To use her to claim the
throne," Matthias said. "You will not take her from me."

"She is not a jewel to be possessed."

"No. She isn't. She is everything to me."

CHAPTER 57

TO FLEE OR TO FIGHT

Avelina

IT WAS TIME. IT HAD to be.

Inspired before by the anonymity of the placeholder, Avelina was ready. First only a thought, an inkling, the idea grew within her. She waited, ready to dart when the opportunity arose. But then the rumors began, whispered between cheers as the tournament progressed.

The Leucerian guard.

They had arrived in Ewigsburg and had challenged an unknown entrant—the archduke's placeholder—to the Feat of Arms, and she was to be awarded as prize to the victor.

Hearing she was to be given to another stranger or handed to Leuceria, her thoughts of escape became a determined plan.

She would flee. Soon, whilst the crowd's attention was diverted, celebrating the champions below, she would feign a trip to the noble's garderobe in the stone tower, and she would run into the cover of the townspeople in the market square.

Pain, be damned. Doubt, be damned. Arrangements and treaties of others, be damned.

She would be pawn to no man.

Avelina laid her hand against her stomach, seeking the reassurance of the prayer book. Finding it, her fingertips curled, pressing against the edge. Another flash of panic stirring within her nerves abated by the habit. Almost obsessive in its frequency now, yet each time the discovery was an oddly welcoming surprise.

Reassuring, calming, with an injection of peaceful strength.

She could do this.

The last lance broken, there was a champion at last.

Breathe, Avelina. Just breathe.

Everyone around her jumped to their feet.

NOW.

She was on her feet in a flash, already a step closer to the exit. Lifting her skirt before her, another step. And another.

"Princess Avelina."

A hand was extended before her, and she stopped in her tracks.

One foot firmly planted on the stone threshold; she was a breath from her victory.

"Ah, Princess Avelina. A moment, please."

Avelina blinked then, looking up, recognized the strong, handsome young face of the Archduke Maximilian. Eager to peek over her shoulder to see who else had noticed her escape, she kept her eyes on the archduke. Carving a sweet smile on her face, she put her hand in his and he pulled her toward him, his aura of confidence steadying her shaking legs. It would be conspicuous to leave one so well revered. She must play along, say her pleasantries, and trust he would soon let her by.

Only for a moment. Soon she would make her move.

"I am the Archduke Maximilian," he said in a pleasant, richly toned voice. Placing his other hand over his heart, he dropped his chin respectfully. He straightened, looking down his nose at her, though smiling warmly. "It is my honor to meet the Daughter of Leuceria."

Only a moment more and she would beg her reprieve.

The archduke carried on, clearly a fan of the tournament and today's results. He was charming and proud, befitting the reputation that proceeded him. Avelina only half listened, waiting for a window to interrupt without rudeness, until he began generously praising another. Leaning toward her, he demanded her attention. "A triumph! What a chivalric example of heroism! What a testament to skill! What a champion I have sponsored."

"Sponsored?" Avelina said, glancing beyond his shoulder to the open hallway. "How magnanimous of you, Your Grace."

The archduke grinned, clearly pleased with himself. "Indeed,

Princess."

Horns blew loud behind her, and the crowds around them settled.

"Ah, Princess Avelina," the archduke said, looking over her head. "Your champion is afield."

"My champion?" *Surely, he spoke not of the Leucerians.*

Tucking her hand into his elbow, Archduke Maximilian turned her on her heel, giving her a view of the grounds below them. Two knights, brilliantly dressed, sat astride their horses below their king, who spoke loudly, introducing them.

"The *Edler* of Metzlingen," Archduke Maximilian said, sitting taller. "The man himself earned the title bestowed upon him by his king. I awarded him my sponsor. The use of my armor and horse. He accepted the challenge against the Leucerian for the promise of your hand."

Avelina's mouth fell open.

Matthias?

This made no sense.

Him, dressed as a knight. Called an *edler*.

She searched his person, looking for some sign of him.

Beneath the title. The armor. That it was indeed him.

She found it at his waist. Sticking out oddly against his glamour was his axe. The axe he had used so many nights to build them a fire. With its worn, smoothed handle and ever dulling blade. That was always, *always*, tied to his belt.

It was him. He was fighting for her. Again.

Why? Why would he do this?

Give away his freedom. Risk his life.

He could be killed.

She was at once elated, body and soul screaming for him, and floored, her bones weakened within her.

Mere moments ago, she had been a step from escape. Part of her begged to flee still, seeing the Leucerian beside him. The Leucerian who had tracked her here and meant to take her. To kill her.

Run, Avelina. Run and don't look back.

But.

What if? What if he was victorious? And she could truly be his? He, hers?

Though riddled with fear, her body would not betray her heart. She would not leave him.

The stadium erupted, and the challengers rode to their respective sides. The king turned a hard look on her. In anger? Frustration? She couldn't read his response, nor did she trust it.

Both eager and terrified to watch the duel, Avelina took a seat beside the archduke, ready to see her future playing out before her. Again, as the barter, the threat of death and the promise of love, so closely intertwined.

The archduke leaned toward her. Her unlikely companion, still securing her hand within his as they set to watch. As Niro had those weeks before. But this time, there was no grinding of her bones. Only a squeeze. Light and encouraging.

"I do this to please my own lovely and virtuous wife, Mary of Burgundy, who sends you her friendship," Archduke Maximilian said. "It was not long ago she herself lost her father and was subject to the quarrels of men. All is well now. We are wed, happily, with a newborn son and heir, and the babe's inheritance and our lines secure." He paused, lifting his proud chin. "My wife's heart is pure and good. It will please her great heart to hear you are well and will marry well. I like your Matthias. He is a brave man."

"You are most generous, Archduke," Avelina said, her voice but a whisper. "A true and godly prince."

The archduke said, *"Amicus fidelis protectio fortis."*

Avelina's heart warmed at the familiar verse, and she responded in kind, *"Qui autem invenit illum, invenit thesaurum."*

Indeed. A faithful friend was a treasure worth far more than their weight in any gold.

Closing her eyes, thankful, terrified yet resilient, Avelina began to silently pray.

CHAPTER 58

TRUTH, REVEALED

———— ❧ ————

Matthias

THE KING RAISED HIS HANDS. "Let it begin."

The crowd, heavy with drink and anticipation, pounded against the wooden rails.

Matthias pulled his horse back. The long tilt barrier between them, their horses squared on opposing sides. Waiting.

The marshal threw the flag, giving the signal to begin.

Matthias roared, pent-up emotion pouring through him as he set his horse at a gallop. He aimed his couched lance at the shield of the Leucerian riding toward him. Their horses pounded toward one another. Each stride quickly shortening the distance. The distance closed, Matthias thrust his lance forward while taking a hit upon his own shield. Neither lance broke, their angles deflecting from the connecting shield. The sudden force of the impact was astounding, shaking him in his seat.

Their first run complete, Matthias reset and grabbed the second lance from his squire. His heart thundering, the charge began. The distance closed. Matthias dug his heels down and thrust his lance forward while taking a direct hit upon his own shield. Both lances shattered. Splinters flew into the air. The impact throttled his shield, sending him slamming back onto his seat. His arms shook.

Forward, man, don't buckle now.

Matthias snarled. His heart was determined, his body rebelling. His limbs shaking afire, raging within the iron flesh. Nauseous from nerves, wishing he could spit.

Again reset, Matthias took the third and last lance. His horse reared, raising its legs high, before thundering along the track at great speed. Determined, he locked his shield and hammered his lance upon the Leucerian's chest. The man was thrust back, and Matthias turned, hoping to see him unhorsed. He wasn't. Matthias threw his broken lance to the side and dismounted. He summoned the sword from the squire.

The noise of the crowd waffled around him, but he kept his eyes on Amis. He squeezed the grip in his hand. Familiarizing himself with its weight, his biceps burning, it became an extension of his arm.

The horns blew, and the king's soldiers poured onto the grounds. Marching along the front line, they then created a square, standing equidistant apart, in the open area before the king's box. Stalwart attendants manned opposing ends, waiting with quarterstaffs to separate the two combatants should they forget themselves and be lost to fury.

Sword at the ready, Matthias marched fiercely across the grounds. The two men stood mere steps apart, waiting for the marshal's signal. Matthias's shoulders shook, rage rippling through his muscles. The king prattled on above them, but Matthias ignored his voice, focusing only on the Leucerian.

This was it. This was his arena. His time.

"Come, son of Avidius," Matthias said, pumping his arms. "I am ready for war. I will fight you all for her."

The marshal dropped the signal.

Matthias closed the distance between them, raising his sword, plunging toward Amis with a strike of wrath. Amis countered from below, deflecting Matthias. The two continued landing blows upon one another.

The Leucerian was a half-head shorter than Matthias. Quick. Agile. His feet moved lightly beneath him, jostling him back and forth. Matthias in turn dug his own, landing each movement surely, intent to control the space between them. Their armor effective against any strikes, Matthias knew he had to get closer.

Still holding the grip in one hand, Matthias grabbed the center of the blade with the other to half-sword. He closed the distance between them and thrust the blade forward as a short spear, knocking Amis in the chin. His head thrown back, Matthias checked him, throwing his elbow into Amis's chest.

Amis faltered, but did not fall. Crouching, he whirled, and as he turned, the pommel of his sword slammed into Matthias's hip. Matthias shifted, catching and righting himself, driving forward with his shoulder, his pommel hitting the Leucerian with the force of a mace.

The close proximity had brought them to a vicious wrestle, working to take advantage of the weak points of the other's armor. The tips of their swords sparked, hitting with such immense force as they tore across metal, looking for entry to gaps in the armor. Hungry for flesh. Thirsty for blood. Kicking and pulling at one another. Animals, brutal and desperate to defeat the other.

Amis's pommel found Matthias's right wrist, and he twisted with vigor. Matthias groaned, fighting the turn, but knew to let go, lest his arm break. His sword was ripped from his hands, landing in the dirt behind him.

Matthias was disarmed.

Amis shifted his weight back and forth, his sword angled and ready. "Do you love her, Sword?"

The thought to dive for his sword was fleeting; instead, Matthias drove toward Amis. Matthias overstepped, leaving himself momentarily exposed. He quickly righted himself, turning straight back on the Leucerian. Matthias lunged forward, ready to sweep Amis's leg with his own, but he shunted away, again creating distance between them.

When he should attack, Amis withdrew. "You heard me, Sword. Do you love her?"

He taunts me.

"Come on!" Matthias yelled. Matthias raised his arms, intentionally exposing a vulnerability beneath his arm.

The Leucerian threw a punch with his left hand, pounding Matthias's face with his iron gauntlet. Matthias answered, grabbing behind the Leucerian's arm with his right hand. Blocking the man's chest with his left hand, Matthias twisted, splitting the Leucerian and his sword apart and toward the ground.

Losing grip on him, Amis somersaulted back onto his heels.

Quickly back on his feet, he lunged at Matthias's legs, barely missing him.

They continued to grapple. Hammering at one another.

"Swear it, Sword. On your honor."

"*Bastard!* Don't play with me!" The words roared, straining the muscles in Matthias's throat.

Amis responded with a rush of force, causing Matthias's heel to slide back through the loosened dirt.

"Answer me."

Matthias growled, heaving himself forward, looking for something.

Anything.

Instead of drawing back, Amis stepped forward, ramming him.

"*Answer me, Sword! Do you love her?*"

Matthias had his right hand at the Leucerian's throat, grabbing the chin of his helmet. Moving, not thinking to answer, the truth fell from his lips anyway.

"Always."

Amis's elbows fell.

His grip eased. "Then she is yours."

Already in motion, Matthias's arm wrapped around the man's knee with his left hand, lifted him, and drove them both to the ground. There was no restriction, no resistance to his movement. The Leucerian's head and extremities bounced beneath Matthias's weight as he landed, pinning him with his elbow across his throat.

Amis had let down his defense. Given Matthias a clear shot. The misstep was purposeful. Only noticeable from up close. Amis had let him win.

The crowd erupted around them. The fight was finished. The Leucerian was on the ground. Matthias had won. But the duel had not been called.

Matthias looked to his king, who remained seated. The king did not throw the baton to end the fight; instead, he sat in his seat, staring at Matthias over the knuckles of his hand. The archduke was on his feet, standing at the rail at the shoulder of his beloved, Avelina.

Shaking, Matthias stared into Amis's face. Matthias had his thrusting dagger in hand. He could end him. He could stab him in his face or cut his throat, both exposed, but something stopped him.

"You left yourself open. You let me win."

The Leucerian looked above Matthias's face, sweat dripping from his brow. "I told you. A wise man must know when to withdraw to win."

The volume of the crowd increased. Matthias looked again to the king's box. The archduke held the baton and, meeting eyes with Matthias, dropped it, declaring the fight won. The cheer reverberated through the ground beneath them. Men, women, children of every class called his name. Knights raised their helmets, yelling hurrah. The soldiers around the pair of them beckoned him to stand, but he couldn't. Not yet.

Astounded and breathless, Matthias threw the dagger aside and fell onto his hip beside Amis.

"Tell me, son of Avidius. What do you gain from this?" Matthias said.

"The promise that she is safe." Amis said. "I'd rather see her live her days with love than on the run, hidden and afraid. My father would know that she is well before he dies. It will bring him peace."

"Safe," Matthias repeated, shaking his head.

Seeing Amis pushing himself into a seated position, Matthias offered him a hand and pulled him upright. They sat side by side.

"Marcus will never be satisfied. He will always be a threat. To her. Those who love her. Those she loves," Amis said. "But you have seen him. You know he is a coward, reckless and predictable. Should she remain here, in your kingdom, with you, she can be protected. And pray God, someday find joy." Amis looked toward the king's box and nodded at Avelina. "This is no small task we entrust to you, Sword. I hope to do so without reservation or regret. She is family to me."

Matthias was dumbfounded. *"Family?"*

"Through her mother, Catherine. She does not know," Amis said. "Her family adopted my father long ago. When he was a child. His ship was driven north in a storm and wrecked off the coast of an island near Leuceria. It was sinking into the Mediterranean when my father was one of a few rescued by a Leucerian trade vessel."

Amis began to remove his gauntlets, and Matthias followed suit.

"Catherine's father was a good and generous man. He brought the survivors to his vineyards. Gave them a home. Work. Friendship. Family. He gave my father respect, his love, and even his name. My father called her mother both sister and friend. The princess is my cousin. Not by blood, but we are bonded nonetheless. Surely, you understand."

Matthias smirked. "Yes, I most certainly do."

"Our family will hold you to your word," Amis said, reached out a hand.

Matthias gripped it. "I swear. I swear with everything that I have."

A smile of mutual respect passed between them.

"Fare-thee-well, Matthias," Amis said, letting go. "The Daughter of Leuceria is yours."

CHAPTER 59

WHAT HAVE YOU DONE

—⚬⚬⚬—

Avelina

IN SILENCE, SHE WAITED. BENEATH the rose arbor of the king's garden, hidden from the view of the court, until hours later she heard the crunch of pebbles beneath his boots.

Matthias.

They were together, alone again.

Avelina hopped to her feet, balking at the dull ache, pronounced from overuse. Steadied, she tried to speak but found herself struck mute.

Matthias looked at her. Eyebrows furrowed, hands on hips, jaw pulsing as if he chewed hard enough to crack bones. His eyes met hers, and the line of his lips disappeared. He dropped his chin and eyes aground.

"Will you not speak?" he muttered.

Avelina stepped toward him. He took a step away, widening the arch he walked around her. The streams of sunlight breaking through the thick branches and yellowing leaves of the arbor cast him in a glow checkered with shadows, making it hard to see his face.

"Matthias."

Avelina's hand reached toward him but then fell. She wanted to touch him. She wanted to throw her arms around him and weep, deliriously happy, but she stood rooted in front of him. Her own lips locked, halting every word but his name.

"Or will you not have me, then?" His voice was so low she almost missed it.

Again, Avelina reached for him, but he took a step back from her, and her hand fell to her side. "Matthias, your freedom?"

It was all he had wanted.

What he had risked his life for over and over again. And his men . . .

"My life is mine to do with what I will," he said.

"But Jorn," she said. "The others. What will happen to them?"

"They have decided to come to Metzlingen."

"Metzlingen? The old ruins? So it is true?"

"*Ja,*" he said. "Very much so."

"Matthias," she said. Taking a step back, the inside of her knee hit the bench, and she sat upon it. "I am . . . I can't let you do this. Not for me."

"I've made my choice."

A lump grew in the back of her throat, and weights pulled on her heart. "The cost is too great."

"You mean my honor?" Matthias said. "I have none if I don't keep my word."

"Your word?"

"I promised you my protection. I swore you an oath, and I don't take them lightly. I failed you once. And again. But I will not fail you a third time."

"What are you . . ." she said, confused. "You've never failed me."

"I left you at Metzlingen. When it was more important to clear my own head."

"But Beatrix . . ."

"You could've been killed," Matthias said. "I led you from danger to danger until death was riding toward you, and I wasn't there . . . I wasn't there to protect you."

Matthias sat on the stone bench beside her.

"You *did* protect me."

"Not last night," he said.

His head hung so low she could not see even the smallest part of his face. The coldness in his voice shocked her, as if she had walked into a wall. He no longer would look at her. His arms were bent and shaking.

Last night. The realization swept over her. How was he to know the king had never visited her chamber? That to her surprise and happiness, she had been left alone.

"Matthias."

"We will not speak of it. You owe no explanation to anyone. Ever. Especially me." He stood, turned his back on her, and walked away. At the great curve of the arbor, he laid his palm against the hilt of his new sword and squeezed.

He was taking her as his, no matter what. But his voice broke her spirit.

Avelina moved toward him. She had touched him. And he, her. Several times. His hand upon hers. His body against hers. She wanted to bury herself in the security and comfort she had felt in his arms. She stood mere inches from him. She wanted to lace her arms through his and press her face into his back. Breathe him in. Give herself to him completely and never let go.

She didn't want to be a queen. She wanted to be his.

When she'd lain in bed last night, waiting, she hadn't mourned the loss of her marriage. She hadn't mourned the loss of yet another crown. The riches. The exaltations. The pageantry. The purported safety of the crown—for she knew better than anyone a crown could be your death sentence as much as your birthright. She had lain there mourning the end of her time with him. With this man who had taken care of her. Risked his life more than once for her. And was now prepared to give up everything for her.

He was getting land and title, but she knew what that meant. For him and his men.

There was no freedom in fealty to a king. There was no peace in a king's service. There was no joy in watching Matthias walk away from his dreams.

Avelina loved him. Truly.

And because she loved him, she would let him go.

"I release you from your oath. From everything." The words broke her. Tears burning her eyes, she cupped one hand over her mouth to silence the sob as her other hand wrapped itself around her waist, lest she touch him. If she touched him, it was over. "Your life is yours now. You have earned your reprieve."

Matthias still wouldn't look at her.

"I will not let you make such a sacrifice for me," she said. "The cost is too great. Your task was to bring me here. You've done that. You don't owe me anything else. I am alive; I will be all right. Thanks to you."

"You would not have me, then? I know I do not deserve you."

"No, Matthias, don't say that."

Matthias fell on his knees in front of her. He took her hand within his and raised it to gently kiss her fingers.

"I earned my freedom. For nine years, on the blood and backs of dead men. I've fought. Buried friends. I've mourned them all and carry them with me. I've done my duty. With honor, I have. I didn't choose this life because I have need for a title. Or a great house with fine things. Or to marry a princess. I fought because it was *right*."

Avelina dropped to her knees on the gravel and leaned forward so her forehead lay against their entwined hands.

His shoulders shuddered. "I chose you, Avelina, but I will never force myself upon you. I do not mean to make you live as my wife." His head shook from side to side. "You will always have a place to call home, should you choose, but I will not see you tied to it. Take this chance, take my name, and I swear it, your life is your own."

"You'd pay this price for me?" she whispered, floored by his words and what he had given her. "And then set me free?"

Matthias efforted a smile and backed away from her onto his heels. He rubbed his palms down his thighs slowly, then pushed to stand tall. He put his hands on his hips and turned sideways from her, avoiding her gaze.

"Yes," he said. "You have my word."

Matthias hurriedly wiped a fresh tear falling down his cheek and turned his face to the sky. He nodded then, turned, and took one step away. She rose quickly to her feet before he could take another.

"Matthias," she said, reaching toward him.

He stopped but didn't turn.

"Unless there were the smallest chance . . ." he said quietly. He turned to face her, and like a wave, his eyes crashed into her, enveloping her in a wash of everything he had to give. "That you'd take me as I am?"

Avelina pushed forward until she crossed over every distance left between them. Her eyes closed, she reached for his face and laid a palm against his damp cheek. Her heart folded in upon itself as she gently ran her thumb beneath his eye and brushed away a tear.

"Matthias . . ."

"I cannot promise you peace. It will be dangerous, but you will have my sword," Matthias said, voice still low but steady. "I cannot promise you perfection. I have land and no money, but I will build you a home." His hands squeezed around hers and drew them to his chest, where she could feel his heart thumping beneath. "Honestly, I know nothing of what I'm doing, but you have my word. I will do my best, for all of you."

Avelina opened her eyes and looked at his face. His lips hung open, the bottom lip shaking. His brown eyes, red and pooled with tears, desperately searched hers.

He was as laid bare, as vulnerable as she had ever seen him.

"Matthias . . ."

"All that I am, Avelina, it's yours. My heart. My devotion. My body. My life. Is yours. Always." He fell to his knees in front of her. "Will you please honor me and be my wife? Will you stay with me?"

His words melted together, pouring over her like a sun-warmed quilt. Bundling her in promises. One after another. Stacking upon one another.

The grandiose offers at her barter from the nobles—endless wealth, treasured and fruitful lands, guards, soldiers, comfort, servants, silks, luxury, great and powerful heirs—his offer included none of those things, yet it included everything.

"I'm yours," she said. She wrapped her arms around his neck, and his arms curled around her back, drawing her to him. She buried her face into his neck, breathing him in, and sighed. "Yours, Matthias. I have been. And always will be."

CHAPTER 60

SOMETHING BORROWED

Avelina

AVELINA WOKE TO A HAND against her cheek. She hadn't planned to sleep. After seeing Matthias, she had been sent to her rooms to prepare for her wedding, but overwhelmed and fatigued, she had fallen fast asleep across an ornate golden chair.

"My dear girl," a warm voice said.

Avelina blinked her eyes open. Disoriented at first, she choked on a rush of emotion, seeing the familiar, kind face. "Madame Flora?"

The lady reached for Avelina and squeezed her hand. "Yes, I'm here."

Avelina was astonished by the change in appearance. The lady appeared brighter. Assured. Sophisticated. Her eyes were wide and colorful. Her swanlike neck tall and perched above the rose-red gown, stitched with a silver thread that accentuated the shine in her hair, upswept beneath a hennin lined with pearls before a wisp of veil. "I thought you'd left."

"I meant to, my dear, but I set myself to one more task." She smiled. "I took a chance and surprised an old friend with a visit last night. I hoped to . . . distract him. To calm his needs for a time, and I do believe I did so."

Avelina paused, confused, and noted the lady's mouth tug at the side.

"A secret. Something for my heart and head alone," Madame Flora said. She scooted in beside Avelina, still holding her hand.

"And besides, my carriage wasn't ready. The stables are a bit hectic, it seems. Lucky for me, a curious red-haired gentleman informed me the delay was caused by his brother getting married to his sweetheart. So here I am."

Tears burned Avelina's eyes, and she drew a sharp breath. "I'm so glad."

"As am I," Madame Flora said, squeezing her hand. "Now. We don't have much time, but it is your wedding day. Let's get you ready, shall we?"

Avelina sat up on the chair and spread out her blue skirt. The gold stitching at the hem was dusted and dull, and she patted nervously at the wrinkles across her lap. "I have this dress. Reymund was so kind to procure it for me."

"It's a lovely color, but I've brought you one of my own as a gift." Madame Flora went to the door. "Come in, Sabine." A lady shuffled in, carrying a package wrapped in linen and tied with string and set it on a table. Madame Flora went eagerly to it.

"Come, mistress," Sabine said, offering Avelina a hand. The round woman's smile reached from ear to ear, where her hair was pulled back beneath a coif. Gray wisps of hair stood on end at her forehead, gleaming against the crisp blue of her eyes. "We move quickly, and with intention, and we'll get you to the chapel in due time to meet that heavenly man of yours."

Avelina was brought to the center of the room, where Sabine buzzed around her. Any lingering doubts or thoughts of home faded as she was stripped of her soiled dress and the ribbons were pulled from her hair.

Modest at first, it was easy to let herself go and join in the infectious and genuine excitement pulsing through the room. The two ladies worked in unison and were methodically attentive to every detail of her dressing. Stockings were tied at the tops of her thighs, and she was covered with layers of dress. First a light linen chemise, then she was fitted into a kirtle, a deep violet silk from its square neckline to where it flared at her hips and fell to her toes. As they tied her into a long lavender overdress, they hummed together, building into a duet in their mother tongue. Vaguely familiar, from somewhere deep within her memory.

"Such rich color you have," Madame Flora said, parting Avelina's hair and gathering it behind her neck. "We will pull some up from the front to show your face, but the rest of this beauty should be left loose in the Leucerian style." She handed Avelina a hand mirror and began separating the locks and combing and braiding and twisting them with ribbons stitched with pearls. Smaller braids framed Avelina's face, while others were pulled back, some knotted and others left long. The lady added a bejeweled cap at the crown of her head, pinning the braid around it. Gathering her hair, she pulled the long braids and the rest of her locks behind her shoulders so it fell loose along the center of her back.

After looping her own circlet around her wrist as a bracelet, Avelina studied the stitched embroidery on her dress. The details were meticulous. She wore a garden of twisting vines, sprouted leaves, and delicate flowers studded with amethysts and pearls. The cream lace along the deep V-neck, leaving a view of the violet beneath, matched the delicate lace peeking from beneath the long sleeves that dipped to the ground, where the same illustrious embroidery danced along the hem to the edges of the train spread behind her.

Avelina had never felt so finely dressed. It was stunning.

And the colors of Leuceria.

When the last pin in her hair was secure, Avelina retrieved a small seam ripper from Sabine's sewing kit. Avelina went to the edge of the bed, where her blue dress and underskirt lay, waiting to be packed. Slowly, carefully, Avelina cut the threads at the hip until she could remove her mother's prayer book.

Holding it in her palm, she began tracing her fingers over the front. The prongs prickling her fingertips brought a glimpse of a memory to mind. Her, quite small, standing on tiptoe to touch the jewels when it sat on her mother's bedside table. Her father had had it made for her mother as a wedding gift. Every morning her mother carried it at her breast to chapel and sat it on her bedside table in the evening. Where Avelina knew she would find it that day. That day she raced, desperate to snatch it before anyone else, and then hid it in her room all those years. The gems were dull, dirty from her journey, compared to the way she remembered them. But it was still a thing of beauty all the same.

Avelina made the sign of the cross on her forehead and pressed the book against her breast. She turned to the ladies, standing side by side, arms linked, watching her. Avelina spread her skirt around her. Warmth and gratitude flooded her soul.

"Madame Flora, Sabine," Avelina whispered. "I'm not sure how to even thank you. I will never forget your kindness."

Madame Flora gently laid a hand on Avelina's cheek and looked her in the eyes. "I learned long ago unexpected kindness is one of the most valuable gifts one can ever receive, my dear. And in turn, one of the most rewarding to bestow on others."

"That's beautiful," Avelina said. "I will remember that always."

"Now, my dear, I have only one question before we go."

"Yes?"

"When I asked you before what it is *you* want for *your own life*, is this part of it? Will this marriage to Matthias please you?"

Avelina smiled.

CHAPTER 61

A SIMPLE MAN

~~~

Matthias

SHIFTING HIS WEIGHT FROM ONE leg to the other, Matthias coughed to clear his throat. Fidgety, Matthias stared at the ring he would soon place on her hand. It sat on a small silk pillow on the carved altar, waiting for her.

Well done, soldier. The ring is yours. May this small token become a symbol of your union, your dedication, and your love for one another.

The archduke had met him privately before the ceremony to offer him the gift formerly spoken of from his own wife. The center stone, a magnificent ruby, was bezel set on a carved gold band, with smaller rubies fashioned around the entirety of the band. It was richly red, with reflections of burgundy light and purple undertones. It was lovely and delicate and far greater than anything he could've given her himself. His jaw had dropped, feeling the need to protest, but the archduke had lain a hand on Matthias's shoulder and squeezed, spinning him.

"Given, and I hope received, in true friendship, Matthias. I'll call upon you soon to visit with us. My wife will be eager to meet yours."

Speechless, Matthias had offered what he could in return—a sheepish smile and nod of thanks.

How could he—a simple man—thank one for such things? For so much?

He was no one. Yet they'd called to him, declaring him "our hero from the arena." Nobles, knights, and servants alike as the archduke had guided him forward. Now at the altar, Matthias's hands curled and uncurled into fists at his sides. His palms grew sweaty. Though groomed and bedecked in well-tailored clothes, he felt like a fraud. He may look the part, but the man beneath was patched with scars and tattooed in shame.

Where was she? He would feel so much better when he saw her face.

Standing here waiting, doubts crept up his skin and sat on his shoulders. Taunting him. He wasn't good enough. He didn't deserve her. He had no idea how to be a husband. It was something he'd never considered. Or wanted. Until Avelina. His own father . . .

Matthias ground his teeth, and pain shot through his jaw.

The only thing his father had taught him was who he did not want to be.

Curse that man. And curse these nerves.

Matthias pulled the ends of his sleeves at his wrists and widened his stance. He looked over the heads of the crowd, where he could see the tops of the carved doors. Closed. Waiting. Members of the court were gathered on both sides of the chapel. Not there for him, or for her, but to be part of the spectacle. They were loud. Laughing. Wearing on his nerves.

Matthias exhaled. He needed to trust, or have faith, as she so often said, that his path had indeed led here. Truly, he had no idea how to do so or what that idea, so abstract, meant, but he decided to try. After a lifetime of running, Matthias closed his eyes, unafraid, and waited for the doors of the chapel to open.

CHAPTER 62

THE WEDDING

Avelina

PRINCESS AVELINA'S HEART POUNDED FURIOUSLY. Years of imprisonment were over. The promise of a future mere footsteps away. The carved chapel doors towered and shook in front of her as the boisterous laughter and garbled voices of the bustling crowd pulsated through them.

A cloud of anxiety, nerves, and exhilaration curled around her, gorging on the enormity of it all. Billowing against the walls of the stone corridor, it grew thicker, darker, and enveloped her young frame. Spidery fingers of panic fought their way through her ribs to squeeze her lungs. Her knees trembled, threatening to buckle and collapse her to the stone floor that made ice of her feet. Beads of sweat peppered her skin. Pooling together, they bled into her silken dress, deepening the violet of the handstitched vines and budding roses. She shivered, the dampened fabric molding to her as a second skin.

This is really happening.

Her future had been tottering for years, and in the last several days it had been thrust from one extreme to the other. Back and forth in front of her, as she felt helpless to control it. Helpless to change it. Again, waiting on the whim of others to set her on the path that she was supposed to take. Or whose bed she was to share.

After everything that had led here, she was going to be a bride.

His bride.

Matthias had chosen her.

And in being his, she was going to be free.

Finally, free.

Avelina would do her best to honor her parents and her past, always, but she could no longer grieve the position she had been born to or who everyone else expected her to be.

She would be true to herself. Without regrets.

Avelina's hand tightened around her mother's book of prayers. Her most prized possession, out in the open now after being successfully saved and hidden for so long. She pulled it closer, thankful for the connection to her parents.

Mother. Father.

Avelina closed her eyes, desperate, aching to remember their faces. They were so long gone. Her heart ached for them, especially at this moment. She imagined they stood beside her. That she was able to grip their hands, and she squeezed. Squeezed until the metal prongs of her prayer book pierced her palm, distracting and comforting and fueling her. Treasured tightly against her breast, it became her armor.

She was ready.

Matthias.

Her heart flipped happily at the thought of his name.

"Are you ready, Princess *Av-e-li-na El-is-a-beth*?"

The king.

Her name dripped from his tongue in bits, each creeping up the bones from the base of her spine, one by one.

Avelina pivoted and fluidly dropped into a low curtsy. "Your Grace."

King Girault sauntered in front of her and leaned down, putting his open palm in front of her face. She placed her hand in it and rose back to her feet, but did not look him in the eye.

Avelina steeled herself, feeling his liquid gaze trace over her, as if she stood naked before him. The back of her throat tightened, and she willed her lungs quiet to control her breathing. Her eyes darted about. She tried to withdraw her fingers from his palm, but his thumb landed hard on them, pinning her hand like a foot caught within a hunter's trap.

They were alone in the corridor. There were no guards. No guests. No members of the court. Only she and the king and the stone walls to stand witness.

"I daresay you look lovely. Like one of the prize roses in my garden. Budded, bloomed, and fresh for a pluck."

King Girault reached his hand into her hair, his fingertips brushing along her throat. He fingered her hair and rubbed the back of her neck. He palmed the base of her skull and jerked her toward him.

He pulled her with such force Avelina hopped onto the tips of her toes to keep from slamming into him. She pushed back against his hand, but the strength of his grip on her startled her. Her blood ran cold in her veins when his hand slid forward to grip her neck and his thumb traced over the front of her throat.

"You," he said, angling her head in his hands until he could see in her eyes. He stared at her with grievous intensity until a wide grin stretched across his face. The slits of his eyes narrowed, and he laughed heartily, the sound rolling and clinging along her limbs like oil. "You make me wonder if I should've kept you for myself. I still could."

"My Matthias von Metzlingen waits for me," Avelina said, looking toward the chapel doors. Willing them to open.

"Ha!" The king let go of her, and she took a few steps back, her hand flying protectively to her throat. He sniggered and put his hands on his hips.

"So he does," King Girault said. "So he does." He started walking a circle around her. "Dear girl, I saw your portrait so long ago and knew of your beauty. I *knew* that was in my favor, but I never counted on him falling in love with you. Christ, I *never* expected him to succeed. That either of you would survive! Ha!"

Avelina vised her jaw and tightened her muscles, desperate not to shake in his presence.

"And then, *there he is.* He both amuses and frustrates me. He's no one, always trying to earn redemption for the sins of others," King Girault snickered. "The farm boy succeeds, and I have to recalculate. But this time, he was ready to give up everything, even those confounded brothers of his. *For you.*" His hand traced along the small of her back and then cupped her bottom. "No matter how the pieces fall, they still fall according to my will."

The king was toying with her. Like a plaything. A doll. A

marionette he could bend and tilt at his will.

Enough.

Avelina wasn't afraid anymore.

No, not in the least.

She'd had enough.

God, it had all been enough.

No more. She was insulted. Disgusted. And so very angry.

Avelina stepped away and turned a sharp eye on him. He sauntered toward her, and she hardened her stance. No longer the young lady mimicking the statue or the cold jewel, but as the woman putting her foot down. She lifted her chin and straightened her shoulders.

"Matthias is a good man," Avelina said. The steadiness in her own voice surprising her, she raised her chin even higher.

King Girault angled his head, grinning at her, and crossed his arms.

"Matthias *is* a good man," he said, running his thumb across his mouth. "And I was counting on that. He can't help but to help others. It's his weakness, and one I knew I could exploit."

He stepped toward her, and she held her ground.

"If it hadn't been you, it would've been Helene. No matter. Instead of Eger's lands, he can bring the *Geisterweg* to heel. Do you see, young lady? I have won. *Again.* My kingdom will be stronger and more secure than ever."

King Girault nodded toward the chapel and offered her his crooked arm. Avelina looked at it, back to his face, and tightened both hands over her prayer book at her breast.

"It pleases me that I have some use for you yet. If I'm not bedding you, at least I gain something from my man doing so," King Girault chuckled. He took another step toward her, leering at her. "Then again, one never knows what the future holds."

Avelina turned, side-stepping him, and quickly moved to the door. She banged her fist on the wooden door. Over and over, her hand throbbing, until the latches sounded and the doors creaked open. King Girault sneered at her.

"I do, Your Grace," Avelina said, turning a cold eye on him. "Not all of it, of course, but I can promise you this, you will *never* touch me again."

Shuffled footsteps resounded, replacing conversations as the entire room turned on a wave to the two of them, standing in the threshold. Their stares crashed into her, their collective curiosity threatening to knock her over and pull her under in their riptide. King Girault's arm quickly dropped, and he preened beside her. Without another look in her direction, he stomped down the aisle and left her alone.

Breathe, Avelina.

Avelina let out a slow breath, expelling the negativity from the previous moments.

Centering her focus, she began to walk the aisle, through the valley of the crowd. Her blood racing, she braced her wobbling knees. She wanted to run. But forward. Anxious to see *him.*

She stifled the last lingering fear threatening each step, keeping them even, steady, as she walked. Eager to move past their scrutinizing gazes, driving to turn her inside out.

None of that mattered. None of them mattered.

The aisle shortening beneath her feet, Avelina looked past those around her. Surrounded by strangers, the chapel itself held a powerful serenity, built on centuries of prayers whispered within its walls. Much simpler and more understated than the Great Hall and gathering rooms, it brought an intimacy and beauty to the moment that straightened her back and lifted her forward.

There, finally, he stood.

Her heart fluttered, and she smiled.

Matthias.

Her betrothed. Her future. *Her* Matthias, storied soldier and now Matthias von Metzlingen.

Luxuriously dressed, decorated with ribbons and gold. His posture was stiff, obviously uncomfortable in the finery he wore; he still stood unrivaled and immense at the altar.

Their eyes met, and he flashed a smile at her. As quickly as it appeared, it was gone.

"My lady," Matthias whispered. Matthias shook his head for a moment. His eyelashes blinked furiously, and his cheeks reddened. He shifted from one leg to another and exhaled.

"Matthias," she whispered.

Matthias offered her his hand, and she happily slipped her

fingers into his bearlike paw. His palm was sweating. He squeezed her hand, raised it to his lips, and gently kissed her knuckles. His chin quivered, and then he cleared his throat.

Was he happy? Truly?

He was.

Happy and overwhelmed. As she was.

Warmth spread across her cheeks as her spirit lifted. She felt taller beside him. Grander than she had ever dared to. And he, beside her—he looked pleased, and it gave her wings to soar.

Closing her eyes, she gave him a slow nod. Deep and respectful, to this man she adored.

In only a matter of moments, she would be his wife. And he, her husband.

Avelina squeezed his hand back and smiled up at him.

His brown eyes glistened, and he blinked again. He lowered her hand and loosened his grip. The friction of his skin, his fingers against hers, his thumb lightly tracing the curve of her knuckles, roared through her like lightning into the pit of her stomach, leaving her breathless.

His touch, firm yet gentle, exhilarating yet innocent, felt so new yet familiar, and she felt awakened, reborn and cherished, beside him.

The clergyman turned them to face one another.

The noise of the guests was lost to her, blending into the background in a room where only they stood. Their eyes were locked on one another. Their breathing in sync, chests rising and falling, becoming one.

Her left hand on top of his right, the two were wrapped in a violet ribbon as the clergyman continued the ceremony.

Matthias was smiling. At least partly.

Her blood warmed, and it pumped through her like liquid courage.

This was it. And this was good. So very good.

She loved this man.

And she was all right.

No matter what happened.

Everything was going to be all right.

They would be one.

Always.

Avelina exhaled.

"I, Princess Avelina Elisabeth, take thee, Matthias von Metzlingen, to my wedded husband and lord," she repeated the vows set out before her, her voice steady and confident. "I am yours. To have and to hold. From this day forward."

He was smiling now.

A wide, open grin lit around his eyes, which were flooded with tears.

"I pledge you my fidelity. To love, cherish, and obey you," she said. "All that I am is yours—my love, my body, my life—that together we shall live and be as one, until death us depart."

Matthias reached into a vest pocket and handed the clergyman a ring. Holding it aloft, he blessed it and handed it back to Matthias.

Matthias stretched to his full height, steadied his stance, and rolled his shoulders wide. A wall in front of her, but open, welcoming her inside. His brows creased; eyes fixated tightly on hers. He leaned in as if speaking only to her.

"I, Matthias von Metzlingen," he said, pausing a moment, steeling himself. "Take thee, Princess Avelina Elisabeth, to my wedded wife and lady."

Matthias took a step toward her and lifted their bound hands against his chest.

"I am yours," he continued. "To have and to hold. From this day forward. I pledge you my fidelity and my protection. To love and cherish you. All that I am to you—my love, my body, my life— that together we shall live and be as one, until death us depart."

Matthias unwrapped their hands and held the ring at the knuckle of her first finger.

"In the name of the Father."

He shifted the ring to her middle finger.

"The Son."

And then to her ring finger and pushed it forward.

"And the Holy Spirit, I thee wed."

Everything. Every word. Poured over her skin. Spreading across her chest, caressing silkily over her skin. Along her limbs. Curling her toes.

Matthias let go of her hand and gently took her face within his two hands. He barely touched her, looking deep into her eyes.

"I love you," he said.

Her heart bounced hard against her ribs. "And I, you."

Matthias bent and put his forehead against hers. "May I kiss you?"

Avelina barely heard him ask. And she didn't wait to answer.

Avelina pushed her lips up to his and kissed him. Lightly. Their lips barely touching, they shook against each other. Their lips parted, and he slid his arms around her, pulling her to him.

"I mean it, Avelina," he whispered against her cheek. "I love you. And I always will."

Her ringed hand held the side of his jaw, and she pressed her face against his. Desire burned deep within her, mounting upon itself. But that was for another time. Far from here.

They clung to one another. Tightly.

Avelina smiled.

Intoxicated. Exhilarated. Invigorated.

Hope—renewed, much more easily recognizable—grounded her.

"And I, always," she said and kissed his cheek. "Let's go home."

CHAPTER 63

THE PATH THAT LEADS US HOME

Matthias

"WELL, IF THAT WASN'T BEAUTIFUL," Jorn said, riding up to Matthias's side. Brom shook his large head and nickered to Jorn's horse.

Matthias snorted.

"I mean it," Jorn said. "You could've squeezed a tear out of the devil himself with the way you two were holding on to each other."

"As long as you were amused," Matthias said.

"Amused, no. Moved, yes."

"Don't mock me, Jorn."

"I do no such thing. And I mean no disrespect."

Matthias rubbed a hand over his face and looked about them. It was evening. Late. Almost dangerous to start on their journey now, to be driving out into the dark wilderness toward Metzlingen, but his gut told him there might be more risk to stay.

There would be time for details later. Reports to the king. Instructions from the king. Right now, his only desire was to put distance between them and Ewigsburg and to see Avelina set safely in their new home.

"All right, then, brother," Matthias said.

"*Edler,*" Jorn replied, twirling his finger in front of his forehead mockingly.

"Bastard," Matthias laughed. "Don't call me that."

Jorn frowned and growled at him. "I have and I will."

Matthias grimaced. He knew well enough it wasn't an argument he would win.

"You better get used to it, you stubborn arse. Does no good for others to hear you addressed differently," Jorn said, gesturing at the throngs of people crowding the streets. The tournament was over, but the celebrations continued. Through the night and at least for another day, until the barrels ran dry and the spits were empty. "Your men won't have it." Jorn cocked his head behind them. "That new wife of yours—*your lady*—she does not deserve any less either."

His wife.

At their last stop within the city walls, Matthias watched Alif bring Rose from the alehouse and lift her into the cart. The young girl wrapped her arms tight around Avelina's neck and didn't let go. Even when her pup, Liesl, and the tiny goat, Lukas, jumped on top of her, nipping jealously at her shoulder. Reymund smiled at him from his spot beside Avelina, and Matthias turned back, ready for them to go.

They rode through the gatehouses, passing the last straggling travelers returning to the city before the watchmen would close and secure the gates at day's end. Their ensemble left Ewigsburg much as they had arrived. A man, a horse, a cart carrying a woman, a girl, and her babes, except now he rode strong with his men at his side.

They had all come. Every one of them. Reymund. Jorn. Alif. Michel, Harock, Boone, and even Lars. They had been waiting in the lower courtyard after the wedding ceremony, with everything prepared so they could leave immediately. Jorn had led the two of them there and turned, taking a knee before them. Every one of them had bent the knee behind him and pledged their service and sword to him. And to Avelina.

"Are you ready for this, brother?" Jorn asked.

Matthias adjusted in his seat. He was much more comfortable without the fancy tunic and jewels, back in his own clothes. He was fidgety. Anxious but excited. So much that Brom beneath him sensed it, whipped his head up, and snorted.

Matthias put a hand on his hip. Turning to Jorn, he was struck by the look on his face. There was no trace of a smirk. The joke that usually sat behind an ornery smile was replaced with a look of genuine concern.

"I think so," Matthias said honestly. "I hope so."

Jorn's head bobbed, and he turned away, looking toward the horizon.

The heavy clip-clop of hooves on cobblestones dissipated as the last of their caravan reached the dirt path. The steady hum of the wheels drumming against the dirt road, mixed with the pounding rhythm of their horses, announced they were officially outside of the city walls and on to their new home.

"I know I devil you, brother. I was angry, but Reymund is right," Jorn said. "You do this for all of us."

"I should've talked to you both first," Matthias said.

"You're wrong," Jorn said. "You had a moment to seize the opportunity, and you did. You did the right thing."

Matthias sighed, nodding his head. Strangely, scarily, it did feel right. "Tell me I won't make a mess of this."

"You will," Jorn said.

Matthias laughed. "Thank you for the encouragement."

"You'll try. You'll fail some," Jorn said with a shrug. "But you'll rise and keep going. A babe who doesn't stumble won't learn to walk. A man who isn't tested won't learn to persevere. Any man who doesn't get shown his arse every now and again becomes one."

Matthias exhaled sharply and rolled his neck.

"All very true," he said, keeping his eyes forward.

"We saw you fight, brother," Jorn said. "You fought like a lion."

"I couldn't find you," Matthias said. "I looked for you."

"We were there, in the stands. We will always be there. You're not alone in this endeavor," Jorn said. "Men follow you because you are true. You give us hope. Reymund isn't the only one of us you saved, brother. I've never forgotten, and I never will. Whatever burden you carry, whatever battle you fight, I will be at your side." He coughed and cleared his throat. "Do not be afraid, brother. I believe in you. And I'm happy for you. For you and your wife."

"Thank you, brother," Matthias said. "Truly. That means a lot."

They rode a while in silence, cresting a hill bathed in the last orange light of the sun.

"You are not your father, brother," Jorn said. "I know he's the reason you feel the need to save those around you. Sometimes, the world entire. But remember that. You are *not* him. Nor will you become him. Nor can you or must you save everyone."

Matthias side-eyed him.

"You know I speak true. Your father was his own man. The king his own as well. *Devils they may be.* The man you are, and what you do, is enough."

Matthias swallowed the stone in his throat. Again, when it became lodged in his chest. He coughed and nodded, finding his voice. "Gold can drive a man to do terrible things."

"But it's not what drives you. Who you were born to doesn't determine the man you will become," Jorn said, rolling his shoulders back. "You are a better man. *Bruder* Klaus saw that in you long ago. Why else would he have dared baptize you with such a name?"

"*Bruder* Klaus?" Matthias said, shocked hearing Jorn speak of him. He'd only thought of the monk himself before the tournament, but Jorn rarely spoke of the *kloster* where they'd secured a safe home for Reymund years ago. Where the monks had taken Reymund in, cared for him, and educated him while the two boys worked his father's farm.

Those were backbreaking days, but good days, spent together, relatively safe. Reymund had given them lessons when they visited, while they'd eaten their apples and *brötchen* in the monastery's garden. Jorn had learned despite himself. Heart hardened and stubborn, Jorn had an anger inside, only wanting to fight, so Matthias had taught him sword and skill, as his father had taught him. Their days had been filled with the ease of routine, honest work, and when spent together, a happiness. Until the day the farmer sold them to the king's armies and the boys had been welcomed as part of Prince Siegfried's retinue.

"The legend himself." Jorn grinned. "I remember the day clearly."

"You mean when you chose your name? Butchering that of the great Dane?"

"Ha! All the better to be remembered as I am, I say," Jorn said. "You, brother, when *Bruder* Klaus gave you the name of the man who replaced Judas, the great betrayer, it was no accident. 'Like the martyr', he said, 'that you should persevere and stand for those who need hope'. *That* is your destiny, brother. *That* is who you are."

Speechless, Matthias looked at his brother. His lip tugged, and he laid a hand on his heart. There was no one who knew better the hell they had come through. Or his fear of losing himself to that darkness.

Jorn's eyes lit in understanding, and he tapped his chest as well. The men bowed their heads to one another.

Everything had changed, but some things would remain the same.

Loyalty. Love. And brotherhood.

"Lead the way, *Edler*," Jorn said with a quick wink. "I'll take position next to your bride and her cart full of wards."

Matthias smirked. Just like that, things were back to normal.

Jorn peeled his horse off to the side and fell behind him. Alif and Boone rode up, taking the flank position behind either side of him.

Matthias looked ahead toward the horizon, where the sun was falling behind the gray mountain wall. The last brilliant hint of yellow remained beside a peak, surrounded by pinks and purples, fading lighter and lighter until they disappeared into the clouds above them. Soon their path would dip into the forest, and then they would follow along the river until they reached the once forgotten land whose name was now his own.

Metzlingen.

Beatrix. The old man, Uhrl.

Matthias had promised to speak on their behalf. That he'd pay them tenfold for their generosity. Here he came—their kin returned with an *edler*, his lady, and men to work and protect the land—hopefully making good on his word. Coins produced by Avelina—from her sacred skirts, no doubt—had purchased two pairs of large horses, each drawing a cart full of grains, provisions, tools, and gifts from the market for those at Metzlingen.

It was a start.

Matthias's cheek tugged, thinking of the motto he'd chosen for their House. *His* House.

We gather strength as we go.

They had no other choice but to. He, and Metzlingen, would push forward. To do right by its people. His men. The land. The mountains. All of them. He would work to ensure their security. Their success. To earn their respect. He wasn't foolish enough to think they belonged to him. That he would conquer it all.

He would do his best.

That's what he had always done. And what still mattered.

Doing his best. Doing what was right.

But when had doing what was right ever been the easy path?

Always. Yet never. So *vires acquirit eundo.*

Matthias smirked and again adjusted himself on his seat. He leaned forward and patted Brom's long neck. He fisted the reins of his horse, and a glint of light lit off his hand.

The ring. The physical reminder of his promise, his pledge, and his oath. Given to so many, but all to honor the vows he made to her.

Matthias had taken oaths before.

Life oaths—those between brothers—unspoken and unbreakable.

Pledging his service, his sword, and life as a boy to his king.

To a stranger. A foreign princess. That he would protect her

Again, taking the knee as he was renamed Matthias von Metzlingen.

This last oath. The vows passing from his lips as he beheld his beloved had both secretly excited and unnerved him. Blissful, Matthias had drunk it all in—the way she looked, the way she had looked at him, their promises to one another—determined to imprint every last detail onto his memory.

It was as if he were seeing her again for the first time.

Not the princess, the jewel, standing before him, but the woman. Whose company he enjoyed. Whom he adored. Whom he loved. Who made him want to be a better man. Who made him believe he could be.

The woman was the sun itself, bringing light to his darkness.

Avelina.

Simply. Perfectly. Astoundingly. Avelina.

Those amber eyes. Dazzling, under dark lashes, almost catlike, round but pulled tightly at the corners, toward her temples. Chestnut hair, swept up at the sides, allowed him to trace the line of her flushed cheek. To her exposed ear. Her bare neck. To the curve of her shoulders, where her gown cut across at an angle. The fitted top with lace the color of milk and stitched with amethysts and tightly twirling flowers rose and fell, not able to hide her own swelling nerves and excitement. The remainder of her hair, thick and wavy, hung loosely along her back to her waist.

When Avelina had given him her small hands, they had been soft and warm and smooth against his weathered skin. Repeating her vows, she'd looked as eager as he, and his heart had soared.

And it still did.

Nothing was certain in their future. Nothing.

No matter what happened, Matthias was hell bent on caring and honoring those with him and before him. He was determined, in the end, that his friends and his brothers would live and die as free men.

And Avelina.

The love he had for Avelina. His *wife*. That love, *their* love, was good.

It was enough, and it was everything.

It was honest. It was real. And worth every last bit of this.

He ran a hand down his throat and drew the autumn air deep into his lungs. The tourniquet of fear, of suffocating self-doubt, always at his neck, had loosened. He could breathe. Deep within his chest, his heart ached with a happiness and hope he had never known before. It was odd. Overpowering. Humbling in its grip on him. But he embraced it.

Tapping Brom's side with his heel and shifting his reins, Matthias turned their caravan away from the last golden fields surrounding Ewigsburg. The days ahead of them unknown, they disappeared into the black forests leading toward the ruins at Metzlingen, where they would build their future together.

Matthias lifted his chin and drove on, unafraid of the dark.

He was ready. He felt filled with purpose. And he was at peace.

The End

EXTRAS FOR

THE KING'S SWORD

AUTHOR'S NOTE

THE KING'S SWORD IS PART of the greater Metzlingen Saga. I've been living in Metzlingen for several years. Unfolding the lines. Interviewing the characters. Sitting at the hearth and listening to each of them. Every family has a story and each person within it, their own voice. It's not a locked puzzle – where each person fits snuggly into their place, but a moving, breathing, living thing – a murmuration of starlings – constantly in movement and affecting one another.

I've been a writer since I was a child. I enjoy the language, building words upon one another to create a story. The music of words, and the artistry they provoke, breathe life into our imagination. I am also a researcher at heart. I enjoy digging through sources to answer all the who, what, when, where, why and how questions, in order to better understand and appreciate things.

Metzlingen is a fictional world, nestled within the very real and endlessly intriguing history of Europe, when the medieval world and the Renaissance intersected. Specifically, I have built my world into the German landscape and culture: where my own familial history originated, where I have traveled and lived, and where I personally wanted to explore and learn more about.

I have long been drawn to history at large, and an avid reader of this time-period, both fictional and non-fictional. I spent the past few years happily researching, reading, and recording ideas and details to build the world of Metzlingen. I've been lucky to travel across the United States. I've been lucky to live in many places. I've also been lucky to travel abroad and to have lived in Germany, where I was able to immerse myself into the culture.

Across towns and borders, I met many wonderful people, who shared their traditions, their hospitality, their stories, and their time with me and my family. We enjoyed joining in alongside, appreciating what opportunities and experiences we could. We listened, learned, and laughed. We explored locally, traveled between towns and across borders, visited museums and landmarks, climbed old city walls and ruins, stood in awe of centuries old buildings and art, hiked through mountains and gorges, attended local markets and events, touching, tasting, and trying new things. I studied old books, theses, sketches, and maps, as I continued to build my library.

The story is a work of fiction, including the majority of the characters, places, and events. The story includes some fictional portrayals of actual historical figures, places, and events, which were researched across several sources. I aimed to present an accurate account of them, but they remain my own fictional and artistic interpretation.

Within the Metzlingen Saga, my characters will walk the path of history, witnessing real events and meeting real historical figures. Some examples within The King's Sword are as follows:

⊛The Battle of Guinegate did take place on August 7, 1749. The battle itself took place primarily between the French troops of King Louis XI and those of the Archduke (later Emperor) Maximilian of Austria and the Hapsburg dynasty, who was determined to secure the Burgundian inheritance through his marriage to Mary of Burgundy. It is my understanding that Maximilian's forces were mainly comprised of Flemish / Burgundian troops, but also included (but were not limited to) various German, Hapsburg, Imperial, and mercenary men-at-arms. It is indeed reported that the Archduke Maximilian fought on foot with a group of nobles. Matthias could have easily been there as part of the allied forces. For the description of the battle, I used a variety of sources, including technical discussions on the history of warfare and the tactics that were used (such as the Swiss pike square formation). I was also able to find and translate old reports of the battle.

⊛My portrayal of Archduke Maximilian is fictional, but reflective of my research. I found him interesting in real life and I based his character on how I believe he would interact with my characters. His support of Matthias mirrored his purported magnanimity and love of all things chivalric. It was also a reflection of his own true love for, and devotion to, his wife at the time, Mary of Burgundy.

Archduke Maximilian's physical description, love of tournaments, description of the ring he sent Mary of Burgundy when they were betrothed (which is said to have been the first recorded engagement ring that contained a diamond), and his tributed words about her kept in line with research. To this point, I have been unable to verify his whereabouts during the time that I have him attending the tournament at Ewigsburg, but as he was such a huge fan of them, it is not outside the scope for him to have attended.

❀The brief mention of the pope, Medici and Pazzi (during the barter) refers to a true event, known as the 'Pazzi Conspiracy', that transpired in Florence, Italy. The plot was an attempt by the Pazzi family to assassinate Lorenzo di' Medici and his brother Giuliano. The brothers were attacked at High Mass within the *Duomo* (cathedral) on April 26, 1478. Lorenzo survived, but his brother did not. There were many conspirators involved in the plot, which is said to have had support from Rome. In my opinion, the conspiracy, the murder, and the fallout from it, would've left Niro incredibly wary of dealing with Rome.

❀The account of the tournament, the Feat of Arms, and the barter / duel were also based on accounts with a focus on German traditions and when Archduke Maximilian was involved. The weapons, armor, and fighting techniques were to the best of my knowledge, what would have been used in Germany in the late 15th century. I used historical materials (sketches, accounts, and books), as well as instructional videos and fighting critiques. I married my own experiences of large stadium events with what I believed it would have been like to witness and attend such an event at that time.

❀There were trade routes used throughout the Alps, but the *Geisterweg* that my characters take is entirely fictional.

❀Maulbronn Monastery (referred to as *Kloster* Maulbronn) is an extremely well-preserved Cistercian monastery in Baden-Württemberg, Germany. My story surrounding the *kloster* is fictional, including the monk known as *Bruder* Klaus, but was based on the history of monasteries taking in and caring for those in need, in places such as their infirmaries. It was one of my favorite places to visit, learn about, and explore during my time living in Germany.

✸Leuceria, and the other city states / kingdoms, are modeled after city states that though they once existed, and may have for hundreds of years, have since disappeared, either absorbed into nearby cities / kingdoms, or simply lost to history. I chose to create them on my own instead of changing an existing city's history / past.

Many of the locations and buildings within the novel were inspired by places that once existed and/or I visited myself, and are fictional portrayals. I attended reconstructed medieval festivals and markets, where I could witness time-period appropriate things, such as wares, techniques, music, food, and games. The marionette that Avelina sees at the market is based off of one that I watched with my daughter, and her own squeals of joy and laughter watching the puppet dance about. The references to flowers, such as the description of the "star of the mountain", also known now as Edelweiss, is based on the ones I bought at a local market and planted in our window-box at our Stuttgart home. The description of the gorge that Rose leads them through was based on a hike I took with my family. Writing that chapter at the time, I remember watching my husband ducking his way through tight cutaways (as I pictured Matthias doing the same) and thinking about how easily my characters could've slipped on wet stones and fallen into the swollen river below. The sound of the bells reflects those we heard carried across the mountain slopes, as we watched the animals grazing or be herded along or driven down from the mountains. Accounts of these things and more - the types of animals, trees, stones, jewelry, clothing, buildings, etc. - were all given as accurately as I could in hopes of immersing the reader into the story. Any errors were unintentional, or taken with literary license, for the purpose of the story.

Thank you for reading The King's Sword. I look forward to exploring the world of Metzlingen further with you in the next installment of The Metzlingen Saga.

All my best,

Rebekah

GLOSSARY OF NON – ENGLISH TERMS

(German unless otherwise indicated)

Ach: Exclamation, various meanings: "oh" or "really" or "obviously."

Agnus Dei, qui tollis peccata mundi, miserere nobis (Latin): "Lamb of God, who takes away the sins of the world, have mercy upon us." Based upon John 1:29 from the Bible; used in Roman Catholic and other Christian liturgies.

Alles gut: "Everything is fine" or "There is no problem"

Amicus fidelis protectio fortis, qui autem, invenit illum, invenit thesaurum (Latin): "A faithful friend is a strong defense: he that hath found him such hath found a treasure." Ecclesiasticus 6:14 from the Bible.

Braver Hund: Good dog.

Bratwurst: A German link sausage typically made from pork (sometimes veal), generally pan-fried, varies by region.

Brötchen: Bread, small crusty rolls.

Bruder: Brother, in this case referring to a monk.

Dona nobis pacem (Latin): "Grant us peace." Round from the Agnus Dei Latin Mass.

Edler: Lowest rank of the titled German nobility, beneath Ritter but above the general servile population. Styled "Edler von X." Like "lord of the manor" or "gentlemen" or "gentry."

Gah: Expresses exasperation or dismay.

Geisterweg: Ghost's way / path

Genau: An affirmation which means "exactly."

Gesegnet ist der Löwe, der dem Lamm dient und die Herde tapfer verteidigt. Wer die Dunkelheit trägt, um anderen Hoffnung zu bringen: "Blessed is the lion who serves the lamb and bravely defends the flock. He who bears the darkness to bring others hope." Blessing bestowed upon Matthias at Maulbronn.

Hai iniziato? Senza di me? (Italian): "Have you started? Without me?"

Heidenhaus: Heath house, old farmhouse typical to Black Forest region.

Himmel, Kreuz, und Sakrament!: "Heaven, cross and sacrament." Version of an old curse, used to express extreme shock and the belief that judgment was pouring down upon them.

Hmpf: Exasperation, expression of scorn or dissatisfaction.

Hochadel: Highest ranks within the German nobility.

Hovawart: Medium to large German herding and working dog. "Yard" or "farm-watcher."

Igitur qui desiderat pacem, praeparet bellum (Latin): "*Therefore let him who desires peace prepare for war.*"

Ja: Yes / Affirmative.

Kloster: Monastery.

Mein Schatz: Term of endearment meaning "my sweetheart" or "my treasure."

Prosit: Cheers, a toast wishing another well or good health.

Quatsch: Exclamation, meaning "nonsense" or "crap."

Ritter: Hereditary knight, second to lowest rank in nobility.

Scheiße: Shit (curse word), exclamation of frustration or surprise.

Scheitholt: Traditional German instrument, oblong wooden stringed box, ancestor of the zither.

Schrank: Two-door tall cabinet or closet used for storage.

Schwarzwald: Black Forest.

Schwein: A pig.

Vati: A male parent.

Vires acquirit eundo (Latin): "We gather strength as we go."

Ziegenglocke: Goat bell

ACKNOWLEDGMENTS

MY WRITING FRIENDS: ALYSSA, MY writing bestie, your friendship and support of me, my characters and their story means the world to me. Someday we WILL kick our feet up for a writing retreat and share that bottle of wine! Rita, thank you for always sharing your humor, knowledge, and endless encouragement. Peaker Writers, you all are amazingly talented and truly lovely people. Thank you all for the chats, the advice, the laughter, and the support. The daily camaraderie of my writing circle of friends is invaluable to me.

Thank you to Miranda Darrow of Book MD Editing for your thoughtful early edits and to Jenny Quinlan of Historical Editorial for your incredible attention to detail. Both of your reviews were instrumental in helping me realize this dream. Thank you to Jennifer Jakes of Killion Group for your formatting expertise with helping to create such a crisp, professional, and lovely layout. Thank you to Dorothea Beck for sharing your expertise and assistance with translations and authenticity. Thank you to Kate Absher Myers for sharing your exceptional, creative artistry for the covers and to Jazlyn for your lovely Edelweiss.

My dear friends (old and new) who have made these years of moving so full of laughter and memories. Thank you for being part of my found family. For always being up for a trip, being patient with me and my million photos, and for easily picking up where we leave off. Everywhere we've lived, wherever we've traveled, someone has welcomed us into their lives. Either for years or for the briefest of moments, (ask me sometime about the mushroom farmers in Poland), we've been repeatedly shown the genuine goodness of people. Whether into their kitchen for delicious *kaffee und kuchen*, into their driveway for family-filled bonfires and ballgames, into their therapies and classrooms with gracious ease and enthusiasm (and lessons on *Agape*), into their bar houses for homespun tales and ales ("History! Tradition! Hofen!"), or into their culture with warmth and an eagerness to share stories (and *grappa*), it's always with neighborliness and kindness. I hope to reflect that back in person and within my stories.

My girls: Andrea, Jamie, Kate, Kathy, Laura, and Shawna - thank you for your decades of true friendship, for always being only a phone call away, for being my constant, and setting me on this journey with a simple question. Almost can't remember a time in my life without you ladies in it. Love you.

My family. Thank you for always being there. Thank you for keeping me grounded, while giving me wings. For giving me everything I needed and teaching me what I didn't. For teaching me about sacrifice and service (and humbly reenforcing that). For teaching me the value of honest, helpful, hard work and early rising. For teaching me how to own mistakes and making me want to do better and be a better person. For showing me early and often how to care for others. For teaching me to think and not to be afraid. For supporting me and listening, even when I know you're shaking your head. For showing up when it matters and for loving my husband and children the way that you do. For being the bedrock of my strength and faith. For each being who you are. And for loving me as I am. Love you all.

My kids. You are priceless to me. Together, and each in your own way. Dear in a way that I'll never be able to properly put into words. Thank you each for being uniquely, perfectly yourselves. For being models of perseverance, kindness, and quiet strength. For inspiring me and giving me purpose and always challenging me to do and be better. For being silly, for being sweet, and for being big hearted in every way. Love you so very much.

My husband. My hero and my best friend. My safe and happy place. You are my home, no matter where we are. Thank you for a beautiful life, even on the hardest days. There are a thousand things to say, and then a thousand more, but I'll save them for your heart alone. My heart is yours, always.

ABOUT THE AUTHOR

A S A MILITARY CHILD, MILITARY spouse, and former public servant, Rebekah Simmers has spent her life in a perpetual state of traveling, moving, meeting people, and learning about new places and things. It's been a humbling, and brilliant, experience – one that she is very thankful for. Rebekah is also a special needs mom for five fantastic children (and three cats). She strives to honor their unique voices and perspective – their perseverance, resilience, struggles, and limitless grace – as well as a life of service both inside and out of the home.

Rebekah is largely inspired by history and loves to incorporate details from her own familial history, as well as her years living, researching, and traveling abroad into her writing. As an author, she hopes to provide immersive, heartfelt stories about authentic experiences for her readers. She enjoys reading in most any genre – a good story is a good story and a great one is a gift!

Rebekah believes there is beauty in broken things. That everyone has a story.
And there is always, always hope.

If you've enjoyed The King's Sword, please consider leaving a review.

Rebekah loves to hear from readers and other writers, so please feel free to contact her. You can find her at *www.rebekahsimmers. com*

Made in the USA
Middletown, DE
07 August 2021